Readers accustomed to H. G. Wells' famous science-fiction tales such as THE WAR OF THE WORLDS, THE TIME MACHINE and THE FIRST MEN IN THE MOON, may be surprised on encountering KIPPS. The novel is a radical departure from the science-fiction genre, for it is a charming love story about a humble draper's apprentice and his rags-to-riches adventures.

Wells himself was the son of a small shopkeeper and was apprenticed to a dry-goods dealer and a druggist before going to college, so the novel is thought to be partially autobiographical. Like the hero of his story, he rose from these humble beginnings to eminence, becoming one of the most popular and prolific writers of his day. Though Wells is now best remembered for his tales of other worlds, KIPPS is considered by many critics to be his masterpiece.

THE LAUREL-LEAF LIBRARY brings together under a single imprint outstanding works of fiction and non-fiction particularly suitable for young adult readers, both in and out of the classroom. This series is under the editorship of M. Jerry Weiss, Chairman, Department of English, Jersey City State College; in association with Ned E. Hoopes, Associate Professor of English, Pace College, and Charles Reasoner, Associate Professor, Elementary Education, New York University.

KIPPS

H. G. WELLS

"Those individuals who have led secluded or isolated lives, or have hitherto moved in other spheres than those wherein well-bred people move, will gather all the information necessary from these pages to render them thoroughly conversant with the manners and amenities of society."

Manners and Rules of Good Society
BY A MEMBER OF THE ARISTOCRACY

Published by Dell Publishing Company, Inc.
750 Third Avenue, New York, N.Y. 10017
Laurel-Leaf Library ® TM 766734
Printed in the U.S.A.
First printing—March, 1968

CONTENTS

1. The Making of Kipps

2. Mr. Coote, the Chaperon

3. Kippses

BOOK ONE

THE MAKING OF KIPPS

I. THE LITTLE SHOP
AT NEW ROMNEY

1

Until he was nearly arrived at adolescence it did not become clear to Kipps how it was that he was under the care of an aunt and uncle instead of having a father and mother like other boys. Yet he had vague memories of a somewhere else that was not New Romney—of a dim room, a window looking down on white buildings—and of a some one else who talked to forgotten people, and who was his mother. He could not recall her features very distinctly, but he remembered with extreme definition a white dress she wore, with a pattern of little sprigs of flowers and little bows of ribbon upon it, and a girdle of straight-ribbed white ribbon about the waist. Linked with this, he knew not how, were clouded half-obliterated recollections of scenes in which there was weeping, weeping in which he was inscrutably moved to join. Some terrible tall man with a loud voice played a part in these scenes, and either before or after them there were impressions of looking for interminable periods out of the windows of railway trains in the company of these two people. . . .

He knew, though he could not remember that he had ever been told, that a certain faded, wistful face, that looked at him from a plush and gilt framed daguerreotype above the mantel of the "sitting-room," was the face of his mother. But that knowledge did not touch his dim memories with any elucidation. In that photograph she was a girlish figure, leaning against a photographer's stile, and with all the self-conscious shrinking natural to that position. She had curly hair and a face far younger and prettier than any other mother in his experience. She swung a Dolly Varden hat by the string, and looked with obedient respectful eyes on the photographer-gentleman who had commanded the pose. She was very slight and pretty. But the phantom mother that haunted his memory so elusively was not like that, though he could not remember how she differed. Perhaps she was older, or a little less shrinking, or, it may be, only dressed in a different way. . . .

It is clear she handed him over to his aunt and uncle at New Romney with explicit directions and a certain endowment. One gathers she had something of that fine sense of social distinctions that subsequently played so large a part in Kipps' career. He was not to go to a "common" school, she provided, but to a certain seminary in Hastings that was not only a "middle-class academy," with mortar boards and every evidence of a higher social tone, but also remarkably cheap. She seems to have been animated by the desire to do her best for Kipps, even at a certain sacrifice of herself, as though Kipps were in some way a superior sort of person. She sent pocket-money to him from time to time for a year or more after Hastings had begun for him, but her face he never saw in the days of his lucid memory.

His aunt and uncle were already high on the hill of life when first he came to them. They had married for comfort in the evening or at any rate in the late afternoon of their days. They were at first no more than vague figures in the background of proximate realities, such realities as familiar chairs and tables, quiet to ride and drive, the newel of the staircase, kitchen furniture, pieces of firewood, the boiler tap, old newspapers, the cat, the High Street, the back yard and the flat fields that are always so near in that little town. He knew all the stones in the yard individually, the creeper in the corner, the dustbin and the mossy wall, better than many men know the faces of their wives. There was a corner under the ironing-board which by means of a shawl could, under propitious gods, be made a very decent cubby-house, a corner that served him for several years as the indisputable hub of the world; and the stringy places in the carpet, the knots upon the dresser, and the several corners of the rag hearthrug his uncle had made, became essential parts of his mental foundations. The shop he did not know so thoroughly—it was a forbidden region to him; yet somehow he managed to know it very well.

His aunt and uncle were, as it were, the immediate gods of this world; and, like the gods of the world of old, occasionally descended right into it, with arbitrary injunctions and disproportionate punishments. And, unhappily, one rose to their Olympian level at meals. Then one had to say one's "grace," hold one's spoon and fork in mad, unnatural ways called "properly," and refrain from eating even nice sweet things "too fast." If he "gobbled" there was trouble, and at the slightest *abandon* with knife, fork, and spoon, his aunt rapped his knuckles, albeit his uncle always finished up his gravy with his knife. Sometimes, moreover, his uncle would come, pipe in hand, out of a sedentary remoteness in the most disconcerting way, when a little boy was doing the most natural and attractive things, with "Drat and drabbit that young rascal! What's he a-doing of now?" And his aunt would appear at door or window to interrupt interesting conversation with children who were upon unknown grounds considered "low" and undesirable, and call him in. The pleasantest little noises, however softly you did them,—drumming on tea-trays, trumpeting your fists, whistling on keys, ringing chimes with a couple of pails, or playing tunes on the window-panes,—brought down the gods in anger. Yet what noise is fainter than your finger on the window—gently done? Sometimes, however, these gods gave him broken toys out of the shop, and then one loved them better—for the shop they kept was, among other things, a toy shop. (The other things included books to read and books to give away and local photographs; it had some pretensions also to be a china shop, and the fascia spoke of glass; it was also a stationer's shop with a touch of haberdashery about it, and in the windows and odd corners were mats and terra-cotta dishes, and milking-stools for painting; and there was a hint of picture-frames, and fire-screens, and fishing tackle, and air-guns, and bathing suits, and tents: various things, indeed, but all cruelly attractive to a small boy's fingers.) Once his aunt gave him a trumpet if he would *promise* faithfully not to blow it, and afterwards took it away again. And his aunt made him say his Catechism and something she certainly called the "Colic for the Day" every Sunday in the year.

As the two grew old while he grew up, and as his impression of them modified insensibly from year to year, it seemed to him at last that they had always been as they were when, in his adolescent days, his impression of things grew fixed. His aunt he thought of as always lean, rather worried-looking, and prone to a certain obliquity of cap, and his uncle massive, many-chinned, and careless about his buttons. They neither visited nor received visitors. They were always very suspicious about their neighbours and other people generally; they feared the "low" and they hated and despised the "stuck-up," and so they "kept themselves *to* themselves," according to the English ideal. Consequently little Kipps had no playmates, except through the sin of disobedience. By inherent nature he had a sociable disposition. When he was in the High Street he made a point of saying "Hello!" to passing cyclists, and he would put his tongue out at the Quodling children whenever their nursemaid was not looking. And he began a friendship with Sid Pornick, the son of the haberdasher next door, that, with wide intermissions, was destined to last his lifetime through.

Pornick, the haberdasher, I may say at once, was, according to old Kipps, a "blaring jackass"; he was a teetotaller, a "nyar, nyar, 'im-singing Methodis'," and altogether distasteful and detrimental, he and his together, to true Kipps ideals, so far as little Kipps could gather them. This Pornick certainly possessed an enormous voice, and he annoyed old Kipps greatly by calling, "You—Arn" and "Siddee," up and down his house. He annoyed old Kipps by private choral services on Sunday, all his family "nyar, nyaring"; and by mushroom culture; by behaving as though the pilaster between the two shops was common property; by making a noise of hammering in the afternoon, when old Kipps wanted to be quiet after his midday meal; by going up and down uncarpeted stairs in his boots; by having a black beard; by attempting to be friendly; and by—all that sort of thing. In fact, he annoyed old Kipps. He annoyed him especially with his shop doormat. Old Kipps never beat his mat, preferring to let sleeping dust lie; and, seeking a motive for a foolish proceeding, he held that Pornick waited until there was a suitable wind in order that the dust disengaged in that operation might defile his neighbour's shop. These issues would frequently develop into loud and vehement quarrels, and on one occasion came so near to violence as to be subsequently described by Pornick (who read his newspaper) as a "Disgraceful Frackass." On that occasion he certainly went into his own shop with extreme celerity.

But it was through one of these quarrels that the friendship of little Kipps and Sid Pornick came about. The two small boys found themselves one day looking through the gate at the doctor's goats together; they exchanged a few contradictions about which goat could fight which, and then young Kipps was moved to remark that Sid's father was a "blaring jackass." Sid said he wasn't, and Kipps repeated that he was, and quoted his authority. Then Sid, flying off at a tangent rather alarmingly, said he could fight young Kipps with one hand, an assertion young Kipps with a secret want of confidence denied. There were some vain repetitions, and the incident might have ended there, but happily a sporting butcher boy chanced on the controversy at this stage, and insisted upon seeing fair play.

The two small boys under his pressing encouragement did at last button up their jackets, square and fight an edifying drawn battle, until it seemed good to the butcher boy to go on with Mrs. Holyer's mutton. Then, according to his directions and under his experienced stage management, they shook hands and made it up. Subsequently, a little tear-stained perhaps, but flushed with the butcher boy's approval ("tough little kids"), and with cold stones down their necks as he advised, they sat side by side on the doctor's gate, projecting very much behind, staunching an honourable bloodshed, and expressing respect for one another. Each had a bloody nose and a black eye—three days later they matched to a shade—neither had given in, and, though this was tacit, neither wanted any more.

It was an excellent beginning. After this first encounter the attributes of their parents and their own relative value in battle never rose between them, and if anything was wanted to complete the warmth of their regard it was found in a joint dislike of the eldest Quodling. The eldest Quodling lisped, had a silly sort of straw hat and a large pink face (all covered over with self-satisfaction), and he went to the National School with a green baize bag—a contemptible thing to do. They called him names and threw stones at him, and when he replied by threatenings ("Look 'ere, young Art Kipth, you better *thtoppit!*") they were moved to attack and put him to flight.

And after that they broke the head of Ann Pornick's doll, so that she went home weeping loudly—a wicked and endearing proceeding. Sid was whacked, but, as he explained, he wore a newspaper tactically adjusted during the transaction, and really it didn't hurt him at all. . . . And Mrs. Pornick put her head out of the shop door suddenly, and threatened Kipps as he passed.

2

"Cavendish Academy," the school that had won the limited choice of Kipps' vanished mother, was established in a battered private house in the part of Hastings remotest from the sea; it was called an Academy for Young Gentlemen, and many of the young gentlemen had parents in "India," and other unverifiable places. Others were the sons of credulous widows, anxious, as Kipps' mother had been, to get something a little "superior" to a board school education as cheaply as possible; and others again were sent to demonstrate the dignity of their parents and guardians. And of course there were boys from France.

Its "principal" was a lean, long creature of indifferent digestion and temper, who proclaimed himself on a gilt-lettered board in his front garden George Garden Woodrow, F.S.Sc., letters indicating that he had paid certain guineas for a bogus diploma. A bleak white-washed outhouse constituted his schoolroom, and the scholastic quality of its carved and worn desks and forms was enhanced by a slippery blackboard and two large yellow out-of-date maps, one of Africa and the other of Wiltshire, that he had picked up cheap at a sale. There were other maps and globes in his study, where he interviewed inquiring parents, but these his pupils never saw. And in a glass cupboard in the passage was several shillingsworth of test tubes and chemicals, a tripod, a glass retort, and a damaged Bunsen burner, manifesting that the "Scientific laboratory" mentioned in the prospectus was no idle boast.

This prospectus, which was in dignified but incorrect English, laid particular stress on the sound preparation for a commercial career given in the Academy, but the army, navy and civil service were glanced at in an ambiguous sentence. There was something vague in the prospectus about "examinational successes"—though Woodrow, of course, disapproved of "cram"—and a declaration that the curriculum included "art," "modern foreign languages" and "a sound technical and scientific training." Then came insistence upon the "moral well-being" of the pupils, and an emphatic boast of the excellence of the religious instruction, "so often neglected nowadays even in schools of wide repute." "That's bound to fetch 'em," Mr. Woodrow had remarked when he drew up the prospectus. And in conjunction with the mortarboards it certainly did. Attention was directed to the "motherly" care of Mrs. Woodrow—in reality a small partially effaced woman with a plaintive face and a mind above cookery; and the prospectus concluded with a phrase intentionally vague, "Fare unrestricted, and our own milk and produce."

The memories Kipps carried from that school into after life were set in an atmosphere of stuffiness and mental muddle; and included countless pictures of sitting on creaking forms bored and idle, of blot licking and the taste of ink, of torn books with covers that set one's teeth on edge, of the slimy surface of the laboured slates, of furtive marble-playing, whispered story-telling, and of pinches, blows, and a thousand such petty annoyances being perpetually "passed on" according to the custom of the place, of standing up in class and being hit suddenly and unreasonably for imaginary misbehaviour, of Mr. Woodrow's raving days, when a scarcely sane injustice prevailed, of the cold vacuity of the hour of preparation before the bread-and-butter breakfast, and of horrible headaches and queer, unprecedented, internal feelings resulting from Mrs. Woodrow's motherly rather than intelligent cookery. There were dreary walks, when the boys marched two by two, all dressed in the mortarboard caps that so impressed the widowed mothers; there were dismal half-holidays when the weather was wet and the spirit of evil temper and evil imagination had the pent boys to work its will on; there were unfair, dishonourable fights and miserable defeats and victories, there was bullying and being bullied. A coward boy Kipps particularly afflicted, until at last he was goaded to revolt by incessant persecution, and smote Kipps to tolerance with whirling fists. There were memories of sleeping three in a bed, of the dense leathery smell of the schoolroom when one returned thither after ten minutes' play, of a playground of mud and incidental sharp flints. And there was much furtive foul language.

"Our Sundays are our happiest days," was one of Woodrow's formulæ with the inquiring parent, but Kipps was not called in evidence. They were to him terrible gaps of inanity—no work, no play, a drear expanse of time with the mystery of church twice and plum duff once in the middle. The afternoon was given up to furtive relaxations, among which "Torture Chamber" games with the less agreeable, weaker boys figured. It was from the difference between this day and common days that Kipps derived his first definite conceptions of the nature of God and heaven. His instinct was to evade any closer acquaintance as long as he could.

The school work varied, according to the prevailing mood of Mr. Woodrow. Sometimes that was a despondent lethargy; copy-books were distributed or sums were "set," or the great mystery of bookkeeping was declared in being, and beneath these superficial activities lengthy conversations and interminable guessing games with marbles went on while Mr. Woodrow sat inanimate at his desk heedless of school affairs, staring in front of him at unseen things. At times his face was utterly inane, at times it had an expression of stagnant amazement, as if he saw before his eyes with pitiless clearness the dishonour and mischief of his being. . . .

At other times the F.S.Sc. roused himself to action, and would stand up a wavering class and teach it, goading it with bitter mockery and blows through a chapter of Ann's "First French Course," or "France and the French," or a Dialogue about a traveller's washing, or the parts of an opera-house. His own knowledge of French had been obtained years ago in another English private school, and he had refreshed it by occasional weeks of loafing and mean adventure in Dieppe. He would sometimes in their lessons hit upon some reminiscence of these brighter days, and then he would laugh inexplicably and repeat French phrases of an unfamiliar type.

Among the commoner exercises he prescribed the learning of long passages of poetry from a "Poetry Book," which he would delegate an elder boy to "hear," and there was reading aloud from the Holy Bible, verse by verse—it was none of your "godless" schools!—so that you counted the verses up to your turn and then gave yourself to conversation—and sometimes one read from a cheap History of this land. They did, as Kipps reported, "loads of catechism." Also there was much learning of geographical names and lists, and sometimes Woodrow in an outbreak of energy would see these names were actually found on a map. And once, just once, there was a chemistry lesson—a lesson of indescribable excitement—glass things of the strangest shape, a smell like bad eggs, something bubbling in something, a smash and stench, and Mr. Woodrow saying quite distinctly —they thrashed it out in the dormitory afterwards— "Damn!" followed by the whole school being kept in, with extraordinary severities, for an hour. . . .

But interspersed with the memories of this grey routine were certain patches of brilliant colour—the holidays, his holidays, which in spite of the feud between their seniors, he spent as much as possible with Sid Pornick, the son of the irascible black-bearded haberdasher next door. They seemed to be memories of a different world. There were glorious days of "mucking about" along the beach, the siege of unresisting Martello towers, the incessant interest of the mystery and motion of windmills, the windy excursions with boarded feet over the yielding shingle to Dungeness lighthouse—Sid Pornick and he far adrift from reality, smugglers and armed men from the moment they left Great Stone behind them—wanderings in the hedgeless reedy marsh, long excursions reaching even to Hythe, where the machine guns of the Empire are forever whirling and tapping, and to Rye and Winchelsea, perched like dream-cities on their little hills. The sky in these memories was the blazing hemisphere of the marsh heavens in summer, or its wintry tumult of sky and sea; and there were wrecks, real wrecks, in it (near Dymchurch pitched high and blackened and rotting were the ribs of a fishing smack flung aside like an empty basket when the sea had devoured its crew); and there was bathing all naked in the sea, bathing to one's armpits and even trying to swim in the warm sea-water (spite of his aunt's prohibition), and (with her indulgence) the rare eating of dinner from a paper parcel miles away from home. Toke and cold ground rice pudding with plums it used to be—there is no better food at all. And for the background, in the place of Woodrow's mean, fretting rule, were his aunt's spare but frequently quite amiable figure—for though she insisted on his repeating the English Church Catechism every Sunday, she had an easy way over dinners that one wanted to take abroad—and his uncle, corpulent and irascible, but sedentary and easily escaped. And freedom!

The holidays were indeed very different from school. They were free, they were spacious, and though he never knew it in these words—they had an element of beauty. In his memory of his boyhood they shone like strips of stained glass window in a dreary waste of scholastic wall, they grew brighter and brighter as they grew remoter. There came a time at last and moods when he could look back to them with a feeling akin to tears.

The last of these windows was the brightest, and instead of the kaleidoscopic effects of its predecessors its glory was a single figure. For in the last of his holidays, before the Moloch of Retail Trade got hold of him, Kipps made his first tentative essays at the mysterious shrine of Love. Very tentative they were, for he had become a boy of subdued passions, and potential rather than actual affectionateness.

And the objects of these first stirrings of the great desire was no other than Ann Pornick, the head of whose doll he and Sid had broken long ago, and rejoiced over long ago, in the days when he had yet to learn the meaning of a heart.

3

Negotiations were already on foot to make Kipps into a draper before he discovered the lights that lurked in Ann Pornick's eyes. School was over, absolutely over, and it was chiefly present to him that he was never to go to school again. It was high summer. The "breaking up" of school had been hilarious; and the excellent maxim, "Last Day's Pay Day," had been observed by him with a scrupulous attention to his honour. He had punched the heads of all his enemies, wrung wrists and kicked shins; he had distributed all his unfinished copybooks, all his school books, his collection of marbles and his mortarboard cap among such as loved him; and he had secretly written in obscure pages of their books, "remember Art Kipps." He had also split the anæmic Woodrow's cane, carved his own name deeply in several places about the premises, and broken the scullery window. He had told everybody so often that he was to learn to be a sea captain that he had come almost to believe the thing himself. And now he was home, and school was at an end for him for evermore.

He was up before six on the day of his return, and out in the hot sunlight of the yard. He set himself to whistle a peculiarly penetrating arrangement of three notes supposed by the boys of the Hastings Academy and himself and Sid Pornick, for no earthly reason whatever, to be the original Huron war-cry. As he did this he feigned not to be doing it, because of the hatred between his uncle and the Pornicks, but to be examining with respect and admiration a new wing of the dustbin recently erected by his uncle—a pretence that would not have deceived a nestling tomtit.

Presently there came a familiar echo from the Pornick hunting-ground. Then Kipps began to sing, "Ar pars eight tra-la, in the lane be'ind the church." To which an unseen person answered, "Ar pars eight it is, in the lane be'ind the church." The "tra-la" was considered to render this sentence incomprehensible to the uninitiated. In order to conceal their operations still more securely, both parties to this duet then gave vent to a vocalisation of the Huron war-cry again, and after a lingering repetition of the last and shrillest note, dispersed severally, as became boys in the enjoyment of holidays, to light the house fires for the day.

Half-past eight found Kipps sitting on the sunlit gate at the top of the long lane that runs towards the sea, clashing his boots in a slow rhythm, and whistling with great violence all that he knew of an excruciatingly pathetic air. There appeared along by the churchyard wall a girl in a short frock, brown-haired, quick-coloured, and with dark blue eyes. She had grown so that she was a little taller than Kipps, and her colour had improved. He scarcely remembered her, so changed was she since last holidays—if indeed he had seen her last holidays, a thing he could not clearly remember. Some vague emotion arose at the sight of her. He stopped whistling and regarded her, oddly tongue-tied.

"He can't come," said Ann, advancing boldly. "Not yet."

"What—not Sid?"

"No. Father's made him dust all his boxes again."

"What for?"

"I dunno. Father's in a stew 'smorning."

"Oh!"

Pause. Kipps looked at her, and then was unable to look at her again. She regarded him with interest. "You left school?" she remarked after a pause.

"Yes."

"So's Sid."

The conversation languished. Ann put her hands on the top of the gate, and began a stationary hopping, a sort of ineffectual gymnastic experiment.

"Can you run?" she said presently.

"Run you any day," said Kipps.

"Gimme a start?"

"Where for?" said Kipps.

Ann considered, and indicated a tree. She walked towards it, and turned. "Gimme to here?" she called.

Kipps, standing now and touching the gate, smiled to express conscious superiority. "Further!" he said.

"Here?"

"Bit more!" said Kipps, and then, repenting of his magnanimity, said "Orf!" suddenly, and so recovered his lost concession.

They arrived abreast at the tree, flushed and out of breath.

"Tie!" said Ann, throwing her hair back from her face with her hand.

"I won," panted Kipps.

They disputed firmly but quite politely.

"Run it again, then," said Kipps. "*I* don't mind."

They returned towards the gate.

"You don't run bad," said Kipps, temperately expressing sincere admiration. "I'm pretty good, you know."

Ann sent her hair back by an expert toss of the head. "You give me a start," she allowed.

They became aware of Sid approaching them.

"You better look out, young Ann," said Sid, with that irreverent want of sympathy usual in brothers. "You been out nearly 'arf-hour. Nothing ain't been done upstairs. Father said he didn't know where you was, but when he did he'd warm y'r young ear."

Ann prepared to go.

"How about that race?" asked Kipps.

"Lor!" cried Sid, quite shocked. "You ain't been racing *her!*"

Ann swung herself round the end of the gate with her

eyes on Kipps, and then turned away suddenly and ran off down the lane.

Kipps' eyes tried to go after her, and came back to Sid's. "I give her a lot of start," said Kipps apologetically. "It wasn't a proper race." And so the subject was dismissed. But Kipps was *distrait* for some seconds, perhaps, and the mischief had begun in him.

4

They proceeded to the question of how two accomplished Hurons might most satisfactorily spend the morning. Manifestly their line lay straight along the lane to the sea.

"There's a new wreck," said Sid, "and my!—don't it smell just!"

"Smell?"

"Fair make you sick. It's rotten wheat."

They fell to talking of wrecks, and so came to ironclads and wars and suchlike manly matters.

Half-way to the wreck Kipps made a casual irrelevant remark. "Your sister ain't a bad sort," he said off-handedly.

"I clout her a lot," said Sidney modestly, and after a pause the talk reverted to more suitable topics.

The new wreck was full of rotting grain, and smelt abominably, even as Sid had said. This was excellent. They had it all to themselves. They took possession of it in force, at Sid's suggestion, and had speedily to defend it against enormous numbers of imaginary "natives," who were at last driven off by loud shouts of *bang, bang,* and vigorous thrusting and shoving of sticks. Then, also at Sid's direction, they sailed with it into the midst of a combined French, German and Russian fleet, demolishing the combination unassisted, and having descended to the beach, clambered up the side and cut out their own vessel in brilliant style, they underwent a magnificent shipwreck (with vocalised thunder) and floated "water-logged"—so Sid insisted—upon an exhausted sea.

These things drove Ann out of mind for a time. But at last, as they drifted without food or water upon a stagnant ocean, haggard-eyed, chins between their hands, looking in vain for a sail, she came to mind again abruptly.

"It's rather nice 'aving sisters," remarked one perishing mariner.

Sid turned round and regarded him thoughtfully. "Not it!" he said.

"No?"

"Not a bit of it." He grinned confidentially. "Know too much," he said; and afterwards, "Get out of things."

He resumed his gloomy scrutiny of the hopeless horizon. Presently he fell to spitting jerkily between his teeth, as he had read was the way with such ripe manhood as chews its quid.

"Sisters," he said, "is rot. That's what sisters are. Girls if you like, but sisters—*no!*"

"But ain't sisters girls?"

"*N-eaow!*" said Sid, with unspeakable scorn.

And Kipps answered, "Of course. I didn't mean—— I wasn't thinking of that."

"You got a girl?" asked Sid, spitting very cleverly again.

Kipps admitted his deficiency. He felt compunction.

"You don't know who *my* girl is, Art Kipps—I bet."

"Who *is*, then?" asked Kipps, still chiefly occupied by his own poverty.

"Ah!"

Kipps let a moment elapse before he did his duty. "Tell us!"

Sid eyed him and hesitated. "Secret?" he said.

"Secret."

"Dying solemn?"

"Dying solemn!" Kipps' self-concentration passed into curiosity.

Sid administered a terrible oath. Even after that precaution he adhered lovingly to his facts. "It begins with a Nem," he said, doling them out parsimoniously. "M A U D," he spelt, with a stern eye on Kipps, "C H A R T E R I S."

Now, Maud Charteris was a young person of eighteen and the daughter of the vicar of St. Bavon's,—besides which she had a bicycle,—so that as her name unfolded the face of Kipps lengthened with respect. "Get out!" he gasped incredulously. "She ain't your girl, Sid Pornick."

"She is!" answered Sid, stoutly.

"What—truth?"

"*Truth.*"

Kipps scrutinised his face. "Reely?"

Sid touched wood, whistled, and repeated a binding doggerel with great solemnity.

Kipps still struggled with the amazing new light on the world about him. "D'you mean—she knows?"

Sid flushed deeply, and his aspect became stern and gloomy. He resumed his wistful scrutiny of the sunlit sea. "I'd die for that girl, Art Kipps," he said presently, and Kipps did not press a question he felt to be ill timed. "I'd do anything she asked me to do," said Sid—"just anything. If she was to ask me to chuck myself into the sea." He met Kipps' eye. "I *would*," he said.

They were pensive for a space, and then Sid began to discourse in fragments of Love, a theme upon which Kipps had already in a furtive way meditated a little, but which, apart from badinage, he had never yet heard talked about in the light of day. Of course many and various aspects of life had come to light in the muffled exchange of knowledge that went on under the shadow of Woodrow, but this of Sentimental Love was not among them. Sid, who was a boy with an imagination, having once broached this topic, opened his heart, or at any rate a new wing of his heart, to Kipps, and found no fault with Kipps for a lack of return. He produced a thumbed novelette that had played a part in his sentimental awakening; he proffered it to Kipps, and confessed there was a character in it, a baronet, singularly like himself. This baronet was a person of volcanic passions which he concealed beneath a demeanour of "icy cynicism." The utmost expression he permitted himself was to grit his teeth; and now his attention was called to it, Kipps remarked that Sid also had a habit of gritting his teeth—and indeed had had all the morning. They read for a time, and presently Sid talked again. The conception of love Sid made evident was compact of devotion and much spirited fighting and a touch of mystery; but through all that cloud of talk there floated before Kipps a face that was flushed and hair that was tossed aside.

So they budded, sitting on the blackening old wreck in which men had lived and died, looking out to sea, talking of that other sea upon which they must presently embark. . . .

They ceased to talk, and Sid read; but Kipps, falling behind with the reading and not wishing to admit that he read slowlier than Sid, whose education was of the inferior elementary school brand, lapsed into meditation.

"I *would* like to 'ave a girl," said Kipps. "I mean just to talk to and all that. . . ."

A floating object distracted them at last from this obscure topic. They abandoned the wreck and followed the new interest a mile along the beach, bombarding it with stones until it came to land. They had inclined to a view that it would contain romantic mysteries, but it was simply an ill-preserved kitten—too much even for them. And at last they were drawn dinnerward and went home hungry and pensive side by side.

5

But Kipps' imagination had been warmed by that talk of love, and in the afternoon, when he saw Ann Pornick in the High Street and said "Hello!" it was a different "hello" from that of their previous intercourse. And when they had passed they both looked back and caught each other doing so. Yes, he *did* want a girl badly. . . .

Afterwards he was distracted by a traction engine going through the town, and his aunt had got some sprats for supper. When he was in bed, however, sentiment came upon him again in a torrent quite abruptly and abundantly, and he put his head under the pillow and whispered very softly, "I love Ann Pornick," as a sort of supplementary devotion.

In his subsequent dreams he ran races with Ann, and they lived in a wreck together, and always her face was flushed and her hair about her face. They just lived in a wreck and ran races, and were very, very fond of one another. And their favourite food was rock-chocolate, dates, such as one buys off barrows, and sprats—fried sprats. . . .

In the morning he could hear Ann singing in the scullery next door. He listened to her for some time, and it was clear to him that he must put things before her.

Towards dusk that evening they chanced on one another at the gate by the church; but though there was much in his mind, it stopped there with a resolute shyness until he and Ann were out of breath catching cockchafers, and were sitting on that gate of theirs again. Ann sat up upon the gate, dark against vast masses of flaming crimson and darkling purple, and her eyes looked at Kipps from a shadowed face. There came a stillness between them, and quite abruptly he was moved to tell his love.

"Ann," he said, "I *do* like you. I wish you was my girl. . . . I say, Ann: will you *be* my girl?"

Ann made no pretence of astonishment. She weighed the proposal for a moment with her eyes on Kipps. "If you like, Artie," she said lightly. "*I* don't mind if I am."

"All right," said Kipps, breathless with excitement, "then you are."

"All right," said Ann.

Something seemed to fall between them, and they no longer looked openly at one another. "Lor'!" cried Ann suddenly, "see that one!" and jumped down and darted after a cockchafer that had boomed within a yard of her face. And with that they were girl and boy again. . . .

They avoided their new relationship painfully.

They did not recur to it for several days, though they met twice. Both felt that there remained something before this great experience was complete, but there was an infinite diffidence about the next step. Kipps talked in fragments of all sorts of matters, telling particularly of the great things that were being done to make a man and a draper of him, how he had two new pairs of trousers and a black coat and four new shirts. And all the while his imagination was urging him to that unknown next step, and when he was alone and in the dark he became even an enterprising wooer. It became evident to him that it would be nice to take Ann by the hand; even the decorous novelettes Sid affected egged him on to that greater nearness of intimacy.

Then a great idea came to him, in a paragraph called "Lovers' Tokens" that he read in a torn fragment of *Tit-Bits*. It fell in to the measure of his courage—a divided sixpence! He secured his aunt's best scissors, fished a sixpence out of his jejune tin money-box, and jabbed his finger in a varied series of attempts to get it in half. When they met again the sixpence was still undivided. He had not intended to mention the matter to her at that stage, but it came up spontaneously. He endeavoured to explain the theory of broken sixpences and his unexpected failure to break one.

"But what you break it for?" said Ann. "It's no good if it's broke."

"It's a Token," said Kipps.

"Like . . . ?"

"Oh, you keep half and I keep half, and when we're sep'rated you look at your half and I look at mine—see! Then we think of each other."

"Oh!" said Ann, and appeared to assimilate this information.

"Only *I* can't get it in 'arf nohow," said Kipps.

They discussed this difficulty for some time without illumination. Then Ann had a happy thought. "Tell you what," she said, starting away from him abruptly and laying a hand on his arm, "you let *me* 'ave it, Artie. I know where father keeps his file."

Kipps handed her the sixpence, and they came upon a pause.

"I'll easy do it," said Ann.

In considering the sixpence side by side, his head had come near her cheek. Quite abruptly he was moved to take his next step into the unknown mysteries of love.

"Ann," he said, and gulped at his temerity, "I *do* love you. Straight. I'd do anything for you, Ann. Reely—I would."

He paused for breath. She answered nothing, but she was no doubt enjoying herself. He came yet closer to her—his shoulder touched hers. "Ann, I wish you'd——"

He stopped.

"What?" said Ann.

"Ann—lemme kiss you."

Things seemed to hang for a space; his tone, the drop of his courage, made the thing incredible as he spoke. Kipps was not of that bold order of wooers who impose conditions.

Ann perceived that she was not prepared for kissing after all. Kissing, she said, was silly, and when Kipps would have displayed a belated enterprise, she flung away from him. He essayed argument. He stood afar off, as it were—the better part of a yard—and said she *might* let him kiss her, and then that he didn't see what good it was for her to be his girl if he couldn't kiss her.

She repeated that kissing was silly. A certain estrangement took them homeward. They arrived in the dusky High Street not exactly together, and not exactly apart, but struggling. They had not kissed, but all the guilt of kissing was between them. When Kipps saw the portly contours of his uncle standing dimly in the shop doorway, his footsteps faltered, and the space between our young couple increased. Above, the window over Pornick's shop was open, and Mrs. Pornick was visible, taking the air. Kipps assumed an expression of extreme innocence. He found himself face to face with his uncle's advanced outposts of waistcoat buttons.

"Where ye bin, my boy?"

"Bin for a walk, uncle."

"Not along of that brat of Pornick's?"

"Along of who?"

"That gell"—indicating Ann with his pipe.

"Oh, no, uncle!"—very faintly.

"Run in, my boy."

Old Kipps stood aside, with an oblique glance upward, and his nephew brushed clumsily by him and vanished out of sight of the street, into the vague obscurity of the little shop. The door closed behind old Kipps with a nervous jangle of its bell, and he set himself to light the single oil lamp that illuminated his shop at nights. It was an operation requiring care and watching, or else it flared and "smelt." Often it smelt after all. Kipps for some reason found the dusky living-room with his aunt in it too populous for his feelings, and went upstairs.

"That brat of Pornick's!" It seemed to him that a horrible catastrophe had occurred. He felt he had identified himself inextricably with his uncle, and cut himself off from her for ever by saying "Oh, no!" At supper he was so visibly depressed that his aunt asked him if he wasn't feeling well. Under this imminent threat of medicine he assumed an unnatural cheerfulness.

He lay awake for nearly half an hour that night, groaning because things had all gone wrong—because Ann wouldn't let him kiss her, and because his uncle had called her a brat. It seemed to Kipps almost as though he himself had called her a brat. . . .

There came an interval during which Ann was alto-

gether inaccessible. One, two, three days passed, and he
did not see her. Sid he met several times; they went fishing,
and twice they bathed; but though Sid lent and received
back two further love stories, they talked no more of love.
They kept themselves in accord, however, agreeing that the
most flagrantly sentimental story was "proper." Kipps was
always wanting to speak of Ann, but never daring to do so.
He saw her on Sunday evening going off to chapel. She was
more beautiful than ever in her Sunday clothes, but she pretended not to see him because her mother was with her. But
he thought she pretended not to see him because she had
given him up for ever. Brat!—who could be expected ever
to forgive that? He abandoned himself to despair, he ceased
even to haunt the places where she might be found.

6

With paralysing unexpectedness came the end.

Mr. Shalford, the draper at Folkestone to whom he was
to be bound apprentice, had expressed a wish to "shape
the lad a bit" before the autumn sale. Kipps became aware
that his box was being packed, and gathered the full truth
of things on the evening before his departure. He became
feverishly eager to see Ann just once more. He made silly
and needless excuses to go out into the yard, he walked
three times across the street without any excuse at all, to
look up at the Pornick windows. Still she was hidden. He
grew desperate. It was within half an hour of his departure
that he came on Sid.

"Hello!" he said; "I'm orf!"

"Business?"

"Yes."

Pause.

"I say, Sid. You going 'ome?"

"Straight now."

"D'you mind? Ask Ann about that."

"About what?"

"She'll know."

And Sid said he would. But even that, it seemed, failed
to evoke Ann.

At last the Folkestone bus rumbled up, and he ascended.
His aunt stood in the doorway to see him off. His uncle

assisted with the box and portmanteau. Only furtively could he glance up at the Pornick windows, and still it seemed Ann hardened her heart against him. "Get up!" said the driver, and the hoofs began to clatter. No—she would not come out even to see him off. The bus was in motion, and old Kipps was going back into his shop. Kipps stared in front of him, assuring himself that he did not care.

He heard a door slam, and instantly craned out his neck to look back. He knew that slam so well. Behold! out of the haberdasher's door a small, untidy figure in homely pink print had shot resolutely into the road, and was sprinting in pursuit. In a dozen seconds she was abreast of the bus. At the sight of her Kipps' heart began to beat very quickly, but he made no immediate motion of recognition.

"Artie!" she cried breathlessly, "Artie! Artie! You know! I got *that!*"

The bus was already quickening its pace, and leaving her behind again, when Kipps realized what "that" meant. He became animated, he gasped, and gathered his courage together, and mumbled an incoherent request to the driver to "stop jest a jiff for sunthin'." The driver grunted, as the disparity of their years demanded, and then the bus had pulled up, and Ann was below.

She leapt up upon the wheel. Kipps looked down into Ann's face, and it was foreshortened and resolute. He met her eyes just for one second as their hands touched. He was not a reader of eyes. Something passed quickly from hand to hand, something that the driver, alert at the corner of his eye, was not allowed to see. Kipps hadn't a word to say, and all she said was, "I done it, 'smorning." It was like a blank space in which something pregnant should have been written and wasn't. Then she dropped down, and the bus moved forward.

After the lapse of about ten seconds it occurred to him to stand and wave his new bowler hat at her over the corner of the bus top, and to shout hoarsely, "Goo-bye, Ann! Don' forget me—while I'm away!"

She stood in the road looking after him, and presently she waved her hand.

He remained standing unstably, his bright, flushed face looking back at her, and his hair fluffing in the wind, and he waved his hat until at last the bend of the road hid her from his eyes. Then he turned about and sat down, and presently he began to put the half-sixpence he held clenched in his hand into his trouser pocket. He looked sideways at the driver, to judge how much he had seen.

Then he fell a-thinking. He resolved that, come what might, when he came back to New Romney at Christmas, he would by hook or by crook kiss Ann.

Then everything would be perfect and right, and he would be perfectly happy.

II. THE EMPORIUM

1

When Kipps left New Romney, with a small yellow tin box, a still smaller portmanteau, a new umbrella, and a keepsake half-sixpence, to become a draper, he was a youngster of fourteen, thin, with whimsical drakes' tails at the poll of his head, smallish features, and eyes that were sometimes very light and sometimes very dark, gifts those of his birth; and by the nature of his training he was indistinct in his speech, confused in his mind, and retreating in his manners. Inexorable fate had appointed him to serve his country in commerce, and the same national bias towards private enterprise and leaving bad alone, which entrusted his general education to Mr. Woodrow, now indentured him firmly into the hands of Mr. Shalford, of the Folkestone Drapery Bazaar. Apprenticeship is still the recognised English way to the distributing branch of the social service. If Mr. Kipps had been so unfortunate as to have been born a German he might have been educated in an elaborate and costly special school ("over-educated—crammed up"—Old Kipps) to fit him for his end—such being their pedagogic way. He might . . . But why make unpatriotic reflections in a novel? There was nothing pedagogic about Mr. Shalford.

He was an irascible, energetic little man, with hairy hands, for the most part under his coat tails, a long, shiny, bald head, a pointed, aquiline nose a little askew, and a neatly trimmed beard. He walked lightly and with a confident jerk, and he was given to humming. He had added to exceptional business "push," bankruptcy under the old dispensation, and judicious matrimony. His establishment was now one of the most considerable in Folkestone, and he insisted on every inch of frontage by alternate stripes of green and yellow down the houses over the shops. His shops were numbered 3, 5 and 7 on the street, and on his billheads 3 to 7. He encountered the abashed and awestricken Kipps with the praises of his system and himself. He spread himself out behind his desk with a grip on the lapel of his coat and made Kipps a sort of speech. "We expect y'r to work, y'r know, and we expect y'r to study our interests," explained Mr. Shalford in the regal and commercial plural. "Our system here is the best system y'r could have. I made it, and I ought to know. I began at the very bottom of the ladder when I was fourteen, and there isn't a step in it I don't know. Not a step. Mr. Booch in the desk will give y'r the card of rules and fines. Jest wait a minute." He pretended to be busy with some dusty memoranda under a paper-weight, while Kipps stood in a sort of paralysis of awe regarding his new master's oval baldness. "Two thous'n three forty-seven pounds," whispered Mr. Shalford audibly, feigning forgetfulness of Kipps. Clearly a place of great transactions!

Mr. Shalford rose, and handing Kipps a blotting-pad and an inkpot to carry—mere symbols of servitude, for he made no use of them—emerged into a counting-house where three clerks had been feverishly busy ever since his door handle had turned. "Booch," said Mr. Shalford, " 'ave y'r copy of the rules?" and a down-trodden, shabby little old man with a ruler in one hand and a quill pen in his mouth, silently held out a small book with green and yellow covers, mainly devoted, as Kipps presently discovered, to a voracious system of fines. He became acutely aware that his hands were full, and that everybody was staring at him. He hesitated a moment before putting the inkpot down to free a hand.

"Mustn't fumble like *that*," said Mr. Shalford as Kipps pocketed the rules. "Won't do here. Come along, come along," and he cocked his coat tails high, as a lady might hold up her dress, and led the way into the shop.

A vast interminable place it seemed to Kipps, with unending shining counters and innumerable faultlessly dressed young men and presently Houri-like young women staring at him. Here there was a long vista of gloves dangling from overhead rods, there ribbons and baby-linen. A short young lady in black mittens was making out the account of a customer, and was clearly confused in her addition by Shalford's eagle eye.

A thickset young man with a bald head and a round, very wise face, who was profoundly absorbed in adjusting all the empty chairs down the counter to absolutely equal distances, awoke out of his preoccupation and answered respectfully to a few Napoleonic and quite unnecessary remarks from his employer. Kipps was told that this young man's name was Mr. Buggins, and that he was to do whatever Mr. Buggins told him to do.

They came round a corner into a new smell, which was destined to be the smell of Kipps' life for many years, the vague, distinctive smell of Manchester goods. A fat man with a large nose jumped—actually jumped—at their appearance, and began to fold a pattern of damask in front of him exactly like an automaton that is suddenly set going.

"Carshot, see to this boy to-morrow," said the master. "See he don't fumble. Smart'n 'im up."

"Yussir," said Carshot fatly, glanced at Kipps, and resumed his pattern-folding with extreme zeal.

"Whatever Mr. Carshot says y'r to do, ye *do*," said Mr. Shalford, trotting onward; and Carshot blew out his face with an appearance of relief.

They crossed a large room full of the strangest things Kipps had ever seen. Ladylike figures, surmounted by black wooden knobs in the place of the refined heads one might have reasonably expected, stood about with a lifelike air of conscious fashion.

"Costume room," said Shalford.

Two voices engaged in some sort of argument—"I can assure you, Miss Mergle, you are entirely mistaken—entirely, in supposing I should do anything so unwomanly," —sank abruptly, and they discovered two young ladies, taller and fairer than any of the other young ladies, and with black trains to their dresses, who were engaged in writing at a little table. Whatever they told him to do, Kipps gathered he was to do. He was also, he understood, to do whatever Carshot and Booch told him to do. And there were also Buggins and Mr. Shalford. And not to forget or fumble!

They descended into a cellar called "The Warehouse," and Kipps had an optical illusion of errand boys fighting. Some aerial voice said, "Teddy!" and the illusion passed. He looked again, and saw quite clearly that they were packing parcels and always would be, and that the last thing in the world that they would or could possibly do was to fight. Yet he gathered from the remarks Mr. Shalford addressed to their busy backs that they had been fighting—no doubt at some past period of their lives.

Emerging in the shop again among a litter of toys and what are called "fancy articles," Shalford withdrew a hand from beneath his coat tails to indicate an overhead change-carrier. He entered into elaborate calculations to show how many minutes in one year were saved thereby, and lost himself among the figures. "Seven tums eight seven nine —was it? Or seven eight nine? Now, *now!* Why, when I was a boy your age I c'd do a sum like that as soon as hear it. We'll soon get y'r into better shape than that. Make you Fishent. Well, y'r must take my word, it comes to pounds and pounds saved in the year—pounds and pounds. System! System everywhere. Fishency." He went on murmuring "Fishency" and "System" at intervals for some time.

They passed into a yard, and Mr. Shalford waved his hand to his three delivery vans all striped green and yellow— "uniform—green, yell'r—System." All over the premises were pinned absurd little cards. "This door locked after 7:30. —By order, Edwin Shalford," and the like.

Mr. Shalford always wrote "By order," though it conveyed no earthly meaning to him. He was one of those people who collect technicalities upon them as the Reduvius bug collects dirt. He was the sort of man who is not only ignorant, but absolutely incapable of English. When he wanted to say he had a sixpenny-ha'penny longcloth to sell, he put it thus to startled customers: "Can DO you one, six half if y'like." He always omitted pronouns and articles and so forth; it seemed to him the very essence of the efficiently businesslike. His only preposition was "as" or the compound "as per." He abbreviated every word he could; he would have considered himself the laughing-stock of Wood Street if he had chanced to spell *socks* in any way but "sox." But, on the other hand, if he saved words here, he wasted them there: he never acknowledged an order that was not an esteemed favour, nor sent a pattern without begging to submit it. He never stipulated for so many months' credit, but bought in November "as Jan." It was not only words he abbreviated in his London communica-

tions. In paying his wholesalers his "System" admitted of a
constant error in the discount of a penny or twopence, and
it "facilitated business," he alleged, to ignore odd pence in
the cheques he wrote. His ledger clerk was so struck with
the beauty of this part of the System, that he started a
private one of his own account with the stamp box, that
never came to Shalford's knowledge.

This admirable British merchant would glow with a
particular pride of intellect when writing his London orders.

"Ah! do y'r think *you*'ll ever be able to write London
orders?" he would say with honest pride to Kipps, waiting
impatiently long after closing time to take these triumphs
of commercial efficiency to post, and so end the interminable day.

Kipps shook his head, anxious for Mr. Shalford to get on.

"Now, here, f' example, I've written—see?—'1 piece
1 in. cott. blk, elas. 1/ or.' What do I mean by that *or*, eh?
—d'ye know?"

Kipps promptly hadn't the faintest idea.

"And then, '2 ea. silk net as per patts herewith': *ea.*, eh?"

"Dunno, sir."

It was not Mr. Shalford's way to explain things. "Dear,
dear! Pity you couldn't get some c'mercial education at
your school. 'Stid of all this lit'ry stuff. Well, my boy, if y'
don't 'ussel a bit y'll never write London orders, *that's* pretty
plain. Jest stick stamps on all those letters, and mind y'r
stick 'em right way up, and try and profit a little more by the
opportunities your aunt and uncle have provided ye. Can't
say *what*'ll happen t'ye if ye don't."

And Kipps, tired, hungry, and belated, set about stamping
with vigour and despatch.

"Lick the *envelope*," said Mr. Shalford, "lick the *envelope*," as though he grudged the youngster the postage-
stamp gum. "It's the little things mount up," he would
say; and, indeed, that was his philosophy of life—to bustle
and save, always to bustle and save. His political creed
linked Reform, which meant nothing, with Efficiency which
meant a sweated service, and Economy which meant a
sweated expenditure, and his conception of a satisfactory
municipal life was to "keep down the rates." Even his religion was to save his soul, and to preach a similar cheese-
paring to the world.

2

The indentures that bound Kipps to Mr. Shalford were
antique and complex: they insisted on the latter gentleman's parental privileges; they forbade Kipps to dice and
game; they made him over body and soul to Mr. Shalford
for seven long years, the crucial years of his life. In return
there were vague stipulations about teaching the whole art
and mystery of the trade to him; but as there was no
penalty attached to negligence, Mr. Shalford, being a sound,
practical business man, considered this a mere rhetorical
flourish, and set himself assiduously to get as much out of
Kipps and to put as little into him as he could in the
seven years of their intercourse.

What he put into Kipps was chiefly bread and margarine,
infusions of chicory and tea-dust, colonial meat by contract
at threepence a pound, potatoes by the sack, and watered
beer. If, however, Kipps chose to buy any supplementary
material for growth, Mr. Shalford had the generosity to
place his kitchen resources at his disposal free—if the fire
chanced to be going. He was also allowed to share a bedroom with eight other young Englishmen, and to sleep in
a bed which, except in very severe weather, could be made
with the help of his overcoat and private underlinen, not
to mention newspapers, quite sufficiently warm for any
reasonable soul. In addition Kipps was taught the list of
fines; and how to tie up parcels; to know where goods were
kept in Mr. Shalford's systematised shop; to hold his hands
extended upon the counter and to repeat such phrases as
"What can I have the pleasure. . . .?" "No trouble, I 'ssure
you," and the like; to block, fold, and measure materials
of all sorts; to lift his hat from his head when he passed
Mr. Shalford abroad, and to practise a servile obedience to
a large number of people. But he was not, of course,
taught the "cost" mark of the goods he sold, nor anything
of the method of buying such goods. Nor was his attention
directed to the unfamiliar social habits and fashions to which
his trade ministered. The use of half the goods he saw
sold and was presently to assist in selling he did not understand; materials for hangings, cretonnes, chintzes, and the
like, serviettes and all the bright, hard white wear of a well-

ordered house, pleasant dress materials, linings, stiffenings—
they were to him from first to last no more than things
heavy and difficult to handle in bulk, that one folded up,
unfolded, cut in lengths, and saw dwindle and pass away
out into that mysterious happy world in which the customer
dwells. Kipps hurried from piling linen table-cloths, that
were collectively as heavy as lead, to eat off oil-cloth in a
gas-lit dining-room underground; and he dreamt of comb-
ing endless blankets beneath his overcoat, spare under-
shirt, and three newspapers. So he had at least the chance
of learning the beginnings of philosophy.

In return for these benefits he worked so that he commonly went to bed exhausted and footsore. His round began at half-past six in the morning, when he would descend
unwashed and shirtless, in old clothes and a scarf, and dust
boxes and yawn, and take down wrappers and clean the
windows until eight. Then in half an hour he would complete
his toilet and take an austere breakfast of bread and margarine and what only an Imperial Englishman would admit
to be coffee, after which refreshment he ascended to the
shop for the labours of the day. Commonly these began
with a mighty running to and fro with planks and boxes
and goods for Carshot, the window-dresser, who, whether
he worked well or ill, nagged persistently by reason of a
chronic indigestion, until the window was done. Sometimes
the costume window had to be dressed, and then Kipps
staggered down the whole length of the shop from the costume room with one after another of those ladylike shapes
grasped firmly, but shamefully, each about her single ankle
of wood. Such days as there was no window-dressing, there
was a mighty carrying and lifting of blocks and bales of
goods into piles and stacks. After this there were terrible
exercises, at first almost despairfully difficult: certain sorts
of goods that came in folded had to be rolled upon rollers,
and for the most part refused absolutely to be rolled, at any
rate by Kipps; and certain other sorts of goods that came
from the wholesalers rolled had to be measured and folded,
which folding makes young apprentices wish they were dead.
All of it, too, quite avoidable trouble, you know, that is
not avoided because of the cheapness of the genteeler sorts
of labour and the dearness of forethought in the world.
And then consignments of new goods had to be marked off

and packed into proper parcels; and Carshot packed like
conjuring tricks, and Kipps packed like a boy with tastes in
some other direction—not ascertained. And always Carshot
nagged.

He had a curious formula of appeal to his visceral
œconomy, had Carshot, that the refinement of the times
and the earnest entreaties of my friends induce me to render
by an anæmic paraphrase.

"My heart and lungs! I never see such a boy," so I
present Carshot's refrain; and even when he was within a
foot or so of the customer's face the disciplined ear of
Kipps would still at times develop a featureless, intercalary
murmur into—well, "my heart and lungs!"

There came a blessed interval when Kipps was sent
abroad "matching." This consisted chiefly in supplying unexpected defects in buttons, ribbon, lining, and so forth in
the dressmaking department. He was given a written paper
of orders with patterns pinned thereto, and discharged into
the sunshine and interest of the street. Then, until he
thought it wise to return and stand the racket of his delay,
he was a free man, clear of all reproach.

He made remarkable discoveries in topography, as for
example that the most convenient way from the establishment of Mr. Adolphus Davis to the establishment of Messrs.
Plummer, Roddis & Tyrrel, two of his principal places of
call, is not as is generally supposed down the Sandgate Road,
but up the Sandgate Road, round by West Terrace, and
along the Leas to the lift, watch the lift up and down
twice, but not longer, because that wouldn't do, back along
the Leas, watch the Harbour for a short time, and then
round by the churchyard, and so (hurrying) into Church
Street and Rendezvous Street. But on some exceptionally
fine days the route lay through Radnor Park to the pond
where the little boys sail ships and there are interesting
swans.

He would return to find the shop settling down to the
business of serving customers. And now he had to stand
by to furnish any help that was necessary to the seniors
who served, to carry parcels and bills about the shop, to clear
away "stuff" after each engagement, to hold up curtains
until his arms ached, and what was more difficult than all,
to do nothing, and not stare disconcertingly at customers

when there was nothing for him to do. He plumbed an abyss of boredom, or stood a mere carcass, with his mind far away, fighting the enemies of the Empire, or steering a dream ship perilously into unknown seas. To be recalled sharply to our higher civilisation by some bustling senior's "Nar then, Kipps. *Look* alive! Ketch 'old. (My heart and lungs!)"

At half-past seven o'clock—except on late nights—a feverish activity of "straightening up" began, and when the last shutter was up outside, Kipps with the speed of an arrow leaving a bow would start hanging wrappers over the fixtures and over the piles of wares upon the counters, preparatory to a vigorous scattering of wet sawdust and the sweeping out of the shop.

Sometimes people would stay long after the shop was closed—"They don't mind a bit at Shalford's," these ladies used to say—it is always ladies do this sort of thing—and while they loitered it was forbidden to touch a wrapper, or take any measures to conclude the day until the doors closed behind them.

Mr. Kipps would watch these later customers from the shadow of a stack of goods, and death and disfigurement was the least he wished for them. Rarely much later than nine, a supper of bread and cheese and watered beer awaited him upstairs, and, that consumed, the rest of the day was entirely at his disposal for reading, recreation, and the improvement of his mind. . . .

The front door was locked at half-past ten, and the gas in the dormitory extinguished at eleven.

3

On Sundays he was obliged to go to church once, and commonly he went twice, for there was nothing else to do. He sat in the free seats at the back; he was too shy to sing, and not always clever enough to keep his place in the prayer-book, and he rarely listened to the sermon. But he had developed a sort of idea that going to church had a tendency to alleviate life. His aunt wanted to have him confirmed, but he evaded this ceremony for some years.

In the intervals between services he walked about Folkestone with an air of looking for something. Folkestone was not so interesting on Sundays as on week-days, because the shops were shut; but on the other hand there was a sort of confusing brilliance along the front of the Leas in the afternoon. Sometimes the apprentice next above him would condescend to go with him; but when the apprentice next but one above him condescended to go with the apprentice next above him, then Kipps, being habited as yet in ready-made clothes without tails, and unsuitable therefore to appear in such company, went alone.

Sometimes he would strike out into the country—still as if looking for something he missed—but the rope of meal-times haled him home again; and sometimes he would invest the major portion of the weekly allowance of a shilling that old Booch handed out to him in a sacred concert on the pier. He would sometimes walk up and down the Leas between twenty and thirty times after supper, desiring much the courage to speak to some other person in the multitude similarly employed. Almost invariably he ended his Sunday footsore.

He never read a book; there were none for him to read, and besides, in spite of Mr. Woodrow's guidance through a cheap and cheaply annotated edition of the *Tempest* (English Literature) he had no taste that way; he never read any newspapers, except occasionally *Tit-Bits* or a ha'penny "comic." His chief intellectual stimulus was an occasional argey-bargey that sprang up between Carshot and Buggins at dinner. Kipps listened as if to unparalleled wisdom and wit, and treasured all the gems of repartee in his heart against the time when he, too, should be a Buggins and have the chance and courage for speech.

At times there came breaks in this routine—sale times, darkened by extra toil and work past midnight, but brightened by a sprat supper and some shillings in the way of "premiums." And every year—not now and then, but every year—Mr. Shalford, with parenthetic admiration of his own generosity and glancing comparisons with the austerer days when *he* was apprenticed, conceded Kipps no less than ten days' holiday—ten whole days every year! Many a poor soul at Portland might well envy the fortunate Kipps. Insatiable heart of man! but how those days were grudged and counted as they snatched themselves away from him one after another!

Once a year came stock-taking, and at intervals gusts of "marking off" goods newly arrived. Then the splendours of Mr. Shalford's being shone with oppressive brilliancy. "System!" he would say, "system. Come! 'ussel!" and issue sharp, confusing, contradictory orders very quickly. Carshot trotted about, confused, perspiring, his big nose up in the air, his little eye on Mr. Shalford, his forehead crinkled, his lips always going to the formula "Oh, my heart and lungs!" The smart junior and the second apprentice vied with one another in obsequious alacrity. The smart junior aspired to Carshot's position, and that made him almost violently subservient to Shalford. They all snapped at Kipps. Kipps held the blotting-pad and the safety inkpot and a box of tickets, and ran and fetched things. If he put the ink down before he went to fetch things Mr. Shalford usually knocked it over, and if he took it away Mr. Shalford wanted it before he returned. "You make my tooth ache, Kipps," Mr. Shalford would say. "You gimme n'ralgia. You got no more System in you than a bad potato." And at the times when Kipps carried off the inkpot Mr. Shalford would become purple in the face and jab round with his dry pen at imaginary inkpots and swear, and Carshot would stand and vociferate, and the smart junior would run to the corner of the department and vociferate, and the second apprentice would pursue Kipps, vociferating, "Look Alive, Kipps! Look Alive! Ink, Man! Ink!"

A vague self-disgust, that shaped itself as an intense hate of Shalford and all his fellow-creatures, filled the soul of Kipps during these periods of storm and stress. He felt that the whole business was unjust and idiotic, but the why and the wherefore was too much for his unfortunate brain. His mind was a welter. One desire, the desire to dodge some at least of a pelting storm of disagreeable comment, guided him through a fumbling performance of his duties. His disgust was infinite! It was not decreased by the inflamed ankles and sore feet that form a normal incident in the business of making an English draper; and the senior apprentice, Minton, a gaunt, sullen-faced youngster with close-cropped, wiry, black hair, a loose, ugly mouth, and a moustache like a smudge of ink, directed his attention to deeper aspects of the question and sealed his misery.

"When you get too old to work they chuck you away,"

said Minton. "Lor! you find old drapers everywhere—tramps, beggars, dock labourers, 'bus conductors—Quod. Anywhere but in a crib."

"Don't they get shops of their own?"

"Lord! *'Ow* are they to get shops of their own? They 'aven't any capital! How's a draper's shopman to save up five hundred pounds even? I tell you it can't be done. You got to stick to cribs until it's over. I tell you we're in a blessed drainpipe, and we've got to crawl along it till we die."

The idea that fermented perpetually in the mind of Minton was to "hit the little beggar slap in the eye"—the little beggar being Mr. Shalford—"and see how his blessed System met that."

The threat filled Kipps with splendid anticipations whenever Shalford went marking off in Minton's department. He would look at Minton and look at Shalford, and decide where he would best like Shalford hit. . . . But for reasons known to himself Shalford never pished and tushed with Minton, as he did at the harmless Carshot, and this interesting experiment upon the System was never attempted.

4

There were times when Kipps would lie awake, all others in the dormitory asleep and snoring, and think dismally of the outlook Minton pictured. Dimly he perceived the thing that had happened to him—how the great, stupid machine of retail trade had caught his life into its wheels, a vast, irresistible force which he had neither strength of will nor knowledge to escape. This was to be his life until his days should end. No adventures, no glory, no change, no freedom. Neither—though the force of that came home to him later—might he dream of effectual love and marriage. And there was a terrible something called the "swap," or "the key of the street," and "crib hunting," of which the talk was scanty but sufficient. Night after night he would resolve to enlist, to run away to sea, to set fire to the warehouse, or drown himself; and morning after morning he rose up and hurried downstairs in fear of a sixpenny fine. He would compare his dismal round of servile drudgery with those windy, sunlit days at Littlestone, those windows of happiness shining ever brighter as they receded. The little figure of Ann seemed in all these windows now.

She, too, had happened on evil things. When Kipps went home for the first Christmas after he was bound, that great suspended resolve of his to kiss her flared up to hot determination, and he hurried out and whistled in the yard. There was a still silence, and then old Kipps appeared behind him.

"It's no good your whistling there, my boy," said old Kipps in a loud, clear tone, designed to be audible over the wall. "They've cleared out all you 'ad any truck with. *She's* gone as help to Ashford, my boy. *Help!* Slavey is what we used to call 'em, but times are changed. Wonder they didn't say lady-'elp while they was about it. It 'ud be like 'em."

And Sid? Sid had gone, too. "Arrand boy or somethink," said old Kipps. "To one of these here brasted bicycle shops."

"*Has* 'e!" said Kipps, with a feeling that he had been gripped about the chest, and he turned quickly and went indoors.

Old Kipps, still supposing him present, went on to further observations of an anti-Pornick hue. . . .

When Kipps got upstairs safe in his own bedroom, he sat down on the bed and stared at nothing. They were caught —they were all caught. All life took on the hue of one perpetual, dismal Monday morning. The Hurons were scattered, the wrecks and the beach had passed away from him, the sun of those warm evenings at Littlestone had set for evermore. . . .

The only pleasure left for the brief remainder of his holiday after that was to think he was not in the shop. Even that was transient. Two more days—one more day— half a day. When he went back there were one or two very dismal nights indeed. He went so far as to write home some vague intimation of his feelings about business and his prospects, quoting Minton. But Mrs. Kipps answered him, "Did he want the Pornicks to say he wasn't good enough to be a draper?" This dreadful possibility was of course conclusive in the matter. "No," he resolved they should not say he failed at that.

He derived much help from a "manly" sermon delivered in an enormous voice by a large, fat, sun-red clergyman, just home from a colonial bishopric he had resigned on the plea of ill-health, exhorting him that whatever his hand found to do, he was to do with all his might; and the revision of his Catechism preparatory to his confirmation reminded him that it behooved him "to do his duty in that state of life unto which it shall please God to call him. . . ."

After a time the sorrows of Kipps grew less acute, and save for a miracle the brief tragedy of his life was over. He subdued himself to his position even as his Church required of him, seeing moreover no way out of it.

The earliest mitigation of his lot was that his soles and ankles became indurated to the perpetual standing. The next was an unexpected weekly whiff of freedom that came every Thursday. Mr. Shalford, after a brave stand for what he called "Innyvishal lib'ty" and the "Idea of my System," a stand which he explained he made chiefly on patriotic grounds, was at last, under pressure of certain of his customers, compelled to fall in line with the rest of the local Early Closing Association, and Mr. Kipps could emerge in daylight and go where he listed for long, long hours. Moreover Minton, the pessimist, reached the end of his appointed time and left—to enlist in a cavalry regiment and go about this planet leading an insubordinate but interesting life, that ended at last in an intimate, vivid and really you know by no means painful or tragic night grapple in the Terah Valley. In a little while Kipps cleaned windows no longer; he was serving customers (of the less important sort) and taking goods out on approval; and presently he was third apprentice, and his moustache was visible, and there were three apprentices whom he might legally snub and cuff. But one was (most dishonestly) too big to cuff in spite of his greener years.

5

There came still other distractions, the natural distractions of adolescence, to take his mind off the inevitable. His costume, for example, began to interest him more; he began to realise himself as a visible object, to find an interest in the costume-room mirrors and the eyes of the girl apprentices.

In this he was helped by counsel and example. Pierce, his immediate senior, was by way of being what was called

a Masher, and preached his cult. During slack times grave
discussions about collars, ties, the cut of trouser legs, and the
proper shape of a boot-toe, were held in the Manchester
department. In due course Kipps went to a tailor, and his
short jacket was replaced by a morning coat with tails.
Stirred by this, he purchased at his own expense three
stand-up collars to replace his former turn-down ones. They
were nearly three inches high, higher than those Pierce
wore, and they made his neck quite sore and left a red
mark under his ears. . . . So equipped, he found himself
fit company even for this fashionable apprentice, who had
now succeeded Minton in his seniority.

Most potent help of all in the business of forgetting his
cosmic disaster was this, that so soon as he was in tail
coats the young ladies of the establishment began to discover that he was no longer a "horrid little boy." Hitherto
they had tossed heads at him and kept him in his place.
Now they discovered that he was a "nice boy," which is next
door at least to being a "feller," and in some ways even
preferable. It is painful to record that his fidelity to Ann
failed at their first onset. I am fully sensible how entirely
better this story would be from a sentimental point of view
if he had remained true to that early love. Only then it
would have been a different story altogether. And at least
Kipps was thus far true, that with none of these later loves
was there any of that particular quality that linked Ann's
flushed face and warmth and the inner things of life so in-
separably together. Though they were not without emotions
of various sorts.

It was one of the young ladies in the costume-room who
first showed by her manner that he was a visible object and
capable of exciting interest. She talked to him, she en-
couraged him to talk to her, she lent him a book she
possessed, and darned a sock for him, and said she would
be his elder sister. She allowed him to escort her to church
with a great air of having induced him to go. Then she investigated his eternal welfare, overcame a certain affecta-
tion of virile indifference to religion, and extorted a promise
that he would undergo "confirmation." This excited the
other young lady in the costumes, her natural rival, and
she set herself with great charm and subtlety to the capture of the ripening heart of Kipps. She took a more

worldly line. She went for a walk with him to the pier on
Sunday afternoon, and explained to him how a gentleman
must always walk "outside" a lady on a pavement, and
how all gentlemen wore, or at least carried gloves, and
generally the broad beginnings of the British social ideal.
Afterwards the ladies exchanged "words," upon Sabbatical
grounds. In this way was the *toga virilis* bestowed on Kipps,
and he became recognised as a suitable object for that
Platonic Eros whose blunted darts devastate even the very
highest-class establishments. In this way, too, did that per-
vading ambition of the British young man to be, if not a
"gentleman," at least mistakably like one, take root in his
heart.

He took to these new interests with quite natural and
personal zest. He became initiated into the mysteries of
"flirting," and—at a slightly later stage, and with some leading hints from Pierce, who was of a communicative disposition in these matters—of the milder forms of "spooning." Very soon he was engaged. Before two years were
out he had been engaged six times, and was beginning to
be rather a desperate fellow, so far as he could make out.
Desperate, but quite gentlemanly, be it understood, and
without let or hindrance to the fact that he was, in four
brief lessons, "prepared" by a distant-mannered and gloomy
young curate, and "confirmed" a member of the Established
Church.

The engagements in drapery establishments do not necessarily involve a subsequent marriage. They are essentially
more refined, less coarsely practical, and altogether less
binding than the engagements of the vulgar rich. These
young ladies do not like not to be engaged—it is so unnatural; and Mr. Kipps was as easy to get engaged to as
one could wish. There are, from the young lady's point of
view, many conveniences in being engaged. You get an escort for church and walks and so forth. It is not quite the
thing to walk abroad with a "feller," much more to "spoon"
with him, when he is neither one's *fiancé* nor an adopted
brother; it is considered either a little *fast*, or else as
savouring of the "walking-out" habits of the servant girls.
Now, such is the sweetness of human charity, that the
shop young lady in England has just the same horror of
doing anything that savours of the servant girl as the lady

journalist, let us say, has of anything savouring of the shop girl, or the really quite nice young lady has of anything savouring of any sort of girl who has gone down into the economic battlefield to earn herself a living. . . . But the very deepest of these affairs was still among the shallow places of love; at best it was paddling where it is decreed that men must sink or swim. Of the deep and dangerous places, and of the huge buoyant lift of its waves, he tasted nothing. Affairs of clothes and vanities they were, jealousies about a thing said, flatteries and mutual boastings, climaxes in the answering grasp of hands, the temerarious use of Christian names, culminations in a walk, or a near confidence, or a little pressure more or less. Close-sitting on a seat after twilight, with some little fondling, was indeed the boldest of a lover's adventures, the utmost limit of his enterprises in the service of that stark Great Lady, who is daughter of Uranus and the sea. The "young ladies" who reigned in his heart came and went like people in an omnibus: there was the vehicle, so to speak, upon the road, and they entered and left it without any cataclysm of emotion. For all that, this development of the sex interest was continuously very interesting to Kipps; and kept him going as much as anything through all these servile years.

6

For a tailpiece to this chapter one may vignette one of those little affairs.

It is a bright Sunday afternoon; the scene is a secluded little seat half-way down the front of the Leas, and Kipps is four years older than when he parted from Ann. There is a quite perceptible down upon his upper lip, and his costume is just as tremendous a "mash" as lies within his means. His collar is so high that it scars his inaggressive jawbone, and his hat has a curly brim, his tie shows taste, his trousers are modestly brilliant, and his boots have light cloth uppers and button at the side. He jabs at the gravel before him with a cheap cane, and glances sideways at Flo Bates, the young lady from the cash desk. She is wearing a brilliant blouse and a gaily trimmed hat. There is an air of fashion about her that might disappear under the analysis of a woman of the world, but which is quite sufficient

to make Kipps very proud to be distingiushed as her particular "feller," and to be allowed at temperate intervals
to use her Christian name.

The conversation is light and gay in the modern style,
and Flo keeps on smiling, good temper being her special
charm.

"Ye see, you don' mean what *I* mean," he is saying.

"Well, what do *you* mean?"

"Not what you mean!"

"Well, tell me."

"*Ah!* That's another story."

Pause. They look meaningly at one another.

"You *are* a one for being roundabout," says the lady.

"Well, you're not so plain, you know."

"Not plain?"

"No."

"You don't mean to say I'm roundabout?"

"No. I mean to say . . . though——"

Pause.

"Well?"

"You're not a bit plain—you're" (his voice jumps up to
a squeak) "pretty. See?"

"Oh, get *out!*" her voice lifts also—with pleasure.

She strikes at him with her glove, then glances suddenly
at a ring upon her finger. Her smile disappears momentarily.
Another pause. Eyes meet and the smile returns.

"I wish I knew——" says Kipps.

"Knew——?"

"Where you got that ring."

She lifts the hand with the ring until her eyes just show
(very prettily) over it. "You'd just *like* to know," she says
slowly, and smiles still more brightly with the sense of successful effect.

"I dessay I could guess."

"I dessay you couldn't."

"Couldn't I?"

"No!"

"Guess it in three."

"Not the name."

"Ah!"

"*Ah!*"

"Well, anyhow lemme look at it."

He looks at it. Pause. Giggles, slight struggle, and a slap on Kipps' coatsleeve. A passerby appears down the path, and she hastily withdraws her hand.

She glances at the face of the approaching man. They maintain a bashful silence until he has passed.

III. THE WOOD-CARVING
CLASS

1

Though these services to Venus Epipontia, the seaside
Venus, and these studies in the art of dress, did much to
distract his thoughts and mitigate his earlier miseries, it
would be mere optimism to present Kipps as altogether
happy. A vague dissatisfaction with life drifted about him
and every now and again enveloped him like a sea fog.
During these periods it was greyly evident that there was
something, something vital in life, lacking. For no earthly
reason that Kipps could discover, he was haunted by a
suspicion that life was going wrong or had already gone
wrong in some irrevocable way. The ripening self-conscious-
ness of adolescence developed this into a clearly felt in-
sufficiency. It was all very well to carry gloves, open doors,
never say "Miss" to a girl, and walk "outside," but were
there not other things, conceivably even deeper things, before the complete thing was attained? For example, certain matters of knowledge. He perceived great bogs of
ignorance about him, fumbling traps, where other people,
it was alleged, *real* gentlemen and ladies, for example, and
the clergy, had knowledge and assurance, bogs which it
was sometimes difficult to elude. A girl arrived in the millinery department who could, she said, *speak* French and
German. She snubbed certain advances, and a realisation
of inferiority blistered Kipps. But he tried to pass the thing
off as a joke by saying, "Parlez-vous Francey," whenever
he met her, and inducing the junior apprentice to say the
same.

He even made some dim half-secret experiments towards
remedying the deficiencies he suspected. He spent five
shillings on five serial numbers of a Home Educator, and
bought (and even thought of reading) a Shakespeare and
a Bacon's "Advancement of Learning" and the poems of

Herrick from a chap who was hard up. He battled with Shakespeare all one Sunday afternoon, and found the "English Literature" with which Mr. Woodrow had equipped him had vanished down some crack in his mind. He had no doubt it was very splendid stuff, but he couldn't quite make out what it was all about. There was an occult meaning, he knew, in literature, and he had forgotten it. Moreover, he discovered one day, while taunting the junior apprentice with ignorance, that his "rivers of England" had also slipped his memory, and he laboriously restored that fabric of rote learning: "Ty Wear Tees 'Umber. . . ."

I suppose some such phase of discontent is a normal thing in every adolescence. The ripening mind seeks something upon which its will may crystallise, upon which its discursive emotions, growing more abundant with each year of life, may concentrate. For many, though not for all, it takes a religious direction, but in those particular years the mental atmosphere of Folkestone was exceptionally free from any revivalistic disturbance that might have reached Kipps' mental being. Sometimes they fall in love. I have known this uneasiness end in different cases in a vow to read one book (not a novel) every week, to read the Bible through in a year, to pass in the Honours division of the London Matriculation examination, to become an accomplished chemist, and never more to tell a lie. It led Kipps finally into Technical Education as we understand it in the south of England.

It was in the last year of his apprenticeship that he had pursued his researches after that missing qualification into the Folkestone Young Men's Association, where Mr. Chester Coote prevailed. Mr. Chester Coote was a young man of semi-independent means who inherited a share in a house agency, read Mrs. Humphry Ward, and took an interest in social work. He was a whitish-faced young man with a prominent nose, pale blue eyes, and a quivering quality in his voice. He was very active upon committees; he was very prominent and useful on all social occasions, in evidence upon platforms and upon all those semi-public occasions when the Great descend. He lived with an only sister. To Kipps and his kind in the Young Men's Association he read a stimulating paper on "Self-Help." He said it was the noblest of all our distinctive English characteris-

tics, and he was very much down upon the "over-educated"
Germans. At the close a young German hairdresser made
a few commendatory remarks which developed somehow
into an oration on Hanoverian politics. As he became excited he became guttural and obscure; the meeting sniggered
cheerfully at such ridiculous English, and Kipps was so
much amused that he forgot a private project to ask this
Chester Coote how he might set about a little self-help on
his own private account in such narrow margins of time as
the System of Mr. Shalford spared him. But afterwards
in the night-time it came to him again.

It was a few months later, and after his apprenticeship
was over and Mr. Shalford had with depreciatory observations taken him on as an improver at twenty pounds a year,
that this question was revived by a casual article on Technical Education in a morning paper that a commercial
traveller had left behind him. It played the *rôle* of the word
in season. Something in the nature of conversion, a faint
sort of concentration of purpose, really occurred in him
then. The article was written with penetrating vehemence,
and it stimulated him to the pitch of inquiring about the
local Science and Art Classes, and after he had told everybody in the shop about it and taken the advice of all who
supported his desperate resolution, he joined. At first he
attended the class in Freehand, that being the subject taught
on early closing night; and he had already made some
progress in that extraordinary routine of reproducing freehand "copies" which for two generations had passed with
English people for instruction in art, when the dates of the
classes were changed. Thereby just as the March winds
were blowing he was precipitated into the wood-carving
class, and his mind diverted first to this useful and broaden-
ing pursuit, and then to its teacher.

2

The class in wood-carving was an extremely select class,
conducted at that time by a young lady named Walshingham, and as this young lady was destined by fortune to
teach Kipps a great deal more than wood-carving, it will
be well if the reader gets the picture of her correctly in
mind. She was only a year or so older than he was; she

had a pale, intellectual face, dark grey eyes, and black hair, which she wore over her forehead in an original and striking way that she had adopted from a picture by Rossetti in the South Kensington Museum. She was slender, so that without ungainliness she had an effect of being tall, and her hands were shapely and white when they came into contrast with hands much exercised in rolling and blocking. She dressed in those loose and pleasant forms and those soft and tempered shades that arose in England in the socialistic-æsthetic epoch and remain to this day among us as the badge of those who read Turgenev's novels, scorn current fiction, and think on higher planes. I think she was as beautiful as most beautiful people, and to Kipps she was altogether beautiful. She had, Kipps learnt, matriculated at London University, an astounding feat to his imagination; and the masterly way in which she demonstrated how to prod and worry honest pieces of wood into useless and unedifying patterns in relief extorted his utmost admiration.

At first, when Kipps had learnt he was to be taught by a "girl," he was inclined to resent it, the more so as Buggins had recently been very strong on the gross injustice of feminine employment.

"We have to keep wives," said Buggins (though as a matter of fact he did not keep even one), "and how are we to do it with a lot of girls coming in to take the work out of our mouths?"

Afterwards Kipps, in conjunction with Pierce, looked at it from another point of view, and thought it would be rather a "lark." Finally, when he saw her, and saw her teaching, and coming nearer to him with an impressive deliberation, he was breathless with awe and the quality of her dark, slender femininity.

The class consisted of two girls and a maiden lady of riper years, friends of Miss Walshingham's, and anxious rather to support her in an interesting experiment than to become really expert wood-carvers; an oldish young man with spectacles and a black beard, who never spoke to any one, and who was evidently too short-sighted to see his work as a whole; a small boy who was understood to have a "gift" for wood-carving; and a lodging-house keeper who "took classes" every winter, she told Mr. Kipps, as though they were a tonic, and "found they did her good." And occasionally Mr. Chester Coote—refined and gentlemanly—would come into the class, with or without papers, ostensibly on committee business, but in reality to talk to the less attractive one of the two girl students; and sometimes a brother of Miss Walshingham's, a slender, dark young man with a pale face, and fluctuating resemblances to the young Napoleon, would arrive just at the end of the class-time to see his sister home.

All these personages impressed Kipps with a sense of inferiority that in the case of Miss Walshingham became positively abysmal. The ideas and knowledge they appeared to have, their personal capacity and freedom, opened a new world to his imagination. These people came and went, with a sense of absolute assurance, against an overwhelming background of plaster casts, diagrams and tables, benches and a blackboard—a background that seemed to him to be saturated with recondite knowledge and the occult and jealously guarded tips and secrets that constitute Art and the Higher Life. They went home, he imagined, to homes where the piano was played with distinction and freedom, and books littered the tables, and foreign languages were habitually used. They had complicated meals, no doubt—with serviettes. They "knew etiquette," and how to avoid all the errors for which Kipps bought penny manuals, "What to Avoid," "Common Errors in Speaking," and the like. He knew nothing about it all—nothing whatever; he was a creature of the outer darkness blinking in an unsuspected light.

He heard them speak easily and freely to one another of examinations, of books and paintings, of "last year's Academy"—a little contemptuously; and once, just at the end of the class-time, Mr. Chester Coote and young Walshingham and the two girls argued about something or other called, he fancied, "Vagner" or "Vargner"—they seemed to say it both ways—and which presently shaped itself more definitely as the name of a man who made up music. (Carshot and Buggins weren't in it with them.) Young Walshingham, it appeared, said something or other that was an "epigram," and they all applauded him. Kipps, I say, felt himself a creature of outer darkness, an inexcusable intruder in an altitudinous world. When the epigram happened, he first of all smiled, to pretend he understood, and instantly suppressed the smile to show he did not listen. Then he became extremely hot and uncomfortable, though nobody had noticed either phase.

It was clear his only chance of concealing his bottomless baseness was to hold his tongue, and meanwhile he chipped with earnest care, and abased his soul before the very shadow of Miss Walshingham. She used to come and direct and advise him, with, he felt, an effort to conceal the scorn she had for him; and, indeed, it is true that at first she thought of him chiefly as the clumsy young man with the red ears.

And as soon as he emerged from the first effect of pure and awestricken humility—he was greatly helped to emerge from that condition to a perception of human equality by the need the lodging-house keeper was under to talk while she worked, and as she didn't like Miss Walshingham and her friends very much, and the young man with spectacles was deaf, she naturally talked to Kipps—he perceived that he was in a state of adoration for Miss Walshingham that it seemed almost a blasphemous familiarity to speak of us being in love.

This state, you must understand, had nothing to do with "flirting" or "spooning" and that superficial passion that flashes from eye to eye upon the leas and pier—absolutely nothing. That he knew from the first. Her rather pallid, intelligent young face, beneath those sombre clouds of hair, put her in a class apart; towards her the thought of "attentions" paled and vanished. To approach such a being, to perform sacrifices and to perish obviously for her, seemed the limit he might aspire to, he or any man. For if his love was abasement, at any rate it had this much of manliness, that it covered all his sex. It had not yet come to Kipps to acknowledge any man as his better in his heart of hearts. When one does that the game is played and one grows old indeed.

The rest of his sentimental interests vanished altogether in this great illumination. He meditated about her when he was blocking cretonne; her image was before his eyes at tea-time, and blotted out the more immediate faces, and made him silent and preoccupied, and so careless in his bearing that the junior apprentice, sitting beside him,

mocked at and parodied his enormous bites of bread and
butter unreproved. He became conspicuously less popular
on the "fancy" side, the "costumes" was chilly with him
and the "millinery" cutting. But he did not care. An in-
termittent correspondent with Flo Bates, that had gone
on since she left Mr. Shalford's desk for a position at Tun-
bridge "nearer home," and which had roused Kipps in its
earlier stages to unparalleled heights of epistolary effort,
died out altogether by reason of his neglect. He heard with
scarcely a pang that, as a consequence perhaps of his neglect, Flo was "carrying on with a chap who managed a
farm."

Every Thursday he jabbed and gouged at his wood,
jabbing and gouging intersecting circles and diamond tracer-
ies, and that laboured inane which our mad world calls
ornament, and he watched Miss Walshingham furtively
whenever she turned away. The circles in consequence
were jabbed crooked; and his panels, losing their symmetry,
became comparatively pleasing to the untrained eye—and
once he jabbed his finger. He would cheerfully have jabbed
all his fingers if he could have found some means of using
the opening to express himself of the vague emotions that
possessed him. But he shirked conversation just as earnestly
as he desired it; he feared that profound general ignorance
of his might appear.

3

There came a time when she could not open one of the
class-room windows. The man with the black beard pored
over his chipping heedlessly. . . .

It did not take Kipps a moment to grasp his opportunity.
He dropped his gouge and stepped forward. "Lem *me*," he
said. . . .

He could not open the window either!

"Oh, please don't trouble," she said.

" 'Sno trouble," he gasped.

Still the sash stuck. He felt his manhood was at stake.
He gathered himself together for a tremendous effort, and
the pane broke with a snap, and he thrust his hand into
the void beyond.

"There!" said Miss Walshingham, and the glass fell ringing into the courtyard below.

Then Kipps made to bring his hand back, and felt the keen touch of the edge of the broken glass at his wrist. He turned dolefully. "I'm tremendously sorry," he said in answer to the accusation in Miss Walshingham's eyes. "I didn't think it would break like that,"—as if he had expected it to break in some quite different and entirely more satisfactory manner. The boy with the gift of wood-carving having stared at Kipps' face for a moment, became involved in a Laocoon struggle with a giggle.

"You've cut your wrist," said one of the girl friends, standing up and pointing. She was a pleasant-faced, greatly freckled girl, with a helpful disposition, and she said "You've cut your wrist," as brightly as if she had been a trained nurse.

Kipps looked down, and saw a swift line of scarlet rush down his hand. He perceived the other man student regarding this with magnified eyes. "You *have* cut your wrist," said Miss Walshingham, and Kipps regarded his damage with greater interest.

"He's cut his wrist," said the maiden lady to the lodging-house keeper, and seemed in doubt what a lady should do. "It's——" she hesitated at the word "bleeding," and nodded to the lodging-house keeper instead.

"Dreadfully," said the maiden lady, and tried to look and tried not to look at the same time.

"Of *course* he's cut his wrist," said the lodging-house keeper, momentarily quite annoyed at Kipps; and the other young lady, who thought Kipps rather common, went on quietly with her wood-cutting with an air of its being the proper thing to do—though nobody else seemed to know it.

"You must tie it up," said Miss Walshingham.

"We must tie it up," said the freckled girl.

"I 'adn't the slightest idea that window was going to break like that," said Kipps, with candour. "Nort the slightest."

He glanced again at the blood on his wrist, and it seemed to him that it was on the very point of dropping on the floor of that cultured class-room. So he very neatly licked it off, feeling at the same time for his handkerchief. "Oh, *don't!*" said Miss Walshingham as he did so, and the girl with the freckles made a movement of horror. The giggle got the better of the boy with the gift, and celebrated its triumph by unseemly noises; in spite of which it seemed to Kipps at the moment that the act that had made Miss Walshingham say "Oh, *don't!*" was rather a desperate and manly treatment of what was after all a creditable injury.

"It ought to be tied up," said the lodging-house keeper, holding her chisel upright in her hand. "It's a bad cut to bleed like that."

"We must tie it up," said the freckled girl, and hesitated in front of Kipps. "Have you got a handkerchief?" she said.

"I dunno 'ow I managed *not* to bring one," said Kipps. "I—— Not 'aving a cold I suppose some'ow I didn't think——"

He checked a further flow of blood.

The girl with the freckles caught Miss Walshingham's eye, and held it for a moment. Both glanced at Kipps' injury. The boy with the gift, who had reappeared with a chastened expression from some noisy pursuit beneath his desk, made the neglected motions of one who proffers shyly. Miss Walshingham under the spell of the freckled girl's eye produced a handkerchief. The voice of the maiden lady could be heard in the background. "I've been through all the technical education ambulance classes twice, and I know you go *so* if it's a vein, and *so* if it's an artery—at least you go *so* for one and *so* for the other, whichever it may be; but . . ."

"If you will give me your hand," said the freckled girl, and proceeded with Miss Walshingham's assistance to bandage Kipps in a most businesslike way. Yes, they actually bandaged Kipps. They pulled up his cuffs—happily they were not a very frayed pair—and held his wrist, and wrapped the soft handkerchief round it, and tightened the knot together. And Miss Walshingham's face, the face of that almost divine Over-human, came close to the face of Kipps.

"We're not hurting you, are we?" she said.

"Not a bit," said Kipps, as he would have said if they had been sawing his arm off.

"We're not experts, you know," said the freckled girl.

"I'm sure it's a dreadful cut," said Miss Walshingham.

"It ain't much reely," said Kipps; "and you're taking a lot of trouble. I'm sorry I broke that window. I can't think what I could have been doing."

"It isn't so much the cut at the time, it's the poisoning afterwards," came the voice of the maiden lady.

"Of course I'm quite willing to pay for the window," panted Kipps opulently.

"We must make it just as tight as possible, to stop the bleeding," said the freckled girl.

"I don't think it's much reely," said Kipps. "I'm awful sorry I broke that window, though."

"Put your finger on the knot, dear," said the freckled girl.

"Eh?" said Kipps; "I mean——"

Both the young ladies became very intent on the knot, and Mr. Kipps was very red and very intent upon the two young ladies.

"Mortified, and had to be sawn off," said the maiden lady.

"Sawn off?" said the lodging-house keeper.

"Sawn *right* off," said the maiden lady, and jabbed at her mangled design.

"*There*," said the freckled girl, "I think that ought to do. You're sure it's not too tight?"

"Not a bit," said Kipps.

He met Miss Walshingham's eye, and smiled to show how little he cared for wounds and pain. "It's only a little cut," he added.

The maiden lady appeared as an addition to their group. "You should have washed the wound, dear," she said. "I was just telling Miss Collis." She peered through her glasses at the bandage. "That doesn't look *quite* right," she remarked critically. "You should have taken the ambulance classes. But I suppose it will have to do. Are you hurting?"

"Not a bit," said Kipps, and he smiled at them all with the air of a brave soldier in hospital.

"I'm sure it *must* hurt," said Miss Walshingham.

"Anyhow, you're a very good patient," said the girl with the freckles.

Mr. Kipps became quite pink. "I'm only sorry I broke the window—that's all," he said. "But who would have thought it was going to break like that?"

Pause.

"I'm afraid you won't be able to go on carving tonight," said Miss Walshingham.

"I'll try," said Kipps. "It reely doesn't hurt—not anything to matter."

Presently Miss Walshingham came to him as he carved heroically with his hand bandaged in her handkerchief. There was a touch of a novel interest in her eyes. "I'm afraid you're not getting on very fast," she said.

The freckled girl looked up and regarded Miss Walshingham.

"I'm doing a little, anyhow," said Kipps. "I don't want to waste any time. A feller like me hasn't much time to spare."

It struck the girls that there was a quality of modest disavowal about that "feller like me." It gave them a light into this obscure person, and Miss Walshingham ventured to commend his work as "promising" and to ask whether he meant to follow it up. Kipps didn't "altogether know"— "things depended on so much," but if he was in Folkestone next winter he certainly should. It did not occur to Miss Walshingham at the time to ask why his progress in art depended upon his presence in Folkestone. There were some more questions and answers—they continued to talk to him for a little time, even when Mr. Chester Coote had come into the room—and when at last the conversation had died out it dawned upon Kipps just how much his cut wrist had done for him. . . .

He went to sleep that night revising that conversation for the twentieth time, treasuring this and expanding that, and inserting things he might have said to Miss Walshingham, things he might still say about himself—in relation more or less explicit to her. He wasn't quite sure if he wouldn't like his arm to mortify a bit, which would make him interesting, or to heal up absolutely, which would show the exceptional purity of his blood.

4

The affair of the broken window happened late in April, and the class came to an end in May. In that interval there were several small incidents and great developments of emotion. I have done Kipps no justice if I have made it seem that his face was unsightly. It was, as the freckled girl pointed out to Helen Walshingham, an "interesting" face, and that aspect of him which presented chiefly erratic hair and glowing ears ceased to prevail.

They talked him over, and the freckled girl discovered there was something "wistful" in his manner. They detected a "natural delicacy," and the freckled girl set herself to draw him out from that time forth. The freckled girl was nineteen, and very wise and motherly and benevolent, and really she greatly preferred drawing out Kipps to wood-carving. It was quite evident to her that Kipps was in love with Helen Walshingham, and it struck her as a queer and romantic and pathetic and extremely interesting phenomenon. And as at that time she regarded Helen as "simply lovely," it seemed only right and proper that she should assist Kipps in his modest efforts to place himself in a state of absolute *abandon* upon her altar.

Under her sympathetic management the position of Kipps was presently defined quite clearly. He was unhappy in his position—misunderstood. He told her he "didn't seem to get on like" with customers, and she translated this for him as "too sensitive." The discontent with his fate in life, the dreadful feeling that education was slipping by him, troubles that time and usage were glazing over a little, revived to their old acuteness but not to their old hopelessness. As a basis for sympathy indeed they were even a source of pleasure.

And one day at dinner it happened that Carshot and Buggins fell talking of "these here writers," and how Dickens had been a labeller of blacking and Thackeray "an artist who couldn't sell a drawing," and how Samuel Johnson had walked to London without any boots, having thrown away his only pair "out of pride." "It's luck," said Buggins, "to a very large extent. They just happen to hit on something that catches on, and there you are!"

"Nice easy life they have of it, too," said Miss Mergle. "Write just an hour or so, and done for the day! Almost like gentlefolks."

"There's more work in it than you'd think," said Carshot, stooping to a mouthful.

"I wouldn't mind changing, for all that," said Buggins.

"I'd like to see one of these here authors marking off with Jimmy."

"I think they copy from each other a good deal," said Miss Mergle.

"Even then (chup, chup, chup)," said Carshot, "there's writing it out in their own hands."

They proceeded to enlarge upon the literary life, on its ease and dignity, on the social recognition accorded to those who led it, and on the ample gratifications their vanity achieved. "Pictures everywhere—never get a new suit without being photographed—almost like Royalty," said Miss Mergle.

And all this talk impressed the imagination of Kipps very greatly. Here was a class that seemed to bridge the gulf. On the one hand essentially Low, but by factitious circumstances capable of entering upon those levels of social superiority to which all true Englishmen aspire, those levels from which one may tip a butler, scorn a tailor, and even commune with those who lead "men" into battle. "Almost like gentlefolks"—that was it! He brooded over these things in the afternoon, until they blossomed into daydreams. Suppose, for example, he had chanced to write a book, a well-known book, under an assumed name, and yet kept on being a draper all the time. . . Impossible, of course, but *suppose*—it made quite a long dream.

And at the next wood-carving class he let it be drawn from him that his real choice in life was to be a Nawther—"only one doesn't get a chance."

After that there were times when Kipps had that pleasant sense that comes of attracting interest. He was a mute, inglorious Dickens, or at any rate something of that sort, and they were all taking him at that. The discovery of this indefinable "something in" him, the development of which was now painfully restricted and impossible, did much to bridge the gulf between himself and Miss Walshingham. He was unfortunate, he was futile, but he was not "common." Even now with help . . .? The two girls, and the freckled girl in particular, tried to "stir him up" to some effort to do his imputed potentialities justice. They were still young enough to believe that to nice and niceish members of the male sex—more especially when under the stimulus of feminine encouragement—nothing is finally impossible.

The freckled girl was, I say, the stage manager of this affair, but Miss Walshingham was the presiding divinity. A touch of proprietorship came in her eyes at times when she looked at him. He was hers—unconditionally—and she knew it.

To her directly Kipps scarcely ever made a speech. The enterprising things that he was continually devising to say to her, he usually did not say, or he said them in a suitably modified form to the girl with the freckles. And one day the girl with the freckles smote him to the heart. She said to him, with the faintest indication of her head across the class-room to where her friend reached a cast from the shelf, "I do think Helen Walshingham is sometimes the most lovely person in the world. Look at her now!"

Kipps gasped for a moment. The moment lengthened, and she regarded him as an intelligent young surgeon might regard an operation without anæsthetics.

"You're right," he said, and then looked at her with an entire abandonment of visage.

She coloured under his glare of silent avowal, and he blushed brightly.

"I think so, too," he said hoarsely, cleared his throat, and after a meditative moment proceeded sacramentally with his wood-carving.

"You *are* wonderful," said the freckled girl to Miss Walshingham, apropos of nothing, as they went on their way home together. "He simply adores you."

"But, my dear, what have I done?" said Helen.

"That's just it," said the freckled girl. "What *have* you done?"

And then with a terrible swiftness came the last class of the course, to terminate this relationship altogether. Kipps was careless of dates, and the thing came upon him with an effect of abrupt surprise. Just as his petals were expanding so hopefully, "Finis," and the thing was at an end. But Kipps did not fully appreciate that the end was indeed and really and truly the end, until he was back in the Emporium after the end was over.

The end began practically in the middle of the last class,

when the freckled girl broached the topic of terminations. She developed the question of just how he was going on after the class ended. She hoped he would stick to certain resolutions of self-improvement he had breathed. She said quite honestly that he owed it to himself to develop his possibilities. He expressed firm resolve, but dwelt on difficulties. He had no books. She instructed him how to get books from the public library. He was to get a form of application for a ticket signed by a ratepayer; and he said "of course," when she said Mr. Shalford would do that, though all the time he knew perfectly well it would "never do" to ask Mr. Shalford for anything of the sort. She explained that she was going to North Wales for the summer, information he received without immediate regret. At intervals he expressed his intention of going on with wood-carving when the summer was over, and once he added "If——"

She considered herself extremely delicate not to press for the completion of that "if——"

After that talk there was an interval of languid wood-carving and watching Miss Walshingham.

Then presently there came a bustle of packing, a great ceremony of hand-shaking all round by Miss Collis and the maiden lady of ripe years, and then Kipps found himself outside the class-room, on the landing with his two friends. It seemed to him he had only just learnt that this was the last class of all. There came a little pause, and the freckled girl suddenly went back into the class-room, and left Kipps and Miss Walshingham alone together for the first time. Kipps was instantly breathless. She looked at his face with a glance that mingled sympathy and curiosity, and held out her white hand.

"Well, good-bye, Mr. Kipps," she said.

He took her hand and held it. "I'd do anything," said Kipps, and had not the temerity to add, "for you." He stopped awkwardly. He shook her hand and said, "Good-bye."

There was a little pause.

"I hope you will have a pleasant holiday," she said.

"I shall come back to the class next year, anyhow," said Kipps valiantly, and turned abruptly to the stairs.

"I hope you will," said Miss Walshingham.

He turned back towards her. "Reelly?" he said.

"I hope everybody will come back."

"I will—anyhow," said Kipps. "You may count on that," and he tried to make his tones significant.

They looked at one another through a little pause.

"Good-bye," she said.

Kipps lifted his hat. She turned towards the class-room.

"Well?" said the freckled girl, coming back towards her.

"Nothing," said Helen. "At least—presently." And she became very energetic about some scattered tools on a desk.

The freckled girl went out and stood for a moment at the head of the stairs. When she came back she looked very hard at her friend. The incident struck her as important— wonderfully important. It was unassimilable, of course, and absurd, but there it was, the thing that is so cardinal to a girl, the emotion, the subservience, the crowning triumph of her sex. She could not help feeling that Helen took it, on the whole, a little too hardly.

IV. CHITTERLOW

1

The hour of the class on the following Thursday found Kipps in a state of nearly incredible despondency. He was sitting with his eyes on the reading room clock, his chin resting on his fists and his elbows on the accumulated comic papers that were comic alas! in vain! He paid no heed to the little man in spectacles glaring opposite to him, famishing for *Fun*. In this place it was he had sat night after night, each night more blissful than the last, waiting until it should be time to go to Her! And then—bliss! And now the hour had come and there was no class! There would be no class now until next October; it might be there would never be a class so far as he was concerned again.

It might be there would never be a class again, for Shalford, taking exception at a certain absent-mindedness that led to mistakes and more particularly to the ticketing of several articles in Kipps' Manchester window upside down, had been "on to" him for the past few days in an exceedingly onerous manner . . .

He sighed profoundly, pushed the comic papers back—they were rent away from him instantly by the little man in spectacles—and tried the old engravings of Folkestone in the past, that hang about the room. But these, too, failed to minister to his bruised heart. He wandered about the corridors for a time and watched the library indicator for awhile. Wonderful thing that! But it did not hold him for long. People came and laughed near him and that jarred with him dreadfully. He went out of the building and a beastly cheerful barrel organ mocked him in the street. He was moved to a desperate resolve to go down to the beach. There it might be he would be alone. The sea might be rough—and attuned to him. It would certainly be dark.

"If I 'ad a penny I'm blest if I wouldn't go and chuck

myself off the end of the pier. . . . *She'd* never miss me. . . ."
He followed a deepening vein of thought.

"Penny though! It's tuppence," he said after a space.

He went down Dover Street in a state of profound melancholia—at the pace and mood as it were of his own funeral procession—and he crossed at the corner of Tontine Street heedless of all mundane things. And there it was that Fortune came upon him, in disguise and with a loud shout, the shout of a person endowed with an unusually rich, full voice, followed immediately by a violent blow in the back.

His hat was over his eyes and an enormous weight rested on his shoulders and something kicked him in the back of his calf.

Then he was on all fours in some mud that Fortune, in conjunction with the Folkestone corporation and in the pursuit of equally mysterious ends, had heaped together even lavishly for his reception.

He remained in that position for some seconds awaiting further developments and believing almost anything broken before his heart. Gathering at last that this temporary violence of things in general was over, and being perhaps assisted by a clutching hand, he arose, and found himself confronting a figure holding a bicycle and thrusting forward a dark face in anxious scrutiny.

"You aren't hurt, Matey?" gasped the figure.

"Was that *you* 'it me?" said Kipps.

"It's these handles, you know," said the figure with an air of being a fellow sufferer. "They're too *low*. And when I go to turn, if I don't remember, Bif!—and I'm *in* to something."

"Well—you give me a oner in the back—anyhow," said Kipps, taking stock of his damages.

"I was coming down hill, you know," explained the bicyclist. "These little Folkestone hills are a Fair Treat. It isn't as though I'd been on the level. I came rather a whop."

"You did *that*," said Kipps.

"I was back pedalling for all I was worth anyhow," said the bicyclist. "Not that I *am* worth much back pedalling."

He glanced round and made a sudden movement almost as if to mount his machine. Then he turned as rapidly to Kipps again, who was now stooping down, pursuing the tale of his injuries.

"Here's the back of my trouser leg all tore down," said Kipps, "and I believe I'm bleeding. You reely ought to be more careful——"

The stranger investigated the damage with a rapid movement. "Holy Smoke, so you are!" He laid a friendly hand on Kipps' arm. "I say—look here! Come up to my diggings and sew it up. I'm——. Of course I'm to blame, and I say——" his voice sank to a confidential friendliness. "Here's a slop. Don't let on I ran you down. Haven't a lamp, you know. Might be a bit awkward, for *me*."

Kipps looked up towards the advancing policeman. The appeal to his generosity was not misplaced. He immediately took sides with his assailant. He stood up as the representative of the law drew nearer. He assumed an air which he considered highly suggestive of an accident not having happened.

"All right," he said, "go on!"

"Right you are," said the cyclist promptly, and led the way, and then, apparently with some idea of deception, called over his shoulder, "I'm tremendous glad to have met you, old chap.

"It really isn't a hundred yards," he said after they had passed the policeman, "it's just round the corner."

"Of course," said Kipps, limping slightly. "I don't want to get a chap into trouble. Accidents *will* happen. Still——"

"Oh! *rather!* I believe you. Accidents *will* happen. Especially when you get *me* on a bicycle." He laughed. "You aren't the first I've run down not by any manner of means! I don't think you can be hurt much either. It isn't as though I was scorching. You didn't see me coming. I was back pedalling like anything. Only naturally it seems to you I must have been coming fast. And I did all I could to ease off the bump as I hit you. It was just the treadle I think came against your calf. But it was All Right of you about that policeman, you know. That was a Fair Bit of All Right. Under the Circs, if you'd told him I was riding it might have been forty bob! Forty bob! I'd have had to tell 'em Time is Money. Just now for Mr. H. C.

"I shouldn't have blamed you either, you know. Most men after a bump like that might have been spiteful. The least I can do is to stand you a needle and thread. And a clothes brush. It isn't everyone who'd have taken it like you.

"Scorching! Why if I'd been scorching you'd have—coming as we did—you'd have been knocked silly.

"But I tell you, the way you caught on about that slop was something worth seeing. When I asked you, I didn't half expect it. Bif! Right off. Cool as a cucumber. Had your line at once. I tell you that there isn't many men would have acted as you have done, I *will* say that. You acted like a gentleman over that slop."

Kipps' first sense of injury disappeared. He limped along a pace or so behind, making depreciatory noises in response to these flattering remarks and taking stock of the very appreciative person who uttered them.

As they passed the lamps he was visible as a figure with a slight anterior plumpness, progressing buoyantly on knickerbockered legs, with quite enormous calves, legs that, contrasting with Kipps' own narrow practise, were even exuberantly turned out at the knees and toes. A cycling cap was worn very much on one side, and from beneath it protruded carelessly straight wisps of dark red hair, and ever and again an ample nose came into momentary view round the corner. The muscular cheeks of this person and a certain generosity of chin he possessed were blue shaven and he had no moustache. His carriage was spacious and confident, his gestures up and down the narrow deserted back street they traversed, were irresistibly suggestive of ownership; a suggestion of broadly gesticulating shadows were born squatting on his feet and grew and took possession of the road and reunited at last with the shadows of the infinite, as lamp after lamp was passed. Kipps saw by the flickering light of one of them that they were in Little Fenchurch Street, and then they came round a corner sharply into a dark court and stopped at the door of a particularly ramshackle looking little house, held up between two larger ones, like a drunken man between policemen.

The cyclist propped his machine carefully against the window, produced a key and blew down it sharply. "The lock's a bit tricky," he said, and devoted himself for some moments to the task of opening the door. Some mechanical catastrophe ensued and the door was open.

"You'd better wait here a bit while I get the lamp," he

remarked to Kipps; "very likely it isn't filled," and vanished
into the blackness of the passage. "Thank God for matches!"
he said, and Kipps had an impression of a passage in the
transitory pink flare and the bicyclist disappearing into a
further room. Kipps was so much interested by these things
that for the time he forgot his injuries altogether.

An interval and Kipps was dazzled by a pink shaded kero-
sene lamp. "You go in," said the red-haired man, "and I'll
bring in the bike," and for a moment Kipps was alone
in the lamp-lit room. He took in rather vaguely the shabby
ensemble of the little apartment, the round table covered
with a torn, red, glass-stained cover on which the lamp
stood, a mottled looking-glass over the fireplace reflecting
this, a disused gas bracket, an extinct fire, a number of
dusty postcards and memoranda stuck round the glass, a
dusty, crowded paper rack on the mantel with a number of
cabinet photographs, a table littered with papers and cigarette ash and a syphon of soda water. Then the cyclist reappeared and Kipps saw his blue-shaved, rather animated
face and bright-reddish, brown eyes for the first time. He
was a man perhaps ten years older than Kipps, but his
beardless face made them in a way contemporary.

"You behaved all right about that policeman—anyhow,"
he repeated as he came forward.

"I don't see 'ow else I could 'ave done," said Kipps quite
modestly. The cyclist scanned his guest for the first time and
decided upon hospitable details.

"We'd better let that mud dry a bit before we brush it.
Whiskey there is, good old Methuselah, Canadian Rye, and
there's some brandy that's all right. Which'll you have?"

"*I* dunno," said Kipps, taken by surprise, and then seeing
no other course but acceptance, "well—whiskey, then."

"Right you are, old boy, and if you'll take my advice
you'll take it neat. I may not be a particular judge of this
sort of thing, but I do know old Methuselah pretty well.
Old Methuselah—four stars. That's me! Good old Harry
Chitterlow and good old Methuselah. Leave 'em together.
Bif! He's gone!"

He laughed loudly, looked about him, hesitated and retired, leaving Kipps in possession of the room and free to
make a more precise examination of its contents.

2

He particularly remarked the photographs that adorned the apartment. They were chiefly photographs of ladies, in one case in tights, which Kipps thought a "bit 'ot," but one represented the bicyclist in the costume of some remote epoch. It did not take Kipps long to infer that the others were probably actresses and that his host was an actor, and the presence of the half of a large, coloured playbill seemed to confirm this. A note framed in an Oxford frame that was a little too large for it, he presently demeaned himself to read. "Dear Mr. Chitterlow," it ran its brief course, "if after all you will send the play you spoke of I will endeavour to read it," followed by a stylish but absolutely illegible signature, and across this was written in pencil, "What price, Harry, now?" And in the shadow by the window was a rough and rather able sketch of the bicyclist in chalk on brown paper, calling particular attention to the curvature of the forward lines of his hull and calves and the jaunty carriage of his nose, and labelled unmistakably "Chitterlow." Kipps thought it "rather a take-off." The papers on the table by the syphon were in manuscript. Kipps observed manuscript of a particularly convulsive and blottesque sort and running obliquely across the page.

Presently he heard the metallic clamour as if of a series of irreparable breakages with which the lock of the front door discharged its function, and then Chitterlow reappeared, a little out of breath as if from running and with a starry labelled bottle in his large, freckled hand.

"Sit down, old chap," he said, "sit down. I had to go out for it after all. Wasn't a solitary bottle left. However, it's all right now we're here. No, don't sit on that chair, there's sheets of my play on that. That's the one—with the broken arm. I think this glass is clean, but anyhow wash it out with a squizz of syphon and shy it in the fireplace. Here! I'll do it! Lend it here!"

As he spoke Mr. Chitterlow produced a corkscrew from a table drawer, attached and overcame good old Methusaleh's cork in a style a bartender might envy, washed out two tumblers in his simple, effectual manner, and poured a

couple of inches of the ancient fluid into each. Kipps took
his tumbler, said "Thenks" in an off-hand way, and after
a momentary hesitation whether he should say "here's to
you!" or not, put it to his lips without that ceremony. For
a space fire in his throat occupied his attention to the exclusion of other matters, and then he discovered Mr. Chitterlow with an intensely bulldog pipe alight, seated on the
opposite side of the empty fireplace and pouring himself out
a second dose of whiskey.

"After all," said Mr. Chitterlow, with his eye on the
bottle and a little smile wandering to hide amidst his larger
features, "this accident might have been worse. I wanted
someone to talk to a bit, and I didn't want to go to a pub,
leastways not a Folkestone pub, because as a matter of fact
I'd promised Mrs. Chitterlow, who's away, not to, for various reasons, though of course if I'd wanted to I'm just that
sort I should have all the same, and here we are! It's curious how one runs up against people out bicycling!"

"Isn't it!" said Kipps, feeling that the time had come for
him to say something.

"Here we are, sitting and talking like old friends, and
half an hour ago we didn't know we existed. Leastways we
didn't know each other existed. I might have passed you in
the street perhaps and you might have passed me, and how
was I to tell that, put to the test, you would have behaved
as decently as you have behaved. Only it happened otherwise, that's all. You're not smoking!" he said. "Have a cigarette?"

Kipps made a confused reply that took the form of not
minding if he did, and drank another sip of old Methusaleh
in his confusion. He was able to follow the subsequent
course of that sip for quite a long way. It was as though the
old gentleman was brandishing a burning torch through his
vitals, lighting him here and lighting him there until at last
his whole being was in a glow. Chitterlow produced a tobacco pouch and cigarette papers and with an interesting
parenthesis that was a little difficult to follow about some
lady named Kitty something or other who had taught him
the art when he was as yet only what you might call a nice
boy, made Kipps a cigarette, and with a consideration that
won Kipps' gratitude suggested that after all he might find a
little soda water an improvement with the whiskey. "Some

people like it that way," said Chitterlow, and then with voluminous emphasis, *"I don't."*

Emboldened by the weakened state of his enemy Kipps promptly swallowed the rest of him and had his glass at once hospitably replenished. He began to feel he was of a firmer consistency than he commonly believed, and turned his mind to what Chitterlow was saying with the resolve to play a larger part in the conversation than he had hitherto done. Also he smoked through his nose quite successfully, an art he had only very recently acquired.

Meanwhile Chitterlow explained that he was a playwright, and the tongue of Kipps was unloosened to respond that he knew a chap, or rather one of their fellows knew a chap, or at least to be perfectly correct this fellow's brother did, who had written a play. In response to Chitterlow's enquiries he could not recall the title of the play, nor where it had appeared nor the name of the manager who produced it, though he thought the title was something about "Love's Ransom" or something like that.

"He made five 'undred pounds by it, though," said Kipps. "I know that."

"That's nothing," said Chitterlow, with an air of experience that was extremely convincing. "Nothing. May seem a big sum to *you*, but *I* can assure you it's just what one gets any day. There's any amount of money, an-ny amount, in a good play."

"I dessay," said Kipps, drinking.

"Any amount of money!"

Chitterlow began a series of illustrative instances. He was clearly a person of quite unequalled gift for monologue. It was as though some conversational dam had burst upon Kipps, and in a little while he was drifting along upon a copious rapid of talk about all sorts of theatrical things by one who knows all about them, and quite incapable of anticipating whither that rapid meant to carry him. Presently somehow they had got to anecdotes about well-known theatrical managers, little Teddy Bletherskite, artful old Chumps, and the magnificent Behemoth, "petted to death, you know, fair sickened, by all these society women." Chitterlow described various personal encounters with these personages, always with modest self-depreciation, and gave Kipps a very amusing imitation of old Chumps in a state of intoxication.

Then he took two more stiff doses of old Methusaleh in rapid succession.

Kipps reduced the hither end of his cigarette to a pulp as he sat "dessaying" and "quite believing" Chitterlow in the sagest manner and admiring the easy way in which he was getting on with this very novel and entertaining personage. He had another cigarette made for him, and then Chitterlow, assuming by insensible degrees more and more of the manner of a rich and successful playwright being interviewed by a young admirer, set himself to answer questions which sometimes Kipps asked and sometimes Chitterlow, about the particulars and methods of his career. He undertook this self-imposed task with great earnestness and vigour, treating the matter indeed with such fulness that at times it seemed lost altogether under a thicket of parentheses, footnotes and episodes that branched and budded from its stem. But it always emerged again, usually by way of illustration to its own digressions. Practically it was a mass of material for the biography of a man who had been everywhere and done everything (including the Hon. Thomas Norgate, which was a Record), and in particular had acted with great distinction and profit (he dated various anecdotes, "when I was getting thirty, or forty or fifty, dollars a week") throughout America and the entire civilised world.

And as he talked on and on in that full, rich, satisfying voice he had, and as old Methusaleh, indisputably a most drunken old reprobate of a whiskey, busied himself throughout Kipps, lighting lamp after lamp until the entire framework of the little draper was illuminated and glowing like some public building on a festival, behold Chitterlow and Kipps with him and the room in which they sat, were transfigured! Chitterlow became in very truth that ripe, full man of infinite experience and humour and genius, fellow of Shakespeare and Ibsen and Maeterlinck (three names he placed together quite modestly far above his own) and no longer ambiguously dressed in a sort of yachting costume with cycling knickerbockers, but elegantly if unconventionally attired, and the room ceased to be a small and shabby room in a Folkestone slum, and grew larger and more richly furnished, and the fly-blown photographs were curious old pictures, and the rubbish on the walls the most rare and costly bric-à-brac, and the indisputable paraffin lamp, a soft and splendid light. A certain youthful heat that to many minds might have weakened old Methusaleh's starry claim to a ripe antiquity, vanished in that glamour, two burnt holes and a claimant darn in the table cloth, moreover, became no more than the pleasing contradictions natural in the house of genius, and as for Kipps!—Kipps was a bright young man of promise, distinguished by recent quick, courageous proceedings not too definitely insisted upon, and he had been rewarded by admission to a sanctum and confidences, for which the common prosperous, for which "society women" even, were notoriously sighing in vain. "Don't *want* them, my boy; they'd simply play old Harry with the work, you know! Chaps outside, bank clerks and university fellows, think the life's all *that* sort of thing. Don't you believe 'em. Don't you believe 'em."

And then——!

"Boom. . . Boom. . . Boom. . . Boom. . . ." right in the middle of a most entertaining digression on flats who join touring companies under the impression that they are actors, Kipps much amused at their flatness as exposed by Chitterlow.

"Lor'!" said Kipps like one who awakens, "that's not eleven!"

"Must be," said Chitterlow. "It was nearly ten when I got that whiskey. It's early yet——"

"All the same I must be going," said Kipps, and stood up. "Even now—maybe. Fact is—I 'ad *no* idea. The 'ouse door shuts at 'arf past ten, you know. I ought to 'ave thought before."

"Well, if you *must* go! I tell you what. I'll come, too. . . . Why! There's your leg, old man! Clean forgot it! You can't go through the streets like that. I'll sew up the tear. And meanwhile have another whiskey."

"I ought to be getting on *now*," protested Kipps feebly, and then Chitterlow was showing him how to kneel on a chair in order that the rent trouser leg should be attainable and old Methuselah on his third round was busy repairing the temporary eclipse of Kipps' arterial glow. Then suddenly Chitterlow was seized with laughter and had to leave off sewing to tell Kipps that the scene wouldn't make a bad bit of business in a farcical comedy, and then he began to sketch out the farcical comedy and that led him to digression about another farcical comedy of which he had written a ripping opening scene which wouldn't take ten minutes to read. It had something in it that had never been done on the stage before, and was yet perfectly legitimate, namely, a man with a live beetle down the back of his neck trying to seem at his ease in a roomful of people. . . .

"*They* won't lock you out," he said, in a singularly reassuring tone, and began to read and act what he explained to be (not because he had written it, but simply because he knew it was so on account of his exceptional experience of the stage) and what Kipps also quite clearly saw to be, one of the best opening scenes that had ever been written.

When it was over Kipps, who rarely swore, was inspired to say the scene was "damned fine" about six times over, whereupon as if by way of recognition, Chitterlow took a simply enormous portion of the inspiring antediluvian, declaring at the same time that he had rarely met a "finer" intelligence than Kipps' (stronger there might be, *that* he couldn't say with certainty as yet, seeing how little after all they had seen of each other, but a finer *never*); that it was a shame such a gallant and discriminating intelligence should be nightly either locked up or locked out at ten—well, ten thirty then—and that he had half a mind to recommend old somebody or other (apparently the editor of a London daily paper) to put on Kipps forthwith as a dramatic critic in the place of the current incapable.

"I don't think I've ever made up anything for print," said Kipps; "——ever. I'd have a thundering good try, though, if ever I got a chance. I would that! I've written window tickets often enough. Made 'em up and everything. But that's different."

"You'd come to it all the fresher for not having done it before. And the way you picked up every point in that scene, my boy, was a Fair Treat! I tell you, you'd knock William Archer into fits. Not so literary, of course, you'd be, but I don't believe in literary critics any more than in literary playwrights. Plays *aren't* literature—that's just the point they miss. Plays are plays. No! That won't hamper you anyhow. You're wasted down here, I tell you. Just as I was, before I took to acting. I'm hanged if I wouldn't like your opinion on these first two acts of that tragedy I'm on to. I haven't told you about that. It wouldn't take me more than an hour to read. . . ."

3

Then so far as he could subsequently remember, Kipps had "another," and then it would seem that suddenly, regardless of the tragedy, he insisted that he "reelly *must* be getting on," and from that point his memory became irregular. Certain things have remained quite clearly, and as it is a matter of common knowledge that intoxicated people forget what happens to them, it follows that he was not intoxicated. Chitterlow came with him partly to see him home and partly for a freshener before turning in. Kipps recalled afterwards very distinctly how in Little Fenchurch Street he discovered that he could not walk straight and also that Chitterlow's needle and thread in his still unmended trouser leg was making an annoying little noise on the pavement behind him. He tried to pick up the needle suddenly by surprise and somehow tripped and fell and then Chitterlow, laughing uproariously, helped him up. "It wasn't a bicycle this time, old boy," said Chitterlow, and that appeared to them both at the time as being a quite extraordinarily good joke indeed. They punched each other about on the strength of it.

For a time after that Kipps certainly pretended to be quite desperately drunk and unable to walk and Chitterlow entered into the pretence and supported him. After that Kipps remembered being struck with the extremely laughable absurdity of going down hill to Tontine Street in order to go up hill again to the Emporium, and trying to get that idea into Chitterlow's head and being unable to do so on account of his own merriment or Chitterlow's evident intoxication, and his next memory after that was of the exterior of the Emporium, shut and darkened, and, as it were, frowning at him with all its stripes of yellow and green. The chilly way in which "Shalford" glittered in the moonlight printed itself with particular vividness on his mind. It appeared to Kipps that that establishment was closed to him for evermore. Those gilded letters, in spite of appearances, spelt FINIS for him and exile from Folkestone. He would never do wood-carving, never see Miss Walshingham again. Not that he had ever hoped to see her again. But this was the knife, this was final. He had stayed out, he had got drunk, there had been that row about the Manchester window dressing only three days ago. . . In the retrospect he was quite sure that he was perfectly sober then and at bottom extremely unhappy, but he kept a brave face on the matter nevertheless, and declared stoutly he didn't care if he *was* locked out.

Whereupon Chitterlow slapped him on the back very hard and told him that was a "Bit of All Right," and assured him that when he himself had been a clerk in Sheffield before he took to acting he had been locked out sometimes for six nights running.

"What's the result?" said Chitterlow. "I could go back to that place now, and they'd be glad to have me. . . . Glad to have me," he repeated, and then added, "that is to say, if they remember me—which isn't very likely."

Kipps asked a little weakly, "What am I to do?"

"Keep out," said Chitterlow. "You can't knock 'em up now—that would give you Right away. You'd better try and sneak in in the morning with the Cat. That'll do you. You'll probably get in all right in the morning if nobody gives you away."

Then for a time—perhaps as the result of that slap in the back—Kipps felt decidedly queer, and acting on Chitterlow's advice went for a bit of a freshener upon the Leas. After a time he threw off the temporary queerness and found Chitterlow patting him on the shoulder and telling him that he'd be all right now in a minute and all the better for it—which he was. And the wind having dropped and the night being now a really very beautiful moonlight night indeed, and all before Kipps to spend as he liked and with only a very little tendency to spin round now and again to mar its splendour, they set out to walk the whole length of the Leas to the Sandgate lift and back, and as they walked Chitterlow spoke first of moonlight transfiguring the sea and then of moonlight transfiguring faces, and so at last he came to the topic of Love, and upon that he dwelt a great while, and with a wealth of experience and illustrative anecdote that seemed remarkably pungent and material to Kipps. He forgot his lost Miss Walshingham and his outraged employer again. He became as it were a desperado by reflection.

Chitterlow had had adventures, a quite astonishing variety of adventures in this direction; he was a man with a past, a really opulent past, and he certainly seemed to like to look back and see himself amidst its opulence.

He made no consecutive history, but he gave Kipps vivid, momentary pictures of relations and entanglements. One moment he was in flight—only too worthily in flight—before the husband of a Malay woman in Cape Town. At the next he was having passionate complications with the daughter of a clergyman in York. Then he passed to a remarkable grouping at Seaford.

"They say you can't love two women at once," said Chitterlow. "But I tell you——" He gesticulated and raised his ample voice. "It's *Rot! Rot!*"

"I know that," said Kipps.

"Why, when I was in the smalls with Bessie Hopper's company there were three." He laughed and decided to add, "Not counting Bessie, that is."

He set out to reveal Life as it is lived in touring companies, a quite amazing jungle of interwoven "affairs" it appeared to be, a mere amorous winepress for the crushing of hearts.

"People say this sort of thing's a nuisance and interferes with Work. I tell you it isn't. The Work couldn't go on without it. They *must* do it. They haven't the Temperament if they don't. If they hadn't the Temperament they wouldn't want to act, if they have—Bif!"

"You're right," said Kipps. "I see that."

Chitterlow proceeded to a close criticism of certain historical indiscretions of Mr. Clement Scott respecting the morals of the stage. Speaking in confidence and not as one who addresses the public, he admitted regretfully the general truth of these comments. He proceeded to examine various typical instances that had almost forced themselves upon him personally, and with especial regard to the contrast between his own character towards women and that of the Hon. Thomas Norgate, with whom it appeared he had once been on terms of great intimacy. . . .

Kipps listened with emotion to these extraordinary recollections. They were wonderful to him, they were incredibly credible. Of course the tumultuous, passionate course was the way life ran—except in high-class establishments! Such things happened in novels, in plays—only he had been fool enough not to understand they happened. His share in the conversation was now indeed no more than faint writing in the margin; Chitterlow was talking quite continuously. He expanded his magnificent voice into huge guffaws, he drew it together into a confidential intensity, it became drawlingly reminiscent, he was frank, frank with the effect of a revelation, reticent also with the effect of a revelation, a stupendously gesticulating, moonlit black figure, wallowing in itself, preaching Adventure and the Flesh to Kipps. Yet withal shot with something of sentiment, with a sort of sentimental refinement very coarsely and egotistically done. The Times he had had!—even before he was as old as Kipps he had had innumerable times.

Well, he said with a sudden transition, he had sown his wild oats—one had to somewhen—and now he fancied he had mentioned it earlier in the evening, he was happily married. She was, he indicated, a "born lady." Her father was a prominent lawyer, a solicitor in Kentish Town, "done a lot of public house business"; her mother was second cousin to the wife of Abel Jones, the fashionable portrait painter— "almost Society people in a way." That didn't count with Chitterlow. He was no snob. What *did* count was that she possessed, what he ventured to assert without much fear of contradiction, was the very finest, completely untrained contralto voice in all the world. ("But to hear it properly," said Chitterlow, "you want a Big Hall.") He became rather vague and jerked his head about to indicate when and how he had entered matrimony. She was, it seemed, "away with her people." It was clear that Chitterlow did not get on with these people very well. It would seem they failed to appreciate his playwright, regarding it as an unremunerative pursuit, whereas as he and Kipps knew, wealth beyond the dreams of avarice would presently accrue. Only patience and persistence were needful.

He went off at a tangent to hospitality. Kipps must come down home with him. They couldn't wander about all night, with a bottle of the right sort pining at home for them. "You can sleep on the sofa. You won't be worried by broken springs anyhow, for I took 'em all out myself two or three weeks ago. I don't see what they even put 'em in for. It's a point I know about. I took particular notice of it when I was with Bessie Hopper. Three months we were and all over England, North Wales and the Isle of Man, and I never struck a sofa in diggings anywhere that hadn't a broken spring. Not once—all the time."

He added almost absently: "It happens like that at times."

They descended the slant road towards Harbour Street and went on past the Pavilion Hotel.

4

They came into the presence of old Methuselah again, and that worthy under Chitterlow's direction at once resumed the illumination of Kipps' interior with the conscientious thoroughness that distinguished him. Chitterlow took a tall portion to himself with an air of asbestos, lit the bulldog pipe again, and lapsed for a space into meditation, from which Kipps roused him by remarking that he expected "an acter 'as a lot of ups and downs like, now and then."

At which Chitterlow seemed to bestir himself. "Ra-ther," he said. "And sometimes it's his own fault and sometimes it isn't. Usually it is. If it isn't one thing it's another. If it isn't the manager's wife it's bar-bragging. I tell you things happen at times. I'm a fatalist. The fact is Character has you. You can't get away from it. You may think you do, but you don't."

He reflected for a moment. "It's that what makes tragedy Psychology really. It's the Greek irony—Ibsen and—all that. Up to date."

He emitted this exhaustive summary of high-toned modern criticism as if he was repeating a lesson while thinking of something else, but it seemed to rouse him as it passed his lips, by including the name of Ibsen.

He became interested in telling Kipps, who was indeed open to any information whatever about this quite novel name, exactly where he thought Ibsen fell short, points where it happened that Ibsen was defective just where it chanced that he, Chitterlow, was strong. Of course he had no desire to place himself in any way on an equality with Ibsen; still the fact remained that his own experience in

England and America and the colonies was altogether more extensive than Ibsen could have had. Ibsen had probably never seen "one decent bar scrap" in his life. That, of course, was not Ibsen's fault or his own merit, but there the thing was. Genius, he knew, was supposed to be able to do anything or to do without anything; still he was now inclined to doubt that. He had a play in hand that might perhaps not please William Archer—whose opinion, after all, he did not value as he valued Kipps' opinion—but which he thought was at any rate as well constructed as anything Ibsen ever did.

So with infinite deviousness Chitterlow came at last to his play. He decided he would not read it to Kipps, but tell him about it. This was the simpler because much of it was still unwritten. He began to explain his plot. It was a complicated plot and all about a nobleman who had seen everything and done everything and knew practically all that Chitterlow knew about women; that is to say, "all about women" and suchlike matters. It warmed and excited Chitterlow. Presently he stood up to act a situation—which could not be explained. It was an extremely vivid situation.

Kipps applauded the situation vehemently. "Tha's dam' fine," said the new dramatic critic, quite familiar with his part now, striking the table with his fist and almost upsetting his third portion (in the second series) of old Methuselah. "Tha's dam' fine, Chit'low!"

"You see it?" said Chitterlow, with the last vestiges of that incidental gloom disappearing. "Good, old boy! I thought you'd see it. But it's just the sort of thing the literary critic can't see. However, it's only a beginning——"

He replenished Kipps and proceeded with his exposition.

In a little while it was no longer necessary to give that over-advertised Ibsen the purely conventional precedence he had hitherto had. Kipps and Chitterlow were friends and they could speak frankly and openly of things not usually admitted. "Any 'ow," said Kipps, a little irrelevantly and speaking over the brim of the replenishment, "what you read jus' now was dam' fine. Nothing can't alter that."

He perceived a sort of faint, buzzing vibration about things that was very nice and pleasant and with a little care he had no difficulty whatever in putting his glass back on the table. Then he perceived Chitterlow was going on with the scenario, and then that old Methuselah had almost entirely left his bottle. He was glad there was so little more Methuselah to drink because that would prevent his getting drunk. He knew that he was not now drunk, but he knew that he had had enough. He was one of those who always know when they have had enough. He tried to interrupt Chitterlow to tell him this, but he could not get a suitable opening. He doubted whether Chitterlow might not be one of those people who did not know when they had had enough. He discovered that he disapproved of Chitterlow. Highly. It seemed to him that Chitterlow went on and on like a river. For a time he was inexplicably and quite unjustly cross with Chitterlow and wanted to say to him, "you got the gift of the gab," but he only got so far as to say "the gift," and then Chitterlow thanked him and said he was better than Archer any day. So he eyed Chitterlow with a baleful eye until it dawned upon him that a most extraordinary thing was taking place. Chitterlow kept mentioning someone named Kipps. This presently began to perplex Kipps very greatly. Dimly but decidedly he perceived this was wrong.

"Look 'ere," he said suddenly, *"what* Kipps?"

"This chap Kipps I'm telling you about."

"What chap Kipps you're telling which about?"

"I told you."

Kipps struggled with a difficulty in silence for a space. Then he reiterated firmly, *"What* chap Kipps?"

"This chap in my play—man who kisses the girl."

"Never kissed a girl," said Kipps; "leastwise——" and subsided for a space. He could not remember whether he had kissed Ann or not—he knew he had meant to. Then suddenly in a tone of great sadness and addressing the hearth he said, *"My* name's Kipps."

"Eh?" said Chitterlow.

"Kipps," said Kipps, smiling a little cynically.

"What about him?"

"He's me." He tapped his breastbone with his middle finger to indicate his essential self.

He leant forward very gravely towards Chitterlow. "Look 'ere, Chit'low," he said, "you haven't no business putting my name into play. You mustn't do things like that. You'd lose me my crib, right away." And they had a little argument—so far as Kipps could remember. Chitterlow entered upon a general explanation of how he got his names. These, he had for the most part got out of a newspaper that was still, he believed, "lying about." He even made to look for it, and while he was doing so Kipps went on with the argument, addressing himself more particularly to the photograph of the girl in tights. He said that at first her costume had not commended her to him, but now he perceived she had an extremely sensible face. He told her she would like Buggins if she met him; he could see she was just that sort. She would admit, all sensible people would admit, that using names in plays was wrong. You could, for example, have the law of him.

He became confidential. He explained that he was already in sufficient trouble for stopping out all night without having his name put in plays. He was certain to be in the deuce of a row, the deuce of a row. Why had he done it? Why hadn't he gone at ten? Because one thing leads to another. One thing, he generalised, always does lead to another. . . .

He was trying to tell her that he was utterly unworthy of Miss Walshingham, when Chitterlow gave up the search and suddenly accused him of being drunk and talking "Rot——."

V. "SWAPPED"

1

He awoke on the thoroughly comfortable sofa that had had all its springs removed, and although he had certainly not been intoxicated, he awoke with what Chitterlow pronounced to be, quite indisputably, a Head and a Mouth. He had slept in his clothes and he felt stiff and uncomfortable all over, but the head and mouth insisted that he must not bother over little things like that. In the head was one large, angular idea that it was physically painful to have there. If he moved his head the angular idea shifted about in the most agonising way. This idea was that he had lost his situation and was utterly ruined and that it really mattered very little. Shalford was certain to hear of his escapade, and that coupled with that row about the Manchester window——!

He raised himself into a sitting position under Chitterlow's urgent encouragement.

He submitted apathetically to his host's attentions. Chitterlow, who admitted being a "bit off it" himself and in need of an egg-cupful of brandy, just an egg-cupful neat, dealt with that Head and Mouth as a mother might deal with the fall of an only child. He compared it with other Heads and Mouths that he had met, and in particular to certain experienced by the Hon. Thomas Norgate. "Right up to the last," said Chitterlow, "he couldn't stand his liquor. It happens like that at times." And after Chitterlow had pumped on the young beginner's head and given him some anchovy paste piping hot on buttered toast, which he preferred to all the other remedies he had encountered, Kipps resumed his crumpled collar, brushed his clothes, tacked up his knee, and prepared to face Mr. Shalford and the reckoning for this wild, unprecedented night, the first "night out" that ever he had taken.

Acting on Chitterlow's advice to have a bit of a freshener before returning to the Emporium, Kipps walked some way along the Leas and back and then went down to a shop near the Harbour to get a cup of coffee. He found that extremely reinvigorating, and he went on up the High Street to face the inevitable terrors of the office, a faint touch of pride in his depravity tempering his extreme self-abasement. After all, it was not an unmanly headache; he had been out all night, and he had been drinking and his physical disorder was there to witness the fact. If it wasn't for the thought of Shalford he would have been even a proud man to discover himself at last in such a condition. But the thought of Shalford was very dreadful. He met two of the apprentices snatching a walk before shop began. At the sight of them he pulled his spirits together, put his hat back from his pallid brow, thrust his hands into his trouser pockets and adopted an altogether more dissipated carriage; he met their innocent faces with a wan smile. Just for a moment he was glad that his patch at the knee was, after all, visible and that some at least of the mud on his clothes had refused to move at Chitterlow's brushing. What wouldn't they think he had been up to? He passed them without speaking. He could imagine how they regarded his back. Then he recollected Mr. Shalford. . . .

The deuce of a row certainly and perhaps——! He tried to think of plausible versions of the affair. He could explain he had been run down by a rather wild sort of fellow who was riding a bicycle, almost stunned for the moment (even now he felt the effects of the concussion in his head) and had been given whiskey to restore him, and "the fact is, sir" —with an upward inflection of the voice, an upward inflection of the eyebrows and an air of its being the last thing one would have expected whiskey to do, the manifestation indeed of a practically unique physiological weakness—"it got into my '*ed!*"

Put like that it didn't look so bad.

He got to the Emporium a little before eight and the housekeeper with whom he was something of a favourite ("There's no harm in Mr. Kipps," she used to say) seemed to like him if anything better for having broken the rules and gave him a piece of dry toast and a good hot cup of tea.

"I suppose the G. V.——" began Kipps.

"He knows," said the housekeeper.

He went down to shop a little before time, and presently Booch summoned him to the presence.

He emerged from the private office after an interval of ten minutes.

The junior clerk scrutinised his visage. Buggins put the frank question.

Kipps answered with one word.

"Swapped!" said Kipps.

2

Kipps leant against the fixtures with his hands in his pockets and talked to the two apprentices under him.

"I don't care if I *am* swapped," said Kipps. "I been sick of Teddy and his System some time. I was a good mind to chuck it when my time was up. Wish I 'ad now."

Afterwards Pierce came round and Kipps repeated this.

"What's it for?" said Pierce. "That row about the window tickets?"

"No fear!" said Kipps and sought to convey a perspective of splendid depravity. "I wasn't in las' night," he said and made even Pierce, "man about town" Pierce, open his eyes.

"Why! where did you get to?" asked Pierce.

He conveyed that he had been "fair round the town." "With a Nactor chap, I know."

"One can't *always* be living like a curit," he said.

"No fear," said Pierce, trying to play up to him.

But Kipps had the top place in that conversation.

"My Lor'!" said Kipps, when Pierce had gone, "but wasn't my mouth and 'ed bad this morning before I 'ad a pick-me-up!"

"Whad jer 'ave?"

"Anchovy on 'ot buttered toast. It's the very best pick-me-up there is. You trust me, Rodgers. I never take no other and I don't advise you to. See?"

And when pressed for further particulars, he said again he had been "fair all *round* the town, with a Nactor chap" he knew. They asked curiously all he had done and he said, "Well, what do *you* think?" And when they pressed for still further details he said there were things little boys ought not to know and laughed darkly and found them some huckaback to roll.

And in this manner for a space did Kipps fend off the contemplation of the "key of the street" that Shalford had presented him.

3

This sort of thing was all very well when junior apprentices were about, but when Kipps was alone with himself it served him not at all. He was uncomfortable inside and his skin was uncomfortable, and Head and Mouth palliated perhaps, but certainly not cured, were still with him. He felt, to tell the truth, nasty and dirty and extremely disgusted with himself. To work was dreadful and to stand still and think still more dreadful. His patched knee reproached him. These were the second best of his three pairs of trousers, and they had cost him thirteen and sixpence. Practically ruined they were. His dusting pair was unfit for shop and he would have to degrade his best. When he was under inspection he affected the slouch of a desperado, but directly he found himself alone, this passed insensibly into the droop.

The financial aspect of things grew large before him. His whole capital in the world was the sum of five pounds in the Post Office Savings Bank and four and sixpence cash. Besides there would be two months' screw. His little tin box upstairs was no longer big enough for his belongings; he would have to buy another, let alone that it was not calculated to make a good impression in a new "crib." Then there would be paper and stamps needed in some abundance for answering advertisements and railway fares when he went "crib hunting." He would have to write letters, and he never wrote letters. There was spelling for example to consider. Probably if nothing turned up before his month was up he would have to go home to his Uncle and Aunt.

How would they take it? . . .

For the present at any rate he resolved not to write to them.

Such disagreeable things as this it was that lurked below the fair surface of Kipps' assertion, "I've been wanting a chance. If 'e 'adn't swapped me, I should very likely 'ave swapped '*im*."

In the perplexed privacies of his own mind he could not understand how everything had happened. He had been the

Victim of Fate, or at least of one as inexorable—Chitter-low. He tried to recall the successive steps that had culminated so disastrously. They were difficult to recall. . . .

Buggins that night abounded in counsel and reminiscence.

"Curious thing," said Buggins, "but every time I've had the swap I've never believed I should get another crib—never. But I have," said Buggins. "Always. So don't lose heart, whatever you do. . . .

"Whatever you do," said Buggins, "keep hold of your collars and cuffs—shirts if you can, but collars anyhow. Spout them last. And anyhow, it's summer!—you won't want your coat. . . . You got a good umbrella. . . .

"You'll no more get a shop from New Romney, than—anything. Go straight up to London, get the cheapest room you can find—and hang out. Don't eat too much. Many a chap's put his prospects in his stomach. Get a cup o' coffee and a slice—egg if you like—but remember you got to turn up at the Warehouse tidy. The best places *now*, I believe, are the old cabmen's eating houses. Keep your watch and chain as long as you can. . . .

"There's lots of shops going," said Buggins. "Lots!"

And added reflectively, "But not this time of year perhaps."

He began to recall his own researches. " 'Stonishing lot of chaps you see," he said. "All sorts. Look like Dukes some of 'em. High hat. Patent boots. Frock coat. All there. All right for a West End crib. Others—Lord! It's a caution, Kipps. Boots been inked in some reading rooms—*I* used to write in a Reading Room in Fleet Street, regular penny club —hat been wetted, collar frayed, tail coat buttoned up, black chest-plaster tie—spread out. Shirt, you know, gone—" Buggins pointed upward with a pious expression.

"No shirt, I expect?"

"Eat it," said Buggins.

Kipps meditated. "I wonder where old Merton is," he said at last. "I often wondered about 'im."

4

It was the morning following Kipps' notice of dismissal that Miss Walshingham came into the shop. She came in with a dark, slender lady, rather faded, rather tightly dressed, whom Kipps was to know some day as her mother.

He discovered them in the main shop at the counter of the ribbon department. He had come to the opposite glove counter with some goods enclosed in a parcel that he had unpacked in his own department. The two ladies were both bent over a box of black ribbon.

He had a moment of tumultuous hesitations. The etiquette of the situation was incomprehensible. He put down his goods very quietly and stood hands on counter, staring at these two ladies. Then, as Miss Walshingham sat back, the instinct of flight seized him. . . .

He returned to his Manchester shop wildly agitated. Directly he was out of sight of her he wanted to see her. He fretted up and down the counter, and addressed some snappish remarks to the apprentice in the window. He fumbled for a moment with a parcel, untied it needlessly, began to tie it up again and then bolted back again into the main shop. He could hear his own heart beating.

The two ladies were standing in the manner of those who have completed their purchases and are waiting for their change. Mrs. Walshingham regarded some remnants with impersonal interest; Helen's eyes searched the shop. They distinctly lit up when they discovered Kipps.

He dropped his hands to the counter by habit and stood for a moment regarding her awkwardly. What would she do? Would she cut him? She came across the shop to him.

"How are *you*, Mr. Kipps?" she said, in her clear, distinct tones, and she held out her hand.

"Very well, thank you," said Kipps; "how are you?"

She said she had been buying some ribbon.

He became aware of Mrs. Walshingham very much surprised. This checked something allusive about the class and he said instead that he supposed she was glad to be having her holidays now. She said she was, it gave her more time for reading and that sort of thing. He supposed that she would be going abroad and she thought that perhaps they *would* go to Knocke or Bruges for a time.

Then came a pause and Kipps' soul surged within him. He wanted to tell her he was leaving and would never see her again. He could find neither words nor voice to say it. The swift seconds passed. The girl in the ribbons was handing Mrs. Walshingham her change. "Well," said Miss Walshingham, "Good-bye," and gave him her hand again.

Kipps bowed over her hand. His manners, his counter manners, were the easiest she had ever seen upon him. She turned to her mother. It was no good now, no good. Her mother! You couldn't say a thing like that before her mother! All was lost but politeness. Kipps rushed for the door. He stood at the door bowing with infinite gravity, and she smiled and nodded as she went out. She saw nothing of the struggle within him, nothing but a satisfactory emotion. She smiled like a satisfied goddess as the incense ascends.

Mrs. Walshingham bowed stiffly and a little awkwardly.

He remained holding the door open for some seconds after they had passed out, then rushed suddenly to the back of the "costume" window to watch them go down the street. His hands tightened on the window rack as he stared. Her mother appeared to be asking discreet questions. Helen's bearing suggested the off-hand replies of a person who found the world a satisfactory place to live in. "Really, Mumsie, you cannot expect me to cut my own students dead," she was in fact saying. . . .

They vanished round Henderson's corner.

Gone! And he would never see her again—never!

It was as though someone had struck his heart with a whip. Never! Never! Never! And she didn't know! He turned back from the window and the department with its two apprentices was impossible. The whole glaring world was insupportable.

He hesitated and made a rush head down for the cellar that was his Manchester warehouse. Rodgers asked him a question that he pretended not to hear.

The Manchester warehouse was a small cellar apart from the general basement of the building and dimly lit by a small gas flare. He did not turn that up, but rushed for the darkest corner, where on the lowest shelf the sale window tickets were stored. He drew out the box of these with trembling hands and upset them on the floor, and so having made himself a justifiable excuse for being on the ground, with his head well in the dark, he could let his poor bursting little heart have its way with him for a space.

And there he remained until the cry of "Kipps! Forward!" summoned him once more to face the world.

VI. THE UNEXPECTED

1

Now in the slack of that same day, after the midday dinner and before the coming of the afternoon customers, this disastrous Chitterlow descended upon Kipps with the most amazing coincidence in the world. He did not call formally, entering and demanding Kipps, but privately, in a confidential and mysterious manner.

Kipps was first aware of him as a dark object bobbing about excitedly outside the hosiery window. He was stooping and craning and peering in the endeavour to see into the interior between and over the socks and stockings. Then he transferred his attention to the door, and after a hovering scrutiny, tried the baby-linen display. His movements and gestures suggested a suppressed excitement.

Seen by daylight, Chitterlow was not nearly such a magnificent figure as he had been by the subdued nocturnal lightings and beneath the glamour of his own interpretation. The lines were the same indeed, but the texture was different. There was a quality about the yachting cap, an indefinable finality of dustiness, a shiny finish on all the salient surfaces of the reefer coat. The red hair and the profile, though still forcible and fine, were less in the quality of Michael Angelo and more in that of the merely picturesque. But it was a bright brown eye still that sought amidst the interstices of the baby-linen.

Kipps was by no means anxious to interview Chitterlow again. If he had felt sure that Chitterlow would not enter the shop he would have hid in the warehouse until the danger was past, but he had no idea of Chitterlow's limitations. He decided to keep up the shop in the shadows until Chitterlow reached the side window of the Manchester department and then to go outside as if to inspect the condition of the window and explain to him that things were unfavourable to immediate intercourse. He might tell him he had already lost his situation. . . .

"Ullo, Chit'low," he said, emerging.

"Very man I want to see," said Chitterlow, shaking with vigour. "Very man I want to see." He laid a hand on Kipps' arm. "How *old* are you, Kipps?"

"One and twenty," said Kipps. "Why?"

"Talk about coincidences! And your name now? Wait a minute." He held out a finger. *"Is* it Arthur?"

"Yes," said Kipps.

"You're the man," said Chitterlow.

"What man?"

"It's about the thickest coincidence I ever struck," said Chitterlow, plunging his extensive hand into his breast coat pocket. "Half a jiff and I'll tell you your mother's Christian name." He laughed and struggled with his coat for a space, produced a washing book and two pencils, which he deposited in his side pocket; then in one capacious handful, a bent but by no means finally disabled cigar, the rubber proboscis of a bicycle pump, some twine and a lady's purse, and finally a small pocket book, and from this, after dropping and recovering several visiting cards, he extracted a carelessly torn piece of newspaper. "Euphemia," he read and brought his face close to Kipps'. "Eh?" He laughed noisily. "It's about as fair a Bit of All Right as anyone *could* have—outside a coincidence play. Don't say her name wasn't Euphemia, Kipps, and spoil the whole blessed show."

"Whose name—Euphemia?" asked Kipps.

"Your mother's."

"Lemme see what it says on the paper."

Chitterlow handed him the fragment and turned away. "You may say what you like," he said, addressing a vast, deep laugh to the street generally.

Kipps attempted to read. " 'WADDY or KIPPS. If Arthur Waddy or Arthur Kipps, the son of Margaret Euphemia Kipps, who——' "

Chitterlow's finger swept over the print. "I went down the column and every blessed name that seemed to fit my play I took. I don't believe in made-up names. As I told you. I'm all with Zola in that. Documents whenever you can. I like 'em hot and real. See? Who was Waddy?"

"Never heard his name."

"Not Waddy?"

"No!"

Kipps tried to read again and abandoned the attempt. "What does it mean?" he said. "I don't understand."

"It means," said Chitterlow, with a momentary note of lucid exposition, "so far as I can make out that you're going to strike it Rich. Never mind about the Waddy—that's a detail. What does it usually mean? You'll hear of something to your advantage—very well. I took that newspaper up to get my names by the merest chance. Directly I saw it again and read that—I knew it was you. I believe in coincidences. People say they don't happen. *I* say they do. Everything's a coincidence. Seen properly. Here you are. Here's one! Incredible? Not a bit of it! See? It's you! Kipps! Waddy be damned! It's a Mascot. There's luck in my play. Bif! You're there. *I'm* there. Fair *in* it! Snap!" And he discharged his fingers like a pistol. "Never you mind about the 'Waddy.'"

"Eh?" said Kipps, with a nervous eye on Chitterlow's fingers.

"You're all right," said Chitterlow; "you may bet the seat of your only breeches on that! Don't you worry about the Waddy—that's as clear as day. You're about as right side up as a billiard ball—whatever you do. Don't stand there gaping, man! Read the paper if you don't believe me. Read it!"

He shook it under Kipps' nose.

Kipps became aware of the second apprentice watching them from the shop. His air of perplexity gave place to a more confident bearing.

——" 'who was born at East Grinstead.' I certainly was born there. I've 'eard my Aunt say——"

"I knew it," said Chitterlow, taking hold of one edge of the paper and bringing his face close alongside Kipps'.

" '——on September the first, eighteen hundred and seventy-eight——' "

"That's all right," said Chitterlow. "It's all, all right, and all you have to do is write to Watson and Bean and get it——"

"Get what?"

"Whatever it is."

Kipps sought his moustache. "You'd write?" he asked.

"Ra-ther."

"But what d'you think it is?"

"That's the fun of it!" said Chitterlow, taking three steps in some as yet uninvented dance. "That's where the joke comes in. It may be anything—it may be a million. If so! Where does little Harry come in? Eh?"

Kipps was trembling slightly. "But——" he said, and thought. "If you was me——" he began. "About that Waddy——?"

He glanced up and saw the second apprentice disappear with amazing swiftness from behind the goods in the window.

"*What?*" asked Chitterlow, but he never had an answer.

"Lor'! There's the guv'nor!" said Kipps, and made a prompt dive for the door.

He dashed in only to discover that Shalford, with the junior apprentice in attendance, had come to mark off remnants of Kipps' cotton dresses and was demanding him. "Hullo, Kipps," he said, "outside——?"

"Seein' if the window was straight, Sir," said Kipps.

"Umph!" said Shalford.

For a space Kipps was too busily employed to think at all of Chitterlow or the crumpled bit of paper in his trouser pocket. He was, however, painfully aware of a suddenly disconcerted excitement at large in the street. There came one awful moment when Chitterlow's nose loomed interrogatively over the ground glass of the department door, and his bright, little, red-brown eye sought for the reason of Kipps' disappearance, and then it became evident that he saw the high light of Shalford's baldness and grasped the situation and went away. And then Kipps (with that advertisement in his pocket) was able to come back to the business in hand.

He became aware that Shalford had asked a question. "Yessir, nosir, rightsir. I'm sorting up zephyrs to-morrow, Sir," said Kipps.

Presently he had a moment to himself again, and, taking up a safe position behind a newly unpacked pile of summer lace curtains, he straightened out the piece of paper and reperused it. It was a little perplexing. That "Arthur

Waddy or Arthur Kipps"—did that imply two persons or one? He would ask Pierce or Buggins. Only——

It had always been impressed upon him that there was something demanding secrecy about his mother.

"Don't you answer no questions about your mother," his aunt had been wont to say. "Tell them you don't know, whatever it is they ask you."

"Now this——?"

Kipps' face became portentously careful and he tugged at his moustache, such as it was, hard.

He had always represented his father as being a "gentleman farmer." "It didn't pay," he used to say with a picture in his own mind of a penny magazine aristocrat prematurely worn out by worry. "I'm a Norfan, both sides," he would explain, with the air of one who had seen trouble. He said he lived with his uncle and aunt, but he did not say that they kept a toy shop, and to tell anyone that his uncle had been a butler—*a servant!*—would have seemed the maddest of indiscretions. Almost all the assistants in the Emporium were equally reticent and vague, so great is their horror of "Lowness" of any sort. To ask about this "Waddy or Kipps" would upset all these little fictions. He was not, as a matter of fact, perfectly clear about his real status in the world (he was not, as a matter of fact, perfectly clear about anything), but he knew that there was a quality about his status that was—detrimental.

Under the circumstances——?

It occurred to him that it would save a lot of trouble to destroy the advertisement there and then.

In which case he would have to explain to Chitterlow!

"Eng!" said Mr. Kipps.

"Kipps," cried Carshot, who was shopwalking; "Kipps, Forward!"

He thrust back the crumpled paper into his pocket and sallied forth to the customers.

"I want," said the customer, looking vaguely about her through glasses, "a little bit of something to cover a little stool I have. Anything would do—a remnant or anything——"

The matter of the advertisement remained in abeyance for half an hour, and at the end the little stool was still a candidate for covering and Kipps had a thoroughly representative collection of the textile fabrics in his department to clear away. He was so angry about the little stool that the crumpled advertisement lay for a space in his pocket, absolutely forgotten.

2

Kipps sat on his tin box under the gas bracket that evening, and looked up the name Euphemia and learnt what it meant in the "Enquire Within About Everything" that constituted Buggins' reference library. He hoped Buggins, according to his habit, would ask him what he was looking for, but Buggins was busy turning out his week's washing. "Two collars," said Buggins, "half pair socks, two dickeys. Shirt? . . . . M'm. There ought to be another collar somewhere."

"Euphemia," said Kipps at last, unable altogether to keep to himself this suspicion of a high origin that floated so delightfully about him, "Eu—phemia; it isn't a name *common* people would give to a girl, is it?"

"It isn't the name any decent people would give to a girl," said Buggins, "——common or not."

"Lor'!" said Kipps. "Why?"

"It's giving girls names like that," said Buggins, "that nine times out of ten makes 'em go wrong. It unsettles 'em. If ever I was to have a girl, if ever I was to have a dozen girls, I'd call 'em all Jane. Every one of 'em. You couldn't have a better name than that. Euphemia indeed! What next? . . . . Good Lord! . . . . That isn't one of my collars there, is it? under your bed? . . . ."

Kipps got him the collar.

"I don't see no great 'arm in Euphemia," he said as he did so.

After that he became restless. "I'm a good mind to write that letter," he said, and then, finding Buggins preoccupied wrapping his washing up in the "half sox," added to himself, "a thundering good mind."

So he got his penny bottle of ink, borrowed the pen from Buggins and with no very serious difficulty in spelling or composition, did as he had resolved.

He came back into the bedroom about an hour afterwards a little out of breath and pale. "Where you been?"

said Buggins, who was now reading the *Daily World Manager,* which came to him in rotation from Carshot.

"Out to post some letters," said Kipps, hanging up his hat.

"Crib hunting?"

"Mostly," said Kipps.

"Rather," he added, with a nervous laugh; "what else?"

Buggins went on reading. Kipps sat on his bed and regarded the back of the *Daily World Manager* thoughtfully.

"Buggins," he said at last.

Buggins lowered his paper and looked.

"I say, Buggins, what do these here advertisements mean that say so-and-so will hear of something greatly to his advantage?"

"Missin' people," said Buggins, making to resume reading.

"How d'yer mean?" asked Kipps. "Money left and that sort of thing?"

Buggins shook his head. "Debts," he said, "more often than not."

"But that ain't to his advantage."

"They put that to get 'old of 'em," said Buggins. "Often it's wives."

"What you mean?"

"Deserted wives, try and get their husbands back that way."

"I suppose it *is* legacies sometimes, eh? Perhaps if someone was left a hundred pounds by someone——"

"Hardly ever," said Buggins.

"Well, 'ow——?" began Kipps and hesitated.

Buggins resumed reading. He was very much excited by a leader on Indian affairs. "By Jove!" he said, "it won't do to give these here Blacks votes."

"No fear," said Kipps.

"They're different altogether," said Buggins. "They 'aven't the sound sense of Englishmen, and they 'aven't the character. There's a sort of tricky dishonesty about 'em—false witness and all that——of which an Englishman has no idea. Outside their courts of law—it's a pos'tive fact, Kipps—there's witnesses waitin' to be 'ired. Reg'lar trade. Touch their 'ats as you go in. Englishmen 'ave no idea, I tell you—not ord'nary Englishmen. It's in their blood. They're too timid to be honest. Too slavish. They aren't used to being free like we are, and if you gave 'em freedom they wouldn't make a proper use of it. Now *we*——. Oh, *Damn!*"

For the gas had suddenly gone out and Buggins had the whole column of Society Club Chat still to read.

Buggins could talk of nothing after that but Shalford's meanness in turning off the gas, and after being extremely satirical indeed about their employer, undressed in the dark, hit his bare toe against a box and subsided after unseemly ejaculations into silent ill-temper.

Though Kipps tried to get to sleep before the affair of the letter he had just posted resumed possession of his mind he could not do so. He went over the whole thing again, quite exhaustively. Now that his first terror was abating he couldn't quite determine whether he was glad or sorry that he had posted that letter. If it *should* happen to be a hundred pounds!

It *must* be a hundred pounds!

If it was he could hold out for a year, for a couple of years even, before he got a Crib.

Even if it was fifty pounds——!

Buggins was already breathing regularly when Kipps spoke again. "*Bug*-gins," he said.

Buggins pretended to be asleep, and thickened his regular breathing (a little too hastily) to a snore.

"I say Buggins," said Kipps after an interval.

"*What's* up now?" said Buggins unamiably.

" 'Spose *you* saw an advertisement in a paper, with your name in it, see, asking you to come and see someone, like, so as to hear of something very much to your——"

"Hide," said Buggins shortly.

"But——"

"I'd hide."

"Er?"

"Goonight, o' man," said Buggins, with convincing earnestness. Kipps lay still for a long time, then blew profoundly, turned over and stared at the other side of the dark.

He had been a fool to post that letter!

Lord! *Hadn't* he been a fool!

3

It was just five days and a half after the light had been turned out while Buggins was reading, that a young man with a white face and eyes bright and wide-open, emerged from a side road upon the Leas front. He was dressed in his best clothes, and, although the weather was fine, he carried his umbrella, just as if he had been to church. He hesitated and turned to the right. He scanned each house narrowly as he passed it, and presently came to an abrupt stop. "Hughenden," said the gateposts in firm, black letters, and the fanlight in gold repeated "Hughenden." It was a stucco house fit to take your breath away, and its balcony was painted a beautiful sea-green, enlivened with gilding. He stood looking up at it.

"Gollys!" he said at last in an awestricken whisper.

It had rich-looking crimson curtains to all the lower windows and brass railed blinds above. There was a splendid tropical plant in a large, artistic pot in the drawing-room window. There was a splendid bronzed knocker (ring also) and two bells—one marked "servants." Gollys! *Servants*, eh?

He walked past away from it, with his eyes regarding it, and then turned and came back. He passed through a further indecision, and finally drifted away to the sea front and sat down on a seat a little way along the Leas and put his arm over the back and regarded "Hughenden." He whistled an air very softly to himself, put his head first on one side and then on the other. Then for a space he scowled fixedly at it.

A very stout old gentleman, with a very red face and very protuberant eyes, sat down beside Kipps, removed a Panama hat of the most abandoned desperado cut, and mopped his brow and blew. Then he began mopping the inside of his hat. Kipps watched him for a space, wondering how much he might have a year, and where he bought his hat. Then "Hughenden" reasserted itself.

An impulse overwhelmed him. "I say," he said, leaning forward, to the old gentleman.

The old gentleman started and stared.

"*Whad* do you say?" he asked fiercely.

"You wouldn't think," said Kipps, indicating with his forefinger, "that that 'ouse there belongs to me."

The old gentleman twisted his neck round to look at "Hughenden." Then he came back to Kipps, looked at his mean, little garments with apoplectic intensity and blew at him by way of reply.

"It does," said Kipps, a little less confidently.

"Don't be a Fool," said the old gentleman, and put his hat on and wiped out the corners of his eyes. "It's hot enough," panted the old gentleman indignantly, "without Fools." Kipps looked from the old gentleman to the house and back to the old gentleman. The old gentleman looked at Kipps and snorted and looked out to sea, and again, snorting very contemptuously, at Kipps.

"Mean to say it doesn't belong to me?" said Kipps.

The old gentleman just glanced over his shoulder at the house in dispute and then fell to pretending Kipps didn't exist. "It's been lef' me this very morning," said Kipps. "It ain't the only one that's been lef' me, neither."

"Aw!" said the old gentleman, like one who is sorely tried. He seemed to expect the passers-by presently to remove Kipps.

"It *'as*," said Kipps. He made no further remark to the old gentleman for a space, but looked with a little less certitude at the house. . . .

"I got——" he said and stopped.

"It's no good telling you if you don't believe," he said.

The old gentleman, after a struggle with himself, decided not to have a fit. "Try that game on with me," he panted. "Give you in charge."

"What game?"

"Wasn't born yesterday," said the old gentleman, and blew. "Besides," he added, *"look* at you! I know you," and the old gentleman coughed shortly and nodded to the horizon and coughed again.

Kipps looked dubiously from the house to the old gentleman and back to the house. Their conversation, he gathered, was over. Presently he got up and went slowly across the grass to its stucco portal again. He stood and his mouth shaped the precious word, "Hughenden." It was all *right!* He looked over his shoulder as if in appeal to the old gentleman, then turned and went his way. The old gentleman was so evidently past all reason!

He hung for a moment some distance along the parade, as though some invisible string was pulling him back. When he could no longer see the house from the pavement he went out into the road. Then with an effort he snapped the string.

He went on down a quiet side street, unbuttoned his coat furtively, took out three bank notes in an envelope, looked at them and replaced them. Then he fished up five new sovereigns from his trouser pocket and examined them. To such a confidence had his exact resemblance to his dead mother's portrait carried Messrs. Watson and Bean.

It was right enough.

It really was *all* right.

He replaced the coins with grave precaution and went his way with a sudden briskness. It was all right—he had it now—he was a rich man at large. He went up a street and round a corner and along another street, and started towards the Pavilion and changed his mind and came round back, resolved to go straight to the Emporium and tell them all.

He was aware of someone crossing a road far off ahead of him, someone curiously relevant to his present extraordinary state of mind. It was Chitterlow. Of course it was Chitterlow who had told him first of the whole thing! The playwright was marching buoyantly along a cross street. His nose was in the air, the yachting cap was on the back of his head and the large freckled hand grasped two novels from the library, a morning newspaper, a new hat done up in paper and a lady's net bag full of onions and tomatoes. . . .

He passed out of sight behind the wine merchant's at the corner, as Kipps decided to hurry forward and tell him of the amazing change in the Order of the Universe that had just occurred.

Kipps uttered a feeble shout, arrested as it began, and waved his umbrella. Then he set off at a smart pace in pursuit. He came round the corner and Chitterlow had gone; he hurried to the next and there was no Chitterlow, he turned back unavailingly and his eyes sought some other possible corner. His hand fluttered to his mouth and he stood for a space at the pavement edge, staring about him. No good!

But the sight of Chitterlow was a wholesome thing, it connected events together, joined him on again to the past at a new point, and that was what he so badly needed. . . .

It was all right—all right.

He became suddenly very anxious to tell everybody at the Emporium, absolutely everybody, all about it. That was what wanted doing. He felt that telling was the thing to make this business real. He gripped his umbrella about the middle and walked very eagerly.

He entered the Emporium through the Manchester department. He flung open the door (over whose ground glass he had so recently, in infinite apprehension, watched the nose of Chitterlow) and discovered the second apprentice and Pierce in conversation. Pierce was prodding his hollow tooth with a pin and talking in fragments about the distinctive characteristics of Good Style.

Kipps came up in front of the counter.

"I say," he said; "what d'yer think?"

"What?" said Pierce over the pin.

"Guess."

"You've slipped out because Teddy's in London."

"Something more."

"What?"

"Been left a fortune."

"Garn!"

"I 'ave."

"Get out!"

"Straight. I been lef' twelve 'undred pounds—twelve 'undred pounds a year!"

He moved towards the little door out of the department into the house, moving, as heralds say, *regardant passant*. Pierce stood with mouth wide open and pin poised in air.

"No!" he said at last.

"It's right," said Kipps, "and I'm going."

And he fell over the doormat into the house.

4

It happened that Mr. Shalford was in London buying summer sale goods—and no doubt also interviewing aspirants to succeed Kipps.

So that there was positively nothing to hinder a wild rush of rumour from end to end of the Emporium. All the masculine members began their report with the same formula. "Heard about Kipps?"

The new girl in the cash desk had had it from Pierce and had dashed out into the fancy shop to be the first with the news on the fancy side. Kipps had been left a thousand pounds a year, twelve thousand pounds a year.

Kipps had been left twelve hundred thousand pounds. The figures were uncertain, but the essential facts they had correct. Kipps had gone upstairs. Kipps was packing his box. He said he wouldn't stop another day in the old Emporium, not for a thousand pounds! It was said that he was singing ribaldry about old Shalford.

He had come down! He was in the counting house. There was a general movement thither. Poor old Buggins had a customer and couldn't make out what the deuce it was all about! Completely out of it was Buggins.

There was a sound of running to and fro and voices saying this, that and the other thing about Kipps. Ring-a-dinger, ring-a-dinger went the dinner bell all unheeded. The whole of the Emporium was suddenly bright-eyed, excited, hungry to tell somebody, to find at any cost somebody who didn't know and be first to tell them, "Kipps has been left thirty—forty—fifty thousand pounds!"

"What!" cried the senior porter, "Him!" and ran up to the counting house as eagerly as though Kipps had broken his neck.

"One of our chaps just been left sixty thousand pounds," said the first apprentice, returning after a great absence, to his customer.

"Unexpectedly?" said the customer.

"Quite," said the first apprentice. . . .

"I'm sure if Anyone deserves it, it's Mr. Kipps," said Miss Mergle, and her train rustled as she hurried to the counting house.

There stood Kipps amidst a pelting shower of congratulations. His face was flushed and his hair disordered. He still clutched his hat and best umbrella in his left hand. His right hand was anyone's to shake rather than his own. (Ring-a-dinger, ring-a-dinger ding, ding, ding, dang you! went the neglected dinner bell.)

"Good old Kipps," said Pierce, shaking; "Good old Kipps."

Booch rubbed one anæmic hand upon the other. "You're sure it's all right, Mr. Kipps," he said in the background.

"I'm sure we all congratulate him," said Miss Mergle.

"Great Scott!" said the new young lady in the glove department. "Twelve hundred a year! Great Scott! You aren't thinking of marrying anyone, are you, Mr. Kipps?"

"Three pounds, five and ninepence a day," said Mr. Booch, working in his head almost miraculously. . . .

Everyone, it seemed, was saying how glad they were it was Kipps, except the junior apprentice, upon whom—he being the only son of a widow and used to having the best of everything as a right—an intolerable envy, a sense of unbearable wrong, had cast its gloomy shade. All the rest were quite honestly and simply glad—gladder perhaps at that time than Kipps because they were not so over-powered. . . .

Kipps went downstairs to dinner, emitting fragmentary, disconnected statements. "Never expected anything of the sort. . . . When this here old Bean told me, you could have knocked me down with a feather. . . . He says, 'You b'en lef' money.' Even then I didn't expect it'd be mor'n a hundred pounds perhaps. Something like that."

With the sitting down to dinner and the handing of plates the excitement assumed a more orderly quality. The housekeeper emitted congratulations as she carved and the maidservant became dangerous to clothes with the plates—she held them anyhow, one expected to see one upside down even—she found Kipps so fascinating to look at. Everyone was the brisker and hungrier for the news (except the junior apprentice) and the housekeeper carved with un-usual liberality. It was High Old Times there under the gaslight, High Old Times. "I'm sure if Anyone deserves it," said Miss Mergle—"pass the salt, please—it's Kipps."

The babble died away a little as Carshot began barking across the table at Kipps. "You'll be a bit of a Swell, Kipps," he said. "You won't hardly know yourself."

"Quite the gentleman," said Miss Mergle.

"Many real gentlemen's families," said the housekeeper, "have to do with less."

"See you on the Leas," said Carshot. "My gu—!" He met the housekeeper's eye. She had spoken about that be-fore. "My eye!" he said tamely, lest words should mar the day.

"You'll go to London, I reckon," said Pierce. "You'll be a man about town. We shall see you mashing 'em, with violets in your button'ole down the Burlington Arcade.

"One of these West End Flats. That'd be *my* style," said Pierce. "And a first-class club."

"Aren't these clubs a bit 'ard to get into?" asked Kipps, open-eyed, over a mouthful of potato.

"No fear. Not for Money," said Pierce. And the girl in the laces who had acquired a cynical view of Modern Society from the fearless exposures of Miss Marie Corelli, said, "Money goes everywhere nowadays, Mr. Kipps."

But Carshot showed the true British strain.

"If I was Kipps," he said, pausing momentarily for a knifeful of gravy, "I should go to the Rockies and shoot bears."

"I'd certainly 'ave a run over to Boulogne," said Pierce, "and look about a bit. I'm going to do that next Easter myself, anyhow—see if I don't."

"Go to Oireland, Mr. Kipps," came the soft insistence of Biddy Murphy, who managed the big workroom, flushed and shining in the Irish way, as she spoke. "Go to Oireland. Ut's the loveliest country in the world. Outside Car-rs. Fishin', shootin', huntin'. An' pretty gals! Eh! You should see the Lakes of Killarney, Mr. Kipps!" And she expressed ecstasy by a facial pantomime and smacked her lips.

And presently they crowned the event.

It was Pierce who said, "Kipps, you ought to stand Sham!"

And it was Carshot who found the more poetical word, "Champagne."

"Rather!" said Kipps hilariously, and the rest was a question of detail and willing emissaries. "Here it comes!" they said as the apprentice came down the staircase. "How about the shop?" said someone. "Oh! *hang* the shop!" said Carshot and made gruntulous demands for a corkscrew with a thing to cut the wire. Pierce, the dog! had a wire cutter in his pocket knife. How Shalford would have stared at the gold tipped bottles if he had chanced to take an early train! Bang with the corks, and bang! Gluck, gluck, gluck, and sizzle!

When Kipps found them all standing about him under the gas flare, saying almost solemnly "Kipps!" with tumblers upheld—"Have it in tumblers," Carshot had said; "have it in tumblers. It isn't a wine like you have in glasses. Not like port and sherry. It cheers you up, but you don't get drunk. It isn't hardly stronger than lemonade. They drink it at dinner, some of 'em, every day."

"What! At three and six a bottle!" said the housekeeper incredulously.

"*They* don't stick at *that*," said Carshot; "not the champagne sort."

The housekeeper pursed her lips and shook her head. . . .

When Kipps, I say, found them all standing up to toast him in that manner, there came such a feeling in his throat and face that for the life of him he scarcely knew for a moment whether he was not going to cry. "Kipps!" they all said, with kindly eyes. It was very good of them, it was very good of them, and hard there wasn't a stroke of luck for them all!

But the sight of upturned chins and glasses pulled him together again. . . .

They did him honour. Unenviously and freely they did him honour.

For example, Carshot being subsequently engaged in serving cretonne and desiring to push a number of rejected blocks up the counter in order to have space for measuring, swept them by a powerful and ill-calculated movement of the arm, with a noise like thunder partly on to the floor and partly on to the foot of the still gloomily preoccupied junior apprentice. And Buggins, whose place it was to shopwalk while Carshot served, shopwalked with quite unparalleled dignity, dangling a new season's sunshade with a crooked handle on one finger. He arrested each customer who came down the shop with a grave and penetrating look. "Showing very 'tractive line new sheason's shunshade," he would remark, and, after a suitable pause, " 'Markable thing, one our 'sistant leg'sy twelve 'undred a year. V'ry 'tractive. Nothing more to-day, mum? No!" And he would then go and hold the door open for them with perfect decorum and with the sunshade dangling elegantly from his left hand. . . .

And the second apprentice, serving a customer with cheap ticking, and being asked suddenly if it was strong, answered remarkably,

"Oo! *no*, mum! Strong! Why it ain't 'ardly stronger than lemonade. . . ."

The head porter, moreover, was filled with a virtuous resolve to break the record as a lightning packer and make up for lost time. Mr. Swaffenham, of the Sandgate Riviera, for example, who was going out to dinner that night at seven, received at half-past six, instead of the urgently needed dress shirt he expected, a corset specially adapted to the needs of persons inclined to embonpoint. A parcel of summer underclothing selected by the elder Miss Waldershawe, was somehow distributed in the form of gratis additions throughout a number of parcels of a less intimate nature, and a box of millinery on approval to Lady Pamshort (at Wampachs) was enriched by the addition of the junior porter's cap. . . .

These little things, slight in themselves, witness perhaps none the less eloquently to the unselfish exhilaration felt throughout the Emporium at the extraordinary and unexpected enrichment of Mr. Kipps.

5

The 'bus that plies between New Romney and Folkestone is painted a British red and inscribed on either side with the word "Tip-top" in gold amidst voluptuous scrolls. It is a slow and portly 'bus. Below it swings a sort of hold, hung by chains between the wheels, and in the summer time the top has garden seats. The front over the two dauntless unhurrying horses rises in tiers like a theatre; there is first a seat for the driver and his company, and above that a seat and above that, unless my memory plays me false, a seat. There are days when this 'bus goes and days when it doesn't go—you have to find out. And so you get to New Romney.

This 'bus it was, this ruddy, venerable and immortal 'bus, that came down the Folkestone hill with unflinching deliberation, and trundled through Sandgate and Hythe, and out into the windy spaces of the Marsh, with Kipps and all his fortunes on its brow. You figure him there. He sat on the highest seat diametrically above the driver and his head was spinning and spinning with champagne and this stupendous Tomfoolery of Luck and his heart was swelling, swelling indeed at times as though it would burst him, and his face towards the sunlight was transfigured. He said never a word, but ever and again as he thought of this or that, he laughed. He seemed full of chuckles for a time, detached and independent chuckles, chuckles that rose and burst in him like bubbles in a wine. . . . He held a banjo sceptre-fashion and restless on his knee. He had always wanted a banjo, and now he had got one at Malchior's while he was waiting for the 'bus.

There sat beside him a young servant who was sucking peppermint and a little boy with a sniff, whose flitting eyes showed him curious to know why ever and again Kipps laughed, and beside the driver were two young men in gaiters talking about "tegs." And there sat Kipps, all unsuspected, twelve hundred a year, as it were, disguised as a common young man. And the young man in gaiters to the left of the driver eyed Kipps and his banjo, and especially his banjo, ever and again as if he found it and him, with his rapt face, an insoluble enigma. And many a King has ridden into a conquered city with a lesser sense of splendour than Kipps.

Their shadows grew long behind them and their faces were transfigured in gold as they rumbled on towards the splendid West. The sun set before they had passed Dymchurch, and as they came lumbering into New Romney past the windmill the dusk had come.

The driver handed down the banjo and the portmanteau, and Kipps having paid him—"That's aw right," he said to the change, as a gentleman should—turned about and ran the portmanteau smartly into Old Kipps, whom the sound of the stopping of the 'bus had brought to the door of the shop in an aggressive mood and with his mouth full of supper.

"Ullo, Uncle, didn't see you," said Kipps.

"Blunderin' ninny," said Old Kipps. "What's brought *you* here? Ain't early closing, is it? Not Toosday?"

"Got some news for you, Uncle," said Kipps, dropping the portmanteau.

"Ain't lost your situation, 'ave you? What's that you got there? I'm blowed if it ain't a banjo. Goo-lord! Spendin' your money on banjoes! Don't put down your portmanty there—anyhow. Right in the way of everybody. I'm blowed if ever I saw such a boy as you've got lately. Here! Molly! And, look here! What you got a portmanty for? Why! Goo-lord! You ain't *really* lost your place, 'ave you?"

"Somethin's happened," said Kipps slightly dashed. "It's all right, Uncle. I'll tell you in a minute."

Old Kipps took the banjo as his nephew picked up the portmanteau again.

The living room door opened quickly, showing a table equipped with elaborate simplicity for supper, and Mrs. Kipps appeared.

"If it ain't young Artie," she said. "Why! Whatever's brought *you* 'ome?"

"Ullo, Aunt," said Artie. "I'm coming in. I got somethin' to tell you. I've 'ad a bit of Luck."

He wouldn't tell them all at once. He staggered with the portmanteau round the corner of the counter, set a bundle of children's tin pails into clattering oscillation, and entered the little room. He deposited his luggage in the corner beside the tall clock, and turned to his Aunt and Uncle again. His Aunt regarded him doubtfully, the yellow light from the little lamp on the table escaped above the shade and lit her forehead and the tip of her nose. It would be all right in a minute. He wouldn't tell them all at once. Old Kipps stood in the shop door with the banjo in his hand, breathing noisily. "The fact is, Aunt, I've 'ad a bit of Luck."

"You ain't been backin' gordless 'orses, Artie?" she asked.

"No fear."

"It's a draw he's been in," said Old Kipps, still panting from the impact of the portmanteau; "it's a dratted draw. Jest look here, Molly. He's won this 'ere trashy banjer and thrown up his situation on the strength of it—that's what he's done. Goin' about singing. Dash and plunge! Jest the very fault poor Pheamy always 'ad. Blunder right in and no one mustn't stop 'er!"

"You ain't thrown up your place, Artie, 'ave you?" said Mrs. Kipps.

Kipps perceived his opportunity. "I 'ave," he said; "I've throwed it up."

"What for?" said Old Kipps.

"So's to learn the banjo!"

"Goo *Lord!*" said Old Kipps, in horror to find himself verified.

"I'm going about playing!" said Kipps with a giggle. "Goin' to black my face, Aunt, and sing on the beach. I'm going to 'ave a most tremenjous lark and earn any amount of money—you see. Twenty-six fousand pounds I'm going to earn just as easy as nothing!"

"Kipps," said Mrs. Kipps, "he's been drinking!"

They regarded their nephew across the supper table with long faces. Kipps exploded with laughter and broke out again when his Aunt shook her head very sadly at him. Then suddenly he fell grave. He felt he could keep it up no longer. "It's all right, Aunt. Reely. I ain't mad and I ain't been drinking. I been lef' money. I been left twenty-six fousand pounds."

Pause.

"And you thrown up your place?" said Old Kipps.

"Yes," said Kipps. "Rather!"

"And bort this banjer, put on your best noo trousers and come right on 'ere?"

"Well," said Mrs. Kipps, "*I* never did."

"These ain't my noo trousers, Aunt," said Kipps regretfully. "My noo trousers wasn't done."

"I shouldn't ha' thought that *even you* could ha' been such a fool as that," said Old Kipps.

Pause.

"It's *all* right," said Kipps a little disconcerted by their distrustful solemnity. "It's all right—reely! Twenny-six fousan' pounds. And a 'ouse——"

Old Kipps pursed his lips and shook his head.

"A 'ouse on the Leas. I could have gone there. Only I didn't. I didn't care to. I didn't know what to say. I wanted to come and tell you."

"How d'yer know the 'ouse——?"

"They told me."

"Well," said Old Kipps, and nodded his head portentously towards his nephew, with the corners of his mouth pulled down in a portentous, discouraging way. "Well, you *are* a young Gaby."

"I didn't *think* it of you, Artie!" said Mrs. Kipps.

"Wadjer mean?" asked Kipps faintly, looking from one to the other with a withered face.

Old Kipps closed the shop door. "They been 'avin' a lark with you," said Old Kipps in a mournful undertone. "That's what I mean, my boy. They jest been seein' what a Gaby like you 'ud do."

"I dessay that young Quodling was in it," said Mrs. Kipps. " 'E's jest that sort."

(For Quodling of the green baize bag had grown up to be a fearful dog, the terror of New Romney.)

"It's somebody after your place very likely," said Old Kipps.

Kipps looked from one sceptical, reproving face to the other, and round him at the familiar shabby, little room, with his familiar cheap portmanteau on the mended chair, and that banjo amidst the supper things like some irrevocable deed. Could he be rich indeed? Could it be that these things had really happened? Or had some insane fancy whirled him hither?

Still—perhaps a hundred pounds——

"But," he said. "It's all right, reely, Uncle. You don't think——? I 'ad a letter."

"Got up," said Old Kipps.

"But I answered it and went to a norfis."

Old Kipps felt staggered for a moment, but he shook his head and chins sagely from side to side. As the memory of old Bean and Shalford revived, the confidence of Kipps came back to him.

"I saw a nold gent, Uncle—perfect gentleman. And 'e told me all about it. Mos' respectable 'e was. Said 'is name was Watson and Bean—leastways 'e was Bean. Said it was lef' me——" Kipps suddenly dived into his breast pocket. "By my Grandfather——"

The old people started.

Old Kipps uttered an exclamation and wheeled round towards the mantel shelf above which the daguerreotype of his lost younger sister smiled its fading smile upon the world.

"Waddy 'is name was," said Kipps, with his hand still deep in his pocket. "It was *'is* son was my father——"

"Waddy!" said Old Kipps.

"Waddy!" said Mrs. Kipps.

"She'd never say," said Old Kipps.

There was a long silence.

Kipps fumbled with a letter, a crumpled advertisement and three bank notes. He hesitated between these items.

"Why! That young chap what was arsting questions——" said Old Kipps, and regarded his wife with an eye of amazement.

"Must 'ave been," said Mrs. Kipps.

"Must 'ave been," said Old Kipps.

"James," said Mrs. Kipps, in an awestricken voice, "after all—perhaps—it's true!"

"'*Ow* much did you say?" asked Old Kipps. " 'Ow much did you say 'ed lef' you, me b'y?"

It was thrilling, though not quite in the way Kipps had expected. He answered almost meekly across the meagre supper things, with his documentary evidence in his hand:

"Twelve 'undred pounds. 'Proximately, he said. Twelve 'undred pounds a year. 'E made 'is will, jest before 'e died— not more'n a month ago. When 'e was dying, 'e seemed to change like, Mr. Bean said. 'E'd never forgiven 'is son, never —not till then. 'Is son 'ad died in Australia, years and years ago, and *then* 'e 'adn't forgiven 'im. You know—'is son what was my father. But jest when 'e was ill and dying 'e seemed to get worried like and longing for someone of 'is own. And 'e told Mr. Bean it was 'im that had prevented them marrying. So 'e thought. That's 'ow it all come about. . . ."

6

At last Kipps' flaring candle went up the narrow un-carpeted staircase to the little attic that had been his shelter and refuge during all the days of his childhood and youth. His head was whirling. He had been advised, he had been warned, he had been flattered and congratulated, he had been given whiskey and hot water and lemon and sugar, and his health had been drunk in the same. He had also eaten two Welsh Rabbits—an unusual supper. His Uncle was chiefly for his going into Parliament, his Aunt was consumed with a great anxiety. "I'm afraid he'll go and marry beneath 'im."

"Y'ought to 'ave a bit o' shootin' somewheer," said Old Kipps.

"It's your *duty* to marry into a county family, Artie. Remember that."

"There's lots of young noblemen'll be glad to 'ang on to you," said Old Kipps. "You mark my words. And borry your money. And then, good day to ye."

"I got to be precious Careful," said Kipps. "Mr. Bean said that."

"And you got to be precious careful of this old Bean,"

said Old Kipps. "We may be out of the world in Noo
Romney, but I've 'eard a bit about s'licitors, for all that.
You keep your eye on old Bean, me b'y.

" 'Ow do we know what 'e's up to, with your money,
even now?" said Old Kipps, pursuing this uncomfortable
topic.

" 'E *looked* very respectable," said Kipps. . . .

Kipps undressed with great deliberation, and with vast
gasps of pensive margin. Twenty-six thousand pounds!

His Aunt's solicitude had brought back certain matters
into the foreground that his "Twelve 'Undred a year!" had
for a time driven away altogether. His thoughts went back
to the wood-carving class. Twelve Hundred a Year. He sat on
the edge of the bed in profound meditation and his boots
fell "whop" and "whop" upon the floor, with a long interval
between each "whop." Twenty-five thousand pounds. "By
Gum!" He dropped the remainder of his costume about him
on the floor, got into bed, pulled the patchwork quilt over
him and put his head on the pillow that had been first to
hear of Ann Pornick's accession to his heart. But he did
not think of Ann Pornick now.

It was about everything in the world except Ann Pornick
that he seemed to be trying to think of—simultaneously. All
the vivid happenings of the day came and went in his over-
taxed brain; "that old Bean" explaining and explaining, the
fat man who wouldn't believe, an overpowering smell of
peppermint, the banjo, Miss Mergle saying he deserved it,
Chitterlow's vanishing round a corner, the wisdom and advice and warnings of his Aunt and Uncle. She was afraid
he would marry beneath him, *was* she? She didn't know. . . .

His brain made an excursion into the wood-carving class
and presented Kipps with the picture of himself amazing that
class by a modest yet clearly audible remark, "I been left
twenty-six thousand pounds." Then he told them all quietly
but firmly that he had always loved Miss Walshingham, always, and so he had brought all his twenty-six thousand
pounds with him to give to her there and then. He wanted
nothing in return. . . . Yes, he wanted nothing in return.
He would give it to her all in an envelope and go. Of
course he would keep the banjo—and a little present for
his Aunt and Uncle—and a new suit perhaps—and one or
two other things she would not miss. He went off at a

tangent. He might buy a motor car, he might buy one of these here things that will play you a piano—that would make old Buggins sit up! He could pretend he had learnt to play—he might buy a bicycle and a cyclist suit. . . .

A terrific multitude of plans of what he might do and in particular of what he might buy, came crowding into his brain, and he did not so much fall asleep as pass into a disorder of dreams in which he was driving a four-horse Tip-top coach down Sandgate Hill ("I shall have to be precious careful"), wearing innumerable suits of clothes, and through some terrible accident wearing them all wrong. Consequently he was being laughed at. The coach vanished in the interest of the costume. He was wearing golfing suits and a silk hat. This passed into a nightmare that he was promenading on the Leas in a Highland costume, with a kilt that kept shrinking, and Shalford was following him with three policemen. "He's my assistant," Shalford kept repeating; "he's escaped. He's an escaped Improver. Keep by him and in a minute you'll have to run him in. I know 'em. We say they wash, but they won't. . . ." He could feel the kilt creeping up his legs. He would have tugged at it to pull it down only his arms were paralysed. He had an impression of giddy crisis. He uttered a shriek of despair. *"Now!"* said Shalford. He woke in horror, his quilt had slipped off the bed.

He had a fancy he had just been called, that he had somehow overslept himself and missed going down for dusting. Then he perceived it was still night and light by reason of the moonlight, and that he was no longer in the Emporium. He wondered where he could be. He had a curious fancy that the world had been swept and rolled up like a carpet and that he was nowhere. It occurred to him that perhaps he was mad. "Buggins!" he said. There was no answer, not even the defensive snore. No room, no Buggins, nothing!

Then he remembered better. He sat on the edge of his bed for some time. Could anyone have seen his face they would have seen it white and drawn with staring eyes. Then he groaned weakly. "Twenty-six thousand pounds?" he whispered.

Just then it presented itself in an almost horribly overwhelming mass.

He remade his bed and returned to it. He was still dreadfully wakeful. It was suddenly clear to him that he need never trouble to get up punctually at seven again. That fact shone out upon him like a star through clouds. He was free to lie in bed as long as he liked, get up when he liked, go where he liked, have eggs every morning for breakfast or rashers or bloater paste or . . . . Also he was going to astonish Miss Walshingham. . . .

Astonish her and astonish her. . . .

. . . .

He was awakened by a thrush singing in the fresh dawn. The whole room was flooded with warm, golden sunshine. "I say!" said the thrush. "I say! I say! Twelve 'undred a year! Twelve 'Undred a Year. Twelve 'UNDRED a Year! I say! I say! I say!"

He sat up in bed and rubbed the sleep from his eyes with his knuckles. Then he jumped out of bed and began dressing very eagerly. He did not want to lose any time in beginning the new life.

END OF BOOK I

BOOK TWO

MR. COOTE, THE CHAPERON

I. THE NEW CONDITIONS

1

There comes a gentlemanly figure into these events and
for a space takes a leading part therein, a Good Influence,
a refined and amiable figure, Mr. Chester Coote. You must
figure him as about to enter our story, walking with a
curious rectitude of bearing through the evening dusk towards
the Public Library, erect, large-headed—he had a great,
big head full of the suggestion of a powerful mind, well
under control—with a large, official-looking envelope in
his white and knuckly hand. In the other he carries a gold-
handled cane. He wears a silken grey jacket suit, buttoned
up, and anon he coughs behind the official envelope. He
has a prominent nose, slatey grey eyes and a certain
heaviness about the mouth. His mouth hangs breathing
open, with a slight protrusion of the lower jaw. His straw
hat is pulled down a little in front, and he looks each person
he passes in the eye, and directly his look is answered looks
away.

Thus Mr. Chester Coote, as he was on the evening when
he came upon Kipps. He was a local house agent and a
most active and gentlemanly person, a conscious gentleman,
equally aware of society and the serious side of life. From
amateur theatricals of a nice, refined sort to science classes,
few things were able to get along without him. He supplied
a fine, full bass, a little flat and quavery perhaps, but very
abundant, to the St. Stylites' choir. . . .

He passes on towards the Public Library, lifts the envelope in salutation to a passing curate, smiles and enters. . . .

It was in the Public Library that he came upon Kipps.

By that time Kipps had been rich a week or more, and the
change in his circumstances was visible upon his person. He
was wearing a new suit of drab flannels, a Panama hat
and a red tie for the first time, and he carried a silver-

mounted stick with a tortoise shell handle. He felt extraordinarily different, perhaps more different than he really was, from the meek Improver of a week ago. He felt as he felt Dukes must feel, yet at bottom he was still modest. He was leaning on his stick and regarding the indicator with a respect that never palled. He faced round to meet Mr. Coote's overflowing smile.

"What are you doang hea?" said Mr. Chester Coote.

Kipps was momentarily abashed. "Oh," he said slowly, and then, "Mooching round a bit."

That Coote should address him with this easy familiarity was a fresh reminder of his enhanced social position. "Jes' mooching round," he said. "I been back in Folkestone free days now. At my 'ouse, you know."

"Ah!" said Mr. Coote. "I haven't yet had an opportunity of congratulating you on your good fortune."

Kipps held out his hand. "It was the cleanest surprise that ever was," he said. "When Mr. Bean told me of it— you could have knocked me down with a feather."

"It must mean a tremendous change for you."

"Oo. Rather. Change. Why, I'm like the chap in the song they sing, I don't 'ardly know where I are. *You* know."

"An extraordinary change," said Mr. Coote. "I can quite believe it. Are you stopping in Folkestone?"

"For a bit. I got a 'ouse, you know. What my gran'father 'ad. I'm stopping there. His housekeeper was kep' on. Fancy—being in the same town and everything!"

"Precisely," said Mr. Coote. "That's it!" and coughed like a sheep behind four straight fingers.

"Mr. Bean got me to come back to see to things. Else I was out in New Romney, where my Uncle and Aunt live. But it's a Lark coming back. In a way . . . ."

The conversation hung for a moment.

"Are you getting a book?" asked Coote.

"Well, I 'aven't got a ticket yet. But I shall get one all right, and have a go in at reading. I've often wanted to. Rather. I was just 'aving a look at this Indicator. Firstclass idea. Tells you all you want to know."

"It's simple," said Coote, and coughed again, keeping his eyes fixed on Kipps. For a moment they hung, evidently disinclined to part. Then Kipps jumped at an idea he had cherished for a day or more,—not particularly in relation to Coote, but in relation to anyone.

"You doing anything?" he asked.

"Just called with a papah about the classes."

"Because———. Would you care to come up and look at my 'ouse and 'ave a smoke and a chat. Eh?" He made indicative back jerks of the head, and was smitten with a horrible doubt whether possibly this invitation might not be some hideous breach of etiquette. Was it, for example, the correct hour? "I'd be awfully glad if you would," he added.

Mr. Coote begged for a moment while he handed the official-looking envelope to the librarian and then declared himself quite at Kipps' service. They muddled a moment over precedence at each door they went through and so emerged to the street.

"It feels awful rum to me at first, all this," said Kipps. "'Aving a 'ouse of my own and all that. It's strange, you know. 'Aving all day. Reely I don't 'ardly know what to do with my time."

"D'ju smoke?" he said suddenly, proffering a magnificent gold decorated pigskin cigarette case, which he produced from nothing, almost as though it was some sort of trick. Coote hesitated and declined, and then, with great liberality, "Don't let me hinder you. . . ."

They walked a little way in silence, Kipps being chiefly concerned to affect ease in his new clothes and keeping a wary eye on Coote. "It's rather a big windfall," said Coote presently. "It yields you an income———?"

"Twelve 'undred a year," said Kipps. "Bit over—if anything."

"Do you think of living in Folkestone?"

"Don't know 'ardly yet. I *may*. Then again, I may not. I got a furnished 'ouse, but I may let it."

"Your plans are undecided?"

"That's jest it," said Kipps.

"Very beautiful sunset it was to-night," said Coote, and Kipps said, "Wasn't it?" and they began to talk of the merits of sunsets. Did Kipps paint? Not since he was a boy. He didn't believe he could now. Coote said his sister was a painter and Kipps received this intimation with respect. Coote sometimes wished he could find time to paint himself,—but one couldn't do everything and Kipps said that was "jest it."

They came out presently upon the end of the Leas and looked down to where the squat dark masses of the Harbour and Harbour Station, gemmed with pinpoint lights, crouched against the twilit grey of the sea. "If one could do *that*," said Coote, and Kipps was inspired to throw his head back, cock it on one side, regard the Harbour with one eye shut and say that it would take some doing. Then Coote said something about "Abend," which Kipps judged to be in a foreign language and got over by lighting another cigarette from his by no means completed first one. "You're right, *puff, puff*."

He felt that so far he had held up his end of the conversation in a very creditable manner, but that extreme discretion was advisable.

They turned away and Coote remarked that the sea was good for crossing, and asked Kipps if he had been over the water very much. Kipps said he hadn't been—"much," but he thought very likely he'd have a run over to Boulogne soon, and Coote proceeded to talk of the charms of foreign travel, mentioning quite a number of unheard-of places by name. He had been to them! Kipps remained on the defensive, but behind his defences his heart sank. It was all very well to pretend, but presently it was bound to come out. *He* didn't know anything of all this. . . .

So they drew near the house. At his own gate Kipps became extremely nervous. It was a fine, impressive door. He knocked neither a single knock nor a double, but about one and a half—an apologetic half. They were admitted by an irreproachable housemaid, with a steady eye, before which Kipps cringed dreadfully. He hung up his hat and fell about over hall chairs and things. "There's a fire in the study, Mary?" he had the audacity to ask, though evidently he knew, and led the way upstairs panting. He tried to shut the door and discovered the housemaid behind him coming to light his lamp. This enfeebled him further. He said nothing until the door closed behind her. Meanwhile to show his *sang froid* he hummed and flitted towards the window, and here and there.

Coote went to the big hearthrug and turned and surveyed his host. His hand went to the back of his head and patted his occiput—a gesture frequent with him.

" 'Ere we are," said Kipps, hands in his pockets and glancing round him.

It was a gaunt Victorian room, with a heavy, dirty cornice, and the ceiling enriched by the radiant plaster ornament of an obliterated gas chandelier. It held two large glass-fronted bookcases, one of which was surmounted by a stuffed terrier encased in glass. There was a mirror over the mantel and hangings and curtains of magnificent crimson patternings. On the mantel were a huge black clock of classical design, vases in the Burslem Etruscan style, spills and toothpicks in large receptacles of carved rock, large lava ash trays and an exceptionally big box of matches. The fender was very great and brassy. In a favourable position, under the window, was a spacious rosewood writing desk, and all the chairs and other furniture were of rosewood and well stuffed.

"This," said Kipps, in something near an undertone, "was the o' gentleman's study—my grandfather that was. 'E used to sit at that desk and write."

"Books?"

"No. Letters to the *Times*, and things like that. 'E's got 'em all cut out—stuck in a book. . . . Leastways, he *'ad*. It's in that bookcase. . . . Won't you sit down?"

Coote did, bowing very slightly, and Kipps secured his vacated position on the extensive black skin rug. He spread out his legs compass-fashion and tried to appear at his ease. The rug, the fender, the mantel and mirror conspired with great success to make him look a trivial and intrusive little creature amidst their commonplace hauteur, and his own shadow on the opposite wall seemed to think everything a great lark and mocked and made tremendous fun of him. . . .

2

For a space Kipps played a defensive game and Coote drew the lines of the conversation. They kept away from the theme of Kipps' change of fortune, and Coote made remarks upon local and social affairs. "You must take an interest in these things now," was as much as he said in the way of personalities. But it speedily became evident that he was a person of wide and commanding social relationships. He spoke of "society" being mixed in the neighbourhood and of the difficulty of getting people to work together, and "do" things; they were chiquish. Incidentally he alluded quite familiarly to men with military titles, and once even to someone with a title, a Lady Punnet. Not snobbishly, you understand, nor deliberately, but quite in passing. He had, it appeared, talked to Lady Punnet about private theatricals! In connection with the Hospitals. She had been unreasonable and he had put her right, gently of course, but firmly. "If you stand up to these people," said Coote, "they like you all the better." It was also very evident he was at his ease with the clergy; "My friend, Mr. Densemore—a curate, you know, and rather curious, the Reverend *and* Honourable." Coote grew visibly in Kipps' eyes as he said these things; he became, not only the exponent of "Vagner or Vargner," the man whose sister had painted a picture to be exhibited at the Royal Academy, the type of the hidden thing called culture, but a delegate, as it were, or at least an intermediary from that great world "up there," where there were men servants, where there were titles, where people dressed for dinner, drank wine at meals, wine costing very often as much as three and sixpence the bottle, and followed through a maze of etiquette, the most stupendous practices. . . .

Coote sat back in the armchair smoking luxuriously and expanding pleasantly, with the delightful sense of Savoir Faire; Kipps sat forward, his elbows on his chair arm alert, and his head a little on one side. You figure him as looking little and cheap and feeling smaller and cheaper amidst his new surroundings. But it was a most stimulating and interesting conversation. And soon it became less general and more serious and intimate. Coote spoke of people who had got on, and of people who hadn't, of people who seemed to be *in* everything and people who seemed to be *out* of everything, and then he came round to Kipps.

"You'll have a good time," he said abruptly, with a smile that would have interested a dentist.

"I dunno," said Kipps.

"There's mistakes, of course."

"That's jest it."

Coote lit a new cigarette. "One can't help being interested in what you will do," he remarked. "Of course—for a young man of spirit, come suddenly into wealth—there's temptations."

"I got to go careful," said Kipps. "O' Bean told me that at the very first."

Coote went on to speak of pitfalls, of Betting, of Bad Companions. "I know," said Kipps. "I know." "There's Doubt again," said Coote. "I know a young fellow—a solicitor—handsome, gifted. And yet, you know—utterly sceptical. Practically altogether a Sceptic."

"Lor'!" said Kipps, "not a Natheist?"

"I fear so," said Coote. "Really, you know, an awfully fine young fellow—Gifted! But full of this dreadful Modern Spirit—Cynical! All this Overman stuff. Nietzsche and all that. . . . I wish I could do something for him."

"Ah!" said Kipps and knocked the ash off his cigarette. "I know a chap—one of our apprentices he was—once. Always scoffing. . . . He lef'!"

He paused. "Never wrote for his refs," he said, in the deep tone proper to a moral tragedy, and then, after a pause —"Enlisted!"

"Ah!" said Coote.

"And often," he said, after a pause, "it's just the most spirited chaps, just the chaps one likes best, who Go Wrong."

"It's temptation," Kipps remarked.

He glanced at Coote, leant forward, knocked the ash from his cigarette into the mighty fender. "That's jest it," he said; "you get tempted. Before you know where you are."

"Modern life," said Coote, "is so—complex. It isn't everyone is Strong. Half the young fellows who go wrong, aren't really bad."

"That's jest it," said Kipps.

"One gets a tone from one's surroundings——"

"That's exactly it," said Kipps.

He meditated. "*I* picked up with a chap," he said. "A Nacter. Leastways he writes plays. Clever fellow. But——"

He implied extensive moral obloquy by a movement of his head. "Of course it's seeing life," he added.

Coote pretended to understand the full implications of Kipps' remark. "Is it *worth* it?" he asked.

"That's jest it," said Kipps.

He decided to give some more. "One gets talking," he said. "Then it's ' 'ave a drink!' Old Methusaleh four stars—and where *are* you? *I* been drunk," he said in a tone of profound humility, and added, "lots of times."

"Tt. Tt.," said Coote.

"Dozens of times," said Kipps, smiling sadly, and added, "lately."

His imagination became active and seductive. "One thing leads to another. Cards, p'raps. Girls——"

"I know," said Coote; "I know."

Kipps regarded the fire and flushed slightly. He borrowed a sentence that Chitterlow had recently used. "One can't tell tales out of school," he said.

"I can imagine it," said Coote.

Kipps looked with a confidential expression into Coote's face. "It was bad enough when money was limited," he remarked. "But now——" He spoke with raised eyebrows, "I got to steady down."

"You *must*," said Coote, protruding his lips into a sort of whistling concern for a moment.

"I must," said Kipps, nodding his head slowly with raised eyebrows. He looked at his cigarette end and threw it into the fender. He was beginning to think he was holding his own in this conversation rather well, after all.

Kipps was never a good liar. He was the first to break silence. "I don't mean to say I been reely bad or reely bad drunk. A 'eadache perhaps—three or four times, say. But there it is!"

"I have never tasted alcohol in my life," said Coote, with an immense frankness, "never!"

"No?"

"Never. I don't feel *I* should be likely to get drunk at all—it isn't that. And I don't go so far as to say even that in small quantities—at meals—it does one harm. But if I take it, someone else who doesn't know where to stop—you see?"

"That's jest it," said Kipps, with admiring eyes.

"I smoke," admitted Coote. "One doesn't want to be a Pharisee."

It struck Kipps what a tremendously Good chap this

Coote was, not only tremendously clever and educated and a gentleman and one knowing Lady Punnet, but Good. He seemed to be giving all his time and thought to doing good things to other people. A great desire to confide certain things to him arose. At first Kipps hesitated whether he should confide an equal desire for Benevolent activities or for further Depravity—either was in his mind. He rather affected the pose of the Good Intentioned Dog. Then suddenly his impulses took quite a different turn, fell indeed into what was a far more serious rut in his mind. It seemed to him Coote might be able to do for him something he very much wanted done.

"Companionship accounts for so much," said Coote.

"That's jest it," said Kipps. "Of course, you know, in my new position——. That's just the difficulty."

He plunged boldly at his most secret trouble. He knew that he wanted refinement—culture. It was all very well—but he knew. But how was one to get it? He knew no one, knew no people——. He rested on the broken sentence. The shop chaps were all very well, very good chaps and all that, but not what one wanted. "I feel be'ind," said Kipps. "I feel out of it. And consequently I feel it's no good. And then if temptation comes along——"

"Exactly," said Coote.

Kipps spoke of his respect for Miss Walshingham and her freckled friend. He contrived not to look too self-conscious. "You know, I'd like to talk to people like that, but I can't. A chap's afraid of giving himself away."

"Of course," said Coote, "of course."

"I went to a middle-class school, you know. You mustn't fancy I'm one of these here board-school chaps, but you know it reely wasn't a first-class affair. Leastways he didn't take pains with us. If you didn't want to learn you needn't—I don't believe it was *much* better than one of these here national schools. We wore mortarboards, o' course. But what's *that?*

"I'm a regular fish out of water with this money. When I got it—it's a week ago—reely I thought I'd got everything I wanted. But I dunno what to *do.*"

His voice went up into a squeak. "Practically," he said, "it's no good shuttin' my eyes to things—I'm a gentleman."

Coote indicated a serious assent.

"And there's the responsibilities of a gentleman," he remarked.

"That's jest it," said Kipps.

"There's calling on people," said Kipps. "If you want to go on knowing Someone you knew before like. People that's refined." He laughed nervously. "I'm a regular fish out of water," he said, with expectant eyes on Coote.

But Coote only nodded for him to go on.

"This actor chap," he meditated, "is a good sort of chap. But 'e isn't what *I* call a gentleman. I got to 'old myself in with 'im. 'E'd make me go it wild in no time. 'E's pretty near the on'y chap I know. Except the shop chaps. They've come round to 'ave supper once already and a bit of a sing song afterwards. I sang. I got a banjo, you know, and I vamp a bit. Vamping—you know. Haven't got far in the book—'Ow to Vamp—but still I'm getting on. Jolly, of course, in a way, but what does it lead to? . . . . Besides that, there's my Aunt and Uncle. *They're* very good old people—very—jest a bit interfering p'r'aps and thinking one isn't grown up, but Right enough. Only——. It isn't what I *want*. I feel I've got be'ind with everything. I want to make it up again. I want to get with educated people who know 'ow to do things—in the regular, proper way."

His beautiful modesty awakened nothing but benevolence in the mind of Chester Coote.

"If I had someone like you," said Kipps, "that I knew regular like——"

From that point their course ran swift and easy. "If I *could* be of any use to you," said Coote. . . .

"But you're so busy and all that."

"Not *too* busy. You know, your case is a very interesting one. It was partly that made me speak to you and draw you out. Here you are with all this money and no experience, a spirited young chap——"

"That's jest it," said Kipps.

"I thought I'd see what you were made of, and I must confess I've rarely talked to anyone that I've found quite so interesting as you have been——"

"I seem able to say things to you like somehow," said Kipps.

"I'm glad. I'm tremendously glad."

"I want a Friend. That's it—straight."

"My dear chap, if I——"

"Yes, but——"

"*I* want a Friend, too."

"Reely?"

"Yes. You know, my dear Kipps—if I may call you that."

"Go on," said Kipps.

"I'm rather a lonely dog myself. *This* to-night——. I've not had anyone I've spoken to so freely of my Work for months."

"No?"

"You. And, my dear chap, if I can do anything to guide or help you——"

Coote displayed all his teeth in a kindly tremulous smile and his eyes were shiny. "Shake 'ands," said Kipps, deeply moved, and he and Coote rose and clasped with mutual emotion.

"It's reely too good of you," said Kipps.

"Whatever I can do I will," said Coote.

And so their compact was made. From that moment they were Friends, intimate, confidential, high-thinking, *sotto voce* friends. All the rest of their talk (and it inclined to be interminable) was an expansion of that. For that night Kipps wallowed in self-abandonment and Coote behaved as one who had received a great trust. That sinister passion for pedagoguery to which the Good Intentioned are so fatally liable, that passion of infinite presumption that permits one weak human being to arrogate the direction of another weak human being's affairs, had Coote in its grip. He was to be a sort of lay confessor and director of Kipps, he was to help Kipps in a thousand ways, he was in fact to chaperon Kipps into the higher and better sort of English life. He was to tell him his faults, advise him about the right thing to do——

"It's all these things I don't know," said Kipps. "I don't know, for instance, what's the right sort of dress to wear—I don't even know if I'm dressed right now——"

"All these things"—Coote stuck out his lips and nodded rapidly to show he understood—"Trust me for that," he said, "trust me."

As the evening wore on Coote's manner changed, became more and more the manner of a proprietor. He began to take up his rôle, to survey Kipps with a new, with a critical affection. It was evident the thing fell in with his ideas. "It will be awfully interesting," he said. "You know, Kipps, you're really good stuff." (Every sentence now he said "Kipps" or "my dear Kipps" with a curiously authoritative intonation.)

"I know," said Kipps, "only there's such a lot of things I don't seem to be up to some'ow. That's where the trouble comes in."

They talked and talked, and now Kipps was talking freely. They rambled over all sorts of things. Among others Kipps' character was dealt with at length. Kipps gave valuable lights on it. "When I'm reely excited," he said, "I don't seem to care *what* I do. I'm like that." And again, "I don't like to do anything under'and. I *must* speak out. . . ."

He picked a piece of cotton from his knee, the fire grimaced behind his back, and his shadow on the wall and ceiling was disrespectfully convulsed.

3

Kipps went to bed at last with an impression of important things settled, and he lay awake for quite a long time. He felt he was lucky. He had known—in fact Buggins and Carshot and Pierce had made it very clear indeed—that his status in life had changed and that stupendous adaptations had to be achieved, but how they were to be effected had driven that adaptation into the incredible. Here in the simplest, easiest way was the adapter. The thing had become possible. Not of course easy, but possible.

There was much to learn, sheer intellectual toil, methods of address, bowing, an enormous complexity of laws. One broken, you are an outcast. How, for example, would one encounter Lady Punnet? It was quite possible some day he might really have to do that. Coote might introduce him. "Lord!" he said aloud to the darkness between grinning and dismay. He figured himself going into the Emporium to buy a tie, for example, and there in the face of Buggins, Carshot, Pierce and the rest of them, meeting "my friend, Lady Punnet!" It might not end with Lady Punnet! His imagination plunged and bolted with him, galloped, took wings and soared to romantic, to poetical altitudes. . . .

Suppose some day one met Royalty. By accident, say!

He soared to that! After all,—twelve hundred a year is a lift, a tremendous lift. How did one address Royalty? "Your Majesty's Goodness," it will be, no doubt—something like that—and on the knees. He became impersonal. Over a thousand a year made him an Esquire, didn't it? He thought that was it. In which case, wouldn't he have to be presented at Court? Velvet cycling breeches like you wear cycling, and a sword! What a curious place a court must be! Kneeling and bowing, and what was it Miss Mergle used to talk about? Of course!—ladies with long trains walking about backward. Everybody walked about backward at court, he knew, when not actually on their knees. Perhaps, though, some people regular stood up to the King! Talked to him, just as one might talk to Buggins, say. Cheek of course! Dukes, it might be, did that—by permission? Millionnaires? . . .

From such thoughts this free citizen of our Crowned Republic passed insensibly into dreams, turgid dreams of that vast ascent which constitutes the true-born Briton's social scheme, which terminates with retrogressive progression and a bending back.

4

The next morning he came down to breakfast looking grave—a man with much before him in the world. . . .

Kipps made a very special thing of his breakfast. Daily once hopeless dreams came true then. It had been customary in the Emporium to supplement Shalford's generous, indeed unlimited, supply of bread and butter-substitute, by private purchases, and this had given Kipps very broad, artistic conceptions of what the meal might be. Now there would be a cutlet or so or a mutton chop—this splendour Buggins had reported from the great London clubs—haddock, kipper, whiting or fish-balls, eggs, boiled or scrambled, or eggs and bacon, kidney also frequently and sometimes liver. Amidst a garland of such themes, sausages, black and white puddings, bubble-and-squeak, fried cabbage and scallops came and went. Always as camp followers came potted meat in all varieties, cold bacon, German sausage, brawn, marmalade and two sorts of jam, and when he had finished these he would sit among his plates and smoke a cigarette and look at all these dishes crowded round him with a beatific approval. It was his principal meal. He was sitting with his cigarette regarding his apartment with that complacency begotten of a generous plan of feeding successfully realised, when newspapers and post arrived.

There were several things by the post, tradesmen's circulars and cards and two pathetic begging letters—his luck had got into the papers—and there was a letter from a literary man and a book to enforce his request for 10/—to put down Socialism. The book made it very clear that prompt action on the part of property owners was becoming urgent, if property was to last out the year. Kipps dipped in it and was seriously perturbed. And there was a letter from old Kipps saying it was difficult to leave the shop and come over and see him again just yet, but that he had been to a sale at Lydd the previous day and bought a few good old books and things it would be difficult to find the equal of in Folkestone. "They don't know the value of these things out here," wrote old Kipps, "but you may depend upon it they are valuable," and a brief financial statement followed. "There is an engraving someone might come along and offer you a lot of money for one of these days. Depend upon it, these old things are about the best investment you could make. . . ."

Old Kipps had long been addicted to sales, and his nephew's good fortune had converted what had once been but a looking and a craving—he had rarely even bid for anything in the old days except the garden tools or the kitchen gallipots or things like that, things one gets for sixpence and finds a use for—into a very active pleasure. Sage and penetrating inspection, a certain mystery of bearing, tactical bids and Purchase!—Purchase!—the old man had had a good time.

While Kipps was rereading the begging letters and wishing he had the sound, clear common sense of Buggins to help him a little, the Parcels Post brought along the box from his uncle. It was a large, insecure looking case held together by a few still loyal nails, and by what the British War Office would have recognised at once as an Army Corps of string, rags and odds and ends tied together. Kipps unpacked it with a table knife, assisted at a critical point by the poker, and found a number of books and other objects of an antique type.

There were three bound volumes of early issues of Chambers' Journal, a copy of Punch's Pocket Book for 1875, Sturm's Reflections, an early version of Gill's Geography (slightly torn), an illustrated work on Spinal Curvature, an early edition of Kirke's Human Physiology, The Scottish Chiefs and a little volume on the Language of Flowers. There was a fine steel engraving, oak-framed and with some rusty spots, done in the Colossal style and representing the Handwriting on the Wall. There were also a copper kettle, a pair of candle snuffers, a brass shoehorn, a tea caddy to lock, two decanters (one stoppered) and what was probably a portion of an eighteenth century child's rattle.

Kipps examined these objects one by one and wished he knew more about them. Turning over the pages of the Physiology again he came upon a striking plate in which a youth of agreeable profile displayed his interior in an unstinted manner to the startled eye. It was a new view of humanity altogether for Kipps, and it arrested his mind.

This anatomised figure made him forget for a space that he was "practically a gentleman" altogether, and he was still surveying its extraordinary complications when another reminder of a world quite outside those spheres of ordered gentility into which his dreams had carried him overnight, arrived (following the servant) in the person of Chitterlow.

5

"Ul-*lo!*" said Kipps, rising.

"Not busy?" said Chitterlow, enveloping Kipps' hand for a moment in one of his own and tossing the yachting cap upon the monumental carved oak sideboard.

"Only a bit of reading," said Kipps.

"Reading, eh?" Chitterlow cocked the red eye at the books and other properties for a moment and then, "I've been expecting you 'round again one night."

"I been coming 'round," said Kipps. "On'y there's a chap 'ere——. I was coming 'round last night on'y I met 'im."

He walked to the hearthrug. Chitterlow drifted around the room for a time, glancing at things as he talked. "I've altered that play tremendously since I saw you," he said. "Pulled it all to pieces."

"What play's that, Chit'low?"

"The one we were talking about. You know. You said something—I don't know if you meant it—about buying half of it. Not the tragedy. I wouldn't sell my twin brother a share in that. That's my investment. That's my Serious Work. No! I mean that new farce I've been on to. Thing with the business about a beetle."

"Oo yes," said Kipps. "*I* remember."

"I thought you would. Said you'd take a fourth share for a hundred pounds. *You* know."

"I seem to remember something——"

"Well, it's all different. Every bit of it. I'll tell you. You remember what you said about a butterfly? You got confused, you know—Old Meth. Kept calling the beetle a butterfly and that set me off. I've made it quite different. Quite different. Instead of Popplewaddle—thundering good farce name that, you know; for all that it came from a Visitors' List—instead of Popplewaddle getting a beetle down his neck and rushing about, I've made him a collector—collects butterflies, and this one you know's a rare one. Comes in at window, centre." Chitterlow began to illustrate with appropriate gestures. "Pop rushes about after it. Forgets he mustn't let on he's in the house. After that——. Tells 'em. Rare butterfly, worth lots of money. Some are, you know. Everyone's on to it after that. Butterfly can't get out of room, every time it comes out to have a try, rush and scurry. Well, I've worked on that. Only——"

He came very close to Kipps. He held up one hand horizontally and tapped it in a striking and confidential manner with the fingers of the other. "Something else," he said. "That's given me a Real Ibsenish Touch—like the Wild Duck. You know that woman—I've made her lighter—and she sees it. When they're chasing the butterfly the third time, she's on! She looks. 'That's me!' she says. Bif! Pestered Butterfly. *She's* the Pestered Butterfly. It's legitimate. Much more legitimate than the Wild Duck—where there isn't a duck!

"Knock 'em! The very title ought to knock 'em. I've been working like a horse at it. . . . You'll have a gold mine in that quarter share, Kipps. . . . *I* don't mind. It's suited me to sell it, and suited you to buy. Bif!"

Chitterlow interrupted his discourse to ask, "You haven't any brandy in the house, have you? Not to drink, you know. But I want just an eggcupful to pull me steady. My liver's a bit queer. . . . It doesn't matter, if you haven't. Not a bit. I'm like that. Yes, whiskey'll do. Better!"

Kipps hesitated for a moment, then turned and fumbled in the cupboard of his sideboard. Presently he disinterred a bottle of whiskey and placed it on the table. Then he put out first one bottle of soda water and after the hesitation of a moment another. Chitterlow picked up the bottle and read the label. "Good old Methusaleh," he said. Kipps handed him the corkscrew and then his hand fluttered up to his mouth. "I'll have to ring now," he said, "to get glasses." He hesitated for a moment before doing so, leaning doubtfully as it were towards the bell.

When the housemaid appeared he was standing on the hearthrug with his legs wide apart, with the bearing of a desperate fellow. And after they had both had whiskeys—"You know a decent whiskey," Chitterlow remarked and took another "just to drink."—Kipps produced cigarettes and the conversation flowed again.

Chitterlow paced the room. He was, he explained, taking a day off; that was why he had come around to see Kipps. Whenever he thought of any extensive change in a play he was writing he always took a day off. In the end it saved time to do so. It prevented his starting rashly upon work that might have to be rewritten. There was no good in doing work when you might have to do it over again, none whatever.

Presently they were descending the steps by the Parade *en route* for the Warren, with Chitterlow doing the talking and going with a dancing drop from step to step. . . .

They had a great walk, not a long one, but a great one. They went up by the Sanatorium, and over the East Cliff and into that queer little wilderness of slippery and tumbling clay and rock under the chalk cliffs, a wilderness of thorn and bramble, wild rose and wayfaring tree, that adds so greatly to Folkestone's charm. They traversed its intricacies and clambered up to the crest of the cliffs at last by a precipitous path that Chitterlow endowed in some mysterious way with suggestions of Alpine adventure. Every now and then he would glance aside at sea and cliffs with a fresh boyishness of imagination that brought back New Romney and the stranded wrecks to Kipps' memory; but mostly he bored on with his great obsession of plays and playwriting,

and that empty absurdity that is so serious to his kind, his
Art. That was a thing that needed a monstrous lot of explaining. Along they went, sometimes abreast, sometimes in
single file, up the little paths, and down the little paths,
and in among the bushes and out along the edge above the
beach, and Kipps went along trying ever and again to get
an insignificant word in edgeways, and the gestures of Chitterlow flew wide and far and his great voice rose and fell,
and he said this and he said that and he biffed and banged
into the circumambient Inane.

It was assumed that they were embarked upon no more
trivial enterprise than the Reform of the British Stage, and
Kipps found himself classed with many opulent and even
royal and noble amateurs—the Honourable Thomas Norgate
came in here—who had interested themselves in the practical realisation of high ideals about the Drama. Only he had
a finer understanding of these things, and instead of being
preyed upon by the common professional—"and they *are*
a lot," said Chitterlow; "I haven't toured for nothing"—
he would have Chitterlow. Kipps gathered few details. It
was clear he had bought the quarter of a farcical comedy—
practically a gold mine—and it would appear it would be
a good thing to buy the half. A suggestion, or the suggestion of a suggestion, floated out that he should buy the
whole play and produce it forthwith. It seemed he was to
produce the play upon a royalty system of a new sort, whatever a royalty system of any sort might be. Then there was
some doubt, after all, whether that farcical comedy was in
itself sufficient to revolutionise the present lamentable state
of the British Drama. Better perhaps for such a purpose
was that tragedy—as yet unfinished—which was to display
all that Chitterlow knew about women, and which was to
centre about a Russian nobleman embodying the funda-
mental Chitterlow personality. Then it became clearer that
Kipps was to produce several plays. Kipps was to produce a
great number of plays. Kipps was to found a National Theatre.

It is probable that Kipps would have expressed some sort
of disavowal, if he had known how to express it. Occasionally his face assumed an expression of whistling meditation,
but that was as far as he got towards protest.

In the clutch of Chitterlow and the Incalculable, Kipps came round to the house in Fenchurch Street and was there made to participate in the midday meal. He came to the house, forgetting certain confidences, and was reminded of the existence of a Mrs. Chitterlow (with the finest completely untrained Contralto voice in England) by her appearance. She had an air of being older than Chitterlow, although probably she wasn't, and her hair was a reddish brown, streaked with gold. She was dressed in one of those complaisant garments that are dressing gowns or tea gowns or bathing wraps or rather original evening robes according to the exigencies of the moment—from the first Kipps was aware that she possessed a warm and rounded neck, and her well-moulded arms came and vanished from the sleeves —and she had large, expressive brown eyes that he discovered ever and again fixed in an enigmatical manner upon his own.

A simple but sufficient meal had been distributed with careless spontaneity over the little round table in the room with the photographs and looking glass, and when a plate had by Chitterlow's direction been taken from under the marmalade in the cupboard and the kitchen fork and a knife that was not loose in its handle had been found for Kipps they began and she had evidently heard of Kipps before, and he made a tumultuous repast. Chitterlow ate with quiet enormity, but it did not interfere with the flow of his talk. He introduced Kipps to his wife very briefly; made it vaguely evident that the production of the comedy was the thing chiefly settled. His reach extended over the table, and he troubled nobody. When Mrs. Chitterlow, who for a little while seemed socially self-conscious, reproved him for taking a potato with a jab of his fork, he answered, "Well, you shouldn't have married a man of Genius," and from a subsequent remark it was perfectly clear that Chitterlow's standing in this respect was made no secret of in his household.

They drank old Methusaleh and syphon soda, and there was no clearing away, they just sat among the plates and things, and Mrs. Chitterlow took her husband's tobacco pouch and made a cigarette and smoked and blew smoke and looked at Kipps with her large, brown eyes. Kipps had seen cigarettes smoked by ladies before, "for fun," but this was real smoking. It frightened him rather. He felt he must not encourage this lady—at any rate in Chitterlow's presence.

They became very cheerful after the repast, and as there was now no waste to deplore, such as one experiences in the windy, open air, Chitterlow gave his voice full vent. He fell to praising Kipps very highly and loudly. He said he had known Kipps was the right sort, he had seen it from the first, almost before he got up out of the mud on that memorable night. "You can," he said, "sometimes. That was why——" he stopped, but he seemed on the verge of explaining that it was his certainty of Kipps being the right sort had led him to confer this great Fortune upon him. He left that impression. He threw out a number of long sentences and material for sentences of a highly philosophical and incoherent character about Coincidences. It became evident he considered dramatic criticism in a perilously low condition. . . .

About four Kipps found himself stranded, as it were, by a receding Chitterlow on a seat upon the Leas.

He was chiefly aware that Chitterlow was an overwhelming personality. He puffed his cheeks and blew.

No doubt this was seeing life, but had he particularly wanted to see life that day? In a way Chitterlow had interrupted him. The day he had designed for himself was altogether different from this. He had been going to read through a precious little volume called "Don't" that Coote had sent round for him, a book of invaluable hints, a summary of British deportment that had only the one defect of being at points a little out of date.

That reminded him he had intended to perform a difficult exercise called an Afternoon Call upon the Cootes, as a preliminary to doing it in deadly earnest upon the Walshinghams. It was no good to-day, anyhow, now.

He came back to Chitterlow. He would have to explain to Chitterlow he was taking too much for granted, he would have to do that. It was so difficult to do in Chitterlow's presence though; in his absence it was easy enough. This half share, and taking a theatre and all of it, was going too far.

The quarter share was right enough, he supposed, but even that——! A hundred pounds! What wealth is there left in the world after one has paid out a hundred pounds from it?

He had to recall that in a sense Chitterlow had indeed brought him his fortune before he could face even that.

You must not think too hardly of him. To Kipps you see there was as yet no such thing as proportion in these matters. A hundred pounds went to his horizon. A hundred pounds seemed to him just exactly as big as any other large sum of money.

II. THE WALSHINGHAMS

1

The Cootes live in a little house in Bouverie Square with a tangle of Virginia creeper up the verandah. ·

Kipps had been troubled in his mind about knocking double or single—it is these things show what a man is made of—but happily there was a bell.

A queer little maid, with a big cap, admitted Kipps and took him through a bead curtain and a door into a little drawing-room, with a black and gold piano, a glazed bookcase, a Moorish cosy corner and a draped looking glass overmantel bright with Regent Street ornaments and photographs of various intellectual lights. A number of cards of invitation to meetings and the match list of a Band of Hope cricket club were stuck into the looking glass frame with Coote's name as a Vice-President. There was a bust of Beethoven over the bookcase and the walls were thick with conscientiously executed but carelessly selected "views" in oil and water colours and gilt frames. At the end of the room facing the light was a portrait that struck Kipps at first as being Coote in spectacles and feminine costume and that he afterwards decided must be Coote's mother. Then the original appeared and he discovered that it was Coote's elder and only sister who kept house for him. She wore her hair in a knob behind, and the sight of the knob suggested to Kipps an explanation for a frequent gesture of Coote's, a patting exploratory movement to the back of his head. And then it occurred to him that this was quite an absurd idea altogether.

She said "Mr. Kipps, I believe," and Kipps laughed pleasantly and said, "That's it!" and then she told him that "Chester" had gone down to the art school to see about sending off some drawings or other and that he would be back soon. Then she asked Kipps if he painted, and showed him the pictures on the wall. Kipps asked her where each one was "of," and when she showed him some of the Leas slopes he said he never would have recognised them. He said it was funny how things looked in a picture very often. "But they're awfully *good*," he said. "Did you do them?" He would look at them with his neck arched like a swan's, his head back and on one side and then suddenly peer closely into them. "They *are* good. I wish I could paint." "That's what Chester says," she answered. "I tell him he has better things to do." Kipps seemed to get on very well with her.

Then Coote came in and they left her and went upstairs together and had a good talk about reading and the Rules of Life. Or rather Coote talked, and the praises of thought and reading were in his mouth. . . .

You must figure Coote's study, a little bedroom put to studious uses, and over the mantel an array of things he had been led to believe indicative of culture and refinement, an autotype of Rossetti's "Annunciation," an autotype of Watt's "Minotaur," a Swiss carved pipe with many joints and a photograph of Amiens Cathedral (these two the spoils of travel), a phrenological bust and some broken fossils from the Warren. A rotating bookshelf carried the Encyclopædia Britannica (tenth edition), and on the top of it a large official looking, age grubby, envelope bearing the mystic words, "On His Majesty's Service," a number or so of the "Bookman," and a box of cigarettes were lying. A table under the window bore a little microscope, some dust in a saucer, some grimy glass slips and broken cover glasses, for Coote had "gone in for" biology a little. The longer side of the room was given over to bookshelves, neatly edged with pinked American cloth, and with an array of books—no worse an array of books than you find in any public library; an almost haphazard accumulation of obsolete classics, contemporary successes, the Hundred Best Books (including Samuel Warren's "Ten Thousand a Year"), old school books, directories, the Times Atlas, Ruskin in bulk, Tennyson complete in one volume, Longfellow, Charles Kingsley, Smiles and Mrs. Humphry Ward, a guide book or so, several medical pamphlets, odd magazine numbers, and much indescribable rubbish—in fact a compendium of the contemporary British mind. And in front of this array stood Kipps, ill-taught and untrained, respectful, awestricken and, for a moment at any rate, willing to learn, while Coote, the exemplary Coote, talked to him like a bishop of reading and the virtue in books.

"Nothing enlarges the mind," said Coote, "like Travel and Books. . . . And they're both so easy nowadays, and so cheap!"

"I've often wanted to 'ave a good go in at reading," Kipps replied.

"You'd hardly believe," Coote said, "how much you can get out of books. Provided you avoid trashy reading, that is. You ought to make a rule, Kipps, and read one Serious Book a week. Of course, we can Learn even from Novels, Nace Novels that is, but it isn't the same thing as serious reading. I made a rule, One Serious Book and One Novel— no more. There's some of the serious books I've been reading lately—on that table; Sartor Resartus—Mrs. Twaddletome's Pond Life, the Scottish Chiefs, Life and Letters of Dean Farrar. . . ."

2

There came at last the sound of a gong and Kipps descended to tea in that state of nervous apprehension at the difficulties of eating and drinking that his Aunt's knuckle rappings had implanted in him forever. Over Coote's shoulder he became aware of a fourth person in the Moorish cosy corner, and he turned, leaving incomplete something incoherent he was saying to Miss Coote about his modest respect and desire for literature to discover this fourth person was Miss Helen Walshingham, hatless and looking very much at home.

She rose at once with an extended hand to meet his hesitation.

"You're stopping in Folkestone, Mr. Kipps?"

" 'Ere on a bit of business," said Kipps. "I thought you was away in Bruges."

"That's later," said Miss Walshingham. "We're stopping until my brother's holiday begins and we're trying to let our house. Where are you staying in Folkestone?"

"I got a 'ouse of mine—on the Leas."

"I've heard all about your good fortune—this afternoon."

"Isn't it a Go!" said Kipps. "I 'aven't nearly got to believe it's reely 'appened yet. When that Mr. Bean told me of it you could 'ave knocked me down with a feather. . . . It's a tremenjous change for me."

He discovered Miss Coote was asking him whether he took milk and sugar. "*I* don't mind," said Kipps. "Just as you like."

Coote became active handing tea and bread and butter. It was thinly cut, and the bread was rather new, and the half of the slice that Kipps took fell upon the floor. He had been holding it by the edge, for he was not used to this migratory method of taking tea without plates or table. This little incident ruled him out of the conversation for a time, and when he came to attend to it again they were talking about something or other prodigious—a performer of some sort—that was coming, called, it seemed, "Padrooski." So Kipps, who had quietly dropped into a chair, ate his bread and butter, said "No, thenk you" to any more, and by this discreet restraint got more freedom with his cup and saucer.

Apart from the confusion natural to tea, he was in a state of tremulous excitement on account of the presence of Miss Walshingham. He glanced from Miss Coote to her brother and then at Helen. He regarded her over the top of his cup as he drank. Here she was, solid and real. It was wonderful. He remarked, as he had done at times before, the easy flow of the dark hair back from her brow over her ears, the shapeliness of the white hands that came out from her simple white cuffs, the delicate pencilling of her brow.

Presently she turned her face to him almost suddenly, and smiled with the easiest assurance of friendship.

"You will go, I suppose," she said, and added, "to the Recital."

"If I'm in Folkestone I shall," said Kipps, clearing away a little hoarseness. "I don't *know* much about music, but what I do know I like."

"I'm sure you'll like Paderewski," she said.

"If you do," he said, "I dessay I shall."

He found Coote very kindly taking his cup.

"Do you think of living in Folkestone?" asked Miss Coote, in a tone of proprietorship, from the hearthrug.

"No," said Kipps, "that's jest it—I hardly know." He also said that he wanted to look around a bit before doing anything. "There's so much to consider," said Coote, smoothing the back of his head.

"I may go back to New Romney for a bit," said Kipps. "I got an Uncle and Aunt there. I reely don't know."

Helen regarded him thoughtfully for a moment.

"You must come and see us," she said, "before we go to Bruges."

"Oo, rather!" said Kipps. "If I may."

"Yes, do," she said, and suddenly stood up before Kipps could formulate an enquiry when he should call.

"You're sure you can spare that drawing board?" she said to Miss Coote, and the conversation passed out of range.

And when he had said "Good-bye" to Miss Walshingham and she had repeated her invitation to call, he went upstairs again with Coote to look out certain initiatory books they had had under discussion. And then Kipps, blowing very resolutely, went back to his own place, bearing in his arm (1) Sesame and Lilies, (2) Sir George Tressady, (3) an anonymous book on "Vitality" that Coote particularly esteemed. And, having got to his own sitting-room, he opened Sesame and Lilies and read it with ruthless determination for some time.

3

Presently he leant back and gave himself up to the business of trying to imagine just exactly what Miss Walshingham could have thought of him when she saw him. Doubts about the precise effect of the grey flannel suit began to trouble him. He turned to the mirror over the mantel, and then got into a chair to study the hang of the trousers. It looked all right. Luckily, she had not seen the Panama hat. He knew that he had the brim turned up wrong, but he could not find out which way the brim was right. However, that she had not seen. He might perhaps ask at the shop where he bought it.

He meditated for awhile on his reflected face—doubtful whether he liked it or not—and then got down again and flitted across to the sideboard where there lay two little books, one in a cheap, magnificent cover of red and gold, and the other in green canvas. The former was called, as its cover witnessed, "Manners and Rules of Good Society, by a Member of the Aristocracy," and after the cover had indulged in a band of gilded decoration, light-hearted but natural under the circumstances, it added "TWENTY-FIRST EDITION." The second was that admirable classic, "The Art of Conversing." Kipps returned with these to his seat, placed the two before him, opened the latter with a sigh and flattened it under his hand.

Then with knitted brows he began to read onward from a mark, his lips moving.

"Having thus acquired possession of an idea, the little ship should not be abruptly launched into deep waters, but should be first permitted to glide gently and smoothly into the shallows, that is to say, the conversation should not be commenced by broadly and roundly stating a fact, or didactically expressing an opinion, as the subject would be thus virtually or summarily disposed of, or perhaps be met with a 'Really' or 'Indeed,' or some equally brief monosyllabic reply. If an opposite opinion were held by the person to whom the remark were addressed, he might not, if a stranger, care to express it in the form of a direct contradiction, or actual dissent. To glide imperceptibly into conversation is the object to be attained."

At this point Mr. Kipps rubbed his fingers through his hair with an expression of some perplexity and went back to the beginning.

4

When Kipps made his call on the Walshinghams, it all happened so differently from the "Manners and Rules" prescription ("Paying Calls") that he was quite lost from the very outset. Instead of the footman or maidservant proper in these cases, Miss Walshingham opened the door to him herself. "I'm so glad you've come," she said, with one of her rare smiles.

She stood aside for him to enter the rather narrow passage.

"I thought I'd call," he said, retaining his hat and stick.

She closed the door and led the way to a little drawing-room, which impressed Kipps as being smaller and less emphatically coloured than that of the Cootes, and in which at first only a copper bowl of white poppies upon the brown tablecloth caught his particular attention.

"You won't think it unconventional to come in, Mr. Kipps, will you?" she remarked. "Mother is out."

"I don't mind," he said, smiling amiably, "if you don't."

She walked around the table and stood regarding him across it, with that same look between speculative curiosity and appreciation that he remembered from the last of the art class meetings.

"I wondered whether you would call or whether you wouldn't before you left Folkestone."

"I'm not leaving Folkestone for a bit, and any'ow, I should have called on you."

"Mother will be sorry she was out. I've told her about you, and she wants, I know, to meet you."

"I saw 'er—if that was 'er—in the shop," said Kipps.

"Yes—you did, didn't you! . . . She has gone out to make some duty calls, and I didn't go. I had something to write. I write a little, you know."

"Reely!" said Kipps.

"It's nothing much," she said, "and it comes to nothing." She glanced at a little desk near the window, on which there lay some paper. "One must do something." She broke off abruptly. "Have you seen our outlook?" she asked and walked to the window, and Kipps came and stood beside her. "We look on the Square. It might be worse, you know. That outporter's truck there is horrid—and the railings, but it's better than staring one's social replica in the face, isn't it? It's pleasant in early spring—bright green, laid on with a dry brush—and it's pleasant in autumn."

"I like it," said Kipps. "That laylock there is pretty, isn't it?"

"Children come and pick it at times," she remarked.

"I dessay they do," said Kipps.

He rested on his hat and stick and looked appreciatively out of the window, and she glanced at him for one swift moment. A suggestion that might have come from the Art of Conversing came into his head. "Have you a garden?" he said.

She shrugged her shoulders. "Only a little one," she said, and then, "perhaps you would like to see it."

"I like gardenin'," said Kipps, with memories of a penny-worth of nasturtiums he had once trained over his uncle's dustbin.

She led the way with a certain relief.

They emerged through a four seasons coloured glass door to a little iron verandah that led by iron steps to a minute walled garden. There was just room for a patch of turf and a flower-bed; one sturdy variegated Euonymus grew in the corner. But the early June flowers, the big narcissus, snow upon the mountains, and a fine show of yellow wall-flowers shone gay.

"That's our garden," said Helen. "It's not a very big one, is it?"

"I like it," said Kipps.

"It's small," she said, "but this is the day of small things." Kipps didn't follow that.

"If you were writing when I came," he remarked, "I'm interrupting you."

She turned round with her back to the railing and rested, leaning on her hands. "I had finished," she said. "I couldn't get on."

"Were you making up something?" asked Kipps.

There was a little interval before she smiled. "I try—quite vainly—to write stories," she said. "One must do something. I don't know whether I shall ever do any good—at that—anyhow. It seems so hopeless. And, of course, one must study the popular taste. But, now my brother has gone to London, I get a lot of leisure."

"I seen your brother, 'aven't I?"

"He came to the class once or twice. Very probably you have. He's gone to London to pass his examinations and become a solicitor. And then, I suppose, he'll have a chance. Not much, perhaps, even then. But he's luckier than I am."

"You got your classes and things."

"They ought to satisfy me. But they don't. I suppose I'm ambitious. We both are. And we hadn't much of a spring-board." She glanced over his shoulder at the cramped little garden with an air of reference in her gesture.

"I should think you could do anything if you wanted to," said Kipps.

"As a matter of fact I can't do anything I want to."

"You done a good deal."

"What?"

"Well, didn't you pass one of these here University things?"

"Oh! I matriculated!"

"I should think I was no end of a swell if *I* did, I know that."

"Mr. Kipps, do you know how many people matriculate into London University every year?"

"How many then?"

"Between two and three thousand."

"Well, just think how many don't!"

Her smile came again, and broke into a laugh. "Oh, *they* don't count," she said, and then, realising that might penetrate Kipps if he was left with it, she hurried on to, "The fact is, I'm a discontented person, Mr. Kipps. Folkestone, you know, is a Sea Front, and it values people by sheer vulgar prosperity. We're not prosperous, and we live in a back street. We have to live here because this is our house. It's a mercy we haven't to 'let.' One feels one hasn't opportunities. If one had, I suppose one wouldn't use them. Still——"

Kipps felt he was being taken tremendously into her confidence. "That's jest it," he said, very sagely.

He leant forward on his stick and said, very earnestly, "I believe you could do anything you wanted to, if you tried."

She threw out her hands in disavowal.

"I know," said he, very sagely and nodding his head. "I watched you once or twice when you were teaching that wood-carving class."

For some reason this made her laugh—a rather pleasant laugh, and that made Kipps feel a very witty and successful person. "It's very evident," she said, "that you're one of those rare people who believe in me, Mr. Kipps," to which he answered, "Oo, I *do!*" and then suddenly they became aware of Mrs. Walshingham coming along the passage. In another moment she appeared through the four seasons door, bonneted and ladylike, and a little faded, exactly as Kipps had seen her in the shop. Kipps felt a certain apprehension at her appearance, in spite of the reassurances he had had from Coote.

"Mr. Kipps has called on us," said Helen, and Mrs.

Walshingham said it was very kind of him, and added that new people didn't call on them very much nowadays. There was nothing of the scandalised surprise Kipps had seen in the shop; she had heard, perhaps, he was a gentleman now. In the shop he had thought her rather jaded and haughty, but he had scarcely taken her hand, which responded to his touch with a friendly pressure, before he knew how mistaken he had been. She then told her daughter that someone called Mrs. Wace had been out, and turned to Kipps again to ask him if he had had tea. Kipps said he had not, and Helen moved towards some mysterious interior. "But *I* say," said Kipps; "don't you on my account——!"

Helen vanished, and he found himself alone with Mrs. Walshingham, which, of course, made him breathless and Boreas-looking for a moment.

"You were one of Helen's pupils in the wood-carving class?" asked Mrs. Walshingham, regarding him with the quiet watchfulness proper to her position.

"Yes," said Kipps, "that's 'ow I 'ad the pleasure——"

"She took a great interest in her wood-carving class. She is so energetic, you know, and it gives her an Outlet."

"I thought she taught something splendid."

"Everyone says she did very well. Helen, I think, would do anything well that she undertook to do. She's so very clever. And she throws herself into things so." ·

She untied her bonnet strings with a pleasant informality.

"She has told me all about her class. She used to be full of it. And about your cut hand."

"Lor'!" said Kipps; "fancy, telling that!"

"Oh, yes! And how brave you were."

(Though, indeed, Helen's chief detail had been his remarkable expedient for checking bloodshed.)

Kipps became bright pink. "She said you didn't seem to feel it a bit."

Kipps felt he would have to spend weeks over "The Art of Conversing."

While he still hung fire Helen returned with the apparatus for afternoon tea upon a tray.

"Do you mind pulling out the table?" asked Mrs. Walshingham.

That, again, was very homelike. Kipps put down his hat

and stick in the corner and, amidst an iron thunder, pulled out a little, rusty, green-painted table, and then in the easiest manner followed Helen in to get chairs.

So soon as he had got rid of his teacup—he refused all food, of course, and they were merciful—he became wonderfully at his ease. Presently he was talking. He talked quite modestly and simply about his changed condition and his difficulties and plans. He spread what indeed had an air of being all his simple little soul before his eyes. In a little while his clipped, defective accent had become less perceptible to their ears, and they began to realise, as the girl with the freckles had long since realised, that there were passable aspects of Kipps. He confided, he submitted, and for both of them he had the realest, the most seductively flattering undertone of awe and reverence.

He stopped about two hours, having forgotten how terribly incorrect it is to stay at such a length. They did not mind at all.

III. ENGAGED

1

Within two months, within a matter of three and fifty days, Kipps had clambered to the battlements of Heart's Desire.

It all became possible by the Walshinghams—it would seem at Coote's instigation—deciding, after all, not to spend the holidays at Bruges. Instead, they remained in Folkestone, and this happy chance gave Kipps just all these opportunities of which he stood in need.

His crowning day was at Lympne, and long before the summer warmth began to break, while indeed August still flamed on high. They had organised—no one seemed to know who suggested it first—a water party on the still reaches of the old military canal at Hythe, the canal that was to have stopped Napoleon if the sea failed us, and they were to picnic by the brick bridge, and afterwards to clamber to Lympne Castle. The host of the gathering, it was understood very clearly, was Kipps.

They went, a merry party. The canal was weedy, with only a few inches of water at the shallows, and so they went in three Canadian canoes. Kipps had learned to paddle—it had been his first athletic accomplishment, and his second —with the last three or four of ten private lessons still to come—was to be cycling. But Kipps did not paddle at all badly; muscles hardened by lifting pieces of cretonne could cut a respectable figure by the side of Coote's executions, and the girl with the freckles, the girl who understood him, came in his canoe. They raced the Walshinghams, brother and sister; and Coote, in a liquefying state and blowing mightily, but still persistent and always quite polite and considerate, toiled behind with Mrs. Walshingham. She could not be expected to paddle (though, of course, she "offered") and she reclined upon specially adjusted cushions under a black and white sunshade and watched Kipps and her daughter, and feared at intervals that Coote was getting hot.

They were all more or less in holiday costume, the eyes of the girls looked out under the shade of wide-brimmed hats; even the freckled girl was unexpectedly pretty, and Helen, swinging sunlit to her paddle, gave Kipps, almost for the first time, the suggestion of a graceful body. Kipps was arrayed in the completest boating costume, and when his fashionable Panama was discarded and his hair blown into disorder he became, in his white flannels, as sightly as most young men. His complexion was a notable asset.

Things favoured him, the day favoured him, everyone favoured him. Young Walshingham, the girl with the freckles, Coote and Mrs. Walshingham, were playing up to him in the most benevolent way, and between the landing place and Lympne, Fortune, to crown their efforts, had placed a small, convenient field entirely at the disposal of an adolescent bull. Not a big, real, resolute bull, but, on the other hand, no calf; a young bull, in the same stage of emotional development as Kipps, "standing where the two rivers meet." Detachedly our party drifted towards him.

When they landed young Walshingham, with the simple directness of a brother, abandoned his sister to Kipps and secured the freckled girl, leaving Coote to carry Mrs. Walshingham's light wool wrap. He started at once, in order to put an effectual distance between himself and his companion, on the one hand, and a certain persuasive chaperonage that went with Coote, on the other. Young Walshingham, I think I have said, was dark, with a Napoleonic profile, and it was natural for him, therefore, to be a bold thinker and an epigrammatic speaker, and he had long ago discovered great possibilities of appreciation in the freckled girl. He was in a very happy frame that day because he had just been entrusted with the management of Kipps' affairs (old Bean inexplicably dismissed), and that was not a bad beginning for a solicitor of only a few months' standing, and, moreover, he had been reading Nietzsche, and he thought that in all probability he was the Non-Moral Overman referred to by that writer. He wore fairly large-sized hats. He wanted to expand the theme of the Non-Moral Overman in the ear of the freckled girl, to say it over, so to speak, and in order to seclude his exposition they went aside from the direct path and trespassed through a coppice, avoiding the youthful bull. They escaped to these higher themes but narrowly, for Coote and Mrs. Walshingham, subtle chaperones both, and each indisposed for excellent reasons to encumber Kipps and Helen, were hot upon their heels. These two kept direct route to the stile of the bull's field, and the sight of the animal at once awakened Coote's innate aversion to brutality in any shape or form. He said the stiles were too high, and that they could do better by going around by the hedge, and Mrs. Walshingham, nothing loath, agreed.

This left the way clear for Kipps and Helen, and they encountered the bull. Helen did not observe the bull, but Kipps did; but, that afternoon at any rate, he was equal to facing a lion. And the bull really came at them. It was not an affair of the bull-ring exactly, no desperate rushes and gorings; but he came; he regarded them with a large, wicked, bluish eye, opened a mouth below his moistly glistening nose and booed, at any rate, if he did not exactly bellow, and he shook his head wickedly and showed that tossing was in his mind. Helen was frightened, without any loss of dignity, and Kipps went extremely white. But he was perfectly calm, and he seemed to her to have lost the last vestiges of his accent and his social shakiness. He directed her to walk quietly towards the stile, and made an oblique advance towards the bull.

"You be orf!" he said. . . .

When Helen was well over the stile Kipps withdrew in good order. He got over the stile under cover of a feint, and the thing was done—a small thing, no doubt, but just enough to remove from Helen's mind an incorrect deduction that a man who was so terribly afraid of a teacup as Kipps must necessarily be abjectly afraid of everything else in the world. In her moment of reaction she went perhaps too far in the opposite direction. Hitherto Kipps had always had a certain flimsiness of effect for her. Now suddenly he was discovered solid. He was discovered possible in many new ways. Here, after all, was the sort of back a woman can get behind! . . .

As so these heirs of the immemorial ages went past the turf-crowned mass of Portus Lemanus up the steep slopes towards the mediæval castle on the crest the thing was also manifest in her eyes.

2

Everyone who stays in Folkestone gets, sooner or later, to
Lympne. The castle became a farmhouse long ago, and the
farmhouse, itself now ripe and venerable, wears the walls
of the castle as a little man wears a big man's coat. The
kindliest of farm ladies entertains a perpetual stream of visitors and shows her vast mangle, and her big kitchen, and
takes you out upon the sunniest little terrace garden in all
the world, and you look down the sheep-dotted slopes to
where, beside the canal and under the trees, the crumpled
memories of Rome sleep forever. For hither to this lonely
spot the galleys once came, the legions, the emperors, mas-
ters of the world. The castle is but a thing of yesterday,
King Stephen's time or thereabout, in that retrospect. One
climbs the pitch of perforation, and there one is lifted to
the centre of far more than a hemisphere of view. Away below one's feet, almost at the bottom of the hill, the Marsh
begins, and spreads and spreads in a mighty crescent that
sweeps about the sea, the Marsh dotted with the church
towers of forgotten mediæval towns and breaking at last
into the low, blue hills of Winchelsea and Hastings; east
hangs France, between the sea and the sky, and round the
north, bounding the wide prospectives of farms and houses
and woods, the Downs, with their hangers and chalk pits,
sustain the passing shadows of the sailing clouds.

And here it was, high out of the world of everyday, and
in the presence of spacious beauty, that Kipps and Helen
found themselves agreeably alone. All six, it had seemed,
had been coming for the Keep, but Mrs. Walshingham had
hesitated at the horrid little stairs, and then suddenly felt
faint, and so she and the freckled girl had remained below,
walking up and down in the shadow of the house, and Coote
had remembered they were all out of cigarettes, and had
taken off young Walshingham into the village. There had
been shouting to explain between ground and parapet, and
then Helen and Kipps turned again to the view, and commended it and fell silent.

Helen sat fearlessly in an embrasure, and Kipps stood
beside her.

"I've always been fond of scenery," Kipps repeated, after
an interval.

Then he went off at a tangent. "D'you reely think that was right what Coote was saying?"

She looked interrogation.

"About my name?"

"Being really C-U-Y-P-S? I have my doubts. I thought at first——. What makes Mr. Coote add an S to Cuyp?"

"I dunno," said Kipps, foiled. "I was just thinking——"

She shot one wary glance at him and then turned her eyes to the sea.

Kipps was out for a space. He had intended to lead from this question to the general question of surnames and change of names; it had seemed a light and witty way of saying something he had in mind, and suddenly he perceived that this was an unutterably vulgar and silly project. The hitch about that "s" had saved him. He regarded her profile for a moment, framed in weather-beaten stone, and backed by the blue elements.

He dropped the question of his name out of existence and spoke again of the view. "When I see scenery, and things that are beautiful, it makes me feel——"

She looked at him suddenly, and saw him fumbling for his words.

"Silly like," he said.

She took him in with her glance, the old look of proprietorship it was, touched with a certain warmth. She spoke in a voice as unambiguous as her eyes. "You needn't," she said. "You know, Mr. Kipps, you hold yourself too cheap."

Her eyes and words smote him with amazement. He stared at her like a man who awakens. She looked down.

"You mean——" he said; and then, "don't you hold me cheap?"

She glanced up again and shook her head.

"But—for instance—you don't think of me—as an equal like."

"Why not?"

"Oo! But reely——"

His heart beat very fast.

"If I thought," he said, and then, "you know so much."

"That's nothing," she said.

Then, for a long time, as it seemed to them, both kept silence, a silence that said and accomplished many things.

"I know what I am," he said, at length. . . . "If I thought it was possible . . . If I thought *you* . . . I believe I could do anything——"

He stopped, and she sat downcast and strikingly still.

"Miss Walshingham," he said, "is it possible that you . . . could care for me enough to—to 'elp me? Miss Walshingham, do you care for me at all?"

It seemed she was never going to answer. She looked up at him. "I think," she said, "you are the most generous —look at what you have done for my brother—the most generous and the most modest of men. And this afternoon —I thought you were the bravest."

She turned her head, glanced down, waved her hand to someone on the terrace below, and stood up.

"Mother is signalling," she said. "We must go down."

Kipps became polite and deferential by habit, but his mind was a tumult that had nothing to do with that.

He moved before her towards the little door that opened on the winding stairs—"always precede a lady down or up stairs"—and then on the second step he turned resolutely. "But," he said, looking up out of the shadow, flannel-clad and singularly like a man.

She looked down on him, with her hand upon the stone lintel.

He held out his hand as if to help her. "Can you tell me?" he said. "You must know——"

"What?"

"If you care for me?"

She did not answer for a long time. It was as if everything in the world had drawn to the breaking point, and in a minute must certainly break.

"Yes," she said, at last, "I know."

Abruptly, by some impalpable sign, he knew what the answer would be, and he remained still.

She bent down over him and softened to her wonderful smile.

"Promise me," she insisted.

He promised with his still face.

"If *I* do not hold you cheap, you will never hold yourself cheap——"

"If you do not hold me cheap, you mean?"

She bent down quite close beside him. "I hold you,"

she said, and then whispered, *"dear."*

"Me?"

She laughed aloud.

He was astonished beyond measure. He stipulated, lest there might be some misconception, "You will marry me?"

She was laughing, inundated by the sense of bountiful power, of possession and success. He looked quite a nice little man to have. "Yes," she laughed. "What else could I mean?" and, "Yes."

He felt as a praying hermit might have felt, snatched from the midst of his quiet devotions, his modest sackcloth and ashes, and hurled neck and crop over the glittering gates of Paradise, smack among the iridescent wings, the bright-eyed Cherubim. He felt like some lowly and righteous man dynamited into Bliss. . . .

His hand tightened upon the rope that steadies one upon the stairs of stone. He was for kissing her hand and did not.

He said not a word more. He turned about, and with something very like a scared expression on his face led the way into the obscurity of their descent.

3

Everyone seemed to understand. Nothing was said, nothing was explained, the merest touch of the eyes sufficed. As they clustered in the castle gateway Coote, Kipps remembered afterwards, laid hold of his arm as if by chance and pressed it. It was quite evident he knew. His eyes, his nose, shone with benevolent congratulations, shone, too, with the sense of a good thing conducted to its climax. Mrs. Walshingham, who had seemed a little fatigued by the hill, recovered, and was even obviously stirred by affection for her daughter. There was, in passing, a motherly caress. She asked Kipps to give her his arm in walking down the steep. Kipps in a sort of dream obeyed. He found himself trying to attend to her, and soon he was attending.

She and Kipps talked like sober, responsible people and went slowly, while the others drifted down the hill together, a loose little group of four. He wondered momentarily what they would talk about and then sank into his conversation with Mrs. Walshingham. He conversed, as it were, out of his superficial personality, and his inner self lay stunned in unsuspected depths within. It had an air of being an

interesting and friendly talk, almost their first long talk together. Hitherto he had had a sort of fear of Mrs. Walshingham, as of a person possibly satirical, but she proved a
soul of sense and sentiment, and Kipps, for all of his ab-
straction, got on with her unexpectedly well. They talked a
little upon scenery and the inevitable melancholy attaching
to the old ruins and the thought of vanished generations.

"Perhaps they jousted here," said Mrs. Walshingham.

"They was up to all sorts of things," said Kipps, and
then the two come round to Helen. She spoke of her daughter's literary ambitions. "She will do something, I feel sure.
You know, Mr. Kipps, it's a great responsibility to a mother
to feel her daughter is—exceptionally clever."

"I dessay it is," said Kipps. "There's no mistake about
that."

She spoke, too, of her son—almost like Helen's twin—
alike, yet different. She made Kipps feel quite fatherly.
"They are so quick, so artistic," she said, "so full of ideas.
Almost they frighten me. One feels they need opportunities
—as other people need air."

She spoke of Helen's writing. "Even when she was quite
a little dot she wrote verse."

(Kipps, sensation.)

"Her father had just the same tastes——" Mrs. Walshingham turned a little beam of half-pathetic reminiscence on
the past. "He was more artist than business man. That was
the trouble. . . . He was misled by his partner, and when
the crash came everyone blamed him. . . . Well, it doesn't
do to dwell on horrid things—especially to-day. There are
bright days, Mr. Kipps, and dark days. And mine have not
always been bright."

Kipps presented a face of Coote-like sympathy.

She diverged to talk of flowers, and Kipps' mind was
filled with the picture of Helen bending down towards him
in the Keep. . . .

They spread the tea under the trees before the little
inn, and at a certain moment Kipps became aware that
everyone in the party was simultaneously and furtively
glancing at him. There might have been a certain tension,
had it not been first of all for Coote and his tact, and afterwards for a number of wasps. Coote was resolved to make
this memorable day pass off well, and displayed an almost

boisterous sense of fun. Then young Walshingham began talking of the Roman remains below Lympne, intending to lead up to the Overman. "These old Roman chaps," he said, and then the wasps arrived. They killed three in the jam alone.

Kipps killed wasps, as if it were in a dream, and handed things to the wrong people, and maintained a thin surface of ordinary intelligence with the utmost difficulty. At times he became aware, aware with an extraordinary vividness, of Helen. Helen was carefully not looking at him and behaving with amazing coolness and ease. But just for that one time there was the faintest suggestion of pink beneath the ivory of her cheeks. . . .

Tacitly the others conceded to Kipps the right to paddle back with Helen; he helped her into the canoe and took his paddle, and, paddling slowly, dropped behind the others. And now his inner self stirred again. He said nothing to her. How could he ever say anything to her again? She spoke to him at rare intervals about reflections and the flowers and the trees, and he nodded in reply. But his mind moved very slowly forward now from the point at which it had fallen stunned in the Lympne Keep, moving forward to the beginnings of realisation. As yet he did not say even in the recesses of his heart that she was his. But he perceived that the goddess had come from her altar amazingly, and had taken him by the hand!

The sky was a vast splendour, and then close to them were the dark, protecting trees and the shining, smooth, still water. He was an erect, black outline to her; he plied his paddle with no unskilful gesture, the water broke to snaky silver and glittered far behind his strokes. Indeed, he did not seem bad to her. Youth calls to youth the wide world through, and her soul rose in triumph over his subjection. And behind him was money and opportunity, freedom and London, a great background of seductively indistinct hopes. To him her face was a warm dimness. In truth, he could not see her eyes, but it seemed to his love-witched brain he did and that they shone out at him like dusky stars.

All the world that evening was no more than a shadowy frame of darkling sky and water and dripping bows about Helen. He seemed to see through things with an extraordinary clearness; she was revealed to him certainly, as the cause and essence of it all.

He was indeed at his Heart's Desire. It was one of those times when there seems to be no future, when Time has stopped and we are at an end. Kipps, that evening, could not have imagined a to-morrow, all that his imagination had pointed towards was attained. His mind stood still and took the moments as they came.

4

About nine that night Coote came around to Kipps' new apartment in the Upper Sandgate Road—the house on the Leas had been let furnished—and Kipps made an effort toward realisation. He was discovered sitting at the open window and without a lamp, quite still. Coote was deeply moved, and he pressed Kipps' palm and laid a knobby, white hand on his shoulder and displayed the sort of tenderness becoming in a crisis. Kipps was too moved that night, and treated Coote like a very dear brother.

"She's splendid," said Coote, coming to it abruptly.

"Isn't she?" said Kipps.

"I couldn't help noticing her face," said Coote. . . . "You know, my dear Kipps, that this is better than a legacy."

"I don't deserve it," said Kipps.

"You can't say that."·

"I don't. I can't 'ardly believe it. I can't believe it at all. No!"

There followed an expressive stillness.

"It's wonderful," said Kipps. "It takes me like that."

Coote made a faint blowing noise, and so again they came for a time of silence.

"And it began—before your money?"

"When I was in 'er class," said Kipps, solemnly.

Coote, speaking out of a darkness which he was illuminating strangely with efforts to strike a match, said that it was beautiful. He could not have *wished* Kipps a better fortune. . . .

He lit a cigarette, and Kipps was moved to do the same, with a sacramental expression. Presently speech flowed more freely.

Coote began to praise Helen and her mother and brother.

He talked of when "it" might be, he presented the thing as concrete and credible. "It's a county family, you know," he said. "She is connected, you know, with the Beaupres family—you know Lord Beaupres."

"No!" said Kipps, "reely!"

"Distantly, of course," said Coote. "Still——"

He smiled a smile that glimmered in the twilight.

"It's too much," said Kipps, overcome. "It's so all like that."

Coote exhaled. For a time Kipps listened to Helen's praises and matured a point of view.

"I say, Coote," he said. "What ought I to do now?"

"What do you mean?" said Coote.

"I mean about calling on 'er and all that."

He reflected. "Naturally, I want to do it all right."

"Of course," said Coote.

"It would be awful to go and do something—now—all wrong."

Coote's cigarette glowed as he meditated. "You must call, of course," he decided. "You'll have to speak to Mrs. Walshingham."

" 'Ow?" said Kipps.

"Tell her you mean to marry her daughter."

"I dessay she knows," said Kipps, with defensive penetration.

Coote's head was visible, shaking itself judiciously.

"Then there's the ring," said Kipps. "What 'ave I to do about that?"

"What ring do you mean?"

" 'Ngagement Ring. There isn't anything at all about that in 'Manners and Rules of Good Society'—not a word."

"Of course you must get something—tasteful. Yes."

"What sort of a ring?"

"Something nace. They'll show you in the shop."

"Of course. I 'spose I got to take it to 'er, eh? Put it on her finger."

"Oh, no! Send it. Much better."

"Ah!" said Kipps, for the first time, with a note of relief.

"Then, 'ow about this call—on Mrs. Walshingham, I mean. 'Ow ought one to go?"

"Rather a ceremonial occasion," reflected Coote.

"Wadyer mean? Frock coat?"

"I *think* so," said Coote, with discrimination.

"Light trousers and all that?"

"Yes."

"Rose?"

"I think it might run to a buttonhole."

The curtain that hung over the future became less opaque to the eyes of Kipps. To-morrow, and then other days, became perceptible at least as existing. Frock coat, silk hat and a rose! With a certain solemnity he contemplated himself in the process of slow transformation into an English gentleman, Arthur Cuyps, frock-coated on occasions of ceremony, the familiar acquaintance of Lady Punnet, the recognised wooer of a distant connection of the Earl of Beaupres.

Something like awe at the magnitude of his own fortune came upon him. He felt the world was opening out like a magic flower in a transformation scene at the touch of this wand of gold. And Helen, nestling beautiful in the red heart of the flower. Only ten weeks ago he had been no more than the shabbiest of improvers and shamefully dismissed for dissipation, the mere soil-burned seed, as it were, of these glories. He resolved the engagement ring should be of expressively excessive quality and appearance, in fact, the very best they had.

"Ought I to send 'er flowers?" he speculated.

"Not necessarily," said Coote. "Though, of course, it's an attention. . . ."

Kipps meditated on flowers.

"When you see her," said Coote, "you'll have to ask her to name the day."

Kipps started. "That won't be just yet a bit, will it?"

"Don't know any reason for delay."

"Oo, but—a year, say."

"Rather a long time," said Coote.

"Is it?" said Kipps, turning his head sharply. "But——"

There was quite a long pause.

"I say," he said, at last, and in an unaltered voice, "you'll 'ave to 'elp me about the wedding."

"Only too happy," said Coote.

"Of course," said Kipps, "I didn't think——" He changed his line of thought. "Coote," he asked, "wot's a 'state-eh-tate'?"

"A 'tate-ah-tay'!" said Coote, improvingly, "is a conversation alone together."

"Lor'!" said Kipps, "but I thought——. It says *strictly* we oughtn't to enjoy a tater-tay, not sit together, walk together, ride together or meet during any part of the day. That don't leave much time for meeting, does it?"

"The books says that?" asked Coote.

"I jest learnt it by 'eart before you came. I thought that was a bit rum, but I s'pose it's all right."

"You won't find Miss Walshingham so strict as all that," said Coote. "I think that's a bit extreme. They'd only do that now in very strict old aristocratic families. Besides, the Walshinghams are so modern—advanced, you might say. I expect you'll get plenty of chances of talking together."

"There's a tremendous lot to think about," said Kipps, blowing a profound sigh. "D'you mean—p'raps we might be married in a few months or so."

"You'll *have* to be," said Coote. "Why not?" . . .

Midnight found Kipps alone, looking a little tired and turning over the leaves of the red-covered textbook with a studious expression. He paused for a moment on page 233, his eye caught by the words:

"FOR AN UNCLE OR AUNT BY MARRIAGE the period is six weeks black, with jet trimmings."

"No," said Kipps, after a vigorous mental effort. "That's not it." The pages rustled again. He stopped and flattened out the little book decisively at the beginning of the chapter on "Weddings."

He became pensive. He stared at the lamp wick. "I suppose I ought to go over and tell them," he said, at last.

5

Kipps called on Mrs. Walshingham, attired in the proper costume for Ceremonial Occasions in the Day. He carried a silk hat, and he wore a deep-skirted frock coat, his boots were patent leather and his trousers dark grey. He had generous white cuffs with gold links, and his grey gloves, one thumb in which had burst when he put them on, he held loosely in his hand. He carried a small umbrella rolled to an exquisite tightness. A sense of singular correctness pervaded his being and warred with the enormity of the occasion for possession of his soul. Anon he touched his silk cravat. The world smelt of his rosebud.

He seated himself on a new re-covered chintz armchair and stuck out the elbow of the arm that held his hat.

"I know," said Mrs. Walshingham, "I know everything," and helped him out most amazingly. She deepened the impression he had already received of her sense and refinement. She displayed an amount of tenderness that touched him.

"This is a great thing," she said, "to a mother," and her hand rested for a moment on his impeccable coat sleeve.

"A daughter, Arthur," she explained, "is so much more than a son."

Marriage, she said, was a lottery, and without love and toleration there was much unhappiness. Her life had not always been bright—there had been dark days and bright days. She smiled rather sweetly. "This is a bright one," she said.

She said very kind and flattering things to Kipps, and she thanked him for his goodness to her son. ("That wasn't anything," said Kipps.) And then she expanded upon the theme of her two children. "Both so accomplished," she said, "so clever. I call them my Twin Jewels."

She was repeating a remark that she had made at Lympne, that she always said her children needed opportunities, as other people needed air, when she was abruptly arrested by the entry of Helen. They hung on a pause, Helen perhaps surprised by Kipps' weekday magnificence. Then she advanced with outstretched hand.

Both the young people were shy. "I jest called 'round," began Kipps, and became uncertain how to end.

"Won't you have some tea?" asked Helen.

She walked to the window, looked out at the familiar outporter's barrow, turned, surveyed Kipps for a moment ambiguously, said "I will get some tea," and so departed again.

Mrs. Walshingham and Kipps looked at one another and the lady smiled indulgently. "You two young people mustn't be shy of each other," said Mrs. Walshingham, which damaged Kipps considerably.

She was explaining how sensitive Helen always had been, even about quite little things, when the servant appeared with the tea things, and then Helen followed, and taking up

a secure position behind the little bamboo tea table, broke
the ice with officious teacup clattering. Then she introduced the topic of a forthcoming open-air performance of
"As You Like It," and steered past the worst of the
awkwardness. They discussed stage illusion. "I mus' say,"
said Kipps, "I don't quite like a play in a theayter. It seems
sort of unreal, some'ow."

"But most plays are written for the stage," said Helen,
looking at the sugar.

"I know," admitted Kipps.

They finished tea. "Well," said Kipps, and rose.

"You mustn't go yet," said Mrs. Walshingham, rising
and taking his hand. "I'm sure you two must have heaps
to say to each other," and so she escaped towards the
door.

6

Among other projects that seemed almost equally correct
to Kipps at that exalted moment was one of embracing Helen
with ardour as soon as the door closed behind her mother
and one of headlong flight through the open window. Then
he remembered he ought to hold the door open for Mrs.
Walshingham, and turned from that duty to find Helen still
standing, beautifully inaccessible, behind the tea things. He
closed the door and advanced towards her with his arms
akimbo and his hands upon his coat skirts. Then, feeling
angular, he moved his right hand to his moustache. Anyhow,
he was dressed all right. Somewhere at the back of his mind,
dim and mingled with doubt and surprise, appeared the
perception that he felt now quite differently towards her,
that something between them had been blown from Lympne
Keep to the four winds of heaven. . . .

She regarded him with an eye of critical proprietorship.

"Mother has been making up to you," she said, smiling
slightly.

She added, "It was nice of you to come around to see
her."

They stood through a brief pause, as though each had
expected something different in the other and was a little
perplexed at its not being there. Kipps found he was at the
corner of the brown covered table, and he picked up a
little flexible book that lay upon it to occupy his mind.

"I bought you a ring to-day," he said, bending the book and speaking for the sake of saying something, and then he was moved to genuine speech. "You know," he said, "I can't 'ardly believe it."

Her face relaxed slightly again. "No?" she said, and may have breathed, "Nor I."

"No," he went on. "It's as though everything 'ad changed. More even than when I got my money. 'Ere we are going to marry. It's like being someone else. What I feel is——"

He turned a flushed and earnest face to her. He seemed to come alive to her with one natural gesture. "I don't *know* things. I'm not good enough. I'm not refined. The more you'll see of me the more you'll find me out."

"But I'm going to help you."

"You'll 'ave to 'elp me a fearful lot."

She walked to the window, glanced out of it, made up her mind, turned and came towards him, with her hands clasped behind her back.

"All these things that trouble you are very little things. If you don't mind—if you will let me tell you things——"

"I wish you would."

"Then I will."

"They're little things to you, but they aren't to me."

"It all depends, if you don't mind being told."

"By you?"

"I don't expect you to be told by strangers."

"Oo!" said Kipps, expressing much.

"You know, there are just a few little things. For instance, you know, you are careless with your pronunciation. . . . You don't mind my telling you?"

"I like it," said Kipps.

"There's aitches."

"I know," said Kipps, and then, endorsingly, "I been told. Fact is, I know a chap, a Nacter, *he's* told me. He's told me, and he's going to give me a lesson or so."

"I'm glad of that. It only requires a little care."

"Of course. On the stage they got to look out. They take regular lessons."

"Of course," said Helen, a little absently.

"I dessay I shall soon get into it," said Kipps.

"And then there's dress," said Helen, taking up her thread again.

Kipps became pink, but he remained respectfully attentive.

"You don't mind?" she said.

"Oo, no."

"You mustn't be too—too dressy. It's possible to be over-conventional, over-elaborate. It makes you look like a shop—like a common, well-off person. There's a sort of easiness that is better. A real gentleman looks right, without looking as though he had tried to be right."

"Jest as though 'e'd put on what came first?" said the pupil, in a faded voice.

"Not exactly that, but a sort of ease."

Kipps nodded his head intelligently. In his heart he was kicking his silk hat about the room in an ecstasy of disappointment.

"And you must accustom yourself to be more at your ease when you are with people," said Helen. "You've only got to forget yourself a little and not be anxious——"

"I'll try," said Kipps, looking rather hard at the teapot. "I'll do my best to try."

"I know you will," she said, and laid a hand for an instant upon his shoulder and withdrew it.

He did not perceive her caress. "One has to learn," he said. His attention was distracted by the strenuous efforts that were going on in the back of his head to translate, "I say, didn't you ought to name the day?" into easy as well as elegant English, a struggle that was still undecided when the time came for them to part. . . .

He sat for a long time at the open window of his sitting-room with an intent face, recapitulating that interview. His eyes rested at last almost reproachfully on the silk hat beside him. " 'Ow *is* one to know?" he asked. His attention was caught by a rubbed place in the nap, and, still thoughtful, he rolled up his handkerchief skilfully into a soft ball and began to smooth this down.

His expression changed slowly.

" 'Ow the Juice is one to know?" he said, putting down the hat with some emphasis.

He rose up, went across the room to the sideboard, and, standing there, opened and began to read "Manners and Rules."

IV. THE BICYCLE
MANUFACTURER

1

So Kipps embarked upon his engagement, steeled himself to the high enterprise of marrying above his breeding. The next morning found him dressing with a certain quiet severity of movement, and it seemed to his landlady's housemaid that he was unusually dignified at breakfast. He meditated profoundly over his kipper and his kidney and bacon. He was going to New Romney to tell the old people what had happened and where he stood. And the love of Helen had also given him courage to do what Buggins had once suggested to him as a thing he would do were he in Kipps' place, and that was to hire a motor car for the afternoon. He had an early cold lunch, and then, with an air of quiet resolution, assumed a cap and coat he had purchased to this end, and thus equipped strolled around, blowing slightly, to the motor shop. The transaction was unexpectedly easy, and within the hour Kipps, spectacled and wrapped about, was tootling through Dymchurch.

They came to a stop smartly and neatly outside the little toy shop. "Make that thing 'oot a bit, will you," said Kipps. "Yes, that's it." "Whup," said the motor car. "Whurrup!"

Both his Aunt and Uncle came out on the pavement. "Why, its Artie," cried his Aunt, and Kipps had a moment of triumph.

He descended to hand claspings, removed wraps and spectacles, and the motor driver retired to take "an hour off." Old Kipps surveyed the machinery and disconcerted Kipps for a moment by asking him in a knowing tone what they asked him for a thing like that. The two men stood inspecting the machine and impressing the neighbours for a time, and then they strolled through the shop into the little parlour for a drink.

"They ain't settled," old Kipps had said to the neighbours. "They ain't got no further than experiments. There's a bit of take-in about each. You take my advice and wait, me boy, even if it's a year or two, before you buy one for your own use."

(Though Kipps had said nothing of doing anything of the sort.)

" 'Ow d'you like that whiskey I sent?" asked Kipps, dodging the old familiar bunch of children's pails.

Old Kipps became tactful. "It's a very good whiskey, my boy," said old Kipps. "I 'aven't the slightest doubt it's a very good whiskey and cost you a tidy price. But—dashed if it soots me! They put this here Foozle Ile in it, my boy, and it ketches me jest 'ere." He indicated his centre of figure. "Gives me the heartburn," he said, and shook his head rather sadly.

"It's a very good whiskey," said Kipps. "It's what the actor manager chaps drink in London, I 'appen to know."

"I dessay they do, my boy," said old Kipps, "but then they've 'ad their livers burnt out, and I 'aven't. They ain't dellicat like me. My stummik always '*as* been extrey dellicat. Sometimes it's almost been as though nothing would lay on it. But that's in passing. I liked those segars. You can send me some of them segars. . . ."

You cannot lead a conversation straight from the gastric consequences of Foozle Ile to Love, and so Kipps, after a friendly inspection of a rare old engraving after Morland (perfect except for a hole kicked through the centre) that his Uncle had recently purchased by private haggle, came to the topic of the old people's removal.

At the outset of Kipps' great fortunes there had been much talk of some permanent provision for them. It had been conceded they were to be provided for comfortably, and the phrase "retire from business" had been very much in the air. Kipps had pictured an ideal cottage, with a creeper always in exuberant flower about the door, where the sun shone forever and the wind never blew and a perpetual welcome hovered in the doorway. It was an agreeable dream, but when it came to the point of deciding upon this particular cottage or that, and on this particular house or that, Kipps was surprised by an unexpected clinging to the little home, which he had always understood to be the worst of all possible houses.

"We don't want to move in a 'urry," said Mrs. Kipps.

"When we want to move, we want to move for life. I've had enough moving about in my time," said old Kipps.

"We can do here a bit more, now we done here so long," said Mrs. Kipps.

"You lemme look about a bit *fust*," said old Kipps.

And in looking about old Kipps found perhaps a finer joy than any mere possession could have given. He would shut his shop more or less effectually against the intrusion of customers, and toddle abroad seeking new matter for his dream; no house was too small and none too large for his knowing enquiries. Occupied houses took his fancy more than vacancies, and he would remark, "You won't be a-livin' 'ere forever, even if you think you will," when irate householders protested against the unsolicited examination of their more intimate premises. . . .

Remarkable difficulties arose of a totally unexpected sort.

"If we 'ave a larger 'ouse," said Mrs. Kipps with sudden bitterness, "we shall want a servant, and I don't want no gells in the place larfin' at me, sniggerin' and larfin' and prancin' and trapesin', lardy da! If we 'ave a smaller 'ouse, there won't be room to swing a cat."

Room to swing a cat it seemed was absolutely essential. It was an infrequent but indispensable operation.

"When we *do* move," said old Kipps, "if we could get a bit of shootin'——. I don't want to sell off all this here stock for nothin'. It's took years to 'cumulate. I put a ticket in the winder sayin' 'sellin' orf,' but it 'asn't brought nothing like a roosh. One of these 'ere dratted visitors pretendin' to want an air gun, was all we 'ad in yesterday. Jest an excuse for spyin' round and then go away and larf at you. No-thanky to everything, it didn't matter what. . . . That's 'ow *I* look at it, Artie."

They pursued meandering fancies about the topic of their future settlement for a space and Kipps became more and more hopeless of any proper conversational opening that would lead to his great announcement, and more and more uncertain how such an opening should be taken. Once indeed old Kipps, anxious to get away from this dangerous subject of removals, began: "And what are you a-doin' of in Folkestone? I shall have to come over and see you one of these days," but before Kipps could get in upon that, his Uncle had passed into a general exposition of the proper treatment of landladies and their humbugging, cheating ways, and so the opportunity vanished. It seemed to Kipps the only thing to do was to go out into the town for a stroll, compose an effectual opening at leisure, and then come back and discharge it at them in its consecutive completeness. And even out of doors and alone, he found his mind distracted by irrelevant thoughts.

2

His steps led him out of the High Street towards the church, and he leant for a time over the gate that had once been the winning post of his race with Ann Pornick, and presently found himself in a sitting position on the top rail. He had to get things smooth again, he knew; his mind was like a mirror of water after a breeze. The image of Helen and his great future was broken and mingled into fragmentary reflections of remoter things, of the good name of Old Methusaleh Three Stars, of long dormant memories the High Street saw fit, by some trick of light and atmosphere, to arouse that afternoon. . . .

Abruptly a fine, full voice from under his elbow shouted, "What—O Art!" and, behold, Sid Pornick was back in his world, leaning over the gate beside him, and holding out a friendly hand.

He was oddly changed and yet oddly like the Sid that Kipps had known. He had the old broad face and mouth, abundantly freckled, the same short nose, and the same blunt chin, the same odd suggestion of his sister Ann without a touch of her beauty; but he had quite a new voice, loud and a little hard, and his upper lip carried a stiff and very fair moustache.

Kipps shook hands. "I was jest thinking of *you,* Sid," he said, "jest this very moment and wondering if ever I should see you again, ever. And 'ere you are!"

"One likes a look 'round at times," said Sid. "How are *you,* old chap?"

"All right," said Kipps. "I just been lef'——"

"You aren't changed much," interrupted Sid.

"Ent I?" said Kipps, foiled.

"I knew your back directly I came 'round the corner.

Spite of that 'at you got on. Hang it, I said, that's Art Kipps or the devil. And so it was."

Kipps made a movement of his neck as if he would look at his back and judge. Then he looked Sid in the face. "You got a moustache, Sid," he said.

"I s'pose you're having your holidays?" said Sid.

"Well, partly. But I just been lef'——"

"*I'm* taking a bit of a holiday," Sid went on. "But the fact is, I have to give *myself* holidays nowadays. I've set up for myself."

"Not down here?"

"No fear! I'm not a turnip. I've started in Hammersmith, manufacturing." Sid spoke offhand as though there was no such thing as pride.

"Not drapery?"

"No fear! Engineer. Manufacture bicycles." He clapped his hand to his breast pocket and produced a number of pink handbills. He handed one to Kipps and prevented him reading it by explanations and explanatory dabs of a pointing finger. "That's our make, my make to be exact, The Red Flag, see?—I got a transfer with my name—Pantocrat tyres, eight pounds—yes, *there*—Clinchers ten, Dunlop's eleven, Ladies' one pound more—that's the lady's. Best machine at a democratic price in London. No guineas and no discounts—honest trade. I build 'em—to order. I've built," he reflected, looking away seaward—"seventeen. Counting orders in 'and. . . . Come down to look at the old place a bit. Mother likes it at times."

"Thought you'd all gone away——"

"What! after my father's death? No! My mother's come back, and she's living at Muggett's cottages. The sea air suits 'er. She likes the old place better than Hammersmith . . and I can afford it. Got an old crony or so here. . . Gossip . . have tea. . . . S'pose *you* ain't married, Kipps?"

Kipps shook his head, "I——" he began.

"*I* am," said Sid. "Married these two years and got a nipper. Proper little chap."

Kipps got his word in at last. "I got engaged day before yesterday," he said.

"Ah!" said Sid airily. "That's all right. Who's the fortunate lady?"

Kipps tried to speak in an offhand way. He stuck his

hands in his pockets as he spoke. "She's a solicitor's daughter," he said, "in Folkestone. Rather'r nice set. County family. Related to the Earl of Beaupres——"

"Steady on!" cried Sid.

"You see, I've 'ad a bit of luck, Sid. Been lef' money."

Sid's eye travelled instinctively to mark Kipps' garments. "How much?" he asked.

"'Bout twelve 'undred a year," said Kipps, more off-handedly than ever.

"Lord!" said Sid, with a note of positive dismay, and stepped back a pace or two.

"My granfaver it was," said Kipps, trying hard to be calm and simple. "'Ardly knew I *'ad* a granfaver. And then—bang! When o' Bean, the solicitor, told me of it, you could 'ave knocked me down——"

"*'Ow* much?" demanded Sid, with a sharp note in his voice.

"Twelve 'undred pound a year—'proximately, that is. . . ."

Sid's attempt at genial unenvious congratulation did not last a minute. He shook hands with an unreal heartiness and said he was jolly glad. "It's a blooming stroke of Luck," he said.

"It's a bloomin' stroke of Luck," he repeated; "that's what it is," with the smile fading from his face. "Of course, better you 'ave it than me, o' chap. So I don't envy you, anyhow. *I* couldn't keep it, if I did 'ave it."

"'Ow's that?" said Kipps, a little hipped by Sid's patent chagrin.

"I'm a Socialist, you see," said Sid. "I don't 'old with Wealth. What *is* Wealth? Labour robbed out of the poor. At most it's only yours in Trust. Leastways, that 'ow *I* should take it." He reflected. "The Present distribution of Wealth," he said and stopped.

Then he let himself go, with unmasked bitterness. "It's no sense at all. It's jest damn foolishness. Who's going to work and care in a muddle like this? Here first you do—something anyhow—of the world's work, and it pays you hardly anything, and then it invites you to do nothing, nothing whatever, and pays you twelve hundred pounds a year. Who's going to respect laws and customs when they come to damn silliness like that?" He repeated, "Twelve hundred pounds a year!"

At the sight of Kipps' face he relented slightly.

"It's not you I'm thinking of, o' man; it's the system. Better you than most people. Still——"

He laid both hands on the gate and repeated to himself, "Twelve 'undred a year. . . . Gee-Whizz, Kipps! You'll be a swell!"

"I shan't," said Kipps with imperfect conviction. "No fear."

"You can't 'ave money like that and not swell out. You'll soon be too big to speak to—'ow do they put it?—a mere mechanic like me."

"No fear, Siddee," said Kipps with conviction. "I ain't that sort."

"Ah!" said Sid, with a sort of unwilling scepticism, "money'll be too much for you. Besides—you're caught by a swell already."

" 'Ow d'you mean?"

"That girl you're going to marry. Masterman says——"

"Oo's Masterman?"

"Rare good chap I know—takes my first floor front room. Masterson says it's always the wife pitches the key. Always. There's no social differences—till women come in."

"Ah!" said Kipps profoundly. "You don't know."

Sid shook his head. "Fancy!" he reflected, "Art Kipps! . . . Twelve 'Undred a Year!"

Kipps tried to bridge that opening gulf. "Remember the Hurons, Sid?"

"Rather," said Sid.

"Remember that wreck?"

"I can smell it now—sort of sour smell."

Kipps was silent for a moment with reminiscent eyes on Sid's still troubled face.

"I say, Sid, 'ow's Ann?"

"*She's* all right," said Sid.

"Where is she now?"

"In a place . . . Ashford."

"Oh!"

Sid's face had become a shade sulkier than before.

"The fact is," he said, "we don't get on very well together. *I* don't hold with service. We're common people, I suppose, but I don't like it. I don't see why a sister of mine should wait at other people's tables. No. Not even if they got Twelve 'Undred a Year."

Kipps tried to change the point of application. "Remember 'ow you came out once when we were racing here? . . . She didn't run bad for a girl."

And his own words raised an image brighter than he could have supposed, so bright it seemed to breathe before him and did not fade altogether, even when he was back in Folkestone an hour or so later.

But Sid was not to be deflected from that other rankling theme by any reminiscences of Ann.

"I wonder what you will do with all that money," he speculated. "I wonder if you will do any good at all. I wonder what you *could* do. You should hear Masterman. He'd tell you things. Suppose it came to me, what should I do? It's no good giving it back to the state as things are. Start an Owenite profit-sharing factory perhaps. Or a new Socialist paper. We want a new Socialist paper."

He tried to drown his personal chagrin in elaborate exemplary suggestions. . . .

3

"I must be gettin' on to my motor," said Kipps at last, having to a large extent heard him out.

"What! Got a motor?"

"No!" said Kipps apologetically. "Only jobbed for the day."

" 'Ow much?"

"Five pounds."

"Keep five families for a week! Good Lord!" That seemed to crown Sid's disgust.

Yet drawn by a sort of fascination he came with Kipps and assisted at the mounting of the motor. He was pleased to note it was not the most modern of motors, but that was the only grain of comfort. Kipps mounted at once, after one violent agitation of the little shop-door to set the bell a-jingle and warn his Uncle and Aunt. Sid assisted with the great furlined overcoat and examined the spectacles.

"Good-bye, o' chap!" said Kipps.

"Good-bye, o' chap!" said Sid.

The old people came out to say good-bye.

Old Kipps was radiant with triumph. " 'Pon my Sammy, Artie! I'm a goo' mind to come with you," he shouted, and then, "I got something you might take with you!"

He dodged back into the shop and returned with the perforated engraving after Morland.

"You stick to this, my boy," he said. "You get it repaired by someone who knows. It's the most vallyble thing I got you so far, you take my word."

"Warrup!" said the motor, and tuff, tuff, tuff, and backed and snorted while old Kipps danced about on the pavement as if foreseeing complex catastrophes, and told the driver, "That's all right."

He waved his stout stick to his receding nephew. Then he turned to Sid. "Now, if you could make something like that, young Pornick, you *might* blow a bit!"

"I'll make a doocid sight better than *that* before I done," said Sid, hands deep in his pockets.

"Not *you*," said old Kipps.

The motor set up a prolonged sobbing moan and vanished around the corner. Sid stood motionless for a space, unheeding some further remark from old Kipps. The young mechanic had just discovered that to have manufactured seventeen bicycles, including orders in hand, is not so big a thing as he had supposed, and such discoveries try one's manhood. . . .

"Oh well!" said Sid at last, and turned his face towards his mother's cottage.

She had got a hot teacake for him, and she was a little hurt that he was dark and preoccupied as he consumed it. He had always been such a boy for teacake, and then when one went out specially and got him one——!

He did not tell her—he did not tell anyone—he had seen young Kipps. He did not want to talk about Kipps for a bit to anyone at all.

V. THE PUPIL LOVER

1

When Kipps came to reflect upon his afternoon's work he had his first inkling of certain comprehensive incompatibilities lying about the course of true love in his particular case. He had felt without understanding the incongruity between the announcement he had failed to make and the circle of ideas of his Aunt and Uncle. It was this rather than the want of a specific intention that had silenced him, the perception that when he travelled from Folkestone to New Romney he travelled from an atmosphere where his engagement to Helen was sane and excellent to an atmosphere where it was only to be regarded with incredulous suspicion. Coupled and associated with this jar was his sense of the altered behaviour of Sid Pornick, the evident shock to that ancient alliance caused by the fact of his enrichment, the touch of hostility in his "You'll soon be swelled too big to speak to a poor mechanic like me." Kipps was unprepared for the unpleasant truth; that the path of social advancement is and must be strewn with broken friendships. This first protrusion of that fact caused a painful confusion in his mind. It was speedily to protrude in a far more serious fashion in relation to the "hands" from the Emporium, and Chitterlow.

From the day at Lympne Castle his relations with Helen had entered upon a new footing. He had prayed for Helen as good souls pray for Heaven, with as little understanding of what it was he prayed for. And now that period of standing humbly in the shadows before the shrine was over, and the Goddess, her veil of mystery flung aside, had come down to him and taken hold of him, a good, strong, firm hold, and walked by his side. . . . She liked him. What was singular was that very soon she had kissed him thrice, whimsically upon the brow, and he had never kissed her at all. He could not analyse his feelings, only he knew the world was wonderfully changed about them, but the truth was that, though he still worshipped and feared her, though his pride in his engagement was ridiculously vast, he loved her now no more. That subtle something woven of the most delicate strands of self-love and tenderness and desire, had vanished imperceptibly; and was gone now for ever. But that she did not suspect in him, nor as a matter of fact did he.

She took him in hand in perfect good faith. She told him things about his accent, she told him things about his bearing, about his costume and his way of looking at things. She thrust the blade of her intelligence into the tenderest corners of Kipps' secret vanity, she slashed his most intimate pride to bleeding tatters. He sought very diligently to anticipate some at least of these informing thrusts by making great use of Coote. But the unanticipated made a brave number. . . .

She found his simple willingness a very lovable thing.

Indeed she liked him more and more. There was a touch of motherliness in her feelings towards him. But his upbringing and his associations had been, she diagnosed, "awful." At New Romney she glanced but little; that was remote. But in her inventory—she went over him as one might go over a newly taken house, with impartial thoroughness—she discovered more proximate influences, surprising intimations of nocturnal "sing-songs"—she pictured it as almost shocking that Kipps should sing to the banjo—much low-grade wisdom treasured from a person called Buggins—"Who *is* Buggins?" said Helen—vague figures of indisputable vulgarity, Pierce and Carshot, and more particularly, a very terrible social phenomenon, Chitterlow.

Chitterlow blazed upon them with unheralded oppressive brilliance the first time they were abroad together.

They were going along the front of the Leas to see a school play in Sandgate—at the last moment Mrs. Walshingham had been unable to come with them—when Chitterlow loomed up into the new world. He was wearing the suit of striped flannel and the straw hat that had followed Kipps' payment in advance for his course in elocution, his hands were deep in his side pockets and animated the corners of his jacket, and his attentive gaze at the passing loungers, the faint smile under his boldly drawn nose, showed him engaged in studying character—no doubt for some forthcoming play.

"What HO!" said he, at the sight of Kipps, and swept off the straw hat with so ample a clutch of his great, flat hand that it suggested to Helen's startled mind a conjurer about to palm a half-penny.

" 'Ello, Chitt'low," said Kipps a little awkwardly and not saluting.

Chitterlow hesitated. "Half a mo', my boy," he said, and arrested Kipps by extending a large hand over his chest. "Excuse me, my dear," he said, bowing like his Russian count by way of apology to Helen and with a smile that would have killed at a hundred yards. He affected a semi-confidential grouping of himself and Kipps while Helen stood in white amazement.

"About that play," he said.

" 'Ow about it?" asked Kipps, acutely aware of Helen.

"It's all right," said Chitterlow. "There's a strong smell of syndicate in the air, I may tell you—Strong."

"That's aw right," said Kipps.

"You needn't tell everybody," said Chitterlow with a transitory, confidential hand to his mouth, which pointed the application of the "everybody" just a trifle too strongly. "But I think it's coming off. However——. I mustn't detain you now. So long. You'll come 'round, eh?"

"Right you are," said Kipps.

"To-night?"

"At eight."

And then, and more in the manner of a Russian prince than any common count, Chitterlow bowed and withdrew. Just for a moment he allowed a conquering eye to challenge Helen's and noted her for a girl of quality. . . .

There was a silence between our lovers for a space.

"That," said Kipps with an allusive movement of the head, "was Chitterlow."

"Is he—a friend of yours?"

"In a way. . . . You see—I met 'im. Leastways 'e met me. Run into me with a bicycle, 'e did, and so we got talking together."

He tried to appear at his ease. The young lady scrutinised his profile.

"What is he?"

" 'E's a Nacter chap," said Kipps. "Leastways 'e writes plays."

"And sells them?"

"Partly."

"Whom to?"

"Different people. Shares he sells. . . . It's all right, reely—I meant to tell you about him before."

Helen looked over her shoulder to catch a view of Chitterlow's retreating aspect. It did not compel her complete confidence.

She turned to her lover and said in a tone of quiet authority, "You must tell me all about Chitterlow. Now."

The explanation began. . . .

The School Play came almost as a relief to Kipps. In the flusterment of going in he could almost forget for a time his Laocoon struggle to explain, and in the intervals he did his best to keep forgetting. But Helen, with a gentle insistence, resumed the explanation of Chitterlow as they returned towards Folkestone.

Chitterlow was confoundedly difficult to explain. You could hardly imagine!

There was an almost motherly anxiety in Helen's manner, blended with the resolution of a schoolmistress to get to the bottom of the affair. Kipps' ears were soon quite brightly red.

"Have you seen one of his plays?"

" 'E's tole me about one."

"But on the stage."

"No. He 'asn't 'ad any on the stage yet. That's all coming. . . ."

"Promise me," she said in conclusion, "you won't do anything without consulting me."

And of course Kipps promised. "Oo—no!"

They went on their way in silence.

"One can't know everybody," said Helen in general.

"Of course," said Kipps; "in a sort of way it was him that helped me to my money." And he indicated in a confused manner the story of the advertisement. "I don't like to drop 'im all at once," he added.

Helen was silent for a space, and when she spoke she

went off at a tangent. "We shall live in London—soon," she remarked. "It's only while we are here."

It was the first intimation she gave him of their post-nuptial prospects.

"We shall have a nice little flat somewhere, not too far west, and there we shall build up a circle of our own."

2

All that declining summer Kipps was the pupil lover. He made an extraordinarily open secret of his desire for self-improvement; indeed Helen had to hint once or twice that his modest frankness was excessive, and all this new circle of friends did, each after his or her manner, everything that was possible to supplement Helen's efforts and help him to ease and skill in the more cultivated circles to which he had come. Coote was still the chief teacher, the tutor—there are so many little difficulties that a man may take to another man that he would not care to propound to the woman he loves—but they were all, so to speak, upon the staff. Even the freckled girl said to him once in a pleasant way, "You mustn't say 'contre temps,' you must say 'contraytom,'" when he borrowed that expression from "Manners and Rules," and she tried at his own suggestion to give him clear ideas upon the subject of "as" and "has." A certain confusion between these words was becoming evident, the first fruits of a lesson from Chitterlow on the aspirate. Hitherto he had discarded that dangerous letter almost altogether, but now he would pull up at words beginning with "h" and draw a sawing breath—rather like a startled kitten—and then aspirate with vigour.

Said Kipps one day, "*As* 'e?—I should say, ah—Has 'e? Ye know I got a lot of difficulty over them two words, which is which?"

"Well, 'as' is a conjunction and 'has' is a verb."

"I know," said Kipps, "but when is 'has' a conjunction and when is 'as' a verb?"

"Well," said the freckled girl, preparing to be very lucid. "It's *has* when it means one has, meaning having, but if it isn't it's *as*. As for instance one says 'e—I mean *he*—He has. But one says 'as he has.'"

"I see," said Kipps. "So I ought to say 'as' 'e?"

"No, if you are asking a question you say *has* 'e—I mean he—'as he?" She blushed quite brightly, but still clung to her air of lucidity.

"I see," said Kipps. He was about to say something further, but he desisted. "I got it much clearer now. *Has* 'e? *Has* 'e as. Yes."

"If you remember about having."

"Oo I will," said Kipps.

Miss Coote specialised in Kipps' artistic development. She had early found an opinion that he had considerable artistic sensibility, his remarks on her work had struck her as decidedly intelligent, and whenever he called around to see them she would show him some work of art, now an illustrated book, now perhaps a colour print of a Botticelli, now the Hundred Best Paintings, now "Academy Pictures," now a German art handbook and now some magazine of furniture and design. "I know you like these things," she used to say, and Kipps said, "Oo I *do*." He soon acquired a little armoury of appreciative sayings. When presently the Walshinghams took him up to the Arts and Crafts, his deportment was intelligent in the extreme. For a time he kept a wary silence and suddenly pitched upon a colour print. "That's rather nace," he said to Mrs. Walshingham. "That lill' thing. There." He always said things like that by preference to the mother rather than the daughter unless he was perfectly sure.

He quite took to Mrs. Walshingham. He was impressed by her conspicuous tact and refinement; it seemed to him that the ladylike could go no further. She was always dressed with a delicate fussiness that was never disarranged and even a sort of faded quality about her hair and face and bearing and emotions contributed to her effect. Kipps was not a big man, and commonly he did not feel a big man, but with Mrs. Walshingham he always felt enormous and distended, as though he was a navvy who had taken some disagreeable poison which puffed him up inside his skin as a preliminary to bursting. He felt, too, as though he had been rolled in clay and his hair dressed with gum. And he felt that his voice was strident and his accent like somebody swinging a crowded pig's pail in a free and careless manner. All this increased and enforced his respect for her. Her hand, which flitted often and again to his hand and arm, was singularly well shaped and cool. "Arthur," she called him from the very beginning.

She did not so much positively teach and tell him as tactfully guide and infect him. Her conversation was not so much didactic as exemplary. She would say, "I *do* like people to do" so and so. She would tell him anecdotes of nice things done, of gentlemanly feats of graceful consideration; she would record her neat observations of people in trains and omnibuses; how, for example, a man had passed her change to the conductor, "quite a common man he looked," but he had lifted his hat. She stamped Kipps so deeply with the hat-raising habit that he would uncover if he found himself in the same railway ticket office with a lady had to stand ceremoniously until the difficulties of change drove him to an apologetic provisional oblique resumption of his headgear. . . . And robbing these things of any air of personal application, she threw about them an abundant talk about her two children—she called them her Twin Jewels quite frequently—about their gifts, their temperaments, their ambition, their need of opportunity. They needed opportunity, she would say, as other people needed air. . . .

In his conversations with her Kipps always assumed, and she seemed to assume, that she was to join that home in London Helen foreshadowed, but he was surprised one day to gather that this was not to be the case. "It wouldn't do," said Helen, with decision. "We want to make a circle of our own."

"But won't she be a bit lonely down here?" asked Kipps.

"There's the Waces, and Mrs. Prebble and Mrs. Bindon Botting and—lots of people she knows." And Helen dismissed this possibility. . . .

Young Walshingham's share in the educational syndicate was smaller. But he shone out when they went to London on that Arts and Crafts expedition. Then this rising man of affairs showed Kipps how to buy the more theatrical weeklies for consumption in the train, how to buy and what to buy in the way of cigarettes with gold tips and shilling cigars, and how to order hock for lunch and sparkling Moselle for dinner, how to calculate the fare of a hansom cab—penny a minute while he goes—how to look intelligently at an hotel tape, and how to sit still in a train

like a thoughtful man instead of talking like a fool and giving yourself away. And he, too, would glance at the good
time coming when they were to be in London for good
and all.

That prospect expanded and developed particulars. It
presently took up a large part of Helen's conversation. Her
conversations with Kipps were never of a grossly sentimental
sort; there was a shyness of speech in that matter with both
of them, but these new adumbrations were at least as interesting and not so directly disagreeable as the clear-cut
intimations of personal defect that for a time had so greatly
chastened Kipps' delight in her presence. The future presented itself with an almost perfect frankness as a joint
campaign of Mrs. Walshingham's Twin Jewels upon the
Great World, with Kipps in the capacity of baggage and
supply. They would still be dreadfully poor, of course—
this amazed Kipps, but he said nothing—until "Brudderkins"
began to succeed, but if they were clever and lucky they
might do a great deal.

When Helen spoke of London a brooding look, as of one
who contemplates a distant country, came into her eyes. Already it seemed they had the nucleus of a set. Brudderkins
was a member of the Theatrical Judges, an excellent and in-
fluential little club of journalists and literary people, and
he knew Shimer and Stargate and Whiffle, of the "Red
Dragon," and besides these were the Revels. They knew the
Revels quite well. Sidney Revel, before his rapid rise to
prominence as a writer of epigrammatic essays that were
quite above the ordinary public, had been an assistant master
at one of the best Folkestone schools, Brudderkins had
brought him home to tea several times, and it was he had
first suggested Helen should try and write. "It's perfectly
easy," Sidney had said. He had been writing occasional things
for the evening papers, and for the weekly reviews even at
that time. Then he had gone up to London and had almost
unavoidedly become a dramatic critic. Those brilliant essays
had followed, and then "Red Hearts a-Beating," the romance
that had made him. It was a tale of spirited adventure, full
of youth and beauty and naïve passion and generous devotion, bold, as the *Bookman* said, and frank in places, but
never in the slightest degree morbid. He had met and married an American widow with quite a lot of money, and

they had made a very distinct place for themselves, Kipps learnt, in the literary and artistic society of London. Helen seemed to dwell on the Revels a great deal; it was her exemplary story, and when she spoke of Sidney—she often called him Sidney—she would become thoughtful. She spoke most of him naturally because she had still to meet Mrs. Revel. . . . Certainly they would be in the world in no time, even if the distant connection with the Beaupres family came to nothing.

Kipps gathered that with his marriage and the movement to London they were to undergo that subtle change of name Coote had first adumbrated. They were to become "Cuyps," Mr. and Mrs. Cuyps. Or, was it Cuyp?

"It'll be rum at first," said Kipps. "I dessay I shall soon get into it. . . ."

So in their several ways they all contributed to enlarge and refine and exercise the intelligence of Kipps. And behind all these other influences, and, as it were, presiding over and correcting these influences, was Kipps' nearest friend, Coote, a sort of master of the ceremonies. You figure his face, blowing slightly with solicitude, his slate coloured, projecting but not unkindly eye intent upon our hero. The thing he thought was going off admirably. He studied Kipps' character immensely. He would discuss him with his sister, with Mrs. Walshingham, with the freckled girl, with anyone who would stand it. "He is an interesting character," he would say, "likable—a sort of gentleman by instinct. He takes to all these things. He improves every day. He'll soon get Sang Froid. We took him up just in time. He wants now—well——. Next year, perhaps, if there is a good Extension Literature course, he might go in for it. He wants to go in for something like that."

"He's going in for his bicycle now," said Mrs. Walshingham.

"That's all right for summer," said Coote, "but he wants to go in for some serious, intellectual interest, something to take him out of himself a little more. Savoir Faire and self-forgetfulness is more than half the secret of Sang Froid."

3

The world as Coote presented it was in part an endorsement, in part an amplification and in part a rectification of the world of Kipps, the world that derived from the old couple in New Romney and had been developed in the Emporium; the world, in fact, of common British life. There was the same subtle sense of social graduation that had moved Mrs. Kipps to prohibit intercourse with labourers' children and the same dread of anything "common" that had kept the personal quality of Mr. Shalford's establishment so high. But now a certain disagreeable doubt about Kipps' own position was removed and he stood with Coote inside the sphere of gentlemen assured. Within the sphere of gentlemen there are distinctions of rank indeed, but none of class; there are the Big People and the modest, refined, gentlemanly little people like Coote, who may even dabble in the professions and counterless trades; there are lords and magnificences, and there are gentle folk who have to manage, but they can all call on one another, they preserve a general equality of deportment throughout, they constitute that great state within the state, Society, or at any rate they make believe they do.

"But reely," said the Pupil, "not what you call being in Society?"

"Yes," said Coote. "Of course, down here one doesn't see much of it, but there's local society. It has the same rules."

"Calling and all that?"

"Precisely," said Coote.

Kipps thought, whistled a bar, and suddenly broached a question of conscience. "I often wonder," he said, "whether I oughtn't to dress for dinner—when I'm alone 'ere."

Coote protruded his lips and reflected. "Not full dress," he adjudicated; "that would be a little excessive. But you should *change,* you know. Put on a mess jacket and that sort of thing—easy dress. That is what *I* should do, certainly, if I wasn't in harness—and poor."

He coughed modestly and patted his hair behind.

And after that the washing bill of Kipps quadrupled, and he was to be seen at times by the bandstand with his light summer overcoat unbuttoned to give a glimpse of his nice white tie. He and Coote would be smoking the gold-tipped cigarettes young Walshingham had prescribed as *chic,* and appreciating the music highly. "That's—puff—a very nice bit," Kipps would say, or better, "That's *nace.*" And at the first grunts of the loyal anthem up they stood with religiously uplifted hats. Whatever else you might call them, you could never call them disloyal.

The boundary of Society was admittedly very close to Coote and Kipps, and a leading solicitude of the true gentleman was to detect clearly those "beneath" him, and to behave towards them in a proper spirit. "It's jest there it's so 'ard for me," said Kipps. He had to cultivate a certain "distance," to acquire altogether the art of checking the presumption of bounders and old friends. It was difficult, Coote admitted. "That's what, so harkward—I mean awkward."

"I got mixed up with this lot 'ere," said Kipps.

"You could give them a hint," said Coote.

" 'Ow?"

"Oh!—the occasion will suggest something."

The occasion came one early closing night when Kipps was sitting in a canopy chair near the bandstand, with his summer overcoat fully open and a new Gibus pulled slightly forward over his brow, waiting for Coote. They were to hear the band for an hour and then go down to assist Miss Coote and the freckled girl in trying over some of Beethoven's duets, if they remembered them, that is, sufficiently well. And as Kipps lounged back in his chair and occupied his mind with his favourite amusement on such evenings, which consisted chiefly in supposing that everyone about him was wondering who he was, came a rude rap at the canvas back and the voice of Pierce.

"It's nice to be a gentleman," said Pierce, and swung a penny chair into position while Buggins appeared smiling agreeably on the other side and leant upon his stick. *He was smoking a common briar pipe!*

Two real ladies, very fashionably dressed and sitting close at hand, glanced quickly at Pierce, and then away again, and it was evident *their* wonder was at an end.

"*He's* all right," said Buggins, removing his pipe and surveying Kipps.

" 'Ello, Buggins!" said Kipps, not too cordially. " 'Ow goes it?"

"All right. Holiday's next week. If you don't look out, Kipps, I shall be on the Continong before you. Eh?"

"You going t' Boologne?"

"Ra-ther. Parley vous Francey. You bet."

"*I* shall 'ave a bit of a run over there one of these days," said Kipps.

There came a pause. Pierce applied the top of his stick to his mouth for a space and regarded Kipps. Then he glanced at the people about them.

"I say, Kipps," he said in a distinct, loud voice, "see 'er Ladyship lately?"

Kipps perceived the audience was to be impressed, but he responded half-heartedly, "No, I 'aven't," he said.

"She was along of Sir William the other night," said Pierce, still loud and clear, "and she asked to be remembered to you."

It seemed to Kipps that one of the two ladies smiled faintly and said something to the other, and then certainly they glanced at Pierce. Kipps flushed scarlet. "*Did* she?" he answered.

Buggins laughed good-humouredly over his pipe.

"Sir William suffers a lot from his gout," Pierce continued unabashed.

(Buggins much amused with his pipe between his teeth.)

Kipps became aware of Coote at hand.

Coote nodded rather distantly to Pierce. "Hope I haven't kept you waiting, Kipps," he said.

"I kep' a chair for you," said Kipps and removed a guardian foot.

"But you've got your friends," said Coote.

"Oh! *we* don't mind," said Pierce cordially, "the more the merrier," and, "why don't you get a chair, Buggins?" Buggins shook his head in a sort of aside to Pierce and Coote coughed behind his hand.

"Been kep' late at business?" asked Pierce.

Coote turned quite pale and pretended not to hear. His eyes sought in space for a time and with a convulsive movement he recognised a distant acquaintance and raised his hat.

Pierce had also become a little pale. He addressed himself to Kipps in an undertone.

"Mr. Coote, isn't he?" he asked.

Coote addressed himself to Kipps directly and exclusively. His manner had the calm of extreme tension.

"I'm rather late," he said. "I think we ought almost to be going on *now*."

Kipps stood up. "That's all right," he said.

"Which way are you going?" said Pierce, standing also, and brushing some crumbs of cigarette ash from his sleeve.

For a moment Coote was breathless. "Thank you," he said, and gasped. Then he delivered the necessary blow; "I don't think we're in need of your society, you know," and turned away.

Kipps found himself falling over chairs and things in the wake of Coote, and then they were clear of the crowd.

For a space Coote said nothing; then he remarked abruptly and quite angrily for him, "I think that was *awful* Cheek!"

Kipps made no reply. . . .

The whole thing was an interesting little object lesson in distance, and it stuck in the front of Kipps' mind for a long time. He had particularly vivid the face of Pierce, with an expression between astonishment and anger. He felt as though he had struck Pierce in the face under circumstances that gave Pierce no power to reply. He did not attend very much to the duets and even forgot at the end of one of them to say how perfectly lovely it was.

4

But you must not imagine that the national ideal of a gentleman, as Coote developed it, was all a matter of deportment and selectness, a mere isolation from debasing associations. There is a Serious Side, a deeper aspect of the true, True Gentleman. The True Gentleman does not wear his heart on his sleeve. He is a polished surface above deeps. For example, he is deeply religious, as Coote was, as Mrs. Walshingham was, but outside the walls of a church it never appears, except perhaps now and then in a pause, in a profound look, in a sudden avoidance. In quite a little while Kipps also had learnt the pause, the profound look, the sudden avoidance, that final refinement of spirituality, impressionistic piety.

And the True Gentleman is patriotic also. When one saw Coote lifting his hat to the National Anthem, then perhaps one got a glimpse of what patriotic emotions, what worship, the polish of a gentleman may hide. Or singing out his deep notes against the Hosts of Midian, in the St. Stylites choir; then indeed you plumbed his spiritual side.

Christian, dost thou heed them,
   On the holy ground,
How the hosts of Mid-i-an,
   Prowl and prowl around!
Christian, up and smai-it them. . . .

But these were but gleams. For the rest, Religion, Nationality, Passion, Money, Politics; much more so those cardinal issues, Birth and Death, the True Gentleman skirted about, and became facially rigid towards and ceased to speak and panted and blew.

"One doesn't talk of that sort of thing," Coote would say with a gesture of the knuckly hand.

"O' course," Kipps would reply, with an equal significance.

Profundities. Deep as it were, blowing to deep.

One does not talk, but on the other hand one is punctilious to do. Actions speak. Kipps—in spite of the fact that the Walshinghams were more than a little lax—Kipps, who had formerly flitted Sunday after Sunday from one Folkestone church to another, had now a sitting of his own, paid for duly at Saint Stylites. There he was to be seen, always at the surplice evening service, and sometimes of a morning, dressed with a sober precision, and with an eye on Coote in the chancel. No difficulties now about finding the place in his book. He became a communicant again—he had lapsed soon after his confirmation when the young lady in the costume-room, who was his adopted sister, left the Emporium—and he would sometimes go around to the Vestry for Coote after the service. One evening he was introduced to the Hon. and Rev. Densemore. He was much too confused to say anything, and the noble cleric had nothing to say, but indisputably they were introduced. . . .

No! you must not imagine our national ideal of a gentleman is without its "serious side," without even its stern and uncompromising side. The imagination no doubt refuses to see Coote displaying extraordinary refinements of courage upon the stricken field, but in the walks of peace there is sometimes sore need of sternness. Charitable as one may be, one must admit there are people who *do* things, impossible things; people who place themselves "out of it" in countless ways; people, moreover, who are by a sort of predestination out of it from the beginning, and against these Society has invented a terrible protection for its Cootery, the Cut. The Cut is no joke for anyone. It is excommunication. You may be cut by an individual, you may be cut by a set or you may be—and this is so tragic that beautiful romances have been written about it—"Cut by the County." One figures Coote discharging this last duty and cutting somebody—Coote, erect and pale, never speaking, going past with eyes of pitiless slate, lower jaw protruding a little, face pursed up and cold and stiff. . . .

It never dawned upon Kipps that he would one day have to face this terrible front, to be to Coote not only as one dead, but as one gone more than a stage or so in decay, cut and passed, banned and outcast for ever.

Yet so it was to be!

One cannot hide any longer that all this fine progress of Kipps is doomed to end in collapse. So far indeed you have seen him ascend. You have seen him becoming more refined and careful day by day, more carefully dressed, less clumsy in the ways and methods of social life. You have seen the gulf widening between himself and his former low associates. I have brought you at last to the vision of him, faultlessly dressed and posed, in an atmosphere of candlelight and chanting, in his own sitting in one of the most fashionable churches in Folkestone. . . . All the time I have refrained from the lightest touch upon the tragic note that must now creep into my tale. Yet the net of his low connections has been about his feet, and moreover there was something interwoven in his being. . . .

VI. DISCORDS

1

One day Kipps set out upon his newly-mastered bicycle to New Romney to break the news of his engagement to his Uncle and Aunt—this time positively. He was now a finished cyclist, but as yet an unseasoned one; the southwest wind, even in its summer guise, as one meets it in the Marsh, is the equivalent of a reasonable hill, and ever and again he got off and refreshed himself by a spell of walking. He was walking just outside New Romney preparatory to his triumphal entry (one hand off) when abruptly he came upon Ann Pornick.

It chanced he was thinking about her at the time. He had been thinking curious things; whether, after all, the atmosphere of New Romney and the Marsh had not some difference, some faint impalpable quality that was missing in the great and fashionable world of Folkestone behind there on the hill. Here there was a homeliness, a familiarity. He had noted as he passed that old Mr. Cliffordown's gate had been mended with a fresh piece of string. In Folkestone he didn't take notice and he didn't care if they built three hundred houses. Come to think of it, that was odd. It was fine and grand to have twelve hundred a year; it was fine to go about on trams and omnibuses and think not a person aboard was as rich as oneself; it was fine to buy and order this and that and never have any work to do and to be engaged to a girl distantly related to the Earl of Beaupres, but yet there had been a zest in the old time out here, a rare zest in the holidays, in sunlight, on the sea beach and in the High Street, that failed from these new things. He thought of those bright windows of holiday that had seemed so glorious to him in the retrospect from his apprentice days. It was strange that now, amidst his present splendours, they were glorious still!

All those things were over now—perhaps that was it! Something had happened to the world and the old light had been turned out. He himself was changed, and Sid was changed, terribly changed, and Ann no doubt was changed.

He thought of her with the hair blown about her flushed cheeks as they stood together after their race. . . .

Certainly she must be changed, and all the magic she had been fraught with to the very hem of her short petticoats gone no doubt for ever. And as he thought that, or before and while he thought it, for he came to all these things in his own vague and stumbling way, he looked up, and there was Ann!

She was seven years older and greatly altered; yet for the moment it seemed to him that she had not changed at all. "Ann!" he said, and she, with a lifting note, "It's Art Kipps!"

Then he became aware of changes—improvements. She was as pretty as she had promised to be, her blue eyes as dark as his memory of them, and with a quick, high colour, but now Kipps by several inches was the taller again. She was dressed in a simple grey dress that showed her very clearly as a straight and healthy little woman, and her hat was Sundayfied with pink flowers. She looked soft and warm and welcoming. Her face was alight to Kipps with her art-less gladness at their encounter.

"It's Art Kipps!" she said.

"Rather," said Kipps.

"You got your holidays?"

It flashed upon Kipps that Sid had not told her of his great fortune. Much regretful meditation upon Sid's be-haviour had convinced him that he himself was to blame for exasperating boastfulness in that affair, and this time he took care not to err in that direction. He erred in the other.

"I'm taking a bit of a 'oliday," he said.

"So'm I," said Ann.

"You been for a walk?" asked Kipps.

Ann showed him a bunch of wayside flowers.

"It's a long time since I seen you, Ann. Why, 'ow long must it be? Seven—eight years nearly."

"It don't do to count," said Ann.

"It don't look like it," said Kipps, with the slightest em-phasis.

"You got a moustache," said Ann, smelling her flowers

and looking at him over them, not without admiration.

Kipps blushed. . . .

Presently they came to the bifurcation of the roads.

"I'm going down this way to mother's cottage," said Ann.

"I'll come a bit your way if I may."

In New Romney social distinctions that are primary realities in Folkestone are absolutely non-existent, and it seemed quite permissible for him to walk with Ann, for all that she was no more than a servant. They talked with remarkable ease to one another, they slipped into a vein of intimate reminiscence in the easiest manner. In a little while Kipps was amazed to find Ann and himself at this:

"You r'ember that half sixpence? What you cut for me?"

"Yes."

"I got it still."

She hesitated. "Funny, wasn't it?" she said, and then, "you got yours, Artie?"

"Rather," said Kipps. "What do *you* think?" and wondered in his heart of hearts why he had never looked at that sixpence for so long.

Ann smiled at him frankly.

"I didn't expect you'd keep it," she said. "I thought often —it was silly to keep mine. Besides," she reflected, "it didn't mean anything really."

She glanced at him as she spoke and met his eye.

"Oh, didn't it!" said Kipps, a little late with his response, and realising his infidelity to Helen even as he spoke.

"It didn't mean much anyhow," said Ann. "You still in the drapery?"

"I'm living at Folkestone," began Kipps and decided that that sufficed. "Didn't Sid tell you he met me?"

"No! Here?"

"Yes. The other day. 'Bout a week or more ago."

"That was before I came."

"Ah! that was it," said Kipps.

" 'E's got on," said Ann. "Got 'is own shop now, Artie."

" 'E tole me."

They found themselves outside Muggett's cottages. "You going in?" said Kipps.

"I s'pose so," said Ann.

They both hung upon the pause. Ann took a plunge.

"D'you often come to New Romney?" she said.

"I ride over a bit at times," said Kipps.

Another pause. Ann held out her hand.

"I'm glad I seen you," she said.

Extraordinary impulses arose in neglected parts of Kipps' being. "Ann," he said and stopped.

"Yes," said she, and was bright to him.

They looked at one another.

All and more than all of those first emotions of his adolescence had come back to him. Her presence banished a multitude of countervaling considerations. It was Ann more than ever. She stood breathing close to him, with her soft-looking lips a little apart and gladness in her eyes.

"I'm awful glad to see you again," he said; "it brings back old times."

"Doesn't it?"

Another pause. He would have liked to have had a long talk to her, to have gone for a walk with her or something, to have drawn nearer to her in any conceivable way, and, above all, to have had some more of the appreciation that shone in her eyes, but a vestige of Folkestone still clinging to him told him it "wouldn't do." "Well," he said, "I must be getting on," and turned away reluctantly, with a will under compulsion. . . .

When he looked back from the corner she was still at the gate. She was perhaps a little disconcerted by his retreat. He felt that. He hesitated for a moment, half turned, stood and suddenly did great things with his hat. That hat! The wonderful hat of our civilisation! . . .

In another minute he was engaged in a singularly absent-minded conversation with his Uncle about the usual topics.

His Uncle was very anxious to buy him a few upright clocks as an investment for subsequent sale. And there were also some very nice globes, one terrestrial and the other celestial, in a shop at Lydd that would look well in a drawing-room and inevitably increase in value. . . . Kipps either did or did not agree to this purchase; he was unable to recollect.

The southwest wind perhaps helped him back, at any rate he found himself through Dymchurch without having noticed the place. There came an odd effect as he drew near Hythe. The hills on the left and the trees on the right seemed to draw together and close in upon him until his way was straight and narrow. He could not turn around on that treacherous, half-tamed machine, but he knew that behind him, he knew so well, spread the wide, vast flatness of the Marsh shining under the afternoon sky. In some way this was material to his thoughts. And as he rode through Hythe he came upon the idea that there was a considerable amount of incompatibility between the existence of one who was practically a gentleman and of Ann.

In the neighbourhood of Seabrook he began to think he had, in some subtle way, lowered himself by walking along by the side of Ann. . . . After all, she was only a servant.

Ann!

She called out all the least gentlemanly instincts of his nature. There had been a moment in their conversation when he had quite distinctly thought it would really be an extremely nice thing for someone to kiss her lips. . . . There was something warming about Ann—at least for Kipps. She impressed him as having somewhen during their vast interval of separation contrived to make herself in some distinctive way his.

Fancy keeping that half sixpence all this time!

It was the most flattering thing that had ever happened to Kipps.

2

He found himself presently sitting over "The Art of Conversing," lost in the strangest musings. He got up, walked about, became stagnant at the window for a space, roused himself and by way of something lighter tried "Sesame and Lilies." From that, too, his attention wandered. He sat back. Anon he smiled, anon sighed. He arose, pulled his keys from his pocket, looked at them, decided and went upstairs. He opened the little yellow box that had been the nucleus of all his possessions in the world, and took out a small "Escritoire," the very humblest sort of present, and opened it— kneeling. And there, in the corner, was a little packet of paper, sealed as a last defence against any prying invader, with red sealing wax. It had gone untouched for years. He held this little packet between finger and thumb for a moment, regarding it, and then put down the escritoire and broke the seal. . . .

As he was getting into bed that night he remembered something for the first time!

"Dash it!" he said. "Dashed if I told 'em *this* time. . . . *Well!* I shall 'ave to go over to New Romney again!"

He got into bed and remained sitting pensively on the pillow for a space.

"It's a rum world," he reflected after a vast interval.

Then he recalled that she had noticed his moustache and embarked upon a sea of egotistical musings.

He imagined himself telling Ann how rich he was. What a surprise that would be for her!

Finally he sighed profoundly, blew out his candle and snuggled down, and in a little while he was asleep. . . .

But the next morning and at intervals afterwards he found himself thinking of Ann—Ann, the bright, the desirable, the welcoming, and with an extraordinary streakiness he wanted quite badly to go and then as badly not to go over to New Romney again.

Sitting on the Leas in the afternoon, he had an idea. "I ought to 'ave told 'er, I suppose, about my being engaged. "Ann!"

All sorts of dreams and impressions that had gone clean out of his mental existence came back to him, changed and brought up to date to fit her altered presence. He thought of how he had gone back to New Romney for his Christmas holidays, determined to kiss her, and of the awful blankness of the discovery that she had gone away.

It seemed incredible now, and yet not wholly incredible, that he had cried real tears for her—how many years was it ago?

3

Daily I should thank my Maker that He did not appoint me Censor of the world of men. I should temper a fierce injustice with a spasmodic indecision that would prolong rather than mitigate the bitterness of the Day. For human dignity, for all conscious human superiority I should lack the beginnings of charity, for bishops, prosperous schoolmasters, judges and all large respect-pampered souls. And more especially bishops, towards whom I bear an atavistic, Viking grudge, dreaming not infrequently and with invari-

able zest of galleys and landings and well known living ornaments of the episcopal bench sprinting inland on twin-
kling gaiters before my thirsty blade—all these people, I
say, should treat below their deserts, but, on the other
hand, for such as Kipps——. There the exasperating inde-
cisions would come in. The Judgment would be arrested
at Kipps. Everyone and everything would wait. *You* would
wait. The balance would sway and sway, and whenever it
heeled towards an adverse decision, my finger would set it
swaying again. Kings, warriors, statesmen, brilliant women
of our first families, personalities, gallants, panting with indignation, headline humanity in general, would stand un-
damned, unheeded, or be damned in the most casual manner for their importunity, while my eye went about for anything possible that could be said on behalf of Kipps. . . .
Albeit I fear nothing can save him from condemnation upon
this present score, that within two days he was talking to
Ann again.

One seeks excuses. Overnight there had been an encounter
of Chitterlow and young Walshingham in his presence, that
had certainly warped his standards. They had called within
a few minutes of each other, and the two swayed by virile
attentions to Old Methuselah Four Stars, had talked against
each other, over and at the hospitable presence of Kipps.
Walshingham had seemed to win at the beginning, but finally
Chitterlow had made a magnificent display of vociferation
and swept him out of existence. At the beginning Chitterlow
had opened upon the great profits of playwrights and young
Walshingham had capped him at once with a cynical, but
impressive, display of knowledge of the High Finance. If
Chitterlow boasted his thousands, young Walshingham
boasted his hundreds of thousands, and was for a space left
in sole possession of the stage, juggling with the wealth of
nations. He was going on by way of Financial Politics to
the Overman, before Chitterlow recovered from his first
check, and came back to victory. "Talking of Women," said
Chitterlow, coming in abruptly upon some things not generally known, beyond Walshingham's more immediate circle,
about a recently departed Empire-builder; "Talking of
Women and the way they Get at a man——"

[Though as a matter of fact they had been talking of
the Corruption of Society by Speculation.]

Upon this new topic Chitterlow was soon manifestly invincible. He knew so much, he had known so many. Young Walshingham did his best with epigrams and reservations, but even to Kipps it was evident that this was a book-learned depravity. One felt Walshingham had never known the inner realities of passion. But Chitterlow convinced and amazed. He had run away with girls, he had been run away with by girls, he had been in love with several at a time—"not counting Bessie"—he had loved and lost, he had loved and refrained, and he had loved and failed. He threw remarkable lights upon the moral state of America—in which country he had toured with great success. He set his talk to the tune of one of Mr. Kipling's best known songs. He told an incident of simple, romantic passion, a delirious dream of love and beauty in a Saturday to Monday steamboat trip up the Hudson, and tagged his end with, "I learnt about women from 'er!" After that he adopted the refrain and then lapsed into the praises of Kipling. "Little Kipling," said Chitterlow, with the familiarity of affection, *"he* knows," and broke into quotation:

> "I've taken my fun where I found it;
> I've rogued and I've ranged in my time;
> I've 'ad my picking of sweet'earts,
> An' four of the lot was Prime."

(These things, I say, affect the moral standards of the best of us.)

"I'd have liked to have written that," said Chitterlow. "That's Life, that is! But go and put it on the Stage, put even a bit of the Realities of Life on the Stage, and see what they'll do to you! Only Kipling could venture on a job like that. That Poem KNOCKED me! I don't say Kipling hasn't knocked me before and since, but that was a Fair Knock Out. And yet—you know—there's one thing in it . . . this:

> "I've taken my fun where I've found it,
> And now I must pay for my fun,
> For the more you 'ave known o' the others,
> The less will you settle to one——"

Well. In my case anyhow—I don't know how much that proves, seeing I'm exceptional in so many things and there's no good denying it—but so far as I'm concerned—I tell you two, but of course you needn't let it go any farther—I've been perfectly faithful to Muriel ever since I married her —ever since. . . . Not once. Not even by accident have I ever said or done anything in the slightest——." His little, brown eye became pensive after this flattering intimacy and the gorgeous draperies of his abundant voice fell into graver folds. *"I learnt about women from 'er,"* he said impressively.

"Yes," said Walshingham, getting into the hinder spaces of that splendid pause, "a man must know about women. And the only sound way of learning is the experimental method."

"If you want to know about the experimental method, my boy," said Chitterlow, resuming. . . .

So they talked. *Ex pede Herculem,* as Coote, that cultivated polyglot, would have put it. And in the small hours Kipps went to bed, with his brain whirling with words and whiskey, and sat for an unconscionable time upon his bed edge, musing sadly upon the unmanly monogamy of soul that had cast its shadow upon his career, musing with his thoughts pointing around more and more certainly to the possibility of at least duplicity with Ann.

4

For some days he had been refraining with some insistence from going off to New Romney again. . .

I do not know if this may count in palliation of his misconduct. Men, real Strong-Souled, Healthy Men, should be, I suppose, impervious to conversational atmospheres, but I have never claimed for Kipps a place at these high levels. The unquenchable fact remains that the next day he spent the afternoon with Ann and found no scruple in displaying himself a budding lover.

He had met her in the High Street, had stopped her, and almost on the spur of the moment had boldly proposed a walk, "for the sake of old times."

"I don't mind," said Ann.

Her consent almost frightened Kipps. His imagination

had not carried him to that. "It would be a lark," said Kipps, and looked up the street and down. "Now?" he said.

"I don't mind a bit, Artie. I was just going for a walk along towards St. Mary's."

"Let's go that way be'ind the church," said Kipps, and presently they found themselves drifting seaward in a mood of pleasant commonplace. For a while they talked of Sid. It went clean out of Kipps' head at that early stage even that Ann was a "girl" according to the exposition of Chitterlow, and for a time he remembered only that she was Ann. But afterwards, with the reek of that talk in his head, he lapsed a little from that personal relation. They came out upon the beach and sat down in a tumbled, pebbly place, where a meagre grass and patches of sea poppy were growing, and Kipps reclined on his elbow and tossed pebbles in his hand, and Ann sat up, sunlit, regarding him. They talked in fragments. They exhausted Sid, they exhausted Ann, and Kipps was chary of his riches.

He declined to a faint love-making. "I got that 'arf sixpence still," he said.

"Reely?"

That changed the key. "I always kept mine, some'ow," said Ann, and there was a pause.

They spoke of how often they had thought of each other during those intervening years. Kipps may have been untruthful, but Ann perhaps was not. "I met people here and there," said Ann; "but I never met anyone quite like you, Artie."

"It's jolly our meeting again, anyhow," said Kipps. "Look at that ship out there. She's pretty close in. . . ."

He had a dull period, became indeed almost pensive, and then he was enterprising for a while. He tossed up his pebbles so that as if by accident they fell on Ann's hand. Then, very penitently, he stroked the place. That would have led to all sorts of coquetries on the part of Flo Banks, for example, but it disconcerted and checked Kipps to find Ann made no objection, smiled pleasantly down on him, with eyes half shut because of the sun. She was taking things very much for granted.

He began to talk, and Chitterlow standards resuming possession of him he said he had never forgotten her.

"I never forgotten you either, Artie," she said. "Funny, isn't it?"

It impressed Kipps also as funny.

He became reminiscent, and suddenly a warm summer's evening came back to him. "Remember them cockchafers, Ann?" he said. But the reality of the evening he recalled was not the chase of cockchafers. The great reality that had suddenly arisen between them was that he had never kissed Ann in his life. He looked up and there were her lips.

He had wanted to very badly, and his memory leaped and annihilated an interval. That old resolution came back to him and all sorts of new resolutions passed out of mind. And he had learnt something since those boyish days. This time he did not ask. He went on talking, his nerves began very faintly to quiver and his mind grew bright.

Presently, having satisfied himself that there was no one to see, he sat up beside her and remarked upon the clearness of the air, and how close Dungeness seemed to them. Then they came upon a pause again.

"Ann," he whispered, and put an arm that quivered about her.

She was mute and unresisting, and, as he was to remember, solemn.

He turned her face towards him, and kissed her lips, and she kissed him back again—kisses frank and tender as a child's.

5

It was curious that in the retrospect he did not find nearly the satisfaction in this infidelity he had imagined was there. It was no doubt desperately doggish, doggish to an almost Chitterlowesque degree to recline on the beach at Littlestone with a "girl," to make love to her and to achieve the triumph of kissing her, when he was engaged to another "girl" at Folkestone, but somehow these two people were not "girls," they were Ann and Helen. Particularly Helen declined to be considered as a "girl." And there was something in Ann's quietly friendly eyes, in her frank smile, in the naïve pressure of her hand, there was something undefended and welcoming that imparted a flavour to the business upon which he had not counted. He had learnt about women from her. That refrain ran through his mind and deflected his thoughts, but as a matter of fact he had learnt about nothing but himself.

He wanted very much to see Ann some more and explain. He did not clearly know what it was he wanted to explain.

He did not clearly know anything. It is the last achievement of the intelligence to get all of one's life into one coherent scheme, and Kipps was only in a measure more aware of himself as a whole than is a tree. His existence was an affair of dissolving and recurring moods. When he thought of Helen or Ann or any of his friends, he thought sometimes of this aspect and sometimes of that—and often one aspect was finally incongruous with another. He loved Helen, he revered Helen. He was also beginning to hate her with some intensity. When he thought of that expedition to Lympne, profound, vague, beautiful emotions flooded his being; when he thought of paying calls with her perforce, or of her latest comment on his bearing, he found himself rebelliously composing fierce and pungent insults, couched in the vernacular. But Ann, whom he had seen so much less of, was a simpler memory. She was pretty, she was almost softly feminine, and she was possible to his imagination just exactly where Helen was impossible. More than anything else, she carried the charm of respect for him, the slightest glance of her eyes was balm for his perpetually wounded self-conceit.

Chance suggestions it was set the tune of his thoughts, and his state of health and repletion gave the colour. Yet somehow he had this at least almost clear in his mind, that to have gone to see Ann a second time, to have implied that she had been in possession of his thoughts through all this interval, and, above all, to have kissed her, was shabby and wrong. Only unhappily this much of lucidity had come now just a few hours after it was needed.

6

Four days after this it was that Kipps got up so late. He got up late, cut his chin while shaving, kicked a slipper into his sponge bath and said, "Desh!"

Perhaps you know those intolerable mornings, dear
Reader, when you seem to have neither the heart nor the
strength to rise, and your nervous adjustments are all wrong
and your fingers thumbs, and you hate the very birds for
singing. You feel inadequate to any demand whatever. Often
such awakenings follow a poor night's rest, and commonly
they mean indiscriminate eating, or those subtle mental influences old Kipps ascribed to "Foozle Ile" in the system,
or worry. And with Kipps—albeit Chitterlow had again been
his guest overnight—assuredly worry had played a leading
rôle. Troubles had been gathering upon him for days, there
had been a sort of concentration of these hosts of Midian
overnight, and in the grey small hours Kipps had held his
review.

The predominating trouble marched under this banner:

Mr. KIPPS

Mrs. BINDON BOTTING

At Home

Thursday, September 16th

Anagrams, 4 to 6:30   R.S.V.P.

---

a banner that was the facsimile of a card upon his looking
glass in the room below. And in relation to this terribly
significant document things had come to a pass with Helen
that he could only describe in his own expressive idiom as
"words."

It had long been a smouldering issue between them that
Kipps was not availing himself with any energy or freedom
of the opportunities he had of social exercises, much less
was he seeking additional opportunities. He had, it was evident, a peculiar dread of that universal afternoon enjoyment, the Call, and Helen made it unambiguously evident
that this dread was "silly" and had to be overcome. His first

display of this unmanly weakness occurred at the Coote's on the day before he kissed Ann. They were all there, chatting very pleasantly, when the little servant with the big cap announced the younger Miss Wace.

Whereupon Kipps manifested a lively horror and rose partially from his chair. "O Gum!" he protested. "Carn't I go upstairs?"

Then he sank back, for it was too late. Very probably the younger Miss Wace had heard him as she came in.

Helen said nothing of that, though her manner may have shown her surprise, but afterwards she told Kipps he must get used to seeing people, and suggested that he should pay a series of calls with Mrs. Walshingham and herself. Kipps gave a reluctant assent at the time and afterwards displayed a talent for evasion that she had not suspected in him. At last she did succeed in securing him for a call upon Miss Punchafer, of Radnor Park—a particularly easy call because Miss Punchafer being so deaf one could say practically what one liked—and then outside the gate he shirked again. "I can't go in," he said in a faded voice.

"You *must*," said Helen, beautiful as ever, but even more than a little hard and forbidding.

"I can't."

He produced his handkerchief hastily, thrust it to his face, and regarded her over it with rounded, hostile eyes.

" 'Possible," he said in a hoarse, strange voice out of the handkerchief. "Nozzez bleedin'."

But that was the end of his power of resistance, and when the rally for the Anagram Tea occurred she bore down his feeble protests altogether. She insisted. She said frankly, "I am going to give you a good talking to about this," and she did. . . .

From Coote he gathered something of the nature of Anagrams and Anagram parties. An anagram, Coote explained, was a word spelt the same way as another, only differently arranged, as, for instance, T. O. C. O. E. would be an anagram for his own name, Coote.

"T. O. C. O. E." repeated Kipps very carefully.

"Or T. O. E. C. O.," said Coote.

"Or T. O. E. C. O.," said Kipps, assisting his poor head by nodding it at each letter.

"Toe Company like," he said in his efforts to comprehend.

When Kipps was clear what an anagram meant, Coote came to the second heading, the Tea. Kipps gathered there might be from thirty to sixty people present, and that each one would have an anagram pinned on. "They give you a card to put your guesses on, rather like a dance programme, and then, you know, you go around and guess," said Coote. "It's rather good fun."

"Oo rather!" said Kipps, with simulated gusto.

"It shakes everybody up together," said Coote.

Kipps smiled and nodded. . . .

In the small hours all his painful meditations were threaded by the vision of that Anagram Tea; it kept marching to and fro and in and out of all his other troubles, from thirty to sixty people, mostly ladies and callers, and a great number of the letters of the alphabet, and more particularly P. I. K. P. S. and T. O. E. C. O., and he was trying to make one word out of the whole interminable procession. . . .

This word, as he finally gave it with some emphasis to the silence of the night, was *"Demn!"*

Then, wreathed as it were in this lettered procession, was the figure of Helen as she had appeared at the moment of "words"; her face a little hard, a little irritated, a little disappointed. He imagined himself going around and guessing under her eye. . . .

He tried to think of other things, without lapsing upon a still deeper uneasiness that was wreathed with yellow sea poppies, and the figures of Buggins, Pierce and Carshot, three murdered Friendships, rose reproachfully in the stillness and changed horrible apprehensions into unspeakable remorse. Last night had been their customary night for the banjo, and Kipps, with a certain tremulous uncertainty, had put old Methuselah amidst a retinue of glasses on the table and opened a box of choice cigars. In vain. They were in no need, it seemed, of *his* society. But instead Chitterlow had come, anxious to know if it was all right about that syndicate plan. He had declined anything but a very weak whiskey and soda, "just to drink," at least until business was settled, and had then opened the whole affair with an effect of great orderliness to Kipps. Soon he was taking another whiskey by sheer inadvertency, and the complex fabric of his conversation was running more easily from the broad loom of his mind. Into that pattern had interwoven a narrative of extensive alterations in the Pestered Butterfly—the neck and beetle business was to be restored—the story of a grave difference of opinion with Mrs. Chitterlow, where and how to live after the play had succeeded, the reasons why the Hon. Thomas Norgate had never financed a syndicate, and much matter also about the syndicate now under discussion. But if the current of their conversation had been vortical and crowded, the outcome was perfectly clear. Kipps was to be the chief participator in the syndicate, and his contribution was to be two thousand pounds. Kipps groaned and rolled over and found Helen, as it were, on the other side. "Promise me," she had said, "you won't do anything without consulting me."

Kipps at once rolled back to his former position, and for a space lay quite still. He felt like a very young rabbit in a trap.

Then suddenly, with extraordinary distinctness, his heart cried out for Ann, and he saw her as he had seen her at New Romney, sitting amidst the yellow sea poppies with the sunlight on her face. His heart called out for her in the darkness as one calls for rescue. He knew, as though he had known it always, that he loved Helen no more. He wanted Ann, he wanted to hold her and be held by her, to kiss her again and again, to turn his back forever on all these other things. . . .

He rose late, but this terrible discovery was still there, undispelled by cockcrow or the day. He rose in a shattered condition, and he cut himself while shaving, but at last he got into his dining-room and could pull the bell for the hot constituents of his multifarious breakfast. And then he turned to his letters. There were two real letters in addition to the customary electric belt advertisement, continental lottery circular and betting tout's card. One was in a slight mourning envelope and addressed in an unfamiliar hand. This he opened first and discovered a note:

Mrs. RAYMOND WACE

Requests the pleasure of

Mr. KIPPS'

Company at Dinner

on Tuesday, September 21st, at 8 o'clock

With a hasty movement Kipps turned his mind to the second letter. It was an unusually long one from his Uncle, and ran as follows:

"My Dear Nephew:

"We are considerably startled by your letter though expecting something of the sort and disposed to hope for the best. If the young lady is a relation to the Earl of Beauprés well and good but take care you are not being imposed upon for there are many who will be glad enough to snap you up now your circumstances are altered—I waited on the old Earl once while in service and he was remarkably close with his tips and suffered from corns. A hasty old gent and hard to please—I daresay he has forgotten me altogether— and anyhow there is no need to rake up bygones. Tomorrow is bus day and as you say the young lady is living near by we shall shut up shop for there is really nothing doing now what with all the visitors bringing everything with them down to their very children's pails and say how de do to her and give her a bit of a kiss and encouragement if we think her suitable—she will be pleased to see your old uncle—We wish we could have had a look at her first but still there is not much mischief done and hoping that all will turn out well yet I am

"Your affectionate Uncle
"Edward George Kipps.

"My heartburn still very bad. I shall bring over a few

bits of rhubub I picked up, a sort you won't get in Folkestone and if possible a good bunch of flowers for the young lady."

"Comin' over to-day," said Kipps, standing helplessly with the letter in his hand.

" 'Ow, the Juice——?

"I carn't.

"Kiss 'er!"

"I carn't even face 'er——!"

A terrible anticipation of that gathering framed itself in his mind—a hideous, impossible disaster.

His voice went up to a note of despair, "And it's too late to telegrarf and stop 'em!"

About twenty minutes after this, an outporter in Castle Hill Avenue was accosted by a young man, with a pale, desperate face, an exquisitely rolled umbrella and a heavy Gladstone bag.

"Carry this to the station, will you?" said the young man. "I want to ketch the nex' train to London. . . . You'll 'ave to look sharp—I 'aven't very much time."

VII. LONDON

1

London was Kipps' third world. There were no doubt other worlds, but Kipps knew only these three; firstly, New Romney and the Emporium, constituting his primary world, his world of origin, which also contained Ann; secondly, the world of culture and refinement, the world of which Coote was chaperon, and into which Kipps was presently to marry, a world it was fast becoming evident absolutely incompatible with the first, and, thirdly, a world still to a large extent unexplored, London. London presented itself as a place of great, grey spaces and incredible multitudes of people, centring about Charing Cross station and the Royal Grand Hotel, and containing at unexpected arbitrary points shops of the most amazing sort, statuary, Squares, Restaurants—where it was possible for clever people like Walshingham to order a lunch item by item, to the waiters' evident respect and sympathy—exhibitions of incredible things—the Walshinghams had taken him to the Arts and Crafts and to a picture gallery—and theatres. London, moreover, is rendered habitable by hansom cabs. Young Walshingham was a natural cab taker, he was an all-round large-minded young man, and he had in the course of their two days' stay taken Kipps into no less than nine, so that Kipps was singularly not afraid of these vehicles. He knew that wherever you were, so soon as you were thoroughly lost you said "Hi!" to a cab, and then "Royal Grand Hotel." Day and night these trusty conveyances are returning the strayed Londoner back to his point of departure, and were it not for their activity in a little while the whole population, so vast and incomprehensible is the intricate complexity of this great city, would be hopelessly lost forever. At any rate, that is how the thing presented itself to Kipps, and I have heard much the same from visitors from America.

His train was composed of corridor carriages, and he forgot his trouble for a time in the wonders of this modern substitute for railway compartments. He went from the non-smoking to the smoking carriage and smoked a cigarette, and strayed from his second-class carriage to a first and back. But presently Black Care got aboard the train and came and sat beside him. The exhilaration of escape had evaporated now, and he was presented with a terrible picture of his Aunt and Uncle arriving at his lodgings and finding him fled. He had left a hasty message that he was called away suddenly on business, "ver' important business," and they were to be sumptuously entertained. His immediate motive had been his passionate dread of an encounter between these excellent but unrefined old people and the Walshinghams, but now that end was secured, he could see how thwarted and exasperated they would be.

How to explain to them?

He ought never to have written to tell them!

He ought to have got married and told them afterwards.

He ought to have consulted Helen.

"Promise me," she had said.

"Oh, *desh!*" said Kipps, and got up and walked back into the smoking car and began to consume cigarettes.

Suppose, after all, they found out the Walshingham's address and went there!

At Charing Cross, however, there were distractions again. He took a cab in an entirely Walshingham manner, and was pleased to note the enhanced respect of the cabman when he mentioned the Royal Grand. He followed Walshingham's routine on their previous visit with perfect success. They were very nice in the office, and gave him an excellent room at fourteen shillings the night.

He went up and spent a considerable time in examining the furniture of his room, scrutinising himself in its various mirrors and sitting on the edge of the bed whistling. It was a vast and splendid apartment, and cheap at fourteen shillings. But, finding the figure of Ann inclined to resume possession of his mind, he roused himself and descended by the staircase after a momentary hesitation before the lift. He had thought of lunch, but he drifted into the great drawing-room and read a guide to the Hotels of Europe for a space, until a doubt whether he was entitled to use this

palatial apartment without extra charge arose in his mind.
He would have liked something to eat very much now, but
his inbred terror of the table was very strong. He did at
last get by a porter in uniform towards the dining-room, but
at the sight of a number of waiters and tables, with remarkable complications of knives and glasses, terror seized him,
and he backed out again, with a mumbled remark to the
waiter in the doorway about this not being the way.

He hovered in the hall and lounge until he thought the
presiding porter regarded him with suspicion, and then went
up to his room again by the staircase, got his hat and umbrella and struck boldly across the courtyard. He would go
to a restaurant instead.

He had a moment of elation in the gateway. He felt all
the Strand must notice him as he emerged through the great
gate of the hotel. "One of these here rich swells," they would
say. "Don't they do it just!" A cabman touched his hat. "No
fear," said Kipps, pleasantly.

Then he remembered he was hungry again.

Yet he decided he was in no great hurry for lunch, in
spite of an internal protest, and turned eastward along the
Strand in a leisurely manner. He tried to find a place to
suit him soon enough. He tried to remember the sort of
things Walshingham had ordered. Before all things he didn't
want to go into a place and look like a fool. Some of these
places rook you dreadful, besides making fun of you. There
was a place near Essex Street where there was a window
brightly full of chops, tomatoes and lettuce. He stopped at
this and reflected for a time, and then it occurred to him
that you were expected to buy these things raw and cook
them at home. Anyhow, there was sufficient doubt in the matter to stop him. He drifted on to a neat window with champagne bottles, a dish of asparagus and a framed menu of a
two shilling lunch. He was about to enter, when fortunately
he perceived two waiters looking at him over the back screen
of the window with a most ironical expression, and he sheered
off at once. There was a wonderful smell of hot food half
way down Fleet Street and a nice looking Tavern with several doors, but he could not decide which door. His nerve
was going under the strain.

He hesitated at Farringdon Street and drifted up to St.
Paul's and round the church yard, full chiefly of dead bar-

gains in the shop windows, to Cheapside. But now Kipps was getting demoralised, and each house of refreshment seemed to promise still more complicated obstacles to food. He didn't know how you went in and what was the correct thing to do with your hat, he didn't know what you said to the waiter or what you called the different things; he was convinced absolutely he would "fumble," as Shalford would have said, and look like a fool. Somebody might laugh at him! The hungrier he got the more unendurable was the thought that anyone should laugh at him. For a time he considered an extraordinary expedient to account for his ignorance. He would go in and pretend to be a foreigner and not know English. Then they might understand. . . . Presently he had drifted into a part of London where there did not seem to be any refreshment places at all.

"Oh, *desh!*" said Kipps, in a sort of agony of indecisiveness. "The very nex' place I see, in I go."

The next place was a fried fish shop in a little side street, where there were also sausages on a gas-lit grill.

He would have gone in, but suddenly a new scruple came to him, that he was too well dressed for the company he could see dimly through the steam sitting at the counter and eating with a sort of nonchalant speed.

2

He was half minded to resort to a hansom and brave the terrors of the dining-room of the Royal Grand—they wouldn't know why he had gone out really—when the only person he knew in London appeared (as the only person one does know will do in London) and slapped him on the shoulder. Kipps was hovering at a window at a few yards from the fish shop, pretending to examine some really strikingly cheap pink baby linen, and trying to settle finally about those sausages.

"Hullo, Kipps!" cried Sid; "spending the millions?"

Kipps turned, and was glad to perceive no lingering vestige of the chagrin that had been so painful at New Romney. Sid looked grave and important, and he wore a quite new silk hat that gave a commercial touch to a generally socialistic costume. For a moment the sight of Sid uplifted Kipps wonderfully. He saw him as a friend and helper, and only presently did it come clearly into his mind that this was the brother of Ann.

He made amiable noises.

"I've just been up this way," Sid explained, "buying a second-hand 'namelling stove. . . . I'm going to 'namel myself."

"Lor'!" said Kipps.

"Yes. Do me a lot of good. Let the customer choose his colour. See? What brings *you* up?"

Kipps had a momentary vision of his foiled Uncle and Aunt. "Jest a bit of a change," he said.

Sid came to a swift decision. "Come down to my little show. I got someone I'd like to see talking to you."

Even then Kipps did not think of Ann in this connection.

"Well," he said, trying to invent an excuse on the spur of the moment. "Fact is," he explained, "I was jest looking 'round to get a bit of lunch."

"Dinner, we call it," said Sid. "But that's all right. You can't get anything to eat hereabout. If you're not too haughty to do a bit of slumming, there's some mutton spoiling for me now——"

The word "mutton" affected Kipps greatly.

"It won't take us 'arf an hour," said Sid, and Kipps was carried.

He discovered another means of London locomotion in the Underground Railway, and recovered his self-possession in that interest. "You don't mind going third?" asked Sid, and Kipps said, "Nort a *bit* of it." They were silent in the train for a time, on account of strangers in the carriage, and then Sid began to explain who it was that he wanted Kipps to meet. "It's a chap named Masterman—do you no end of good.

"He occupies our first floor front room, you know. It isn't so much for gain I let as company. We don't *want* the whole 'ouse, and another, I knew the man before. Met him at our Sociological, and after a bit he said he wasn't comfortable where he was. That's how it came about. He's a first-class chap—first-class. Science! You should see his books!

"Properly he's a sort of journalist. He's written a lot of things, but he's been too ill lately to do very much. Poetry

he's written, all sorts. He writes for the *Commonweal* sometimes, and sometimes he reviews books. 'E's got 'eaps of
books—'eaps. Besides selling a lot.

"He knows a regular lot of people, and all sorts of things.
He's been a dentist, and he's a qualified chemist, an' I
seen him often reading German and French. Taught 'im-
self. He was here——"

Sid indicated South Kensington, which had come oppor-
tunely outside the carriage windows, with a nod of his
head, "—three years. Studying science. But you'll see 'im.
When he really gets to talking—he *pours* it out."

"Ah!" said Kipps, nodding sympathetically, with his two
hands on his umbrella knob.

"He'll do big things some day," said Sid. "He's written a
book on science already. 'Physiography,' it's called. 'Elementary Physiography'! Some day he'll write an Advanced—
when he gets time."

He let this soak into Kipps.

"I can't introduce you to Lords and swells," he went on,
"but I *can* show you a Famous Man, that's going to be. I
can do that. Leastways—unless——"

Sid hesitated.

"He's got a frightful cough," he said.

"He won't care to talk with me," weighed Kipps.

"That's all right; *he* won't mind. He's fond of talking.
He'd talk to anyone," said Sid, reassuringly, and added a
perplexing bit of Londonized Latin. "He doesn't *pute* anything, *non alienum*. You know."

"*I* know," said Kipps, intelligently, over his umbrella
knob, though of course that was altogether untrue.

3

Kipps found Sid's shop a practical looking establishment,
stocked with the most remarkable collection of bicycles and
pieces of bicycle that he had ever beheld. "My hiring stock,"
said Sid, with a wave to this ironmongery, "and there's the
best machine at a democratic price in London, The Red-
Flag, built by *me*. See?"

He indicated a graceful, grey-brown framework in the
window. "And there's my stock of accessories—store prices.

"Go in for motors a bit," added Sid.

"Mutton?" said Kipps, not hearing him distinctly.

"Motors, I *said*. . . . 'Owever, Mutton Department 'ere," and he opened a door that had a curtain guarded window in its upper panel, to reveal a little room with red walls and green furniture, with a white clothed table and the generous promise of a meal. "Fanny!" he shouted. "Here's Art Kipps."

A bright-eyed young woman of five or six and twenty in a pink print appeared, a little flushed from cooking, and wiped a hand on an apron and shook hands and smiled, and said it would all be ready in a minute. She went on to say she had heard of Kipps and his luck, and meanwhile Sid vanished to draw the beer, and returned with two glasses for himself and Kipps.

"Drink that," said Sid, and Kipps felt all the better for it.

"I give Mr. Masterman *'is* upstairs a hour ago," said Mrs. Sid. "I didn't think 'e ought to wait."

A rapid succession of brisk movements on the part of everyone, and they were all four at dinner—the fourth person being Master Walt Whitman Pornick, a cheerful young gentleman of one and a half, who was given a spoon to hammer on the table with to keep him quiet, and who got "Kipps" right at the first effort and kept it all through the meal, combining it first with this previous acquisition, and then that. "Peacock Kipps" said Master Walt, at which there was great laughter, and also "More Mutton, Kipps."

"He's a regular oner," said Mrs. Sid, "for catching up words. You can't say a word but what 'e's on to it."

There were no serviettes and less ceremony, and Kipps thought he had never enjoyed a meal so much. Everyone was a little excited by the meeting and chatting, and disposed to laugh, and things went off easily from the very beginning. If there was a pause Master Walt filled it in. Mrs. Sid, who tempered her enormous admiration for Sid's intellect and his socialism and his severe business methods by a motherly sense of her sex and seniority, spoke of them both as "you boys," and dilated—when she was not urging Kipps to have some more of this or that—on the disparity between herself and her husband.

"Shouldn't ha' thought there was a year between you," said Kipps; "you seem jest a match."

"*I'm his* match, anyhow," said Mrs. Sid, and no epigram of young Walshingham's was ever better received.

"Match," said young Walt, coming in on the trail of the joke and getting a round for himself.

Any sense of superior fortune had long vanished from Kipps' mind, and he found himself looking at host and hostess with enormous respect. Really, old Sid was a wonderful chap, here in his own house at two and twenty, carving his own mutton and lording it over wife and child. No legacies needed by him! And Mrs. Sid, so kind and bright and hearty! And the child, old Sid's child! Old Sid had jumped round a bit. It needed the sense of his fortune at the back of his mind to keep Kipps from feeling abject. He resolved he'd buy young Walt something tremendous in toys at the first opportunity.

"Drop more beer, Art?"

"Right you are, old man."

"Cut Mr. Kipps a bit more bread, Sid."

"Can't I pass *you* a bit?"

Sid was all right, Sid was, and there was no mistake about that.

It was growing up in his mind that Sid was the brother of Ann, but he said nothing about her for excellent reasons. After all, because he remembered Sid's irritation at her name when they had met in New Romney seemed to show a certain separation. They didn't tell each other much. . . . He didn't know how things might be between Ann and Sid, either.

Still, for all that, Sid was Ann's brother.

The furniture of the room did not assert itself very much above the cheerful business at the table, but Kipps was impressed with the idea that it was pretty. There was a dresser at the end with a number of gay plates and a mug or so, a Labour Day poster, by Walter Crane, on the wall, and through the glass and over the blind of the shop door one had a glimpse of the bright coloured advertisement cards of bicycle dealers, and a shelfful of boxes labelled, The Paragon Bell, The Scarum Bell, and The Patent Omi! Horn. . . .

It seemed incredible that he had been in Folkestone that morning, and even now his Aunt and Uncle——!

Brrr. It didn't do to think of his Aunt and Uncle.

4

When Sid repeated his invitation to come and see Masterman, Kipps, now flushed with beer and Irish stew, said he didn't mind if he did, and after a preliminary shout from Sid that was answered by a voice and a cough, the two went upstairs.

"Masterman's a rare one," said Sid over his arm and in an undertone. "You should hear him speak at a meeting. . . . If he's in form, that is."

He rapped and went into a large, untidy room.

"This is Kipps," he said. "You know. The chap I told you of. With twelve 'undred a year."

Masterman sat gnawing at an empty pipe and as close to the fire as though it was alight and the season midwinter. Kipps concentrated upon him for a space, and only later took in something of the frowsy furniture, the little bed half behind, and evidently supposed to be wholly behind, a careless screen, the spittoon by the fender, the remains of a dinner on the chest of drawers and the scattered books and papers. Masterman's face showed him a man of forty or more, with curious hollows at the side of his forehead and about his eyes. His eyes were very bright; there was a spot of red in his cheeks, and the wiry black moustache under his short, red nose had been trimmed with scissors into a sort of brush along his upper lip. His teeth were darkened ruins. His jacket collar was turned up about a knitted white neck wrap, and his sleeves betrayed no cuffs. He did not rise to greet Kipps, but held out a thin wristed hand and pointed with the other to a bedroom arm chair.

"Glad to see you," he said. "Sit down and make yourself at home. Will you smoke?"

Kipps said he would, and produced his store. He was about to take one, and then, with a civil afterthought, handed the packet first to Masterman and Sid. Masterman pretended surprise to find his pipe out before he took one. There was an interlude of matches. Sid pushed the end of the screen out of his way, sat down on the bed thus frankly admitted, and prepared, with a certain quiet satisfaction of manner, to witness Masterman's treatment of Kipps.

"And how does it feel to have twelve hundred a year?"

asked Masterman, holding his cigarette to his nose tip in a curious manner.

"It's rum," confided Kipps, after a reflective interval. "It feels juiced rum."

"I never felt it," said Masterman.

"It takes a bit of getting into," said Kipps. "I can tell you that."

Masterman smoked and regarded Kipps with curious eyes.

"I expect it does," he said presently.

"And has it made you perfectly happy?" he asked, abruptly.

"I couldn't 'ardly say *that*," said Kipps.

Masterman smiled. "No," he said. "Has it made you much happier?"

"It did at first."

"Yes. But you got used to it. How long, for example, did the real delirious excitement last?"

"Oo, *that!* Perhaps a week," said Kipps.

Masterman nodded his head. "That's what discourages *me* from amassing wealth," he said to Sid. "You adjust yourself. It doesn't last. I've always had an inkling of that, and it's interesting to get it confirmed. I shall go on sponging for a bit longer on *you,* I think."

"You don't," said Sid. "No fear."

"Twenty-four thousand pounds," said Masterman, and blew a cloud of smoke. "Lord! Doesn't it worry you?"

"It is a bit worrying at times. . . . Things 'appen."

"Going to marry?"

"Yes."

"H'm. Lady, I guess, of a superior social position?"

"Rather," said Kipps. "Cousin to the Earl of Beaupres."

Masterman readjusted his long body with an air of having accumulated all the facts he needed. He snuggled his shoulder-blades down into the chair and raised his angular knees. "I doubt," he said, flicking cigarette ash into the atmosphere, "if any great gain or loss of money does—as things are at present—make more than the slightest difference in one's happiness. It ought to—if money was what it ought to be, the token for given service; one ought to get an increase in power and happiness for every pound one got. But the plain fact is the times are out of joint, and money—

money, like everything else, is a deception and a disappointment."

He turned his face to Kipps and enforced his next words with the index finger of his lean, lank hand. "If I thought otherwise," he said, "I should exert *myself* to get some. But, if one sees things clearly, one is so discouraged. So confoundedly discouraged. . . . When you first got your money, you thought that it meant you might buy just anything you fancied?"

"I was a bit that way," said Kipps.

"And you found that you couldn't. You found that for all sorts of things it was a question of where to buy and how to buy, and what you didn't know how to buy with your money, straight away this world planted something else upon you——"

"I got rather done over a banjo first day," said Kipps. "Leastways, my Uncle says."

"Exactly," said Masterman.

Sid began to speak from the bed. "That's all very well, Masterman," he said, "but, after all, money *is* Power, you know. You can do all sorts of things——"

"I'm talking of happiness," said Masterman. "You can do all sorts of things with a loaded gun in the Hammersmith Broadway, but nothing—practically—that will make you or any one else very happy. Nothing. Power's a different matter altogether. As for happiness, you want a world in order before money or property, or any of those things that have any real value, and this world, I tell you, is hopelessly out of joint. Man is a social animal with a mind nowadays that goes around the globe, and a community cannot be happy in one part and unhappy in another. It's all or nothing, no patching any more for ever. It is the standing mistake of the world not to understand that. Consequently people think there is a class or order somewhere, just above them or just below them, or a country or place somewhere, that is really safe and happy. The fact is, Society is one body, and it is either well or ill. That's the law. This society we live in is ill. It's a fractious, feverish invalid, gouty, greedy and ill-nourished. You can't have a happy left leg with neuralgia, or a happy throat with a broken leg. That's my position, and that's the knowledge you'll come to. I'm so satisfied of it that I sit here and wait for my end quite calmly, sure that I can't better things by bothering—in my time, and so far as I am concerned, that is. I'm not even greedy any more—my egotism's at the bottom of a pond, with a philosophical brick around its neck. The world is ill, my time is short and my strength is small. I'm as happy here as anywhere."

He coughed and was silent for a moment, then brought the index finger around to Kipps again. You've had the opportunity of sampling two grades of society, and you don't find the new people you're among much better or any happier than the old?"

"No," said Kipps, reflectively. "No. I 'aven't seen it quite like that before, but——. No. They're not."

"And you might go all up the scale and down the scale and find the same thing. Man's a gregarious beast, a gregarious beast, and no money will buy you out of your own time—any more than out of your own skill. All the way up and all the way down the scale there's the same discontent. No one is quite sure where they stand, and everyone's fretting. The herd's uneasy and feverish. All the old tradition goes or has gone, and there's no one to make a new tradition. Where are your nobles now? Where are your gentlemen? They vanished directly the peasant found out he wasn't happy and ceased to be a peasant. There's big men and little men mixed up together, that's all. None of us know where we are. Your cads in a bank holiday train and your cads on a two thousand pound motor; except for a difference in scale, there's not a pin to choose between them. Your smart society is as low and vulgar and uncomfortable for a balanced soul as a gin palace, no more and no less; there's no place or level of honour or fine living left in the world; so what's the good of climbing?"

" 'Ear, 'ear," said Sid.

"It's true," said Kipps.

"*I* don't climb," said Masterman, and accepted Kipps' silent offer of another cigarette.

"No," he said. "This world is out of joint. It's broken up, and I doubt if it will heal. I doubt very much if it'll heal. We're in the beginning of the Sickness of the World."

He rolled his cigarette in his lean fingers and repeated with satisfaction: "The Sickness of the World."

"It's we've got to make it better," said Sid, and looked at Kipps.

"Ah, Sid's an optimist," said Masterman.

"So are you, most times," said Sid.

Kipps lit another cigarette with an air of intelligent participation.

"Frankly," said Masterman, recrossing his legs and expelling a jet of smoke luxuriously, "frankly, I think thas civilisation of ours is on the topple."

"There's Socialism," said Sid.

"There's no imagination to make use of it."

"We've got to *make* one," said Sid.

"In a couple of centuries perhaps," said Masterman. "But meanwhile we're going to have a pretty acute attack of confusion. Universal confusion. Like one of those crushes when men are killed and maimed for no reason at all, going into a meeting or crowding for a train. Commercial and Industrial Stresses. Political Exploitation. Tariff Wars. Revolutions. All the bloodshed that will come of some fools calling half the white world yellow. These things alter the attitude of everybody to everybody. Everybody's going to feel 'em. Every fool in the world panting and shoving. *We're* all going to be as happy and comfortable as a household during a removal. What else can we expect?"

Kipps was moved to speak, but not in answer to Masterman's enquiry. "I've never rightly got the 'eng of this Socialism," he said. "What's it going to do, like?"

They had been imagining that he had some elementary idea in the matter, but as soon as he had made it clear that he hadn't, Sid plunged at exposition, and in a little while Masterman, abandoning his pose of the detached man ready to die, joined in. At first he joined in only to correct Sid's version, but afterwards he took control. His manner changed. He sat up and rested his elbow on his knees, and his cheek flushed a little. He expanded his case against Property and the property class with such vigour that Kipps was completely carried away, and never thought of asking for a clear vision of the thing that would fill the void this abolition might create. For a time he quite forgot his own private opulence. And it was as if something had been lit in Masterman. His languor passed. He enforced his words by gestures of his long, thin hands. And as he passed swiftly from point to point of his argument it was evident he grew angry.

"To-day," he said, "the world is ruled by rich men; they may do almost anything they like with the world. And what are they doing? Laying it waste!"

"Hear, hear!" said Sid, very sternly.

Masterman stood up, gaunt and long, thrust his hands in his pockets and turned his back to the fireplace.

"Collectively, the rich to-day have neither heart nor imagination. No! They own machinery, they have knowledge and instruments and powers beyond all previous dreaming, and what are they doing with them? Think what they are doing with them, Kipps, and think what they might do. God gives them a power like the motor car, and all they can do with it is to go careering about the roads in goggled masks killing children and making machinery hateful to the soul of man! ("True," said Sid, "true.") God gives them means of communication, power unparalleled of every sort, time and absolute liberty! They waste it all in folly! Here under their feet (and Kipps' eyes followed the direction of a lean index finger to the hearthrug) under their accursed wheels, the great mass of men festers and breeds in darkness, darkness those others make by standing in the light. The darkness breeds and breeds. It knows no better. . . . Unless you can crawl or pander or rob you must stay in the stew you are born in. And those rich beasts above claw and clutch as though they had nothing! They grudge us our schools, they grudge us a gleam of light and air, they cheat us and then seek to forget us. . . . There is no rule, no guidance, only accidents and happy flukes. . . . Our multitudes of poverty increase, and this crew of rulers makes no provision, foresees nothing, anticipates nothing. . . ."

He paused and made a step, and stood over Kipps in a white heat of anger. Kipps nodded in a non-committal manner and looked hard and rather gloomily at his host's slipper as he talked.

"It isn't as though they had something to show for the waste they make of us, Kipps. They haven't. They are ugly and cowardly and mean. Look at their women! Painted, dyed and drugged, hiding their ugly shapes under a load of dress! There isn't a woman in the swim of society at the present time, who wouldn't sell herself, body and soul, who wouldn't lick the boots of a Jew or marry a nigger, rather than live decently on a hundred a year! On what would be wealth for you and me! They know it. They know we know it. . . . No one believes in them. No one believes in nobility any more. Nobody believes in kingship any more. Nobody believes there is justice in the law. . . . But people have habits, people go on in the old grooves, as long as there's work, as long as there's weekly money. . . . It won't last, Kipps."

He coughed and paused. "Wait for the lean years," he cried. "Wait for the lean years." And suddenly he fell into a struggle with his cough and spat a gout of blood. "It's nothing," he said to Kipps' note of startled horror.

He went on talking, and the protests of his cough interlaced with his words, and Sid beamed in an ecstasy of painful admiration.

"Look at the fraud they have let life become, the miserable mockery of the hope of one's youth. What have *I* had? I found myself at thirteen being forced into a factory like a rabbit into a chloroformed box. Thirteen!—when *their* children are babies. But even a child of that age could see what it meant, that Hell of a factory! Monotony and toil and contempt and dishonour! And then death. So I fought—at thirteen!"

Minton's "crawling up a drain pipe until you die" echoed in Kipps' mind, but Masterman, instead of Minton's growl, spoke in a high, indignant tenor.

"I got out at last—somehow," he said, quietly, suddenly plumping back in his chair. He went on after a pause. "For a bit. Some of us get out by luck, some by cunning, and crawl on to the grass, exhausted and crippled to die. That's a poor man's success, Kipps. Most of us don't get out at all. I worked all day and studied half the night, and here I am with the common consequences. Beaten! And never once have I had a fair chance, never once!" His lean, clenched fist flew out in a gust of tremulous anger. "These Skunks shut up all the university scholarships at nineteen for fear of men like me. And then—do *nothin'*. . . . We're wasted for nothing. By the time I'd learnt something the doors were locked. I thought knowledge would do it—I did think that! I've fought for knowledge as other men fight for bread. I've starved for knowledge. I've turned my back on women; I've done even that. I've burst my accursed lung. . ." His voice rose with impotent anger. "I'm a better man than any ten princes alive! And I'm beaten and wasted. I've been crushed, trampled and defiled by a drove of hogs. I'm no use to myself or the world. I've thrown my life away to make myself too good for use in this huckster's scramble. If I had gone in for business, if I had gone in for plotting to cheat my fellow men—ah, well! It's too late. It's too late for that, anyhow. It's too late for anything now! And I couldn't have done it. . . . And over in New York now there's a pet of society making a corner in wheat!

"By God!" he cried hoarsely, with a clutch of the lean hand. "By God! If I had his throat! Even now I might do something for the world."

He glared at Kipps, his face flushed deep, his sunken eyes glowing with passion, and then suddenly he changed altogether.

There was a sound of tea things rattling upon a tray outside the door, and Sid rose to open it.

"All of which amounts to this," said Masterman, suddenly quiet and again talking against time. "The world is out of joint, and there isn't a soul alive who isn't half waste or more. You'll find it the same with you in the end, wherever your luck may take you. . . . I suppose you won't mind my having another cigarette?"

He took Kipps' cigarette with a hand that trembled so violently it almost missed its object, and stood up, with something of guilt in his manner as Mrs. Sid came into the room.

Her eye met his and marked the flush upon his face.

"Been talking Socialism?" said Mrs. Sid, a little severely.

5

Six o'clock that day found Kipps drifting eastward along the southward margin of Rotten Row. You figure him a small, respectably attired figure going slowly through a sometimes immensely difficult and always immense world. At times he becomes pensive and whistles softly. At times he looks about him. There are a few riders in the Row, a carriage flashes by every now and then along the roadway, and among the great rhododendrons and laurels and upon the greensward there are a few groups and isolated people dressed in the style Kipps adopted to call upon the Walsinghams when first he was engaged. Amid the complicated confusion of Kipps' mind was a regret that he had not worn his other things. . . .

Presently he perceived that he would like to sit down; a green chair tempted him. He hesitated at it, took possession of it, and leant back and crossed one leg over the other.

He rubbed his under lip with his umbrella handle and reflected upon Masterman and his denunciation of the world.

"Bit orf 'is 'ead, poor chap," said Kipps, and added: "I wonder."

He thought intently for a space.

"I wonder what he meant by the lean years?"

The world seemed a very solid and prosperous concern just here, and well out of reach of Masterman's dying clutch. And yet——

It was curious he should have been reminded of Minton.

His mind turned to a far more important matter. Just at the end Sid had said to him, "Seen Ann?" and as he was about to answer, "You'll see a bit more of her now. She's got a place in Folkestone."

It had brought him back from any concern about the world being out of joint or anything of that sort.

Ann!

One might run against her any day.

He tugged at his little moustache.

He would like to run against Ann very much. . .

"And it would be juiced awkward if I did!"

In Folkestone! It was a jolly sight too close. . .

Then, at the thought that he might run against Ann in his beautiful evening dress on the way to the band, he fluttered into a momentary dream, that jumped abruptly into a nightmare.

Suppose he met her when he was out with Helen! "Oh, Lor'!" said Kipps. Life had developed a new complication that would go on and go on. For some time he wished with the utmost fervour that he had not kissed Ann, that he had not gone to New Romney the second time. He marvelled at his amazing forgetfulness of Helen on that occasion. Helen took possession of his mind. He would have to write to Helen, an easy, off-hand letter, to say that he had come to London for a day or so. He tried to imagine her reading it. He would write just such another letter to the old people, and say he had had to come up on business. That might do for *them* all right, but Helen was different. She would insist on explanations.

He wished he could never go back to Folkestone again. That would settle the whole affair.

A passing group attracted his attention, two faultlessly dressed gentlemen and a radiantly expensive lady. They were talking, no doubt, very brilliantly. His eyes followed them. The lady tapped the arm of the left hand gentleman with a daintily tinted glove. Swells! No end. . . .

His soul looked out upon life in general as a very small nestling might peep out of its nest. What an extraordinary thing life was, to be sure, and what a remarkable variety of people there were in it!

He lit a cigarette and speculated upon that receding group of three, and blew smoke and watched them. They seemed to do it all right. Probably they all had incomes of very much over twelve hundred a year. Perhaps not. Probably none of them suspected, as they went past, that he, too, was a gentleman of independent means, dressed, as he was, without distinction. Of course things were easier for them. They were brought up always to dress well and do the right thing from their very earliest years; they started clear of all his perplexities; they had never got mixed up with all sorts of different people who didn't go together. If, for example, that lady there got engaged to that gentleman, she would be quite safe from any encounter from a corpulent, osculatory Uncle, or Chitterlow, or the dangerously insignificant eye of Pierce.

His thoughts came round to Helen.

When they were married and Cuyps, or Cuyp—Coote had failed to justify his "s"—and in that West End flat and shaken free of all these low class associations, would he and she parade here of an afternoon dressed like that? It would be rather fine to do so. If one's dress was all right.

Helen!

She was difficult to understand at times.

He blew extensive clouds of cigarette smoke.

There would be teas, there would be dinners, there would be calls. Of course he would get into the way of it.

But Anagrams were a bit stiff to begin with!

It was beastly confusing at first to know when to use your fork at dinner, and all that. Still——

He felt an extraordinary doubt whether he would get into the way of it. He was interested for a space by a girl and groom on horseback, and then he came back to his personal preoccupations.

He would have to write to Helen. What could he say to explain his absence from the Anagram Tea? She had been pretty clear she wanted him to come. He recalled her resolute face without any great tenderness. He *knew* he would look like a silly ass at that confounded tea! Suppose he shirked it and went back in time for the dinner! Dinners were beastly difficult, too, but not as bad as Anagrams. The very first thing that might happen when he got back to Folkestone would be to run against Ann. Suppose, after all, he did meet Ann when he was with Helen!

What queer encounters were possible in the world!

Thank goodness, they were going to live in London!

But that brought him around to Chitterlow. The Chitterlows were coming to London, too. If they didn't get money they'd come after it; they weren't the sort of people to be choked off easily, and if they did they'd come to London to produce their play. He tried to imagine some seemly social occasion invaded by Chitterlow and his rhetoric, by his torrential thunder of self-assertion, the whole company flattened thereunder like wheat under a hurricane.

Confound and hang Chitterlow! Yet, somehow, somewhen, one would have to settle accounts with him! And there was Sid! Sid was Ann's brother. He realised with sudden horror the social indiscretion of accepting Sid's invitation to dinner.

Sid wasn't the sort of chap one could snub or cut, and besides—Ann's brother! He didn't want to cut him. It would be worse than cutting Buggins and Pierce—a sight worse. And after that lunch!

It would be the next thing to cutting Ann herself. And even as to Ann!

Suppose he was with Helen or Coote! . . .

"Oh, Blow!" he said, at last, and then, viciously, *"Blow!"*
and so rose and flung away his cigarette end, and pursued
his reluctant, dubiating way towards the really quite un-
congenial splendours of the Royal Grand. . . .

And it is vulgarly imagined that to have money is to
have no troubles at all!

<h2 style="text-align:center">6</h2>

Kipps endured splendour at the Royal Grand Hotel for
three nights and days, and then he retreated in disorder.
The Royal Grand defeated and overcame and routed Kipps,
not of intention, but by sheer royal grandeur, grandeur
combined with an organisation for his comfort carried to
excess. On his return he came upon a difficulty; he had lost
his circular piece of cardboard with the number of his
room, and he drifted about the hall and passages in a state
of perplexity for some time, until he thought all the porters
and officials in gold lace caps must be watching him and
jesting to one another about him. Finally, in a quiet corner,
down below the hairdresser's shop, he found a kindly looking personage in bottle green, to whom he broached his
difficulty. "I say," he said, with a pleasant smile, "I can't
find my room nohow." The personage in bottle green, instead of laughing in a nasty way, as he might well have
done, became extremely helpful, showed Kipps what to do,
got his key, and conducted him by lift and passage to his
chamber. Kipps tipped him half a crown.

Safe in his room, Kipps pulled himself together for dinner. He had learnt enough from young Walshingham to
bring his dress clothes, and now he began to assume them.
Unfortunately, in the excitement of his flight from his Aunt
and Uncle, he had forgotten to put in his other boots, and
he was some time deciding between his purple cloth slippers,
with a golden marigold, and the prospect of cleaning the
boots he was wearing with the towel, but finally, being a little
footsore, he took the slippers.

Afterwards, when he saw the porters and waiters and
the other guests catch a sight of the slippers, he was sorry
he had not chosen the boots. However, to make up for any

want of style at that end, he had his crush hat under his arm.

He found the dining-room without excessive trouble. It was a vast and splendidly decorated place, and a number of people, evidently quite *au fait*, were dining there at little tables lit with electric, red shaded candles, gentlemen in evening dress, and ladies with dazzling, astonishing necks. Kipps had never seen evening dress in full vigour before, and he doubted his eyes. And there were also people not in evening dress who, no doubt, wondered what noble family Kipps represented. There was a band in a decorated recess, and the band looked collectively at the purple slippers, and so lost any chance they may have had of a collection, so far as Kipps was concerned. The chief drawback to this magnificent place was the excessive space of floor that had to be crossed before you got your purple slippers hid in under a table.

He selected a little table—not the one where a rather impudent looking waiter held a chair, but another—sat down, and finding his gibus in his hand, decided after a moment of thought to rise slightly and sit on it. (It was discovered in his abandoned chair at a late hour by a supper party, and restored to him next day.)

He put the napkin carefully on one side, selected his soup without difficulty, "Clear, please," but he was rather floored by the presentation of a quite splendidly bound wine card. He turned it over, discovered a section devoted to whiskey, and had a bright idea.

" 'Ere," he said to the waiter, with an encouraging movement of his head, and then in a confidential manner, "you haven't any Old Methuselah Three Stars, 'ave you?"

The waiter went away to enquire, and Kipps went on with his soup with an enhanced self-respect. Finally, Old Methuselah being unobtainable, he ordered a claret from about the middle of the list. "Let's 'ave some of this," he said. He knew claret was a good sort of wine.

"A half bottle?" said the waiter.

"Right you are," said Kipps.

He felt he was getting on. He leant back after his soup, a man of the world, and then slowly brought his eyes around to the ladies in evening dress on his right. . . .

He couldn't have thought it!

They were scorchers. Jest a bit of black velvet over the shoulders!

He looked again. One of them was laughing with a glass of wine half raised—wicked-looking woman she was—the other, the black velvet one, was eating bits of bread with nervous quickness and talking fast.

He wished old Buggins could see them.

He found a waiter regarding him and blushed deeply. He did not look again for some time, and became confused about his knife and fork over the fish. Presently he remarked a lady in pink to the left of him eating the fish with an entirely different implement.

It was over the *vol au vent* that he began to go to pieces. He took a knife to it; then saw the lady in pink was using a fork only, and hastily put down his knife, with a considerable amount of rich creaminess on the blade, upon the cloth. Then he found that a fork in his inexperienced hand was an instrument of chase rather than capture. His ears became violently red, and then he looked up, to discover the lady in pink glancing at him and then smiling as she spoke to the man beside her.

He hated the lady in pink very much.

He stabbed a large piece of the *vol au vent* at last, and was too glad of his luck not to take a mouthful of it. But it was an extensive fragment, and pieces escaped him. Shirt front! "Desh it!" he said, and had resort to his spoon. His waiter went and spoke to two other waiters, no doubt jeering at him. He became very fierce suddenly. " 'Ere!" he said, gesticulating, and then, "clear this away!"

The entire dinner party on his right, the party of the ladies in advanced evening dress, looked at him. . . . He felt that everyone was watching him and making fun of him, and the injustice of this angered him. After all, they had every advantage he hadn't. And then, when they got him there doing his best, what must they do but glance and sneer and nudge one another. He tried to catch them at it, and then took refuge in a second glass of wine.

Suddenly and extraordinarily he found himself a socialist. He did not care how close it was to the lean years when all these things would end.

Mutton came with peas. He arrested the hand of the

waiter. "No peas," he said. He knew something of the difficulty and danger of eating peas. Then, when the peas went away again he was embittered again. . . . Echoes of Masterman's burning rhetoric began to reverberate in his mind. Nice lot of people these were to laugh at anyone! Women half undressed. It was that made him so beastly uncomfortable. How could one eat one's dinner with people about him like that? Nice lot they were. He was glad he wasn't one of them, anyhow. Yes, they might look. He resolved if they looked at him again he would ask one of the men who he was staring at. His perturbed and angry face would have concerned anyone. The band by an unfortunate accident was playing truculent military music. The mental change Kipps underwent was, in its way, what psychologists call a conversion. In a few moments all Kipps' ideals were changed. He who had been "practically a gentleman," the sedulous pupil of Coote, the punctilious raiser of hats, was instantly a rebel, an outcast, the hater of everything "stuck up," the foe of Society and the social order of to-day. Here they were among the profits of their robbery, these people who might do anything with the world. . . .

"No, thenks," he said to a dish.

He addressed a scornful eye at the shoulders of the lady to his left.

Presently he was refusing another dish. He didn't like it— fussed up food! Probably cooked by some foreigner. He finished up his wine and his bread.

"No, thenks."

"No, thenks. . . ."

He discovered the eye of a diner fixed curiously upon his flushed face. He responded with a glare. Couldn't he go without things if he liked?

"What's this?" said Kipps to a great green cone.

"Ice," said the waiter.

"I'll 'ave some," said Kipps.

He seized a fork and spoon and assailed the bombe. It cut rather stiffly. "Come up!" said Kipps, with concentrated bitterness, and the truncated summit of the bombe flew off suddenly, travelling eastward with remarkable velocity. Flop, it went upon the floor a yard away, and for awhile time seemed empty.

At the adjacent table they were laughing together.

Shy the rest of the bombe at them?

Flight?

At any rate a dignified withdrawal.

"No!" said Kipps, "no more," arresting the polite attempt of the waiter to serve him with another piece. He had a vague idea he might carry off the affair as though he had meant the ice to go on the floor—not liking ice, for example, and being annoyed at the badness of his dinner. He put both hands on the table, thrust back his chair, disengaged a purple slipper from his napkin, and rose. He stepped carefully over the prostrate ice, kicked the napkin under the table, thrust his hands deep into his pockets, and marched out—shaking the dust of the place, as it were, from his feet. He left behind him a melting fragment of ice upon the floor, his gibus hat, warm and compressed in his chair, and in addition every social ambition he had ever entertained in the world.

7

Kipps went back to Folkestone in time for the Anagram Tea. But you must not imagine that the change of heart that came to him in the dining-room of the Royal Grand Hotel involved any change of attitude toward this promised social and intellectual treat. He went back because the Royal Grand was too much for him.

Outwardly calm, or at most a little flushed and ruffled, inwardly Kipps was a horrible, tormented battleground of scruples, doubts, shames and self-assertions during that three days of silent, desperate grappling with the big hotel. He did not intend the monstrosity should beat him without a struggle, but at last he had sullenly to admit himself overcome. The odds were terrific. On the one hand himself—with, among other things, only one pair of boots; on the other a vast wilderness of rooms, covering several acres, and with over a thousand people, staff and visitors, all chiefly occupied in looking queerly at Kipps, in laughing at him behind his back, in watching for difficult corners at which to confront and perplex him, and inflict humiliations upon him. For example, the hotel scored over its electric light. After the dinner the chambermaid, a hard, unsympathetic young woman with a superior manner, was summoned by a bell Kipps had rung under the impression the button was the electric light switch. "Look 'ere," said Kipps, rubbing a shin that had suffered during his search in the dark, "why aren't there any candles or matches?" The hotel explained and scored heavily.

"It isn't everyone is up to these things," said Kipps.

"No, it isn't," said the chambermaid, with ill-concealed scorn, and slammed the door at him.

"S'pose I ought to have tipped her," said Kipps.

After that Kipps cleaned his boots with a pocket-handkerchief and went for a long walk and got home in a hansom, but the hotel scored again by his not putting out his boots and so having to clean them again in the morning. The hotel also snubbed him by bringing him hot water when he was fully dressed and looking surprised at his collar, but he got a breakfast, I must admit, with scarcely any difficulty.

After that the hotel scored heavily by the fact that there are twenty-four hours in the day and Kipps had nothing to do in any of them. He was a little footsore from his previous day's pedestrianism, and he could make up his mind for no long excursions. He flitted in and out of the hotel several times, and it was the polite porter who touched his hat every time that first set Kipps tipping.

"What 'e wants is a tip," said Kipps.

So at the next opportunity he gave the man an unexpected shilling, and having once put his hand in his pocket, there was no reason why he should not go on. He bought a newspaper at the book-stall and tipped the boy the rest of the shilling, and then went up by the lift and tipped the man a sixpence, leaving his newspaper inadvertently in the lift. He met his chambermaid in the passage and gave her half a crown. He resolved to demonstrate his position to the entire establishment in this way. He didn't like the place; he disapproved of it politically, socially, morally, but he resolved no taint of meanness should disfigure his sojourn in its luxurious halls. He went down by the lift (tipping again), and, being accosted by a waiter with his gibus, tipped the finder half a crown. He had a vague sense that he was making a flank movement upon the hotel and buying over its staff. They would regard him as a character. They would get to like him. He found his stock of small silver diminishing, and replenished it at a desk in the hall. He tipped a man in bottle green who looked like the man who had shown him his room the day before, and then he saw a visitor eyeing him, and doubted whether he was in this instance doing right. Finally he went out and took chance 'buses to their destinations, and wandered a little in remote, wonderful suburbs and returned. He lunched at a chop house in Islington, and found himself back in the Royal Grand, now unmistakably footsore and London weary, about three. He was drawn towards the drawing-room by a neat placard about afternoon tea.

It occurred to him that the campaign of tipping upon which he had embarked was perhaps after all a mistake. He was confirmed in this by observing that the hotel officials were watching him, not respectfully, but with a sort of amused wonder, as if to see whom he would tip next. However, if he backed out now, they would think him an awful fool. Everyone wasn't so rich as he was. It was his way to tip. Still——

He grew more certain the hotel had scored again.

He pretended to be lost in thought and so drifted by, and having put hat and umbrella in the cloak-room went into the drawing-room for afternoon tea.

There he did get what for a time he held to be a point in his favour. The room was large and quiet at first, and he sat back restfully until it occurred to him that his attitude brought his extremely dusty boots too prominently into the light, so instead he sat up, and then people of the upper and upper middle classes began to come and group themselves about him and have tea likewise, and so revive the class animosities of the previous day.

Presently a fluffy, fair-haired lady came into prominent existence a few yards away. She was talking to a respectful, low-voiced clergyman, whom she was possibly entertaining at tea. "No," she said, "dear Lady Jane wouldn't like that!"

"Mumble, mumble, mumble," from the clergyman.

"Poor dear Lady Jane was always so sensitive," the voice of the lady sang out clear and emphatic.

A fat, hairless, important-looking man joined this group, took a chair and planted it firmly with its back in the face of Kipps, a thing that offended Kipps mightily. "Are you telling him," gurgled the fat, hairless man, "about dear

Lady Jane's affliction?" A young couple, lady brilliantly attired and the man in a magnificently cut frock coat, arranged themselves to the right, also with an air of exclusion towards Kipps. "I've told him," said the gentleman in a flat, abundant voice. "My!" said the young lady, with an American smile. No doubt they all thought Kipps was out of it. A great desire to assert himself in some way surged up in his heart. He felt he would like to cut in on the conversation in some dramatic way. A monologue something in the manner of Masterman? At any rate, abandoning that as impossible, he would like to appear self-centred and at ease. His eyes, wandering over the black surfaces of a noble architectural mass close by, discovered a slot—an enamelled plaque of directions.

It was some sort of musical box! As a matter of fact, it was the very best sort of Harmonicon and specially made to the scale of the Hotel.

He scrutinised the plaque with his head at various angles and glanced about him at his neighbours.

It occurred to Kipps that he would like some music, that to inaugurate some would show him a man of taste and at his ease at the same time. He rose, read over a list of tunes, selected one haphazard, pressed his sixpence—it was sixpence!—home, and prepared for a confidential, refined little melody.

Considering the high social tone of the Royal Grand, it was really a very loud instrument indeed. It gave vent to three deafening brays and so burst the dam of silence that had long pent it in. It seemed to be chiefly full of the greatuncles of trumpets, megalotrombones and railway brakes. It made sounds like shunting trains. It did not so much begin as blow up your counter-scarp or rush forward to storm under cover of melodious shrapnel. It had not so much an air as a *ricochette*. The music had, in short, the inimitable quality of Sousa. It swept down upon the friend of Lady Jane and carried away something socially striking into the eternal night of the unheard; the American girl to the left of it was borne shrieking into the inaudible. "HIGH cockalorum Tootletootle tootle loo. HIGH cockalorum tootle lootle loo. BUMP, bump, bump—BUMP." Joyous, exorbitant music it was from the gigantic nursery of the Future, bearing the hearer along upon its torrential succession of sounds, as if he was in a cask on Niagara. Whiroo! Yah and have at you! The strenuous Life! Yaha! Stop! A Reprieve! A Reprieve! No! Bang! Bump!

Everybody looked around, conversation ceased and gave place to gestures.

The friend of Lady Jane became terribly agitated.

"Can't it be stopped?" she vociferated, pointing a gloved finger and saying something to the waiter about "That dreadful young man."

"Ought not to be working," said the clerical friend of Lady Jane.

The waiter shook his head at the fat, hairless gentleman. People began to move away. Kipps leant back luxurious, and then tipped with a half crown to pay. He paid, tipped like a gentleman, rose with an easy gesture, and strolled towards the door. His retreat evidently completed the indignation of the friend of Lady Jane, and from the door he could still discern her gestures as asking, "Can't it be stopped?" The music followed him into the passage and pursued him to the lift and only died away completely in the quiet of his own room, and afterwards from his window he saw the friend of Lady Jane and her party having their tea carried out to a little table in the court. BUMP, bump, bump, BUMP floated up to him, and certainly that was a point to him. But it was his only score; all the rest of the game lay in the hands of the upper classes and the big hotel. And presently he was doubting whether even this was really a point. It seemed a trifle vulgar, come to think it over, to interrupt people when they were talking.

He saw a clerk peering at him from the office, and suddenly it occurred to him that the place might get back at him tremendously over the bill.

They would probably take it out of him by charging pounds and pounds.

Suppose they charged more than he had!

The clerk had a particularly nasty face, just the face to take advantage of a vacillating Kipps.

He became aware of a man in a cap touching it, and produced his shilling automatically, but the strain was beginning to tell. It was a deuce and all of an expense—this tipping.

If the hotel chose to stick it on to the bill something

tremendous what was Kipps to do? Refuse to pay? Make a
row?

If he did he couldn't fight all these men in bottle
green. . . .

He went out about seven and walked for a long time
and dined at last upon a chop in the Euston Road; then he
walked along to the Edgeware Road and sat and rested in
the Metropolitan Music Hall for a time until a trapeze performance unnerved him and finally he came back to bed.
He tipped the lift man sixpence and wished him good-night.
In the silent watches of the night he reviewed the tale of
the day's tipping, went over the horrors of the previous
night's dinner, and heard again the triumphant bray of the
harmonicon devil released from its long imprisonment.
Everyone would be told about him tomorrow. He couldn't
go on! He admitted his defeat. Never in their whole lives
had any of these people seen such a Fool as he! Ugh! . . .

His method of announcing his withdrawal to the clerk
was touched with bitterness.

"I'm going to get out of this," said Kipps, blowing windily.
"Let's see what you got on my bill."

"One breakfast?" asked the clerk.

"Do I *look* as if I'd ate two?" . . .

At his departure Kipps, with a hot face, convulsive gestures and an embittered heart, tipped everyone who did not
promptly and actively resist, including an absent-minded
South African diamond merchant, who was waiting in the
hall for his wife and succumbed to old habit. He paid his
cabman a four shilling piece at Charing Cross, having no
smaller change, and wished he could burn him alive. Then
in a sudden reaction of economy he refused the proffered
help of a porter and carried his bag quite violently to the
train.

VIII. KIPPS ENTERS SOCIETY

1

Submission to Inexorable Fate took Kipps to the Anagram Tea.

At any rate he would meet Helen there in the presence of other people and be able to carry off the worst of the difficulty of explaining his little jaunt to London. He had not seen her since his last portentous visit to New Romney. He was engaged to her, he would have to marry her, and the sooner he faced her again the better. Before wild plans of turning socialist, defying the world and repudiating all calling for ever, his heart on second thoughts sank. He felt Helen would never permit anything of the sort. As for the Anagrams he could do no more than his best and that he was resolved to do. What had happened at the Royal Grand, what had happened at New Romney, he must bury in his memory and begin again at the reconstruction of his social position. Ann, Buggins, Chitterlow, all these, seen in the matter-of-fact light of the Folkestone train, stood just as they stood before; people of an inferior social position who had to be eliminated from his world. It was a bother about Ann, a bother and a pity. His mind rested so for a space on Ann until the memory of these Anagrams drew him away. If he could see Coote that evening he might, he thought, be able to arrange some sort of connivance about the Anagrams, and his mind was chiefly busy sketching proposals for such an arrangement. It would not, of course, be ungentlemanly cheating, but only a little mystification. Coote very probably might drop him a hint of the solution of one or two of the things, not enough to win a prize, but enough to cover his shame. Or failing that he might take a humorous, quizzical line and pretend he was pretending to be very stupid. There were plenty of ways out of it if one kept a sharp lookout. . . .

The costume Kipps wore to the Anagram Tea was designed as a compromise between the strict letter of high fashion and seaside laxity, a sort of easy, semi-state for afternoon. Helen's first reproof had always lingered in his mind. He wore a frock coat, but mitigated it by a Panama hat of romantic shape with a black band, grey gloves, but for relaxation brown button boots. The only other man besides the clergy present, a new doctor with an attractive wife, was in full afternoon dress. Coote was not there.

Kipps was a little pale, but quite self-possessed, as he approached Mrs. Bindon Botting's door. He took a turn while some people went in and then faced it manfully. The door opened and revealed—Ann!

In the background through a draped doorway behind a big fern in a great art pot the elder Miss Botting was visible talking to two guests; the auditory background was a froth of feminine voices. . . .

Our two young people were much too amazed to give one another any formula of greeting, though they had parted warmly enough. Each was already in a state of extreme tension to meet the demands of this great and unprecedented occasion of an Anagram Tea. "Lor'!" said Ann, her sole remark, and then the sense of Miss Botting's eye ruled her straight again. She became very pale, but she took his hat mechanically, and he was already removing his gloves. "Ann," he said in a low tone, and then "Fency!" The eldest Miss Botting knew Kipps was the sort of guest who requires nursing, and she came forward vocalising charm. She said it was "Awfully jolly of him to come, awfully jolly. It was awfully difficult to get any good men!"

She handed Kipps forward, mumbling in a dazed condition, to the drawing-room, and there he encountered Helen looking unfamiliar in an unfamiliar hat. It was as if he had not met her for years.

She astonished him. She didn't seem to mind in the least his going to London. She held out a shapely hand, and smiled encouragingly. "You've faced the anagrams?" she said.

The second Miss Botting accosted them, a number of oblong pieces of paper in her hand, mysteriously inscribed. "Take an anagram," she said; "take an anagram," and boldly pinned one of these brief documents to Kipps' lapel. The letters were "Cypshi," and Kipps from the very beginning suspected this was an anagram for Cuyps. She also left a thing like a long dance programme, from which dangled a little pencil in his hand. He found himself being introduced to people, and then he was in a corner with the short lady in a big bonnet, who was pelting him with gritty little bits of small talk that were gone before you could take hold of them and reply. "Very hot," said this lady. "Very hot, indeed—hot all the summer—remarkable year—all the years remarkable now—don't know what we're coming to—don't you think so, Mr. Kipps?"

"Oo rather," said Kipps, and wondered if Ann was still in the hall. Ann!

He ought not to have stared at her like a stuck fish and pretended not to know her. That couldn't be right. But what *was* right?

The lady in the big bonnet proceeded to a second discharge. "Hope you're fond of anagrams, Mr. Kipps—difficult exercise—still one must do something to bring people together—better than Ludo anyhow. Don't you think so, Mr. Kipps?"

Ann fluttered past the open door. Her eyes met his in amazed enquiry. Something had got dislocated in the world for both of them. . . .

He ought to have told her he was engaged. He ought to have explained things to her. Perhaps even now he might be able to drop her a hint.

"Don't you think so, Mr. Kipps?"

"Oo rather," said Kipps for the third time.

A lady with a tired smile, who was labelled conspicuously "Wogdelenk," drifted towards Kipps' interlocutor and the two fell into conversation. Kipps found himself socially aground. He looked about him. Helen was talking to a curate and laughing. Kipps was overcome by a vague desire to speak to Ann. He was for sidling doorward.

"What are *you,* please?" said an extraordinarily bold, tall girl, and arrested him while she took down "Cypshi."

"I'm sure I don't know what it means," she explained. "I'm Sir Bubh. Don't you think anagrams are something chronic?"

Kipps made stockish noises, and the young lady suddenly became the nucleus of a party of excited friends who were forming a syndicate to guess, and barred his escape. She took no further notice of him. He found himself jammed against an occasional table and listening to the conversation of Mrs. "Wogdelenk" and his lady with the big bonnet.

"She packed her two beauties off together," said the lady in the big bonnet. "Time enough, too. Don't think much of this girl; she's got as housemaid now. Pretty, of course, but there's no occasion for a housemaid to be pretty— none whatever. And she doesn't look particularly up to her work either. Kind of 'mazed expression."

"You never can tell," said the lady labelled "Wogdelenk;" "you never can tell. My wretches are big enough, Heaven knows, and do they work? Not a bit of it! . . ."

Kipps felt dreadfully out of it with regard to all these people, and dreadfully in it with Ann.

He scanned the back of the big bonnet and concluded it was an extremely ugly bonnet indeed. It got jerking forward as each short, dry sentence was snapped off at the end and a plume of osprey on it jerked excessively. "She hasn't guessed even one!" followed by a shriek of girlish merriment, came from the group about the tall, bold girl. They'd shriek at him presently, perhaps. Beyond thinking his own anagram might be Cuyps, he hadn't a notion. What a chatter they were all making! It was just like a summer sale! Just the sort of people who'd give a lot of trouble and swap you! And suddenly the smouldering fires of rebellion leapt to flame again. These were a rotten lot of people, and the anagrams were rotten nonsense, and he, Kipps, had been a rotten fool to come. There was Helen away there, still laughing, with her curate. Pity she couldn't marry a curate and leave him (Kipps) alone! Then he'd know what to do. He disliked the whole gathering collectively and in detail. Why were they all trying to make him one of themselves? He perceived unexpected ugliness everywhere about him. There were two great pins jabbed through the tall girl's hat, and the swirls of her hair below the brim with the minutest piece of tape tie-up showing did not repay close examination. Mrs. "Wogdelenk" wore a sort of mumps bandage of lace, and there was another lady perfectly dazzling with beads, and jewels and bits of trimming. They were all flaps and angles and flounces—these women. Not one of them looked as neat and decent a shape as Ann's clean, trim, little figure. Echoes of Masterman woke up in him again. Ladies indeed! Here were all these chattering people, with money, with leisure, with every chance in the world, and all they could do was to crowd like this into a couple of rooms and jabber nonsense about anagrams.

"Could Cypshi really mean Cuyps?" floated like a dissolving wreath of mist across his mind.

Abruptly resolution stood armed in his heart. He was going to get out of this!

" 'Scuse me," he said, and began to wade neck deep through the bubbling tea party.

He was going to get out of it all!

He found himself close by Helen. "I'm orf," he said, but she gave him the briefest glance. She did not appear to hear him. "Still, Mr. Spratlingdown, you *must* admit there's a limit even to conformity," she was saying. . . .

He was in a curtained archway, and Ann was before him carrying a tray supporting several small sugar bowls.

He was moved to speech. *"What* a Lot!" he said, and then mysteriously, "I'm engaged to *her."* He indicated Helen's new hat, and became aware of a skirt he had stepped upon.

Ann stared at him helplessly, borne past in the grip of incomprehensible imperatives.

Why shouldn't they talk together?

He was in a small room, and then at the foot of the staircase in the hall. He heard the rustle of a dress, and what was conceivable his hostess was upon him.

"But you're not going, Mr. Kipps?" she said.

"I must," he said; "I got to."

"But, Mr. Kipps!"

"I must," he said. "I'm not well."

"But before the guessing! Without any tea!"

Ann appeared and hovered behind him.

"I got to go," said Kipps.

If he parleyed with her Helen might awake to his desperate attempt.

"Of course if you *must* go."

"It's something I've forgotten," said Kipps, beginning to feel regrets. "Reely I must."

Mrs. Botting turned with a certain offended dignity, and

Ann in a state of flushed calm that evidently concealed much
came forward to open the door.

"I'm very sorry," he said; "I'm very sorry," half to his
hostess and half to her, and was swept past her by superior
social forces—like a drowning man in a mill-race—and into
the Upper Sandgate Road. He half turned upon the step,
and then slam went the door. . . .

He retreated along the Leas, a thing of shame and perplexity—Mrs. Botting's aggrieved astonishment uppermost
in his mind. . . .

Something—reinforced by the glances of the people he
was passing—pressed its way to his attention through the
tumultuous disorder of his mind.

He became aware that he was still wearing his little
placard with the letters "Cypshi."

"Desh it!" he said, clutching off this abomination. In another moment its several letters, their task accomplished,
were scattering gleefully before the breeze down the front
of the Leas.

2

Kipps was dressed for Mrs. Wace's dinner half an hour
before it was time to start, and he sat waiting until Coote
should come to take him around. "Manners and Rules of
Good Society" lay before him neglected. He had read the
polished prose of the Member of the Aristocracy, on page
96, as far as—

> "the acceptance of an invitation is in the eyes of
> "diners out, a binding obligation which only ill-
> "health, family bereavement, or some all-important
> "reason justifies its being set on one side or other-
> "wise evaded"—

and then he had lapsed into gloomy thoughts.

That afternoon he had had a serious talk with Helen.

He had tried to express something of the change of heart
that had happened to him. But to broach the real state of
the matter had been altogether too terrible for him. He had
sought a minor issue. "I don't like all this Society," he had
said.

"But you must *see* people," said Helen.

"Yes, but——. It's the sort of people you see." He nerved himself. "I didn't think much of that lot at the Enegram Tea."

"You have to see all sorts of people if you want to see the world," said Helen.

Kipps was silent for a space and a little short of breath.

"My dear Arthur," she began, almost kindly, "I shouldn't ask you to go to these affairs if I didn't think it good for you, should I?"

Kipps acquiesced in silence.

"You will find the benefit of it all when we get to London. You learn to swim in a tank before you go out into the sea. These people here are good enough to learn upon. They're stiff and rather silly and dreadfully narrow and not an idea in a dozen of them, but it really doesn't matter at all. You'll soon get Savoir Faire."

He made to speak again, and found his powers of verbal expression lacking. Instead he blew a sigh.

"You'll get used to it all very soon," said Helen helpfully. . . .

As he sat meditating over that interview and over the vistas of London that opened before him, on the little flat, and teas and occasions and the constant presence of Brudderkins and all the bright prospect of his new and better life, and how he would never see Ann any more, the housemaid entered with a little package, a small, square envelope to "Arthur Kipps, Esquire."

"A young woman left this, Sir," said the housemaid, a little severely.

"Eh?" said Kipps; "what young woman?" and then suddenly began to understand.

"She looked an ordinary young woman," said the housemaid coldly.

"Ah!" said Kipps. *"That's* orlright."

He waited till the door had closed behind the girl, staring at the envelope in his hand, and then, with a curious feeling of increasing tension, tore it open. As he did so, some quicker sense than sight or touch told him its contents. It was Ann's half sixpence. And, besides, not a word!

Then she must have heard him——!

She had kept the half sixpence all these years!

He was standing with the envelope in his hand, trying to get on from that last inference, when Coote became audible without.

Coote appeared in evening dress, a clean and radiant Coote, with large, greenish, white gloves and a particularly large white tie, edged with black. "For a third cousin," he presently explained. "Nace, isn't it?" He could see Kipps was pale and disturbed and put this down to the approaching social trial. "You keep your nerve up, Kipps, my dear chap, and you'll be all right," said Coote, with a big, brotherly glove on Kipps' sleeve.

3

The dinner came to a crisis so far as Kipps' emotions were concerned, with Mrs. Bindon Botting's talk about servants, but before that there had been several things of greater or smaller magnitude to perturb and disarrange his social front. One little matter that was mildly insurgent throughout the entire meal was, if I may be permitted to mention so intimate a matter, the behaviour of his left brace. The webbing—which was of a cheerful scarlet silk—had slipped away from its buckle, fastened no doubt in agitation, and had developed a strong tendency to place itself obliquely in the manner rather of an official decoration, athwart his spotless front. It first asserted itself before they went in to dinner. He replaced this ornament by a dexterous thrust when no one was looking and thereafter the suppression of his novel innovation upon the stereotyped sombreness of evening dress became a standing preoccupation. On the whole, he was inclined to think his first horror excessive; at any rate no one remarked upon it. However you imagine him constantly throughout the evening, with one eye and one hand, whatever the rest of him might be doing, predominantly concerned with the weak corner.

But this, I say, was a little matter. What exercised him much more was to discover Helen quite terribly in evening dress.

The young lady had let her imagination rove Londonward, and this costume was perhaps an anticipation of that clever little flat not too far west which was to become the centre of so delightful a literary and artistic set. It was, of all the feminine costumes present, most distinctly an evening dress. One was advised Miss Walshingham had arms and shoulders of a type by no means despicable, one was advised Miss Walshingham was capable not only of dignity but charm, even a certain glow of charm. It was, you know, her first evening dress, a tribute paid by Walshingham finance to her brightening future. Had she wanted keeping in countenance, she would have had to have fallen back upon her hostess, who was resplendent in black and steel. The other ladies had to a certain extent compromised. Mrs. Walshingham had dressed with just a refined, little V and Mrs. Bindon Botting, except for her dear mottled arms, confided scarcely more of her plump charm to the world. The elder Miss Botting stopped short of shoulders, and so did Miss Wace. But Helen didn't. She was—had Kipps had eyes to see it—a quite beautiful human figure; she knew it and she met him with a radiant smile that had forgotten all the little difference of the afternoon. But to Kipps her appearance was the last release. With that, she had become as remote, as foreign, as incredible as a wife and mate, as though the Cnidian Venus herself, in all her simple elegance, was, before witnesses, declared to be his. If, indeed, she had ever been credible as a wife and mate.

She ascribed his confusion to modest reverence, and having blazed smiling upon him for a moment turned a shapely shoulder towards him and exchanged a remark with Mrs. Bindon Botting. Ann's poor little half sixpence came against Kipps' fingers in his pocket and he clutched at it suddenly as though it was a talisman. Then he abandoned it to suppress his Order of the Brace. He was affected by a cough. "Miss Wace tells me Mr. Revel is coming," Mrs. Botting was saying.

"Isn't it delightful?" said Helen. "We saw him last night. He's stopped on his way to Paris. He's going to meet his wife there."

Kipps' eyes rested for a moment on Helen's dazzling deltoid, and then went enquiringly, accusingly almost to Coote's face. Where, in the presence of this terrible emergency, was the gospel of suppression now—that Furtive treatment of Religion and Politics, and Birth and Death and Bathing and Babies, and "all those things" which constitutes your True Gentleman? He had been too modest even to discuss this question with his Mentor, but surely, surely this quintessence of all that is good and nice could regard these unsolicited confidences only in one way. With something between relief and the confirmation of his worst fears he perceived, by a sort of twitching of the exceptionally abundant muscles about Coote's lower jaw, in a certain deliberate avoidance of one particular direction by these pale, but resolute, grey eyes, by the almost convulsive grip of the ample, greenish white gloves behind him, a grip broken at times for controlling pats at the black-bordered tie and the back of that spacious head, and by a slight but increasing disposition to cough, that *Coote did not approve!*

To Kipps Helen had once supplied a delicately beautiful dream, a thing of romance and unsubstantial mystery. But this was her final materialisation, and the last thin wreath of glamour about her was dispelled. In some way (he had forgotten how and it was perfectly incomprehensible) he was bound to this dark, solid and determined young person whose shadow and suggestion he had once loved. He had to go through with the thing as a gentleman should. Still——

And when he was sacrificing Ann!

He wouldn't stand this sort of thing, whatever else he stood. . . . Should he say something about her dress to her—to-morrow?

He could put his foot down firmly. He could say, "Look 'ere. I don't care. I ain't going to stand it. See?"

She'd say something unexpected, of course. She always did say something unexpected.

Suppose for once he overrode what she said? Simply repeated his point?

He found these thoughts battling with certain conversational aggressions from Mrs. Wace, and then Revel arrived and took the centre of the stage.

The author of that brilliant romance, "Red Hearts a-Beating," was a less imposing man than Kipps had anticipated, but he speedily effaced that disappointment by his predominating manners. Although he lived habitually in the vivid world of London, his collar and tie were in no way remarkable, and he was neither brilliantly handsome nor curly nor long-haired. His personal appearance suggested

arm chairs, rather than the equestrian exercises and amorous toyings and passionate intensities of his masterpiece; he
was inclined to be fat, with whitish flesh, muddy coloured
straight hair, he had a rather shapeless and truncated nose
and his chin was asymmetrical. One eye was more inclined to stare than the other. He might have been esteemed a little undistinguished looking were it not for his
beeswaxed moustache, which came amidst his features with
a pleasing note of incongruity, and the whimsical wrinkles
above and about his greater eye. His regard sought and
found Helen's as he entered the room and they shook
hands presently with an air of intimacy Kipps, for no clear
reason, found objectionable. He saw them clasp their hands,
heard Coote's characteristic cough—a sound rather more
like a very, very old sheep, a quarter of a mile away, being
blown to pieces by a small charge of gunpowder than anything else in the world—did some confused beginnings of a
thought, and then they were all going in to dinner and
Helen's shining bare arm lay along his sleeve. Kipps was in
no state for conversation. She glanced at him, and, though
he did not know it, very slightly pressed his elbow. He
struggled with strange respiratory dislocations. Before them
went Coote, discoursing in amiable reverberations to Mrs.
Walshingham, and at the head of the procession was Mrs.
Bindon Botting talking fast and brightly beside the erect
military figure of little Mr. Wace. (He was not a soldier
really, but he had caught a martinet bearing by living
so close to Shorncliffe.) Revel came last, in charge of
Mrs. Wace's queenly black and steel, politely admiring in a
flute-like cultivated voice the mellow wall paper of the staircase. Kipps marvelled at everybody's self-possession.

From the earliest spoonful of soup it became evident
that Revel considered himself responsible for the table talk.
And before the soup was over it was almost as manifest
that Mrs. Bindon Botting inclined to consider his sense of
responsibility excessive. In her circle Mrs. Bindon Botting
was esteemed an agreeable rattle, her manner and appearance were conspicuously vivacious for one so plump, and she
had an almost Irish facility for humourous description. She
would keep people amused all through an afternoon call,
with the story of how her jobbing gardener had got himself
married and what his home was like, or how her favourite

butt, Mr. Stigson Warder, had all his unfortunate children taught almost every conceivable instrument because they had the phrenological bump of music abnormally large. "They got to trombones, my dear!" she would say, with her voice coming to a climax. Usually her friends conspired to draw her out, but on this occasion they neglected to do so, a thing that militated against her keen desire to shine in Revel's eyes. After a time she perceived that the only thing for her to do was to cut in on the talk, on her own account, and this she began to do. She made several ineffectual snatches at the general attention and then Revel drifted towards a topic she regarded as particularly her own, the ordering of households.

They came to the thing through talk about localities. "We are leaving our house in The Boltons," said Revel, "and taking a little place at Wimbledon, and I think of having rooms in Dane's Inn. It will be more convenient in many ways. My wife is furiously addicted to golf and exercise of all sorts, and I like to sit about in clubs—I haven't the strength necessary for these hygienic proceedings—and the old arrangement suited neither of us. And, besides, no one could imagine the demoralisation the domestics of West London have undergone during the last three years."

"It's the same everywhere," said Mrs. Bindon Botting.

"Very possibly it is. A friend of mine calls it the servile tradition in decay and regards it all as a most hopeful phenomenon——"

"He ought to have had my last two criminals," said Mrs. Bindon Botting.

She turned to Mrs. Wace while Revel came again a little too late with a "Possibly——"

"And I haven't told you, my dear," she said, speaking with voluble rapidity, "I'm in trouble again."

"The last girl?"

"The last girl. Before I can get a cook, my hard won housemaid"—she paused—"chucks it."

"Panic?" asked young Walshingham.

"Mysterious grief! Everything merry as a marriage bell until my Anagram Tea! Then in the evening a portentous rigour of bearing, a word or so from my Aunt, and immediately—Floods of Tears and Notice!" For a moment her eye rested thoughtfully on Kipps, as she said: "Is there anything heartrending about Anagrams?"

"I find them so," said Revel. "I——"

But Mrs. Bindon Botting got away again. "For a time it made me quite uneasy——"

Kipps jabbed his lip with his fork rather painfully, and was recalled from a fascinated glare at Mrs. Botting to the immediate facts of dinner.

"——whether anagrams might not have offended the good domestic's Moral Code—you never can tell. We made enquiries. No. No. No. She *must* go and that's all!"

"One perceives," said Revel, "in these disorders, dimly and distantly, the last dying glow of the age of Romance. Let us suppose, Mrs. Botting, let us at least try to suppose—it is Love."

Kipps clattered with his knife and fork.

"It's love," said Mrs. Botting; "what else can it be? Beneath the orderly humdrum of our lives these romances are going on, until at last they bust up and give Notice and upset our humdrum altogether. Some fatal, wonderful soldier——"

"The passions of the common or house domestic," said Revel, and recovered possession of the table.

Upon the troubled disorder of Kipps' table manners there had supervented a quietness, an unusual calm. For once in his life he had distinctly made up his mind on his own account. He listened no more to Revel. He put down his knife and fork and refused anything that followed. Coote regarded him with tactful concern and Helen flushed a little.

4

About half-past nine that night came a violent pull at the bell of Mrs. Bindon Botting, and a young man in a dress suit, a gibus and other marks of exalted social position stood without. Athwart his white expanse of breast lay a ruddy bar of patterned silk that gave him a singular distinction and minimised the glow of a few small stains of burgundy. His gibus was thrust back and exposed a disorder of hair that suggested a reckless desperation. He had, in fact, burnt his boats and refused to join the ladies. Coote, in the subsequent conversation, had protested quietly, "You're going on all right, you know," to which Kipps had answered he didn't care a "Eng" about that, and so, after a brief tussel with Walshingham's detaining arm, had got away. "I got something to do," he said. " 'Ome." And here he was—panting an extraordinary resolve. The door opened, revealing the pleasantly furnished hall of Mrs. Bindon Botting, lit by rose-tinted lights, and in the centre of the picture, neat and pretty in black and white, stood Ann. At the sight of Kipps her colour vanished.

"Ann," said Kipps, "I want to speak to you. I got something to say to you right away. See? I'm——"

"This ain't the door to speak to me at," said Ann.

"But, Ann! It's something special."

"You spoke enough," said Ann.

"Ann!"

"Besides. That's my door, down there. Basement. If I was caught talking at *this* door——!"

"But, Ann, *I'm*——"

"Basement after nine. Them's my hours. I'm a servant and likely to keep one. If you're calling here, what name please? But you got your friends and I got mine and you mustn't go talking to *me*."

"But, Ann, I want to ask you——"

Someone appeared in the hall behind Ann. "Not here," said Ann. "Don't know anyone of that name," and incontinently slammed the door in his face.

"What was that, Ann?" said Mrs. Bindon Botting's invalid Aunt.

"Ge'm a little intoxicated, Ma'am—asking for the wrong name, Ma'am."

"What name did he want?" asked the lady, doubtfully.

"No name that *we* know, Ma'am," said Ann, hustling along the hall towards the kitchen stairs.

"I hope you weren't too short with him, Ann."

"No shorter than he deserved, considering 'ow he be'aved," said Ann, with her bosom heaving.

And Mrs. Bindon Botting's invalid Aunt, perceiving suddenly that this call had some relation to Ann's private and sentimental trouble, turned, after one moment of hesitating scrutiny, away.

She was an extremely sympathetic lady, was Mrs. Bindon

Botting's invalid Aunt; she took an interest in the servants, imposed piety, extorted confessions and followed human nature, blushing and lying defensively, to its reluctantly revealed recesses, but Ann's sense of privacy was strong and her manner under drawing out and encouragement, sometimes even alarming. . . .

So the poor old lady went upstairs again.

5

The basement door opened and Kipps came into the kitchen. He was flushed and panting.

He struggled for speech.

" 'Ere," he said, and held out two half sixpences.

Ann stood behind the kitchen table—face pale and eyes round, and now—and it simplified Kipps very much—he could see she had indeed been crying.

"Well?" she said.

"Don't you see?"

Ann moved her head slightly.

"I kep' it all these years."

"You kep' it too long."

His mouth closed and his flush died away. He looked at her. The amulet, it seemed, had failed to work.

"Ann!" he said.

"Well?"

"Ann."

The conversation still hung fire.

"Ann," he said, made a movement with his hands that suggested appeal, and advanced a step.

Ann shook her head more defiantly, and became defensive.

"Look here, Ann," said Kipps. "I been a fool."

They stared into each other's miserable eyes.

"Ann," he said. "I want to marry you."

Ann clutched the table edge. "You can't," she said faintly.

He made as if to approach her around the table, and she took a step that restored their distance.

"I must," he said.

"You can't."

"I must. You *got* to marry me, Ann."

"You can't go marrying everybody. You got to marry 'er."

"I shan't."

Ann shook her head. "You're engaged to that girl. Lady, rather. You can't be engaged to me."

"I don't want to be engaged to you. I *been* engaged. I want to be married to you. See? Right away."

Ann turned a shade paler. "But what d'you mean?" she asked.

"Come right off to London and marry me. Now."

"What d'you mean?"

Kipps became extremely lucid and earnest.

"I mean come right off and marry me now before anyone else can. See?"

"In London?"

"In London."

They stared at one another again. They took things for granted in the most amazing way.

"I couldn't," said Ann. "For one thing my month's not up for mor'n free weeks yet."

They hung before that for a moment as though it was insurmountable.

"Look 'ere, Ann! Arst to go. Arst to go!"

"*She* wouldn't," said Ann.

"Then come without arsting," said Kipps.

"She's keep my box——"

"She won't."

"She will."

"She won't."

"You don't know 'er."

"Well, desh 'er—let 'er! LET 'ER! Who cares? I'll buy you a 'undred boxes if you'll come."

"It wouldn't be right towards Her."

"It isn't Her you got to think about, Ann. It's me."

"And you 'aven't treated me properly," she said. "You 'aven't treated me properly, Artie. You didn't ought to 'ave——"

"I didn't say I '*ad*," he interrupted, "did I, Ann?" he appealed. "I didn't come to arguefy. I'm all wrong. I never said I wasn't. It's yes or no. Me or not. . . . I been a fool. There! See? I been a fool. Ain't that enough? I got myself all tied up with everyone and made a fool of myself all around. . . ."

He pleaded, "It isn't as if we didn't care for one another, Ann."

She seemed impassive and he resumed his discourse.

"I thought I wasn't likely ever to see you again, Ann. I reely did. It isn't as though I was seein' you all the time. I didn't know what I wanted, and I went and be'aved like a fool—jest as anyone might. I know what I want and I know what I don't want now.

"Ann!"

"Well?"

"Will you come? . . . Will you come? . . ."

Silence.

"If you don't answer me, Ann—I'm desprit—if you don't answer me now, if you don't say you'll come I'll go right out now——"

He turned doorward passionately as he spoke, with his threat incomplete.

"I'll go," he said; "I 'aven't a friend in the world! I been and throwed everything away. I don't know why I done things and why I 'aven't. All I know is I can't stand nothing in the world any more." He choked. "The pier," he said.

He fumbled with the door latch, grumbling some inarticulate self-pity, as if he sought a handle, and then he had it open.

Clearly he was going.

"Artie!" said Ann, sharply.

He turned about and the two hung, white and tense.

"I'll do it," said Ann.

His face began to work, he shut the door and came a step back to her, staring; his face became pitiful and then suddenly they moved together. "Artie!" she cried, "don't go!" and held out her arms, weeping.

They clung close to one another. . . .

"Oh! I *been* so mis'bel," cried Kipps, clinging to this lifebuoy, and suddenly his emotion, having no further serious work in hand, burst its way to a loud *boohoo*! His fashionable and expensive gibus flopped off and fell and rolled and lay neglected on the floor.

"I been so mis'bel," said Kipps, giving himself vent. "Oh! I *been* so mis'bel, Ann."

"Be quiet," said Ann, holding his poor, blubbering head

tightly to her heaving shoulder, and herself all a-quiver; "be quiet. She's there! Listenin'. She'll 'ear you, Artie, on the stairs. . . ."

6

Ann's last words when, an hour later, they parted, Mrs. and Miss Bindon Botting having returned very audibly upstairs, deserve a section to themselves.

"I wouldn't do this for everyone, mind you," whispered Ann.

IX. THE LABYRINTHODON

1

You imagine them fleeing through our complex and difficult social system, as it were, for life, first on foot and severally to the Folkestone Central Station; then in a first-class carriage, with Kipps' bag as sole chaperone to Charing Cross, and then in a four-wheeler, a long, rumbling, palpitating, slow flight through the multitudinous swarming London streets to Sid. Kipps kept peeping out of the window. "It's the next corner after this, I believe," he would say. For he had a sort of feeling that at Sid's he would be immune from the hottest pursuits. He paid the cabman in a manner adequate to the occasion and turned to his prospective brother-in-law. "Me and Ann," he said, "we're going to marry."

"But I thought——" began Sid.

Kipps motioned him towards explanations in the shop. . . .

"It's no good, my arguing with you," said Sid, smiling delightedly as the case unfolded. "You done it now." And Masterman being apprised of the nature of the affair descended slowly in a state of flushed congratulation.

"I thought you might find the Higher Life a bit difficult," said Masterman, projecting a bony hand. "But I never thought you'd have the originality to clear out. . . . Won't the young lady of the superior classes swear! Never mind—it doesn't matter anyhow.

"You were starting a climb," he said at dinner, "that doesn't lead anywhere. You would have clambered from one refinement of vulgarity to another and never got to any satisfactory top. There isn't a top. It's a squirrel's cage. Things are out of joint, and the only top there is is a lot of blazing card playing women and betting men—you should read Modern Society—seasoned with archbishops and officials and all that sort of glossy, pandering Bosh. . . . You'd have hung on, a disconsolate, dismal, little figure, somewhere up the ladder, far below even the motor-car class, while your wife larked about—or fretted because she wasn't a bit higher than she was. . . . I found it all out long ago. I've seen women of that sort. And I don't climb any more."

"I often thought about what you said last time I saw you," said Kipps.

"I wonder what I said," said Masterman in parenthesis. "Anyhow, you're doing the right and sane thing, and that's a rare spectacle. You're going to marry your equal, and you're going to take your own line, quite independently of what people up there, or people down there, think you ought or ought not to do. That's about the only course one can take nowadays with everything getting more muddled and upside down every day. Make your own little world and your own house first of all, keep that right side up whatever you do, and marry your mate. . . . That, I suppose, is what *I* should do—if *I* had a mate. . . . But people of my sort, luckily for the world, don't get made in pairs. No!

"Besides——! However——" And abruptly, taking advantage of an interruption by Master Walt, he lapsed into thought.

Presently he came out of his musings.

"After all," he said, "there's hope."

"What about?" said Sid.

"Everything," said Masterman.

"Where there's life there's hope," said Mrs. Sid. "But none of you aren't eating anything like you ought to."

Masterman lifted his glass.

"Here's to Hope!" he said, "The Light of the World!"

Sid beamed at Kipps as who should say, "You don't meet a character like *this* every dinner time."

"Here's to Hope," repeated Masterman. "The best thing one can have. Hope of life—yes."

He imposed his movement of magnificent self-pity on them all. Even young Walt was impressed.

They spent the days before their marriage in a number of agreeable excursions together. One day they went to Kew by steamboat, and admired the house full of paintings of flowers extremely; and one day they went early to have a good, long day at the Crystal Palace, and enjoyed them-

selves very much indeed. They got there so early that nothing was open inside, all the stalls were wrappered up and
all the minor exhibitions locked and barred; they seemed
the minutest creatures even to themselves in that enormous
empty aisle and their echoing footsteps indecently loud.
They contemplated realistic groups of plaster savages, and
Ann thought they'd be queer people to have about. She
was glad there were none in this country. They meditated
upon replicas of classical statuary without excessive comment. Kipps said at large, it must have been a queer world
then, but Ann very properly doubted if they really went
about like that. But the place at that early hour was really
lonely. One began to fancy things. So they went out into the
October sunshine of the mighty terraces, and wandered
amidst miles of stucco tanks and about those quiet Gargan-
tuan grounds. A great, grey emptiness it was, and it seemed
marvellous to them, but not nearly so marvellous as it might
have seemed. "I never see a finer place, never," said Kipps,
turning to survey the entirety of the enormous glass front
with Paxton's vast image in the centre.

"What it must 'ave cost to build!" said Ann, and left
her sentence eloquently incomplete.

Presently they came to a region of caves and waterways,
and amidst these waterways strange reminders of the possibilities of the Creator. They passed under an arch made
of a whale's jaws, and discovered amidst herbage, as if they
were browsing or standing unoccupied and staring as if
amazed at themselves, huge effigies of iguanodons and deino-
theria and mastodons and suchlike cattle, gloriously done in
green and gold.

"They got everything," said Kipps. "Earl's Court isn't a
patch on it."

His mind was very greatly exercised by these monsters, and
he hovered about them and returned to them. "You'd wonder
'ow they ever got enough to eat," he said several times.

2

It was later in the day, and upon a seat in the presence
of the green and gold Labyrinthodon that looms so splendidly above the lake, that the Kippses fell into talk about
their future. They had made a sufficient lunch in the pal-

ace, they had seen pictures and no end of remarkable things, and that and the amber sunlight made a mood for them, quiet and philosophical, a heaven mood. Kipps broke a contemplative silence with an abrupt illusion to one principal preoccupation. "I shall offer an 'pology and I shall offer 'er brother damages. If she likes to bring an action for Breach after that, well—I done all I can. . . . They can't get much out of reading my letters in court, because I didn't write none. I dessay a thousan' or two'll settle all that, anyhow. I ain't much worried about that. That don't worry me very much, Ann—No."

And then, "It's a lark, our marrying. It's curious 'ow things come about. If I 'adn't run against you, where should I 'ave been now. Eh? . . . Even after we met, I didn't seem to see it like—not marrying you I mean—until that night I came. I didn't—reely."

"I didn't neither," said Ann, with thoughtful eyes on the water.

For a time Kipps' mind was occupied by the prettiness of her thinking face. A faint, tremulous network of lights reflected from the ripples of a passing duck, played subtly over her cheek and faded away.

Ann reflected. "I s'pose things 'ad to be," she said.

Kipps mused. "It's curious 'ow ever I got on to be engaged to 'er."

"She wasn't suited to you," said Ann.

"Suited. No fear! That's jest it. 'Ow did it come about?"

"I expect she led you on," said Ann.

Kipps was half-minded to assent. Then he had a twinge of conscience. "It wasn't that, Ann," he said. "It's curious. I don't know what it was, but it wasn't that. I don't recollect. . . No. . . Life's jolly rum; that's one thing any'ow. And I suppose I'm a rum sort of feller. I get excited sometimes, and then I don't seem to care *what* I do. That's about what it was reely. Still——"

They meditated, Kipps with his arms folded and pulling at his scanty moustache. Presently a faint smile came over his face.

"We'll get a nice little 'ouse out Ithe way."

"It's 'omelier than Folkestone," said Ann.

"Jest a nice *little* 'ouse," said Kipps. There's Hughenden, of course. But that's let. Besides being miles too big. And I wouldn't live in Folkestone again some'ow—not for anything."

"I'd like to 'ave a 'ouse of my own," said Ann. "I've often thought, being in service, 'ow much I'd like to manage a 'ouse of my own."

"You'd know all about what the servants was up to, anyhow," said Kipps, amused.

"Servants! We don't want no servants," said Ann, startled.

"You'll 'ave to 'ave a servant," said Kipps. "If it's only to do the 'eavy work of the 'ouse."

"What! and not be able 'ardly to go into my own kitchen?" said Ann.

"You ought to 'ave a servant," said Kipps.

"One could easy 'ave a woman in for anything that's 'eavy," said Ann. "Besides—— If I 'ad one of the girls one sees about nowadays I should want to be taking the broom out of 'er 'and and do it all over myself. I'd manage better without 'er."

"We ought to 'ave one servant anyhow," said Kipps, "else 'ow should we manage if we wanted to go out together or anything like that?"

"I might get a *young* girl," said Ann, "and bring 'er up in my own way."

Kipps left the matter at that and came back to the house.

"There's little 'ouses going into Hythe, just the sort we want, not too big and not too small. We'll 'ave a kitching and a dining-room and a little room to sit in of a night."

"It mustn't be a 'ouse with a basement," said Ann.

"What's a basement?"

"It's a downstairs, where there's not arf enough light and everything got to be carried—up and down, up and down, all day—coals and everything. And it's got to 'ave a watertap and sink and things upstairs. You'd 'ardly believe, Artie, if you 'adn't been in service, 'ow cruel and silly some 'ouses are built—you'd think they 'ad a spite against servants the way the stairs are made."

"We won't 'ave one of that sort," said Kipps. . .

"We'll 'ave a quiet little life. Now go out a bit—now come 'ome again. Read a book perhaps if we got nothing else to do. 'Ave old Buggins in for an evening at times. 'Ave

Sid down. There's bicycles——"

"I don't fancy myself on a bicycle," said Ann.

"'Ave a trailer," said Kipps, "and sit like a lady. I'd take you out to New Romney easy as anything jest to see the old people."

"I wouldn't mind that," said Ann.

"We'll jest 'ave a sensible little 'ouse, and sensible things. No art or anything of that sort, nothing stuck-up or anything, but jest sensible. We'll be as right as anything, Ann."

"No socialism," said Ann, starting a lurking doubt.

"No socialism," said Kipps; "just sensible, that's all."

"I dessay it's all right for them that understand it, Artie, but I don't agree with this socialism."

"I don't neither, reely," said Kipps. "I can't argue about it, but it don't seem real like to me. All the same Masterman's a clever fellow, Ann."

"I didn't like 'im at first, Artie, but I do now—in a way. You don't understand 'im all at once."

"'E's so clever," said Kipps. "Arf the time I can't make out what 'e's up to. 'E's the cleverest chap I ever met. I never 'eard such talking. 'E ought to write a book. . . . It's a rum world, Ann, when a chap like that isn't 'ardly able to earn a living."

"It's 'is 'ealth," said Ann.

"I expect it is," said Kipps, and ceased to talk for a little while.

Then he spoke with deliberation, "Sea air might be the saving of 'im, Ann."

He glanced doubtfully at Ann, and she was looking at him even fondly.

"You think of other people a lot," said Ann. "I been looking at you sittin' there and thinking."

"I suppose I do. I suppose when one's 'appy one does."

"*You* do," said Ann.

"We shall be 'appy in that little 'ouse, Ann. Don't y' think?"

She met his eyes and nodded.

"I seem to see it," said Kipps, "sort of cosy like. 'Bout tea time and muffins, kettle on the 'ob, cat on the 'earth-rug. We must get a cat, Ann, and *you* there. Eh?"

They regarded each other with appreciative eyes and

Kipps became irrelevant.

"I don't believe, Ann," he said, "I 'aven't kissed you not for 'arf an hour. Leastways not since we was in those caves."

For kissing had already ceased to be a matter of thrilling adventure for them.

Ann shook her head. "You be sensible and go on talking about Mr. Masterman," she said. . . .

But Kipps had wandered to something else. "I like the way your 'air turns back just there," he said, with an indicative finger. "It was like that, I remember, when you was a girl. Sort of wavy. I've often thought of it—— . . . 'Member when we raced that time—out be'ind the church?"

Then for a time they sat idly, each following out agreeable meditations.

"It's rum," said Kipps.

"What's rum?"

" 'Ow everything's 'appened," said Kipps. "Who'd 'ave thought of our being 'ere like this six weeks ago? . . . Who'd 'ave thought of my ever 'aving any money?"

His eyes went to the big Labyrinthodon. He looked first carelessly and then suddenly with a growing interest in its vast face.

"I'm deshed," he murmured. Ann became interested. He laid a hand on her arm and pointed. Ann scrutinised the Labyrinthodon and then came around to Kipps' face in mute interrogation.

"Don't you see it?" said Kipps.

"See what?"

" 'E's jest *like* old Coote."

"It's extinct," said Ann, not clearly apprehending.

"I dessay 'e is. But 'e's jest like old Coote all the same for that."

Kipps meditated on the monstrous shapes in sight. "I wonder 'ow all these old antediluvium animals *got* extinct," he asked. "No one couldn't possibly 'ave killed 'em."

"Why! *I* know that," said Ann. "They was overtook by the Flood. . . ."

Kipps meditated for a while. "But I thought they had to take two of everything there was——"

"Within reason they 'ad," said Ann. . . .

The Kippses left it at that.

The great green and gold Labyrinthodon took no notice of their conversation. It gazed with its wonderful eyes over their heads into the infinite—inflexibly calm. It might indeed have been Coote himself there, Coote, the unassuming, cutting them dead. . .

5

And in due course these two simple souls married, and Venus Urania, the Goddess of Wedded Love, the Goddess of Tolerant Kindliness or Meeting Half Way, to whom all young couples should pray and offer sacrifices of self, who is indeed a very great and noble and kindly goddess, was in some manner propitiated, and bent down and blessed them in their union.

END OF BOOK II.

BOOK THREE

KIPPSES

I. THE HOUSING PROBLEM

1

Honeymoons and all things come to an end, and you see at last Mr. and Mrs. Arthur Kipps descending upon the Hythe platform—coming to Hythe to find that nice *little* house—to realise that bright dream of a home they had first talked about in the grounds of the Crystal Palace. They are a valiant couple, you perceive, but small, and the world is a large incongruous system of complex and difficult things. Kipps wears a grey suit, with a wing-poke collar and a neat, smart tie. Mrs. Kipps is the same bright and healthy little girl woman you saw in the marsh; not an inch has been added to her stature in all my voluminous narrative. Only now she wears a hat.

It is a hat very unlike the hats she used to wear on her Sundays out, a flourishing hat with feathers and buckle and bows and things. The price of that hat would take many people's breath away—it cost two guineas! Kipps chose it. Kipps paid for it. They left the shop with flushed cheeks and smarting eyes, glad to be out of range of the condescending saleswoman.

"Artie," said Ann, "you didn't ought to 'ave——"

That was all. And you know, the hat didn't suit Ann a bit. Her clothes did not suit her at all. The simple, cheap, clean brightness of her former style had given place not only to this hat, but to several other things in the same key. And out from among these things looked her pretty face, the face of a wise little child—an artless wonder struggling through a preposterous dignity.

They had bought that hat one day when they had gone to see the shops in Bond Street. Kipps had looked at the passers-by and it had suddenly occurred to him that Ann was dowdy. He had noted the hat of a very proud-looking lady passing in an electric brougham and had resolved to get Ann the nearest thing to that.

The railway porters perceived some subtle incongruity in Ann, the knot of cabmen in the station doorway, the two golfers and the lady with daughters, who had also got out of the train. And Kipps, a little pale, blowing a little, not in complete possession of himself, knew that they noticed her and him. And Ann——. It is hard to say just what Ann observed of these things.

" 'Ere!" said Kipps to a cabman, and regretted too late a vanished "H."

"I got a trunk up there," he said to a ticket inspector, "marked A. K."

"Ask a porter," said the inspector, turning his back.

"Demn!" said Kipps, not altogether inaudibly.

2

It is all very well to sit in the sunshine and talk of the house you will have, and another altogether to achieve it. We English—all the world indeed to-day—live in a strange atmosphere of neglected great issues, of insistent, triumphant petty things, we are given up to the fine littlenesses of intercourse; table manners and small correctitudes are the substance of our lives. You do not escape these things for long even by so catastrophic a proceeding as flying to London with a young lady of no wealth and inferior social position. The mists of noble emotion swirl and pass and there you are divorced from all your deities and grazing in the meadows under the Argus eyes of the social system, the innumerable mean judgments you feel raining upon you, upon your clothes and bearing, upon your pretensions and movements.

Our world to-day is a meanly conceived one—it is only an added meanness to conceal that fact. For one consequence, it has very few nice little houses, such things do not come for the asking, they are not to be bought with money during ignoble times. Its houses are built on the ground of monstrously rich, shabbily extortionate landowners, by poor, parsimonious, greedy people in a mood of elbowing competition. What can you expect from such ridiculous conditions? To go househunting is to spy out the nakedness of this pretentious world, to see what our civilization amounts to when you take away curtains and flounces and carpets and all the fluster and distraction of people and fittings. It is to see mean plans meanly executed for mean ends, the conventions torn aside, the secrets stripped, the substance underlying all such Chester Cootery, soiled and worn and left.

So you see our poor, dear Kippses going to and fro, in Hythe, in Sandgate, in Ashford and Canterbury and Deal and Dover—at last even in Folkestone, with "orders to view," pink and green and white and yellow orders to view, and labelled keys in Kipps' hand and frowns and perplexity upon their faces. . . . They did not clearly know what they wanted, but whatever it was they saw, they knew they did not want that. Always they found a confusing multitude of houses they could not take, and none they could. Their dreams began to turn mainly on empty, abandoned-looking rooms, with unfaded patches of paper to mark the place of vanished pictures and doors that had lost their keys. They saw rooms floored with boards that yawned apart and were splintered, skirtings eloquent of the industrious mouse, kitchens with a dead black-beetle in the empty cupboard, and a hideous variety of coal holes and dark cupboards under the stairs. They stuck their little heads through roof trap-doors and gazed at disorganised ball taps, at the bleak filthiness of unstoppered roofs. There were occasions when it seemed to them that they must be the victims of an elaborate conspiracy of house agents, so bleak and cheerless is a second-hand empty house in comparison with the humblest of inhabited dwellings.

Commonly the houses were too big. They had huge windows that demanded vast curtains in mitigation, countless bedrooms, acreage of stone steps to be cleaned, kitchens that made Ann protest. She had come so far towards a proper conception of Kipps' social position as to admit the prospect of one servant—"but lor'!" she would say, "you'd want a manservant in this 'ouse." When the houses were not too big, then they were almost invariably the product of speculative building, of that multitudinous hasty building for the extravagant multitude of new births that was the essential disaster of the nineteenth century. The new houses Ann refused as damp, and even the youngest of these that had been

in use showed remarkable signs of a sickly constitution, the
plaster flaked away, the floors gaped, the paper mouldered
and peeled, the doors dropped, the bricks scaled and the
railings rusted, Nature in the form of spiders, earwigs, cock-
roaches, mice, rats, fungi and remarkable smells, was already
fighting her way back. . . .

And the plan was invariably inconvenient, invariably.
All the houses they saw had a common quality for which
she could find no word, but for which the proper word is
incivility. "They build these 'ouses," she said, "as though
girls wasn't 'uman beings." Sid's social democracy had got
into her blood perhaps, and anyhow they went about discov-
ering the most remarkable inconsiderateness in the contemporary house. "There's kitching stairs to go up, Artie!" Ann
would say. "Some poor girl's got to go up and down, up
and down, and be tired out, jest because they haven't the
sense to leave enough space to give their steps a proper rise
—and no water upstairs anywhere—every drop got to be
carried! It's 'ouses like this wear girls out.

"It's 'aving 'ouses built by men, I believe, makes all the
work and trouble," said Ann. . . .

The Kippses, you see, thought they were looking for a
reasonably simple little contemporary house, but indeed they
were looking either for dreamland or 1975 A.D. or there-
abouts, and it hadn't come.

3

But it was a foolish thing of Kipps to begin building a
house.

He did that out of an extraordinary animosity for house
agents he had conceived.

Everybody hates house agents just as everybody loves
sailors. It is no doubt a very wicked and unjust hatred, but
the business of a novelist is not ethical principle but facts.
Everybody hates house agents because they have everybody
at a disadvantage. All other callings have a certain amount
of give and take; the house agent simply takes. All other
callings want you; your solicitor is afraid you may change
him, your doctor cannot go too far, your novelist—if only
you knew it—is mutely abject towards your unspoken wishes
—and as for your tradespeople, milkmen will fight outside
your front door for you, and green-grocers call in tears if

you discard them suddenly; but who ever heard of a house agent struggling to serve anyone? You want to get a house; you go to him, you dishevelled and angry from travel, anxious, enquiring; he calm, clean, inactive, reticent, quietly doing nothing. You beg him to reduce rents, whitewash ceilings, produce other houses, combine the summer house of No. 6 with the conservatory of No. 4—much he cares! You want to dispose of a house; then he is just the same, serene, indifferent—on one occasion I remember he was picking his teeth all the time he answered me. Competition is a mockery among house agents, they are all alike, you cannot wound them by going to the opposite office, you cannot dismiss them, you can at most dismiss yourself. They are invulnerably placed behind mahogany and brass, too far usually even for a sudden swift lunge with an umbrella, and to throw away the keys they lend you instead of returning them is larceny and punishable as such.

It was a house agent in Dover who finally decided Kipps to build. Kipps, with a certain faltering in his voice, had delivered his ultimatum, no basement, not more than eight rooms, hot and cold water upstairs, coal cellar in the house but with intervening doors to keep dust from the scullery and so forth. He stood blowing. "You'll have to build a house," said the house agent, sighing wearily, "if you want all that." It was rather for the sake of effective answer than with any intention at the time that Kipps mumbled, "That's about what I shall do—this goes on."

Whereupon the house agent smiled. He smiled!

When Kipps came to turn the thing over in his mind he was surprised to find quite a considerable intention had germinated and was growing up in him. After all, lots of people *have* built houses. How could there be so many if they hadn't? Suppose he "reely" did! Then he would go to the house agent and say, " 'Ere, while you been getting me a sootable 'ouse, blowed if I 'aven't built one!" Go round to all of them; all the house agents in Folkestone, in Dover, Ashford, Canterbury, Margate, Ramsgate, saying that! Perhaps then they might be sorry. It was in the small hours that he awoke to a realisation that he had made up his mind in the matter.

"Ann," he said, "Ann," and also used the sharp of his elbow.

Ann was at last awakened to the pitch of an indistinct enquiry what was the matter.

"I'm going to build a house, Ann."

"Eh?" said Ann, suddenly, as if awake.

"Build a house."

Ann said something incoherent about he'd better wait until the morning before he did anything of the sort, and immediately with a fine trustfulness went fast asleep again.

But Kipps lay awake for a long while building his house, and in the morning at breakfast he made his meaning clear. He had smarted under the indignities of house agents long enough, and this seemed to promise revenge—a fine revenge. "And, you know, we might reely make rather a nice little 'ouse out of it—like we want."

So resolved, it became possible for them to take a house for a year, with a basement, no service lift, blackleading to do everywhere, no water upstairs, no bathroom, vast sash windows to be cleaned from the sill, stone steps with a twist and open to the rain into the coal cellar, insufficient cupboards, unpaved path to the dustbin, no fireplace to the servant's bedroom, no end of splintery wood to scrub—in fact, a very typical English middle-class house. And having added to this house some furniture, and a languid young person with unauthentic golden hair named Gwendolen, who was engaged to a sergeant-major and had formerly been in an hotel, having "moved in" and spent some sleepless nights varied by nocturnal explorations in search of burglars, because of the strangeness of being in a house for which they were personally responsible, Kipps settled down for a time and turned himself with considerable resolution to the project of building a home.

4

At first Kipps had gathered advice, finding an initial difficulty in how to begin. He went into a builder's shop at Seabrook one day, and told the lady in charge that he wanted a house built; he was breathless but quite determined, and he was prepared to give his order there and then, but she temporised with him and said her husband was out, and he left without giving his name. Also he went and talked to a man in a cart who was pointed out to him by a workman as the builder of a new house near Saltwood, but he found him first sceptical and then overpoweringly sarcastic. "I suppose you build a 'ouse every 'oliday," he said, and turned from Kipps with every symptom of contempt.

Afterwards Carshot told alarming stories about builders, and shook Kipps' expressed resolution a good deal, and then Pierce raised the question whether one ought to go in the first instance to a builder at all and not rather to an architect. Pierce knew a man at Ashford whose brother was an architect, and as it is always better in these matters to get someone you know, the Kippses decided, before Pierce had gone, and Carshot's warning had resumed their sway, to apply to him. They did so—rather dubiously.

The architect who was brother of Pierce's friend appeared as a small, alert individual with a black bag and a cylindrical silk hat, and he sat at the dining-room table, with his hat and his bag exactly equidistant right and left of him, and maintained a demeanour of impressive woodenness, while Kipps on the hearthrug, with a quaking sense of gigantic enterprise, vacillated answers to his enquiries. Ann held a watching brief for herself, in a position she had chosen as suitable to the occasion beside the corner of the carved oak sideboard. They felt, in a sense, at bay.

The architect began by asking for the site, and seemed a little discomposed to discover this had still to be found. "I thought of building just anywhere," said Kipps. "I 'aven't made up my mind about that yet." The architect remarked that he would have preferred to see the site in order to know where to put what he called his "ugly side," but it was quite possible of course to plan a house "in the air," on the level, "simply with back and front assumed"— if they would like to do that. Kipps flushed slightly, and secretly hoping it would make no great difference in the fees, said a little doubtfully that he thought that would be all right.

The architect then marked off as it were the first section of his subject, with a single dry cough, opened his bag, took out a spring tape measure, some hard biscuits, a metal flask, a new pair of dogskin gloves, a clockwork motor-car partially wrapped in paper, a bunch of violets, a paper of small brass screws, and finally a large, distended notebook; he replaced the other objects carefully, opened his notebook, put a pencil to his lips and said: "And what accommodation will you require?" To which Ann, who had followed his every movement with the closest attention and a deepening dread, replied with the violent suddenness of one who has long lain in wait, "Cubbuds!"

"Anyhow," she added, catching her husband's eye.

The architect wrote it down.

"And how many rooms?" he said, coming to secondary matters.

The young people regarded one another. It was dreadfully like giving an order.

"How many bedrooms, for example?" asked the architect.

"One?" suggested Kipps, inclined now to minimise at any cost.

"There's Gwendolen," said Ann.

"Visitors perhaps," said the architect, and temperately, "You never know."

"Two, p'raps?" said Kipps. "We don't want no more than a *little* 'ouse, you know."

"But the merest shooting-box——," said the architect.

They got to six; he beat them steadily from bedroom to bedroom, the word "nursery" played across their imaginative skies—he mentioned it as the remotest possibility—and then six being reluctantly conceded, Ann came forward to the table, sat down and delivered herself of one of her prepared conditions: " 'Ot and cold water," she said, "laid on to each room—any'ow."

It was an idea long since acquired from Sid.

"Yes," said Kipps, on the hearthrug, " 'Ot and cold water laid on to each bedroom—we've settled on that."

It was the first intimation to the architect that he had to deal with a couple of exceptional originality, and as he had spent the previous afternoon in finding three large houses in *The Builder*, which he intended to combine into an original and copyright design of his own, he naturally struggled against these novel requirements. He enlarged on the extreme expensiveness of plumbing, on the extreme expensiveness of everything not already arranged for in his scheme, and only when Ann declared she'd as soon not have the house as not have her requirements, and Kipps, blenching the while, had said he didn't mind what a thing cost him so long as he got what he wanted, did he allow a kindred originality of his own to appear beneath the acquired professionalism of his methods. He dismissed their previous talk with his paragraphic cough. "Of course," he said, "if you don't mind being unconventional——"

He explained that he had been thinking of a Queen Anne style of architecture (Ann directly she heard her name shook her head at Kipps in an aside) so far as the exterior went. For his own part, he said, he liked to have the exterior of a house in a style, not priggishly in a style, but mixed, with one style uppermost, and the gables and dormers and casements of the Queen Anne style, with a little rough cast and sham timbering here and there and perhaps a bit of an overhang diversified a house and made it interesting. The advantages of what he called a Queen Anne style was that it had such a variety of features. . . . Still, if they were prepared to be unconventional it could be done. A number of houses were now built in the unconventional style and were often very pretty. In the unconventional style one frequently had what perhaps he might call Internal Features, for example, an Old English oak staircase and gallery. White rough-cast and green paint were a good deal favoured in houses of this type.

He indicated that this excursus on style was finished by a momentary use of his cough, and reopened his notebook, which he had closed to wave about in a moment of descriptive enthusiasm while expatiating on the unbridled wealth of External Features associated with Queen Anne. "Six bedrooms," he said, moistening his pencil. "One with barred windows suitable for a nursery if required."

Kipps endorsed this huskily and reluctantly.

There followed a most interesting discussion upon house building, in which Kipps played a minor part. They passed from bedrooms to the kitchen and scullery, and there Ann displayed an intelligent exactingness that won the expressed admiration of the architect. They were particularly novel upon the position of the coal cellar, which Ann held to be altogether too low in the ordinary house, necessitating much heavy carrying. They dismissed as impracticable the idea of having coal cellar and kitchen at the top of the house, because that would involve carrying all the coal through the house, and therewith much subsequent cleaning, and for a time they dealt with a conception of a coal cellar on the ground floor with a light staircase running up outside to an exterior shoot. "It might be made a Feature," said the architect, a little doubtfully, jotting down a note of it. "It would be apt to get black, you know."

Thence they passed to the alternative of service lifts, and then by an inspiration of the architect to the possibilities of gas heating. Kipps did a complicated verbal fugue on the theme, "gas heating heats the air," with variable aspirates; he became very red and was lost to the discussion altogether for a time, though his lips kept silently on.

Subsequently the architect wrote to say that he found in his notebook very full and explicit directions for bow windows to all rooms, for bedrooms, for water supply, lift, height of stairs and absence of twists therein, for a well-ventilated kitchen twenty feet square, with two dressers and a large box-window seat, for scullery and outhouses and offices, but nothing whatever about drawing-room, dining-room, library or study, or approximate cost, and he awaited further instructions. He presumed there would be a breakfast-room, dining-room, drawing-room, and study for Mr. Kipps, at least that was his conception, and the young couple discussed this matter long and ardently.

Ann was distinctly restrictive in this direction. "I don't see what you want a drawin'-room and a dinin' *and* a kitchen for. If we was going to let in summer—well and good. But we're not going to let. Consequently we don't want so many rooms. Then there's a 'all. What use is a 'all? It only makes work. And a study!"

Kipps had been humming and stroking his moustache since he had read the architect's letter. "I think I'd like a little bit of a study—not a big one, of course, but one with a desk and book-shelves, like there was in Hughenden. I'd like that."

It was only after they had talked to the architect again and seen how scandalised he was at the idea of not having a drawing-room that they consented to that Internal Feature. They consented to please him. "But we shan't never use it," said Ann.

Kipps had his way about a study. "When I get that study," said Kipps, "I shall do a bit of reading I've long wanted to do. I shall make a nabit of going in there and reading something an hour every day. There's Shakespeare and a lot of things a man like me ought to read. Besides, we got to 'ave *somewhere* to put the Encyclopædia. I've always thought a study was about what I've wanted all along. You can't 'elp reading if you got a study. If you 'aven't, there's nothing for it, so far's *I* can see, but treshy novels."

He looked down at Ann and was surprised to see a joyless thoughtfulness upon her face.

"Fency, Ann!" he said, not too buoyantly, " 'aving a little 'ouse of our own!"

"It won't be a little 'ouse," said Ann, "not with all them rooms."

5

Any lingering doubt in that matter was dispelled when it came to plans.

The architect drew three sets of plans on a transparent bluish sort of paper that smelt abominably. He painted them very nicely; brick red and ginger, and arsenic green and a leaden sort of blue, and brought them over to show our young people. The first set were very simple, with practically no External Features—"a plain style," he said it was —but it looked a big sort of house nevertheless; the second had such extras as a conservatory, bow windows of various sorts, one rough-cast gable and one half-timbered ditto in plaster, and a sort of overhung verandah, and was much more imposing; and the third was quite fungoid with External Features, and honeycombed with Internal ones; it was, he said, "practically a mansion," and altogether a very noble fruit of the creative mind of man. It was, he admitted, perhaps almost too good for Hythe; his art had run away with him and produced a modern mansion in the "best Folkestone style"; it had a central hall with a staircase, a Moorish gallery, and Tudor stained glass window, crenelated battlements to the leading over the portico, an octagonal bulge with octagonal bay windows, surmounted by an oriental dome of metal, lines of yellow bricks to break up the red and many other richnesses and attractions. It was the sort of house, ornate and in its dignified way voluptuous, that a city magnate might build, but it seemed excessive to the Kippses. The first plan had seven bedrooms, the second eight, the third eleven; that had, the architect explained, "worked in" as if they were pebbles in a mountaineer's boat.

"They're big 'ouses," said Ann directly the elevations were unrolled.

Kipps listened to the architect with round eyes and an exuberant caution in his manner, anxious not to commit himself further than he had done to the enterprise, and the architect pointed out the Features and other objects of interest with the scalpel belonging to a pocket manicure set that he carried. Ann watched Kipps' face and communicated with him furtively over the architect's head. *"Not so big,"* said Ann's lips.

"It's a bit big for what I meant," said Kipps, with a reassuring eye on Ann.

"You won't think it big when you see it up," said the architect; "you take my word for that."

"We don't want no more than six bedrooms," said Kipps.

"Make this one a box-room, then," said the architect.

A feeling of impotence silenced Kipps for a time.

"Now which," said the architect, spreading them out, "is it to be?"

He flattened down the plans of the most ornate mansion to show it to better effect.

Kipps wanted to know how much each would cost "at the outside," which led to much alarmed signalling from Ann. But the architect could estimate only in the most general way.

They were not really committed to anything when the architect went away; Kipps had promised to think it over, that was all.

"We can't 'ave that 'ouse," said Ann.

"They're miles too big—all of them," agreed Kipps.

"You'd want——. Four servants wouldn't be 'ardly enough," said Ann.

Kipps went to the hearthrug and spread himself. His tone was almost offhand. "Nex' time 'e comes," said Kipps, "I'll 'splain to him. It isn't at all the sort of thing we want. It's—it's a misunderstanding. You got no occasion to be anxious 'bout it, Ann."

"I don't see much good reely in building an 'ouse at all," said Ann.

"Oo, we *got* to build a 'ouse now we begun," said Kipps. "But, now, supposin' we 'ad——."

He spread out the most modest of the three plans and scratched his cheek.

6

It was unfortunate that old Kipps came over the next day. Old Kipps always produced peculiar states of mind in his nephew, a rash assertiveness, a disposition towards display unlike his usual self. There had been great difficulty in reconciling both these old people to the Pornick mesalliance, and at times the controversy echoed in old Kipps' expressed thoughts. This perhaps it was, and no ignoble vanity, that set the note of florid successfulness going in Kipps' conversation whenever his uncle appeared. Mrs. Kipps was, as a matter of fact, not reconciled at all, she had declined all invitations to come over on the 'bus, and was a taciturn hostess on the one occasion when the young people called at the toy shop *en route* for Mrs. Pornick. She displayed a tendency to sniff that was clearly due to pride rather than catarrh, and except for telling Ann she hoped she would not feel too "stuck up" about her marriage, confined her conversation to her nephew or the infinite. The call was a brief one and made up chiefly of pauses, no refreshment was offered or asked for, and Ann departed with a singularly high colour. For some reason she would not call at the toy shop when they found themselves again in New Romney.

But old Kipps, having adventured over and tried the table of the new *menage* and found it to his taste, showed many signs of softening towards Ann. He came again and then again. He would come over by the 'bus, and except when his mouth was absolutely full, he would give his nephew one solid and continuous mass of advice of the most subtle and disturbing description, until it was time to toddle back to the High Street for the afternoon 'bus. He would walk with him to the sea front, and commence *pourparlers* with boatmen for the purchase of one of their boats. "You ought to keep a boat of your own," he said, though Kipps was a singularly poor sailor—or he would pursue a plan that was forming in his mind in which he should own and manage what he called "weekly" property in the less conspicuous streets of Hythe. The cream of that was to be a weekly collection of rents in person, the nearest approach to feudal splendour left in this democratised country. He gave no hint of the source of the capital he designed for this investment and at times it would appear he intended it as an occupation for his nephew rather than himself.

But there remained something in his manner towards Ann; in the glances of scrutiny he gave her unawares, that kept Kipps alertly expansive whenever he was about. And in all sorts of ways. It was on account of old Kipps, for example, that our Kipps plunged one day, a golden plunge, and brought home a box of cummerbundy ninepenny cigars, and substituted blue label old Methuselah Four Stars for the common and generally satisfactory white brand.

"Some of this is whiskey, my boy," said old Kipps when he tasted it, smacking critical lips.

"Saw a lot of young officer fellers coming along," said old Kipps. "You ought to join the volunteers, my boy, and get to know a few."

"I dessay I shall," said Kipps. "Later."

"They'd make you an officer, you know, 'n no time. They want officers," said old Kipps. "It isn't everyone can afford it. They'd be regular glad to 'ave you. . . . Ain't bort a dog yet?"

"Not yet, uncle. 'Ave a segar?"

"Not a moty car?"

"Not yet, uncle."

"There's no 'urry 'bout that. And don't get one of these 'ere trashy cheap ones when you do get it, my boy. Get one as'll last a lifetime. . . . I'm surprised you don't 'ire a bit more."

"Ann don't seem to fency a moty car," said Kipps.

"Ah!" said old Kipps, "I expect not," and glanced a comment at the door. "She ain't used to going out," he said. "More at 'ome indoors."

"Fact is," said Kipps, hastily, "we're thinking of building a 'ouse."

"I wouldn't do that, my boy," began old Kipps, but his nephew was routing in the cheffonier drawer amidst the plans. He got them in time to check some further comment on Ann. "Um," said the old gentleman, a little impressed by the extraordinary odour and the unusual transparency of the tracing paper Kipps put into his hands. "Thinking of building a 'ouse, are you?"

Kipps began with the most modest of the three projects. Old Kipps read slowly through his silver-rimmed spectacles: "Plan of a 'ouse for Arthur Kipps Esquire—Um."

He didn't warm to the project all at once, and Ann drifted into the room to find him still scrutinising the architect's proposals a little doubtfully.

"We couldn't find a decent 'ouse anywhere," said Kipps, leaning against the table and assuming an offhand note. "I didn't see why we shouldn't run up one for ourselves." Old Kipps could not help liking the tone of that.

"We thought we might see——" said Ann.

"It's a spekerlation, of course," said old Kipps, and held the plan at a distance of two feet or more from his glasses and frowned. "This isn't exactly the 'ouse I should expect you to 'ave thought of, though," he said. "Practically it's a villa. It's the sort of 'ouse a bank clerk might 'ave. 'Tisn't what I should call a gentleman's 'ouse, Artie."

"It's plain, of course," said Kipps, standing beside his uncle and looking down at this plan, which certainly did seem a little less magnificent now than it had at the first encounter.

"You mustn't 'ave it too plain," said old Kipps.

"If it's comfortable——," Ann hazarded.

Old Kipps glanced at her over his spectacles. "You ain't comfortable, my gal, in this world, not if you don't live up to your position," so putting compactly into contemporary English that fine old phrase, *noblesse oblige.* "A 'ouse of this sort is what a retired tradesman might 'ave, or some little whippersnapper of a s'liciter. But *you*——"

"Course that isn't the o'ny plan," said Kipps, and tried the middle one.

But it was the third one which won over old Kipps. "Now that's a *'ouse,* my boy," he said at the sight of it.

Ann came and stood just behind her husband's shoulder while old Kipps expanded upon the desirability of the larger scheme. "You ought to 'ave a billiard-room," he said: "I don't see that, but all the rest's all right. A lot of these 'ere officers 'ere 'ud be glad of a game of billiards. . . ."

"What's all these dots?" said old Kipps.

"S'rubbery," said Kipps. "Flow'ing s'rubs."

"There's eleven bedrooms in that 'ouse," said Ann. "It's a bit of a lot, ain't it, uncle?"

"You'll want 'em, my girl. As you get on, you'll be 'aving visitors. Friends of your 'usband, p'raps, from the School of Musketry, what you want 'im to get on with. You can't never tell."

"If we 'ave a great s'rubbery," Ann ventured, "we shall 'ave to keep a gardener."

"If you don't 'ave a s'rubbery," said old Kipps, with a note of patient reasoning, "'ow are you to prevent every jackanapes that goes by, starin' into your drorin'-room winder—p'raps when you get someone a bit special to entertain?"

"We ain't *used* to a s'rubbery," said Ann, mulishly; "we get on very well 'ere."

"It isn't what you're used to," said old Kipps, "it's what you ought to 'ave *now*." And with that Ann dropped out of the discussion.

"Study and lib'ry," old Kipps read. "That's right. I see a Tantalus the other day over Brookland, the very thing for a gentleman's study. I'll try and get over and bid for it. . . ."

By 'bus time old Kipps was quite enthusiastic about the house building, and it seemed to be definitely settled that the largest plan was the one decided upon. But Ann had said nothing further in the matter.

7

When Kipps returned from seeing his uncle into the 'bus—there always seemed a certain doubt whether that portly figure would go into the little red "Tip-Top" box—he found Ann still standing by the table, looking with an expression of comprehensive disapproval at the three plans.

"There don't seem much the matter with uncle," said Kipps, assuming the hearthrug, "spite of 'is 'eartburn. 'E 'opped up them steps like a bird."

Ann remained staring at the plans.

"You don't like them plans?" hazarded Kipps.

"No, I don't, Artie."

"We got to build somethin' now."

"But—it's a gentleman's 'ouse, Artie!"

"It's—it's a decent size, o' course."

Kipps took a flirting look at the drawing and went to the window.

"Look at the cleanin'. Free servants'll be lost in that 'ouse, Artie."

"We must *'ave* servants," said Kipps.

Ann looked despondently at her future residence.

"We got to keep up our position, any'ow," said Kipps, turning towards her. "It stands to reason, Ann, we got a position. Very well! I can't 'ave you scrubbin' floors. You got to 'ave a servant and you got to manage a 'ouse. You wouldn't 'ave me ashamed——"

Ann opened her lips and did not speak.

"What?" asked Kipps.

"Nothing," said Ann, "only I did want it to be a *little* 'ouse, Artie. I wanted it to be a 'andy little 'ouse, jest for us."

Kipps' face was suddenly flushed and mulish. He took up the curiously smelling tracings again. "I'm not a-going to be looked down upon," he said. "It's not only Uncle I'm thinking of!"

Ann stared at him.

Kipps went on. "I won't 'ave that young Walshingham f'r instance, sneering and sniffling at me. Making out as if we was all wrong. I see 'im yesterday. . . . Nor Coote neether. I'm as good—we're as good. Whatever's 'appened."

Silence and the rustle of plans.

He looked up and saw Ann's eyes bright with tears. For a moment the two stared at one another.

"We'll 'ave the big 'ouse," said Ann, with a gulp. "I didn't think of that, Artie."

Her aspect was fierce and resolute, and she struggled with emotion. "We'll 'ave the big 'ouse," she repeated. "They shan't say I dragged you down wiv' me—none of them shan't say that. I've thought—I've always been afraid of that."

Kipps looked again at the plan, and suddenly the grand house had become very grand indeed. He blew.

"No, Artie, none of them shan't say that," and with something blind in her motions Ann tried to turn the plan round to her. . . .

After all, Kipps thought there might be something to

say for the milder project. . . . But he had gone so far that now he did not know how to say it.

And so the plans went out to the builders, and in a little while Kipps was committed to two thousand five hundred pounds worth of building. But then, you know, he had an income of twelve hundred a year.

8

It is extraordinary what minor difficulties cluster about house building.

"I say, Ann," remarked Kipps one day, "we shall 'ave to call this little 'ouse by a name. I was thinking of 'Ome Cottage. But I dunno whether 'Ome Cottage is quite the thing like. All these little fishermen's places are called Cottages."

"I like cottage," said Ann.

"It's got eleven bedrooms, d'see," said Kipps. "I don't see 'ow you can call it a cottage with more bedrooms than four. Prop'ly speaking, it's a Large Villa. Prop'ly, it's almost a Big 'Ouse. Leastways a 'Ouse."

"Well," said Ann, "if you must call it Villa—Home Villa. . . . I wish it wasn't."

Kipps meditated.

" 'Ow about Eureka Villa?" he said, raising his voice.

"What's Eureka?"

"It's a name," he said. "There used to be Eureka Dress Fasteners. There's lots of names, come to think of it, to be got out of a shop. There's Pyjama Villa. I remember that in the hosiery. No, come to think, that wouldn't do. But Maraposa—sort of oatmeal cloth, that was. . . . No! Eureka's better."

Ann meditated. "It seems silly like to 'ave a name that don't mean much."

"Perhaps it does," said Kipps. "Though it's what people 'ave to do."

He became meditative. "I got it!" he cried.

"Not Oreeka!" said Ann.

"No! There used to be a 'ouse at Hastings opposite our school—quite a big 'ouse it was—St. Ann's. Now *that*——"

"No," said Mrs. Kipps with decision. "Thanking you

kindly, but I don't have no butcher boys making game of me. . . ."

They consulted Carshot, who suggested after some days of reflection, Waddycombe, as a graceful reminder of Kipps' grandfather; Old Kipps, who was for "Upton Manor House," where he had once been second footman; Buggins, who favoured either a stern simple number, "Number One"—if there were no other houses there, or something patriotic, as "Empire Villa," and Pierce, who inclined to "Sandringham"; but in spite of all this help they were still undecided when, amidst violent perturbations of the soul, and after the most complex and difficult hagglings, wranglings, fears, muddles and goings to and fro, Kipps became the joyless owner of a freehold plot of three-eights of an acre, and saw the turf being wheeled away from the site that should one day be his home.

II. THE CALLERS

1

The Kippses sat at their midday dinner-table and amidst the vestiges of rhubarb pie, and discussed two postcards the one o'clock post had brought. It was a rare bright moment of sunshine in a wet and windy day in the March that followed their marriage. Kipps was attired in a suit of brown, with a tie of fashionable green, while Ann wore one of those picturesque loose robes that are usually associated with sandals and advanced ideas. But there weren't any sandals on Ann or any advanced ideas, and the robe had come quite recently through the counsels of Mrs. Sid Pornick. "It's Artlike," said Kipps, giving way. "It's more comfortable," said Ann. The room looked out by French windows upon a little patch of green and the Hythe parade. The parade was all shiny wet with rain, and the green-grey sea tumbled and tumbled between parade and sky.

The Kipps' furniture, except for certain chromo lithographs of Kipps' incidental choice that struck a quiet note amidst the wall paper, had been tactfully forced by an expert salesman, and it was in a style of mediocre elegance. There was a sideboard of carved oak that had only one fault, it reminded Kipps at times of wood-carving, and its panel of bevelled glass now reflected the back of his head. On its shelf were two books from Parsons' Library, each with a "place" marked by a slip of paper; neither of the Kippses could have told you the title of either book they read, much less the author's name. There was an ebonised overmantel set with phials and pots of brilliant colour, each duplicated by looking-glass, and bearing also a pair of Chinese jars made in Birmingham, a wedding present from Mr. and Mrs. Sidney Pornick, and several sumptuous Japanese fans. And there was a Turkey carpet of great richness. In addition to these modern exploits of Messrs. Bunt and Bubble, there were two inactive tall clocks, whose extreme dilapidation appealed to the connoisseur; a terrestrial and a celestial globe, the latter deeply indented; a number of good old iron moulded and dusty books, and a stuffed owl wanting one (easily replaceable) glass eye, obtained by the exertions of Uncle Kipps. The table equipage was as much as possible like Mrs. Bindon Botting's, only more costly, and in addition there were green and crimson wine glasses—though the Kippses never drank wine.

Kipps turned to the more legible of his two postcards again.

" 'Unavoidably prevented from seein' me to-day,' 'e says. I like 'is cheek. After I give 'im 'is start and everything."

He blew.

" 'E certainly treats you a bit orf'and," said Ann.

Kipps gave vent to his dislike of young Walshingham. "He's getting too big for 'is britches," he said. "I'm beginning to wish she 'ad brought an action for breach. Ever since 'e said she wouldn't, 'e's seemed to think I've got no right to spend my own money."

" 'E's never liked your building the 'ouse," said Ann.

Kipps displayed wrath. "What the goodness 'as it got to do wiv' 'im?"

"Overman indeed!" he added. "Overmantel! . . . 'E trys that on with me, I'll tell 'im something 'e won't like."

He took up the second card. "Dashed if I can read a word of it. I can jest make out Chit-low at the end and that's all."

He scrutinised it. "It's like someone in a fit writing. This here might be W H A T—*what*. P R I C E—*I* got it! What price Harry now? It was a sort of saying of 'is. I expect 'e's either done something or not done something towards starting that play, Ann."

"I expect that's about it," said Ann.

Kipps grunted with effort. "I can't read the rest," he said at last, "nohow."

A thoroughly annoying post. He pitched the card on the table, stood up and went to the window, where Ann, after a momentary reconnaisance at Chitterlow's hieroglyphics, came to join him.

"Wonder what I shall do this afternoon," said Kipps, with his hands deep in his pockets.

He produced and lit a cigarette.

"Go for a walk, I s'pose," said Ann.

"I *been* for a walk this morning.

"S'pose I must go for another," he added, after an interval.

They regarded the windy waste of sea for a space.

"Wonder why it is 'e won't see me," said Kipps, returning to the problem of young Walshingham. "It's all lies about 'is being too busy."

Ann offered no solution.

"Rain again!" said Kipps, as the lash of the little drops stung the window.

"Oo, bother!" said Kipps, "you got to do something. Look 'ere, Ann! I'll go orf for a reg'lar tramp through the rain, up by Saltwood, 'round by Newington, over the camp, and so 'round and back, and see 'ow they're getting on about the 'ouse. See? And look 'ere! you get Gwendolen to go out a bit before I come back. If it's still rainy, she can easy go 'round and see 'er sister. Then we'll 'ave a bit of tea, with tea cake—all buttery, see? Toce it ourselves, p'raps. Eh?"

"I dessay I can find something to do in the 'ouse," said Ann, considering. "You'll take your mackintosh and leggin's, I s'pose. You'll get wet without your mackintosh over those roads."

"Righ-O," said Kipps, and went to ask Gwendolen for his brown leggings, and his other pair of boots.

2

Things conspired to demoralise Kipps that afternoon.

When he got outside the house everything looked so wet under the drive of the southwester that he abandoned the prospect of the clay lanes towards Newington altogether, and turned east to Folkestone along the Seabrook digue. His mackintosh flapped about him, the rain stung his cheek; for a time he felt a hardy man. And then as abruptly the rain ceased and the wind fell, and before he was through Sandgate High Street it was a bright spring day. And there was Kipps in his mackintosh and squeaky leggings, looking like a fool!

Inertia carried him another mile to the Leas, and there

the whole world was pretending there had never been such
a thing as rain—ever. There wasn't a cloud in the sky;
except for an occasional puddle the asphalt paths looked as
dry as a bone. A smartly dressed man in one of those
overcoats that look like ordinary cloth and are really most
deceitfully and unfairly waterproof, passed him and glanced
at the stiff folds of his mackintosh. "Demn!" said Kipps.
His mackintosh swished against his leggings, his leggings
piped and whistled over his boot-tops.

"Why do I never get anything right?" Kipps asked of a
bright implacable universe.

Nice old ladies passed him, refined people with tidy um-
brellas, bright, beautiful, supercilious-looking children. Of
course! the right thing for such a day as this was a light
overcoat and an umbrella. A child might have known that.
He had them at home, but how could one explain that? He
decided to turn down by the Harvey monument and escape
through Clifton Gardens towards the hills. And thereby he
came upon Coote.

He already felt the most abject and propitiatory of social
outcasts when he came upon Coote, and Coote finished him.
He passed within a yard of Coote. Coote was coming along
towards the Leas, and when Kipps saw him his legs hesitated about their office and he seemed to himself to stag-
ger about all over the footpath. At the sight of him Coote
started visibly. Then a sort of *rigor vitae* passed through
his frame, his jaw protruded and errant bubbles of air seemed
to escape and run about beneath his loose skin. (Seemed I
say—I am perfectly well aware that there is really con-
nective tissue in Coote as in all of us to prevent anything
of the sort.) His eyes fixed themselves on the horizon and
glazed. As he went by Kipps could hear his even, resolute
breathing. He went by, and Kipps staggered on into a universe of dead cats and dust heaps, rind and ashes—*cut!*
Cut!

It was part of the inexorable decrees of Providence that
almost immediately afterwards the residuum of Kipps had to
pass a very, very long and observant-looking girls' school.

Kipps recovered consciousness again on the road between
Shorncliffe Station and Cheriton, though he cannot remember, indeed to this day he has never attempted to re-

member, how he got there. And he was back at certain
thoughts suggested by his last night's novel reading, that
linked up directly with the pariah-like emotions of these
last encounters. The novel lay at home upon the cheffonier;
it was one of society and politics—there is no need whatever to give the title or name the author—written with a
heavy-handed thoroughness that overrode any possibility of
resistance on the part of the Kipps mind. It had crushed
all his poor little edifice of ideals, his dreams of a sensible,
unassuming existence, of snugness, of not caring what people
said and all the rest of it, to dust; it had reinstated, squarely
and strongly again, the only proper conception of English
social life. There was a character in the book who trifled
with Art, who was addicted to reading French novels,
who dressed in a loose, careless way, who was a sorrow to
his dignified, silvery-haired, politico-religious mother, and
met the admonitions of bishops with a front of brass. He
treated a "nice girl," to whom they had got him engaged,
badly; he married beneath him—some low thing or other.
And sank. . .

Kipps could not escape the application of the case. He
was enabled to see how this sort of thing looked to decent
people; he was enabled to gauge the measure of the penalties
due. His mind went from that to the frozen marble of
Coote's visage.

He deserved it! . . .

That day of remorse! Later it found him coming upon
the site of his building operations and surveying it in a mood
near to despair, his mackintosh over his arm.

Hardly anyone was at work that day—no doubt the
builders were having him in some obscure manner—and
the whole place seemed a dismal and depressing litter. The
builder's shed, black-lettered WILKINS, BUILDER, HYTHE,
looked like a stranded thing amidst a cast-up disorder of
wheelbarrows and wheeling planks, and earth and sand and
bricks. The foundations of the walls were trenches full of
damp concrete, drying in patches; the rooms—it was incredible they could ever be rooms—were shaped out as
squares and oblongs of coarse, wet grass and sorrel. They
looked absurdly small—dishonestly small. What could you
expect? Of course the builders were having him, building
too small, building all wrong, using bad materials! Old

Kipps had told him a wrinkle or two. The builders were having him, young Walshingham was having him, everybody was having him! They were having him and laughing at him because they didn't respect him. They didn't respect him because he couldn't do things right. Who could respect him? . . .

He was an outcast, he had no place in the world. He had had his chance in the world and turned his back on it. He had "behaved badly"—that was the phrase.

Here a great house was presently to arise, a house to be paid for, a house neither he nor Ann could manage—with eleven bedrooms, and four disrespectful servants having them all the time!

How had it all happened exactly?

This was the end of his great fortune! What a chance he had had! If he had really carried out his first intentions and stuck to things, how much better everything might have been! If he had got a tutor—that had been in his mind originally—a special sort of tutor to show him everything right; a tutor for gentlemen of neglected education. If he had read more and attended better to what Coote had said!

Coote, who had just cut him! . . .

Eleven bedrooms! What had possessed him? No one would ever come to see them, no one would ever have anything to do with them. Even his aunt cut him! His uncle treated him with a half-contemptuous sufferance. He had not a friend worth counting in the world! Buggins, Carshot, Pierce; shop assistants! The Pornicks—a low socialist lot! He stood among his foundations like a lonely figure among ruins; he stood among the ruins of his future, and owned himself a foolish and mistaken man. He saw himself and Ann living out their shameful lives in this great crazy place—as it would be—with everybody laughing secretly at them and their eleven rooms, and nobody approaching them—nobody nice and right that is, for ever. And Ann!

What was the matter with Ann? She'd given up going for walks lately, got touchy and tearful, been fitful with her food. Just when she didn't ought to. It was all a part of the judgment upon wrongdoing, it was all part of the social penalties that Juggernaut of a novel had brought home to his mind.

3

He let himself in with his latchkey. He went moodily into the dining-room and got out the plans to look at them. He had a vague hope that there would prove to be only ten bedrooms. But he found there were still eleven. He became aware of Ann standing over him. "Look 'ere, Artie!" said Ann.

He looked up and found her holding a number of white oblongs. His eyebrows rose.

"It's Callers," said Ann.

He put his plans aside slowly and took and read the cards in silence, with a sort of solemnity. Callers after all! Then perhaps he wasn't to be left out of the world after all. Mrs. G. Porrett Smith, Miss Porrett Smith, Miss Mabel Porrett Smith, and two smaller cards of the Rev. G. Porrett Smith. "Lor'!" he said, *"Clergy!"*

"There was a lady," said Ann, "and two growed-up gals—all dressed up!"

"And 'im?"

"There wasn't no *'im.*"

"Not——?" He held out the little card.

"No; there was a lady and two young ladies."

"But—these cards! Wad they go and leave these two little cards with the Rev. G. Smith on for? Not if 'e wasn't with 'em."

" 'E wasn't with 'em."

"Not a little chap—dodgin' about be'ind the others? And didn't come in?"

"I didn't see no gentleman with them at all," said Ann.

"Rum!" said Kipps. A half-forgotten experience came back to him. *"I* know," he said, waving the reverend gentleman's card; " 'e give 'em the slip, that's what he'd done. Gone off while they was rapping before you let 'em in. It's a fair call, any'ow." He felt a momentary base satisfaction at his absence. "What did they talk about, Ann?"

There was a pause. "I didn't let 'em in," said Ann.

He looked up suddenly and perceived that something unusual was the matter with Ann. Her face was flushed, her eyes were red and hard.

"Didn't let 'em in?"

"No! They didn't come in at all."

He was too astonished for words.

"I answered the door," said Ann; "I'd been upstairs 'namelling the floor. 'Ow was I to think about Callers, Artie? We ain't never 'ad Callers all the time we been 'ere. I'd sent Gwendolen out for a bref of fresh air, and there I was upstairs 'namelling that floor she done so bad, so's to get it done before she came back. I thought I'd 'namel that floor and then get tea and 'ave it quiet with you, toce and all, before she came back. 'Ow was I to think about Callers?"

She paused. "Well," said Kipps, "what them?"

"They came and rapped. 'Ow was I to know? I thought it was a tradesman or something. Never took my apron off, never wiped the 'namel off my 'ands—nothing. There they was!"

She paused again. She was getting to the disagreeable part.

"Wad they say?" said Kipps.

"She says, 'Is Mrs. Kipps at home?' See? To me."

"Yes."

"And me all painty and no cap on and nothing, neither missis nor servant like. There, Artie, I could 'a sunk through the floor with shame, I really could. I could 'ardly get my voice. I couldn't think of nothing to say but just 'Not at 'Ome,' and out of 'abit like I 'eld the tray. And they give me the cards and went, and 'ow I shall ever look that lady in the face again I don't know. . . . And that's all about it, Artie! They looked me up and down, they did, and then I shut the door on 'em."

"Goo!" said Kipps.

Ann went and poked the fire needlessly with a passion quivering hand.

"I wouldn't 'ave 'ad that 'appen for five pounds," said Kipps. "A clergyman and all!"

Ann dropped the poker into the fender with some *éclat* and stood up and looked at her hot face in the glass. Kipps' disappointment grew. "You did ought to 'ave known better than that, Ann! You reely did."

He sat forward, cards in hand, with a deepening sense of social disaster. The things were laid upon the table, toast sheltered under a cover, at mid fender, the teapot warmed beside it, and the kettle just lifted from the hob, sang amidst the coals. Ann glanced at him for a moment, then stooped with the kettle-holder to wet the tea.

"Tcha!" said Kipps, with his mental state developing.

"I don't see it's any use getting in a state about it now," said Ann.

"Don't you? I do. See? 'Ere's these people, good people, want to 'sociate with us, and 'ere you go and slap 'em in the face!"

"I didn't slap 'em in the face."

"You do—practically. You slams the door in their face, and that's all we see of 'em ever. I wouldn't 'ave 'ad this 'appen not for a ten-pound note."

He rounded his regrets with a grunt. For a while there was silence, save for the little stir of Ann's movements preparing the tea.

"Tea, Artie," said Ann, handing him a cup.

Kipps took it.

"I put sugar *once*," said Ann.

"Oo, dash it! Oo cares?" said Kipps, taking an extraordinarily large additional lump with fury quivering fingers, and putting his cup with a slight excess of force on the recess cupboard. "Oo cares?

"I wouldn't 'ave 'ad that 'appen," he said, bidding steadily against accomplished things, "for twenty pounds."

He gloomed in silence through a long minute or so.

Then Ann said the fatal thing that exploded him. "Artie!" she said.

"What?"

"There's Buttud Toce down there! By your foot!"

There was a pause, husband and wife regarded one another.

"Buttud Toce!" he said. "You go and mess up them callers and then you try and stuff me up with Buttud Toce! Buttud Toce indeed! 'Ere's our first chance of knowing anyone that's at all fit to 'sociate with——. Look 'ere, Ann! Tell you what it is—you got to return that call."

"Return that call!"

"Yes, you got to return that call. That's what you got to do! I know—— He waved his arm vaguely towards the miscellany of books in the recess. "It's in Manners and Rools of Good S'ity. You got to find jest 'ow many cards to leave and you got to go and leave 'em. See?"

Ann's face expressed terror. "But, Artie, 'ow *can* I?"

" 'Ow *can* you? 'Ow *could* you? You got to do it, any'ow. They won't know you—not in your Bond Street 'at! If they do, they won't say anything."

His voice assumed a note of entreaty. "You mus', Ann."

"I can't."

"You mus'."

"I can't and I won't. Anything in reason I'll do, but face those people again I can't—after what 'as 'appened."

"You won't?"

"No! . . ."

"So there they go—orf! And we never see them again! And so it goes on! So it goes on! We don't know anybody and we *shan't* know anybody! And you won't put yourself out not a little bit, or take the trouble to find out anything 'ow it ought to be done."

Terrible pause.

"I never ought to 'ave merried you, Artie, that's the troof."

"Oh! *don't* go into that."

"I never ought to 'ave merried you, Artie. I'm not equal to the position. If you 'adn't said you'd drown yourself——" She choked.

"I don' see why you shouldn't *try*, Ann. *I've* improved. Why don't you? 'Stead of which you go sending out the servant and 'namelling floors, and then when visitors come——"

" 'Ow was *I* to know about y'r old visitors?" cried Ann in a wail, and suddenly got up and fled from amidst their ruined tea, the tea of which "toce, all buttery," was to be the crown and glory.

Kipps watched her with a momentary consternation. Then he hardened his heart. "Ought to 'ave known better," he said, "goin' on like that!" He remained for a space rubbing his knees and muttering. He emitted scornfully: "I carn't an' I won't." He saw her as the source of all his shames.

Presently, quite mechanically, he stooped down and lifted the flowery china cover. "Ter dash 'er Buttud Toce!" he shouted at the sight of it, and clapped the cover down again hard. . . .

When Gwendolen came back she perceived things were in a slightly unusual poise. Kipps sat by the fire in a rigid attitude reading a casually selected volume of the *Encyclopædia Britannica,* and Ann was upstairs and inaccessible —to reappear at a later stage with reddened eyes. Before the fire and still in a perfectly assimilable condition was what was evidently an untouched supply of richly buttered toast under a cracked cover.

"They've 'ad a bit of a tiff," said Gwendolen, attending to her duties in the kitchen, with her outdoor hat still on and her mouth full. "They're rummùns—if ever! My eye!"

And she took another piece of Ann's generously buttered toast.

4

The Kippses spoke no more that day to one another.

The squabble about cards and buttered toast was as serious to them as the most rational of differences. It was all rational to them. Their sense of wrong burnt within them; their sense of what was owing to themselves, the duty of implacability, the obstinacy of pride. In the small hours Kipps lay awake at the nadir of unhappiness and came near groaning. He saw life as an extraordinarily desolating muddle; his futile house, his social discredit, his bad behaviour to Helen, his low marriage to Ann. . . .

He became aware of something irregular in Ann's breathing. . . .

He listened. She was awake and quietly and privately sobbing!

He hardened his heart; resolutely he hardened his heart.

The stupid little tragedies of these clipped and limited lives!

What is the good of keeping up the idyllic sham and pretending that ill-educated, misdirected people "get along very well," and that all this is harmlessly funny and nothing more? You think I'm going to write fat, silly, grinning novels about half-educated, under-trained people and keep it up all the time, that the whole thing's nothing but funny!

As I think of them lying unhappily there in the darkness, my vision pierces the night. See what I can see! Above them, brooding over them, I tell you there is a monster, a lumpish monster, like some great, clumsy griffin thing, like the Crystal Palace labyrinthodon, like Coote, like the leaden goddess Dulness Pope Abhorred, like some fat, proud flunkey, like pride, like indolence, like all that is darkening and heavy and obstructive in life. It is matter and darkness, it is anti-soul, Stupidity. My Kippses live in its shadow. Shalford and his apprenticeship system, the Hastings Academy, the ideas of Coote, the ideas of the old Kippses, all the ideas that have made Kipps what he is, all these are in its shadow. But for that monster they might not be groping among false ideas and hurt one another so sorely and so stupidly; but for that, the glowing promise of childhood and youth might have had a happier fruition, thought might have awakened in them to meet *the* thought of the world, the quickening sunshine of literature pierced to the substance of their souls, their lives might not have been divorced, as now they are divorced for ever, from the apprehension of beauty that we favoured ones are given —the vision of the Grail that makes life fine for ever. I have laughed, and I laugh at these two people; I have sought to make you laugh. . . .

But I see through the darkness the souls of my Kippses, as they are, as little pink strips of living stuff, like the bodies of little, ill-nourished, ailing, ignorant children, children who feel pain, who are naughty and muddled and suffer and do not understand why. And the claw of this Beast rests upon them!

III. TERMINATIONS

1

Next morning came a remarkable telegram from Folkestone. "Please come at once, urgent, Walshingham," said
the telegram, and Kipps, after an agitated but still ample
breakfast, departed. . . .

When he returned his face was very white and his
countenance disordered. He let himself in with his latchkey
and came into the dining-room where Ann sat, affecting to
work at a little thing she called a bib. She heard his hat fall
in the hall before he entered, as though he had missed the
peg. "I got something to tell you, Ann," he said, disregard-
ing their overnight quarrel, and went to the hearthrug and
took hold of the mantel, and stared at Ann as though the
sight of her was novel.

"Well?" said Ann, not looking up and working a little
faster.

" 'E's gone!"

Ann looked up sharply and her hands stopped. *Who's*
gone?" For the first time she perceived Kipps' pallor.

"Young Walshingham—I saw 'er and she tole me."

"Gone? What d'you mean?"

"Cleared out! Gone off for good!"

"What for?"

"For 'is 'ealth," said Kipps, with sudden bitterness. " 'E's
been speckylating. He's speckylated our money and 'e's
speckylated their money, and now 'e's took 'is 'ook. That's
all about it, Ann."

"You mean?"

"I mean 'e's orf and our twenty-four thousand's orf, too!
And 'ere we are! Smashed up! That's all about it, Ann."
He panted.

Ann had no vocabulary for such an occasion. "Oh, Lor'!"
she said, and sat still.

Kipps came about and stuck his hands deeply in his trouser pockets. "Speckylated every penny—lorst it all—and gorn."

Even his lips were white.

"You mean we ain't got nothin' left, Artie?"

"Not a penny! Not a bloomin' penny, Ann. No!"

A gust of passion whirled across the soul of Kipps. He flung out a knuckly fist. "If I 'ad 'im 'ere," he said, "I'd—I'd—I'd wring 'is neck for 'im. I'd—I'd——" His voice rose to a shout. He thought of Gwendolen in the kitchen and fell to "Ugh!"

"But, Artie," said Ann, trying to grasp it, "d'you mean to say he's took our money?"

"Speckylated it!" said Kipps, with an illustrative flourish of the arm, that failed to illustrate. "Bort things dear and sold 'em cheap, and played the 'ankey-pankey jackass with everything we got. That's what I mean 'e's done, Ann." He repeated this last sentence with the addition of violent adverbs.

"D'you mean to say our money's *gone*, Artie?"

"Ter-dash it, *Yes*, Ann!" swore Kipps, exploding in a shout. "Ain't I tellin' you?"

He was immediately sorry. "I didn't mean to 'oller at you, Ann," he said, "but I'm all shook up. I don't 'ardly know what I'm sayin'. Ev'ry penny. . . ."

"But, Artie——"

Kipps grunted. He went to the window and stared for a moment at a sunlit sea. "Gord!" he swore.

"I mean," he said, coming back to Ann and with an air of exasperation, "that he's 'bezzled and 'ooked it. That's what I mean, Ann."

Ann put down the bib. "But wot are we going to *do*, Artie?"

Kipps indicated ignorance, wrath and despair with one comprehensive gesture of his hands. He caught an ornament from the mantel and replaced it. "I'm going to bang about," he said, "if I ain't precious careful."

"You saw '*er*, you say?"

"Yes."

"What did she say 'xactly?" said Ann.

"Told me to see a s'licitor—tole me to get someone to 'elp me at once. She was there in black—like she used to

be—and speaking cool and careful-like. 'Elen! . . . She's
precious 'ard, is 'Elen. She looked at me straight. 'It's my
fault,' she said, 'I ought to 'ave warned you. . . . Only under
the circumstances it was a little difficult.' Straight as anything. I didn't 'ardly say anything to 'er. I didn't seem to
begin to take it in until she was showing me out. I 'adn't
anything to say. Jest as well, perhaps. She talked like a
call a'most. She said—what *was* it she said about her mother?
'My mother's overcome with grief,' she said, 'so naturally
everything comes on me.' "

"And she told you to get someone to 'elp you?"

"Yes. I been to old Bean."

"O' Bean?"

"Yes. What I took my business away from!"

"What did he say?"

"He was a bit off'and at first, but then 'e come 'round.
He couldn't tell me anything till 'e knew the facts. What
I know of young Walshingham, there won't be much 'elp in
the facts. No!"

He reflected for a space. "It's a smash-up, Ann. More
likely than not, Ann, 'e's left us over'ead in debt. We
got to get out of it just 'ow we can. . . .

"We got to begin again," he went on. " '*Ow*, I don't
know. All the way 'ome my 'ead's been going. We got to
get a living some'ow or other. 'Aving time to ourselves,
and a bit of money to spend, and no hurry and worry, it's
all over for ever, Ann. We was fools, Ann. We didn't know
our benefits. We been caught. Gord! . . . Gord!"

He was on the verge of "banging about" again.

They heard a jingle in the passage, the large soft impact
of a servant's indoor boots. As if she were a part, a
mitigatory part of Fate, came Gwendolen to lay the midday
meal. Kipps displayed self-control forthwith. Ann picked
up the bib again and bent over it, and the Kippses bore
themselves gloomily perhaps, but not despairfully, while
their dependant was in the room. She spread the cloth and
put out the cutlery with a slow inaccuracy, and Kipps, after
a whisper to himself, went again to the window. Ann got
up and put away her work methodically in the cheffonier.

"When I think," said Kipps, as soon as the door closed
again behind Gwendolen, "when I think of the 'ole people
and 'aving to tell 'em of it all—I want to smesh my 'ead

against the nearest wall. Smesh my silly brains out! And Buggins—Buggins what I'd 'arf promised to start in a lill' outfitting shop in Rendezvous Street. . . ."

Gwendolen returned and restored dignity.

The midday meal spread itself slowly before them. Gwendolen, after her custom, left the door open and Kipps closed it carefully before sitting down.

He stood for a moment, regarding the meal doubtfully.

"I don't feel as if I could swaller a moufful," he said.

"You got to eat," said Ann. . . .

For a time they said little, and once swallowing was achieved, ate on with a sort of melancholy appetite. Each was now busy thinking.

"After all," said Kipps, presently, "whatever 'appens, they can't turn us out or sell us up before nex' quarter-day. I'm pretty sure about that."

"Sell us up!" said Ann.

"I dessey we're bankrup'," said Kipps, trying to say it easily and helping himself with a trembling hand to unnecessary potatoes.

Then a long silence. Ann ceased to eat, and there were silent tears.

"More potatoes, Artie?" choked Ann.

"I couldn't," said Kipps. "No."

He pushed back his plate, which was indeed replete with potatoes, got up and walked about the room. Even the dinner-table looked distraught and unusual.

"What to do, I *don't* know," he said.

"Oh, *Lord!*" he ejaculated, and picked up and slapped down a book.

Then his eye fell upon another postcard that had come from Chitterlow by the morning's post, and which now lay by him on the mantel-shelf. He took it up, glanced at its imperfectly legible message, and put it down.

"Delayed!" he said, scornfully. "Not prodooced in the smalls. Or is it smells 'e says? 'Ow can one understand that? Any'ow 'e's 'umbugging again. . . . Somefing about the Strand. No! Well, 'e's 'ad all the money 'e'll ever get out of me! . . . I'm done."

He seemed to find a momentary relief in the dramatic effect of his announcement. He came near to a swagger of despair upon the hearthrug, and then suddenly came and sat down next to Ann and rested his chin on the knuckles of his two clenched hands.

"I been a fool, Ann," he said in a gloomy monotone. "I been a brasted fool. But it's 'ard on us, all the same. It's 'ard."

" 'Ow was you to know?" said Ann.

"I ought to 'ave known. I did in a sort of way know. And 'ere we are! I wouldn't care so much if it was myself, but it's *you*, Ann! 'Ere we are! Regular smashed up! And you——" He checked at an unspeakable aggravation of their disaster. "I knew 'e wasn't to be depended upon and there I left it! And you got to pay. . . . What's to 'appen to us all, I don't know."

He thrust out his chin and glared at fate.

" 'Ow do you know 'e's speckylated everything?" said Ann, after a silent survey of him.

" 'E 'as," said Kipps, irritably, holding firm to disaster.

"She says so?"

"She don't know, of course, but you depend upon it that's it. She told me she knew something was on, and when she found 'im gone and a note lef' for her she knew it was up with 'im. 'E went by the night boat. She wrote that telegram off to me straight away."

Ann surveyed his features with tender, perplexed eyes; she had never seen him so white and drawn before, and her hand rested an inch or so away from his arm. The actual loss was still, as it were, afar from her. The immediate thing was his enormous distress.

" 'Ow do you know——?" she said and stopped. It would irritate him too much.

Kipps' imagination was going headlong.

"Sold up!" he emitted presently, and Ann flinched.

"Going back to work, day after day—I can't stand it, Ann, I can't. And you——"

"It don't do to think of it," said Ann.

Presently he came upon a resolve. "I keep on thinking of it, and thinking of it, and what's to be done and what's to be done. I shan't be any good 'ome s'arfernoon. It keeps on going 'round and 'round in my 'ead, and 'round and 'round. I better go for a walk or something. I'd be no comfort to you, Ann. I should want to 'owl and 'ammer things if I 'ung about 'ome. My fingers is all atwitch. I shall keep on thinking 'ow I might 'ave stopped it and callin' myself a fool. . . ."

He looked at her between pleading and shame. It seemed like deserting her.

Ann regarded him with tear-dimmed eyes.

"You'd better do what's good for you, Artie," she said. . . . "*I'll* be best cleaning. It's no use sending off Gwendolen before her month, and the top room wants turning out." She added with a sort of grim humour: "May as well turn it out now while I got it."

"I *better* go for a walk," said Kipps. . . .

And presently our poor exploded Kipps was marching out to bear his sudden misery. Habit turned him up the road towards his growing house, and then suddenly he perceived his direction—"Oh, Lor'!"—and turned aside and went up the steep way to the hill crest and the Sandling Road, and over the line by that tree-embowered Junction, and athwart the wide fields towards Postling—a little, black, marching figure—and so up the Downs and over the hills, whither he had never gone before. . . .

2

He came back long after dark, and Ann met him in the passage.

"Where you been, Artie?" she asked, with a strained note in her voice.

"I been walking and walking—trying to tire myself out. All the time I been thinking what shall I do. Trying to fix something up all out of nothing."

"I didn't know you meant to be out all this time."

Kipps was gripped by compunction. . . .

"I can't think what we ought to do," he said, presently.

"You can't do anything much, Artie, not till you hear from Mr. Bean."

"No; I can't do anything much. That's jest it. And all this time I keep feelin' if I don't do something the top of my 'ead'll bust. . . . Been trying to make up advertisements 'arf the time I been out—'bout finding a place, good salesman and stockkeeper, and good Manchester dresses, windowdressing—Lor'! Fancy that all beginning again! . . . If you went to stay with Sid a bit—if I sent every penny I got to you—I dunno! I dunno!"

When they had gone to bed there was an elaborate attempt to get to sleep. . . . In one of their great waking pauses Kipps remarked in a muffled tone: "I didn't mean to frighten you, Ann, being out so late. I kep' on walking and walking, and some'ow it seemed to do me good. I went out to the 'illtop ever so far beyond Stanford, and sat there ever so long, and it seemed to make me better. Just looking over the marsh like, and seeing the sun set. . . ."

"Very likely," said Ann, after a long interval, "it isn't so bad as you think it is, Artie."

"It's bad," said Kipps.

"Very likely, after all, it isn't quite so bad. If there's only a little——"

There came another long silence.

"Ann," said Kipps in the quiet darkness.

"Yes," said Ann.

"Ann," said Kipps, and stopped as though he had hastily shut a door upon speech.

"I kep' thinking," he said, trying again, "I kep' thinking —after all—I been cross to you and a fool about things— about them cards, Ann; but"—his voice shook to pieces— "we *'ave* been 'appy, Ann . . . . some'ow . . . . togever."

And with that he and then she fell into a passion of weeping. They clung very tightly together—closer than they had been since ever the first brightness of their married days turned to the grey of common life again.

All the disaster in the world could not prevent their going to sleep at last with their poor little troubled heads close together on one pillow. There was nothing more to be done, there was nothing more to be thought; Time might go on with his mischiefs, but for a little while at least they still had one another.

3

Kipps returned from his second interview with Mr. Bean in a state of strange excitement. He let himself in with his latchkey and slammed the door. "Ann!" he shouted, in an unusual note; "Ann!"

Ann replied distantly.

"Something to tell you," said Kipps; "something noo!"

Ann appeared apprehensive from the kitchen.

"Ann," he said, going before her into the little dining-room, for his news was too dignified for the passage, "very likely, Ann, o' Bean says, we shall 'ave——" He decided to prolong the suspense. "Guess!"

"I can't, Artie."

"Think of a lot of money!"

"A 'undred pounds p'raps?"

He spoke with immense deliberation. "O v e r   a   f o u s - a n d   p o u n d s !"

Ann stared and said nothing, only went a shade whiter.

"Over," he said. "A'most certainly over."

He shut the dining-room door and came forward hastily, for Ann, it was clear, meant to take this mitigation of their disaster with a complete abandonment of her self-control. She came near flopping; she fell into his arms.

"Artie," she got to at last and began to weep, clinging tightly to him.

"Pretty near certain," said Kipps, holding her. "A fousand pounds!"

"I *said*, Artie," she wailed on his shoulder with the note of accumulated wrongs, "very likely it wasn't so bad. . . ."

"There's things," he said, when presently he came to particulars, " 'e couldn't touch. The noo place! It's freehold and paid for, and with the bit of building on it, there's five or six 'undred pound p'raps—say worf free 'undred, for safety. We can't be sold up to finish it, like we thought. O' Bean says we can very likely sell it and get money. 'E says you often get a chance to sell a 'ouse lessen 'arf done, 'specially free'old. *Very* likely, 'e say. Then there's Hughenden. Hughenden 'asn't been mortgaged not for more than 'arf its value. There's a 'undred or so to be got on that, and the furniture and the rent for the summer still coming in. 'E says there's very likely other things. A fousand pounds, that's what 'e said. 'E said it might even be more."

They were sitting now at the table.

"It alters everything," said Ann.

"I been thinking that, Ann, all the way 'ome. I came in the motor car. First ride I've 'ad since the smash. We needn't send off Gwendolen, leastways not till *after*. You know. We needn't turn out of 'ere—not for a long time. What we been doing for the o' people we can go on doing a'most as much. And your mother! . . . I wanted to 'oller coming along. I pretty near run coming down the road by the hotel."

"Oh, I *am* glad we can stop 'ere and be comfortable a bit," said Ann. "I *am* glad for that."

"I pretty near told the driver on the motor—only 'e was the sort won't talk. . . . You see, Ann, we'll be able to start a shop, we'll be able to get *into* something like. All about our 'aving to go back to places and that; all that doesn't matter any more."

For a while they abandoned themselves to ejaculating transports. Then they fell talking to shape an idea to themselves of the new prospect that opened before them.

"We must start a sort of shop," said Kipps, whose imagination had been working. "It'll 'ave to be a shop."

"Drapery?" said Ann.

"You want such a lot of capital for the drapery, mor'n a thousand pounds you want by a long way—to start it anything like proper."

"Well, outfitting. Like Buggins was going to do."

Kipps glanced at that for a moment, because the idea had not occurred to him. Then he came back to his prepossession.

"Well, I thought of something else, Ann," he said. "You see, I've always thought a little book-shop. It isn't like the drapery—'aving to be learnt. I thought—even before this smash-up—'ow I'd like to 'ave something to do, instead of always 'aving 'olidays always like we 'ave been 'aving."

He reflected.

"You don't know *much* about books, do you, Artie?"

"You don't want to." He illustrated. "I noticed when we used to go to that Lib'ry at Folkestone, ladies weren't anything like what they was in a draper's—if you 'aven't got *just* what they want it's 'Oh, no!' and out they go. But in a book-shop it's different. One book's very like another—after all, what is it? Something to read and done with. It's not a thing that matters like print dresses or serviettes—where you either like 'em or don't, and people judge you by. They take what you give 'em in books and lib'ries, and glad to be told *what* to. See 'ow we was—up at that lib'ry." . . .

He paused. "You see, Ann——

"Well, I read 'n 'dvertisement the other day. I been asking Mr. Bean. It said—five 'undred pounds."

"What did?"

"Branches," said Kipps.

Ann failed to understand. "It's a sort of thing that gets up book-shops all over the country," said Kipps. "I didn't tell you, but I arst about it a bit. On'y I dropped it again. Before this smash, I mean. I'd thought I'd like to keep a shop for a lark, on'y then I thought it silly. Besides it 'ud 'ave been beneath me."

He blushed vividly. "It was a sort of projek of mine, Ann.

"On'y it wouldn't 'ave done," he added.

It was a tortuous journey when the Kippses set out to explain anything to each other. But through a maze of fragmentary elucidations and questions, their minds did presently begin to approximate to a picture of a compact, bright, little shop, as a framework for themselves.

"I thought of it one day when I was in Folkestone. I thought of it one day when I was looking in at a window. I see a chap dressin' a window and he was whistlin' reg'lar light-'arted. . . . I thought then I'd like to keep a book-shop, any'ow, jest for something to do. And when people weren't about, then you could sit and read the books. See? It wouldn't be 'arf bad. . . ."

They mused, each with elbows on table and knuckles to lips, looking with speculative eyes at each other.

"Very likely we'll be 'appier than we should 'ave been with more money," said Kipps presently.

"We wasn't 'ardly suited," reflected Ann, and left her sentence incomplete.

"Fish out of water like," said Kipps. . . .

"You won't 'ave to return that call now," said Kipps, opening a new branch of the question. "That's one good thing."

"Lor'!" said Ann, visibly brightening, "no more I shan't!"

"I don't s'pose they'd want you to, even if you did —with things as they are."

A certain added brightness came into Ann's face. "Nobody won't be able to come leaving cards on us, Artie, now, any more. We are out of *that!*"

"There isn't no necessity for us to be stuck up," said Kipps, "any more for ever! 'Ere we are, Ann, common people, with jest no position at all, as you might say, to keep up. No sev'nts, not if you don't like. No dressin' better than other people. If it wasn't we been robbed—dashed if I'd care a rap about losing that money. I b'lieve"—his face shone with the rare pleasure of paradox—"I reely b'lieve, Ann, it'll prove a savin' in the end."

4

The remarkable advertisement which had fired Kipps' imagination with this dream of a book-shop opened out in the most alluring way. It was one little facet in a comprehensive scheme of transatlantic origin, which was to make our old-world methods of book-selling "sit up," and it displayed an imaginative briskness, a lucidity and promise that aroused the profoundest scepticism in the mind of Mr. Bean. To Kipps' renewed investigation it presented itself in an expository illustrated pamphlet (far too well printed, Mr. Bean thought, for a reputable undertaking) of the most convincing sort. Mr. Bean would not let him sink his capital in shares in its projected company that was to make all things new in the world of books, but he could not prevent Kipps becoming one of their associated booksellers. And so when presently it became apparent that an epoch was not to be made, and the "Associated Booksellers' Trading Union (Limited)" receded and dissolved and liquidated (a few drops) and vanished and went away to talk about something else, Kipps remained floating undamaged in this interestingly uncertain universe as an independent bookseller.

Except that it failed, the Associated Booksellers' Trading Union had all the stigmata of success. Its fault, perhaps, was that it had them all instead of only one or two. It was to buy wholesale for all its members and associates and exchange stock, having a common books-in-stock list and a common lending library, and it was to provide a uniform registered shop front to signify all these things to the intelligent passer-by. Except that it was controlled by buoyant young Over-men with a touch of genius in their arithmetic, it was, I say, a most plausible and hopeful project. Kipps went several times to London and an agent came to Hythe; Mr. Bean made some timely interventions, and then behind a veil of planks and an announcement in the High Street, the uniform registered shop front came rapidly into being. "Associated Booksellers' Trading Union," said this shop front, in a refined, artistic lettering that bookbuyers were going to value, as wise men over forty value the proper label for Berncasteler Doctor, and then, "Arthur Kipps."

Next to starting a haberdasher's shop I doubt if Kipps could have been more truly happy than during those weeks of preparation.

There is, of course, nothing on earth, and I doubt at times if there is a joy in Heaven, like starting a small haberdasher's shop. Imagine, for example, having a drawerful of tapes (one whole piece most exquisitely blocked of every possible width of tape), or, again, an army of neat, large packages, each displaying one sample of hooks and eyes. Think of your cottons, your drawer of coloured silks, the little, less, least of the compartments and thin packets of your needle drawer! Poor princes and wretched gentlefolk mysteriously above retail trade, may taste only the faint unsatisfactory shadow of these delights with trays of stamps or butterflies. I write, of course, for those to whom these things appeal; there are clods alive who see nothing, or next to nothing, in spools of mercerised cotton and endless bands of paper-set pins. I write for the wise, and as I write I wonder that Kipps resisted haberdashery. He did. Yet even starting a book-shop is at least twenty times as interesting as building your own house to your own design in unlimited space and time, or any possible thing people with indisputable social position and sound securities can possibly find to do. Upon that I rest.

You figure Kipps "going to have a look to see how the little shop is getting on," the shop that is not to be a loss and a spending of money, but a gain. He does not walk too fast towards it; as he comes into view of it his paces slacken and his head goes to one side. He crosses to the pavement opposite in order to inspect the fascia better, already his name is adumbrated in faint white lines; stops in the middle of the road and scrutinises imaginary details for the benefit of his future next door neighbour, the curiosity-shop man, and so at last, in. . . . A smell of paint and of the shavings of imperfectly seasoned pinewood! The shop is already glazed and a carpenter is busy over the fittings for adjustable shelves in the side windows. A painter is busy on the fixtures round about (shelving above and drawers below), which are to accommodate most of the stock, and the counter—the counter and desk are done. Kipps goes inside the desk, the desk which is to be the strategic centre of the shop, brushes away some sawdust, and draws out the marvellous till; here gold is to be, here silver, here copper—notes locked up in a cash-box in the well below. Then he leans his elbows on the desk, rests his chin on his fist and fills the shelves with imaginary stock; books beyond reading. Every day a man who cares to wash his hands and read uncut pages artfully may have his cake and eat it, among that stock. Under the counter to the right, paper and string are to lurk ready to leap up and embrace goods sold; on the table to the left, art publications, whatever they may prove to be! He maps it out, serves an imaginary customer, receives a dream seven and six pence, packs, bows out. He wonders how it was he ever came to fancy a shop a disagreeable place.

"It's different," he says at last, after musing on that difficulty, "being your own."

It *is* different. . . .

Or, again, you figure Kipps with something of the air of a young sacristan, handling his brightly virginal account-books, and looking, and looking again, and then still looking, at an unparalleled specimen of copperplate engraving, ruled money below and above, bearing the words "In Account with, ARTHUR KIPPS" (loud flourishes), "The Booksellers' Trading Union" (temperate decoration). You figure Ann sitting and stitching at one point of the circumference of the light of the lamp, stitching queer little garments for some unknown stranger, and over against her sits Kipps. Before him is one of those engraved memorandum forms, a moist pad, wet with some thick and greasy greenish purple ink that is also spreading quietly but steadily over his fingers, a cross-nibbed pen for first-aid surgical assistance to the patient in his hand, a dating rubber stamp. At intervals he brings down this latter with great care and emphasis upon the paper, and when he lifts it there appears a beautiful oval design of which "Paid, Arthur Kipps, The Associated Booksellers' Trading Union," and a date, are the essential ingredients, stamped in purple ink.

Anon he turns his attention to a box of small, round, yellow labels, declaring "This book was bought from the Associated Booksellers' Trading Union." He licks one with

deliberate care, sticks it on the paper before him and de-
faces it with great solemnity. "I can do it, Ann," he says,
looking up brightly. For the Associated Booksellers' Trading Union, among other brilliant notions and inspirations,
devised an ingenious system of taking back its books again
in part payment for new ones within a specified period.
When it failed, all sorts of people were left with these un-
redeemed pledges in hand.

5

Amidst all this bustle and interest, all this going to and
fro before they "moved in" to the High Street, came the
great crisis that hung over the Kippses, and one morning
in the small hours Ann's child was born. . . .

Kipps was coming to manhood swiftly now. The once
rabbit-like soul that had been so amazed by the discovery
of "chubes" in the human interior and so shocked by the
sight of a woman's shoulder-blades, that had found shame
and anguish in a mislaid Gibus and terror in an Anagram
Tea, was at last facing the greater realities. He came suddenly upon the master thing in life, birth. He passed through
hours of listening, hours of impotent fear in the night and
in the dawn, and then there was put into his arms something most wonderful, a weak and wailing creature, incredibly, heart-stirringly soft and pitiful, with minute appealing
hands that it wrung his heart to see. He held this miracle in
his arms and touched its tender cheek as if he feared his
lips might injure it. And this marvel was his Son!

And there was Ann, with a greater strangeness and a
greater familiarity in her quality than he had ever found
before. There were little beads of perspiration on her temples
and her lips, and her face was flushed, not pale as he had
feared to see it. She had the look of one who emerges
from some strenuous and invigorating act. He bent down
and kissed her, and he had no words to say. She wasn't to
speak much yet, but she stroked his arm with her hand
and had to tell him one thing:

"He's over nine pounds, Artie," she whispered. "Bessie's
—Bessie's wasn't no more than eight."

To have given Kipps a pound of triumph over Sid seemed
to her almost to justify Nunc Dimittis. She watched his face
for a moment, then closed her eyes in a kind of blissful

exhaustion as the nurse, with something motherly in her
manner, pushed Kipps out of the room.

6

Kipps was far too much preoccupied with his own life to
worry about the further exploits of Chitterlow. The man had
got his two thousand; on the whole Kipps was glad he had
had it rather than young Walshingham, and there was an
end to the matter. As for the complicated transactions he
achieved and proclaimed by mainly illegible and always incomprehensible postcards, they were like passing voices
heard in the street as one goes about one's urgent concerns.
Kipps put them aside and they got in between the pages of
the stock and were lost forever and sold in with the goods
to customers who puzzled over them mightily.

Then one morning as he was dusting round before breakfast, Chitterlow returned, appeared suddenly in the shop
doorway.

Kipps was overcome with amazement.

It was the most unexpected thing in the world. The man
was in evening dress, evening dress in that singularly
crumpled state it assumes after the hour of dawn, and above
his dishevelled red hair, a smallish Gibus hat tilted remarkably forward. He opened the door and stood, tall and
spread, with one vast white glove flung out as if to display
how burst a glove might be, his eyes bright, such wrinkling
of brow and mouth as only an experienced actor can produce, and a singular radiance of emotion upon his whole
being, an altogether astonishing spectacle.

It was amazing beyond the powers of Kipps. The bell
jangled for a bit and then gave it up and was silent. For a
long, great second everything was quietly attentive. Kipps
was amazed to his uttermost; had he had ten times the
capacity he would still have been fully amazed. "It's
Chit'low!" he said at last, standing duster in hand.

But he doubted whether it was not a dream.

"Tzit!" gasped that most excitable and extraordinary
person, still in an incredibly expanded attitude, and then
with a slight forward jerk of the starry split glove, "Bif!"

He could say no more. The tremendous speech he had
had ready vanished from his mind. Kipps stared at his extraordinary facial changes, vaguely conscious of the truth

of the teachings of Nisbet and Lombroso concerning men of genius.

Then suddenly Chitterlow's features were convulsed, the histrionic fell from him like a garment, and he was weeping. He said something indistinct about "Old Kipps! *Good* old Kipps! Oh, old Kipps!" and somehow he managed to mix a chuckle and a sob in the most remarkable way. He emerged from somewhere near the middle of his original attitude, a merely life-size creature. "My play, boo-hoo!" he sobbed, clutching at his friend's arm. "My play, Kipps! (sob) You know?"

"Well?" cried Kipps, with his heart sinking in sympathy, "it ain't——"

"No," howled Chitterlow; "no. It's a success! My dear chap! my dear boy! oh! it's a—bu—boo-hoo!—a big success!" He turned away and wiped streaming tears with the back of his hand. He walked a pace or so and turned. He sat down on one of the specially designed artistic chairs of the Associated Booksellers' Trading Union and produced an exiguous lady's handkerchief, extraordinarily belaced. He choked. "*My* play," and covered his face here and there.

He made an unsuccessful effort to control himself, and shrank for a space to the dimensions of a small and pathetic creature. His great nose suddenly came through a careless place in the handkerchief.

"I'm knocked," he said in a muffled voice, and so remained for a space—wonderful—veiled.

He made a gallant effort to wipe his tears away. "I had to tell you," he said, gulping.

"Be all right in a minute," he added, "calm," and sat still. . . .

Kipps stared in commiseration of such success. Then he heard footsteps and went quickly to the house doorway. "Jest a minute," he said. "Don't go in the shop, Ann, for a minute. It's Chitterlow. He's a bit essited. But he'll be better in a minute. It's knocked him over a bit. You see"—his voice sank to a hushed note as one who announces death— " 'e's made a success with his play."

He pushed her back lest she should see the scandal of another male's tears. . . .

Soon Chitterlow felt better, but for a little while his manner was even alarmingly subdued. "I *had* to come and tell you," he said. "I *had* to astonish someone. Muriel—she'll be firstrate, of course. But she's over at Dymchurch." He blew his nose with enormous noise, and emerged instantly a merely garrulous optimist.

"I expect she'll be precious glad."

"She doesn't know yet, my dear boy. She's at Dymchurch —with a friend. She's seen some of my first nights before. . . Better out of it. . . . I'm going to her now. I've been up all night—talking to the boys and all that. I'm a bit off it just for a bit. But—it Knocked 'em. It Knocked everybody."

He stared at the floor and went on in a monotone. "They laughed a bit at the beginning—but nothing like a settled laugh—not until the second act—you know—the chap with the beetle down his neck. Little Chisholme did that bit to rights. Then they began—*to* rights." His voice warmed and increased. "Laughing! It made *me* laugh! We jumped 'em into the third act before they had time to cool. Everybody was on it. I never saw a first night go so fast. Laugh, laugh, l a u g h, L A U G H, L A U G H, L A U G H" (he howled the last word with stupendous violence). "Everything they laughed at. They laughed at things that we hadn't meant to be funny—not for one moment. Bif! Bizz! Curtain. A Fair Knock-Out! . . . I went on—but I didn't say a word. Chisholme did the patter. Shouting! It was like walking under Niagara—going across that stage. It was like never having seen an audience before. . . .

"Then afterwards—the Boys!"

His emotion held him for a space. "Dear old Boys!" he murmured.

His words multiplied, his importance increased. In a little while he was restored to something of his old self. He was enormously excited. He seemed unable to sit down anywhere. He came into the breakfast-room so soon as Kipps was sure of him, shook hands with Mrs. Kipps parenthetically, sat down and immediately got up again. He went to the bassinette in the corner and looked absentmindedly at Kipps, junior, and said he was glad if only for the youngster's sake. He immediately resumed the thread of his discourse. . . . He drank a cup of coffee noisily and walked up and down the room talking, while they attempted breakfast amidst the gale of his excitement. The infant slept marvellously through it all.

"You won't mind my sitting down, Mrs. Kipps. I couldn't sit down for anyone, or I'd do it for you. It's you I'm thinking of more than anyone, you and Muriel, and all Old Pals and Good Friends. It means wealth, it means money—hundreds and thousands. . . . If you'd heard 'em, *you'd know.*"

He was silent through a portentous moment while topics battled for him and finally he burst and talked of them all together. It was like the rush of water when a dam bursts and washes out a fair-sized provincial town; all sorts of things floated along on the swirl. For example, he was discussing his future behaviour. "I'm glad it's come now. Not before. I've had my lesson. I shall be very discreet now, trust me. We've learnt the value of money." He discussed the possibility of a country house, of taking a Martello tower as a swimming-box (as one might say a shooting-box), of living in Venice because of its artistic associations and scenic possibilities, of a flat in Westminster or a house in the West End. He also raised the question of giving up smoking and drinking, and what classes of drink were especially noxious to a man of his constitution. But discourses on all this did not prevent a parenthetical computation of the probable profits on the supposition of a thousand nights here and in America, nor did it ignore the share Kipps was to have, nor the gladness with which Chitterlow would pay that share, nor the surprise and regret with which he had learnt, through an indirect source which awakened many associations, of the turpitude of young Walshingham, nor the distaste Chitterlow had always felt for young Walshingham and men of his type. An excursus upon Napoleon had got into the torrent somehow and kept bobbing up and down. The whole thing was thrown into the form of a single complex sentence, with parenthetical and subordinate clauses fitting one into the other like Chinese boxes, and from first to last it never even had an air of approaching anything in the remotest degree partaking of the nature of a full stop.

Into this deluge came the *Daily News,* like the gleam of light in Watts' picture, the waters were assuaged while its sheet was opened, and it had a column, a whole column, of praise. Chitterlow held the paper and Kipps read over his left hand, and Ann under his right. It made the affair more real to Kipps; it seemed even to confirm Chitterlow against lurking doubts he had been concealing. But it took him away. He departed in a whirl, to secure a copy of every morning paper, every blessed rag there is, and take them all to Dymchurch and Muriel forthwith. It had been the send-off the Boys had given him that had prevented his doing as much at Charing Cross—let alone that he only caught it by the skin of his teeth. . . . Besides which the bookstall wasn't open. His white face, lit by a vast excitement, bid them a tremendous farewell, and he departed through the sunlight, with his buoyant walk, buoyant almost to the tottering pitch. His hair, as one got it sunlit in the street, seemed to have grown in the night.

They saw him stop a newsboy.

"Every blessed rag," floated to them on the notes of that gorgeous voice.

The newsboy, too, had happened on luck. Something like a faint cheer from the newsboy came down the air to terminate that transaction.

Chitterlow went on his way swinging a great budget of papers, a figure of merited success. The newsboy recovered from his emotion with a jerk, examined something in his hand again, transferred it to his pocket, watched Chitterlow for a space, and then in a sort of hushed silence resumed his daily routine. . . .

Ann and Kipps watched that receding happiness in silence, until he vanished round the bend of the road.

"I *am* glad," said Ann at last, speaking with a little sigh.

"So'm I," said Kipps, with emphasis. "For if ever a feller 'as worked and waited—it's 'im. . . ."

They went back through the shop rather thoughtfully, and after a peep at the sleeping baby, resumed their interrupted breakfast. "If ever a feller 'as worked and waited, it's 'im," said Kipps, cutting bread.

"Very likely it's true," said Ann, a little wistfully.

"What's true?"

"About all that money coming."

Kipps meditated. "I don't see why it shouldn't be," he decided, and handed Anna piece of bread on the tip of his knife.

"But we'll keep on the shop," he said after an interval for further reflection, "all the same. . . . I 'aven't much trust in money after the things we've seen."

7

That was two years ago, and as the whole world knows, the "Pestered Butterfly" is running still. It *was* true. It has made the fortune of a once declining little theatre in the Strand, night after night the great beetle scene draws happy tears from a house packed to repletion, and Kipps—for all that Chitterlow is not what one might call a business man —is almost as rich as he was in the beginning. People in Australia, people in Lancashire, Scotland, Ireland, in New Orleans, in Jamaica, in New York and Montreal, have crowded through doorways to Kipps' enrichment, lured by the hitherto unsuspected humours of the entomological drama. Wealth rises like an exhalation all over our little planet, and condenses, or at least some of it does, in the pockets of Kipps.

"It's rum," said Kipps.

He sat in the little kitchen out behind the book-shop and philosophised and smiled, while Ann gave Arthur Waddy Kipps his evening tub before the fire. Kipps was always present at this ceremony unless customers prevented; there was something in the mixture of the odours of tobacco, soap and domesticity that charmed him unspeakably.

"Chuckerdee, o' man," he said, affably, wagging his pipe at his son, and thought incidentally, after the manner of all parents, that very few children could have so straight and clean a body.

"Dadda's got a cheque," said Arthur Waddy Kipps, emerging for a moment from the towel.

" 'E gets 'old of everything," said Ann. "You can't say a word——"

"Dadda got a cheque," this marvellous child repeated.

"Yes, o' man, I got a cheque. And it's got to go into a bank for you, against when you got to go to school. See? So's you'll grow up knowing your way about a bit."

"Dadda's got a cheque," said the wonder son, and then gave his mind to making mighty splashes with his foot. Every time he splashed, laughter overcame him, and he had to be

held up for fear he should tumble out of the tub in his
merriment. Finally he was towelled to his toe-tips, wrapped
up in warm flannel, and kissed, and carried off to bed by
Ann's cousin and lady help, Emma. And then after Ann had
carried away the bath into the scullery, she returned to find
her husband with his pipe extinct and the cheque still in his
hand.

"Two fousand pounds," he said. "It's dashed rum. Wot
'ave *I* done to get two fousand pounds, Ann?"

"What 'aven't you—not to?" said Ann.

He reflected upon this view of the case.

"I shan't never give up this shop," he said at last.

"We're very 'appy 'ere," said Ann.

"Not if I 'ad *fifty* fousand pounds."

"No fear," said Ann.

"You got a shop," said Kipps, "and you come along in a
year's time and there it is. But money—look 'ow it come
and goes! There's no sense in money. You may kill yourself
trying to get it, and then it comes when you aren't looking.
There's my 'riginal money! Where is it now? Gone! And it's
took young Walshingham with it, and 'e's gone, too. It's
like playing skittles. 'Long comes the ball, right and left you
fly, and there it is rolling away and not changed a bit. No
sense in it! 'E's gone, and she's gone—gone off with that
chap Revel, that sat with me at dinner. Merried man! And
Chit'low rich! Lor'!—what a fine place that Gerrik Club is,
to be sure, where I 'ad lunch wiv' 'im! Better'n *any* 'otel.
Footmen in powder they got—not waiters, Ann—footmen!
'E's rich and me rich—in a sort of way. . . . Don't seem
much sense in it, Ann, 'owever you look at it." He shook
his head.

"I know one thing," said Kipps.

"What?"

"I'm going to put it in jest as many different banks as I
can. See? Fifty 'ere, fifty there. 'Posit. I'm not going to
'nvest it—no fear."

"It's only frowing money away," said Ann.

"I'm 'arf a mind to bury some of it under the shop. Only
I expect one 'ud always be coming down at nights to make
sure it was there. . . . I don't seem to trust anyone—not
with money." He put the cheque on the table corner and
smiled and tapped his pipe on the grate with his eyes on

that wonderful document. "S'pose old Bean started orf," he reflected. . . . "One thing, 'e *is* a bit lame."

" 'E wouldn't," said Ann; "not 'im."

"I was only joking like." He stood up, put his pipe among the candlesticks on the mantel, took up the cheque and began folding it carefully to put it back in his pocket-book.

A little bell jangled.

"Shop!" said Kipps. "That's right. Keep a shop and the shop'll keep you. That's 'ow I look at it, Ann."

He drove his pocket-book securely into his breast pocket before he opened the living-room door. . . .

But whether indeed it is the bookshop that keeps Kipps or whether it is Kipps who keeps the bookshop is just one of those commercial mysteries people of my unarithmetical temperament are never able to solve. They do very well, the dears, anyhow, thank Heaven!

The bookshop of Kipps is on the left-hand side of the Hythe High Street coming from Folkestone, between the yard of the livery stable and the shop-window full of old silver and such like things—it is quite easy to find—and there you may see him for yourself and speak to him and buy this book of him if you like. He has it in stock, I know. Very delicately I've seen to that. His name is not Kipps, of course, you must understand that, but everything else is exactly as I have told you. You can talk to him about books, about politics, about going to Boulogne, about life, and the ups and downs of life. Perhaps he will quote you Buggins— from whom, by the bye, one can now buy everything a gentleman's wardrobe should contain at the little shop in Rendezvous Street, Folkestone. If you are fortunate to find Kipps in a good mood he may even let you know how he inherited a fortune "once." "Run froo it," he'll say with a not unhappy smile. "Got another afterwards—speckylating in plays. Needn't keep this shop if I didn't like. But it's something to do. . . ."

Or he may be even more intimate. "I seen some things," he said to me once. "Raver! Life! Why! once I—I 'loped! I did—reely!"

(Of course you will not tell Kipps that he *is* "Kipps," or that I have put him in this book. He does not know. And you know, one never knows how people are going to take that sort of thing. I am an old and trusted customer now, and for many amiable reasons I should prefer that things remained exactly on their present footing.)

8

One early-closing evening in July they left the baby to the servant cousin, and Kipps took Ann for a row on the Hythe canal. It was a glorious evening, and the sun set in a mighty blaze and left a world warm, and very still. The twilight came. And there was the water, shining bright, and the sky a deepening blue, and the great trees that dipped their boughs towards the water, exactly as it had been when he paddled home with Helen, when her eyes had seemed to him like dusky stars. He had ceased from rowing and rested on his oars, and suddenly he was touched by the wonder of life, the strangeness that is a presence stood again by his side.

Out of the darknesses beneath the shallow, weedy stream of his being rose a question, a question that looked up dimly and never reached the surface. It was the question of the wonder of the beauty, the purposeless, inconsecutive beauty, that falls so strangely among the happenings and memories of life. It never reached the surface of his mind, it never took to itself substance or form, it looked up merely as the phantom of a face might look, out of deep waters, and sank again to nothingness.

"Artie," said Ann.

He woke up and pulled a stroke. "What?" he said.

"Penny for your thoughts, Artie."

He considered.

"I reely don't think I was thinking of anything," he said at last with a smile. "No."

He still rested on his oars.

"I expect," he said, "I was thinking jest what a Rum Go everything is. I expect it was something like that."

"Queer old Artie!"

"Ain't I? I don't suppose there ever was a chap quite like me before."

He reflected for just another minute. "Oo! I dunno," he said, and roused himself to pull.